Divided Sky
Book 1

Daniel Harrell

ISBN: 979-8-9986539-0-2

Cover design by: M.waqas
Printed in the United States of America

To learn more about this series, please visit: www.dividedskybooks.com

This book is dedicated to my first storytellers, my mom and dad, and to you dear reader. Although we may not have met, you kept me writing.

CHAPTER ONE

Miho opened her eyes and knew she was alive because it hurt so much. She hadn't thought she would be alive, not after that fall. When she tried to move, everything ached, so she decided that lying still was fine for now. She was having trouble breathing, so she focused on that rather than the pain. She guessed the fall had knocked the wind out of her. After a few minutes, she realized she was going to continue breathing, so she went back to thinking about her aching body. That made her want to cry, so she looked around to see where she landed.

It wasn't the Ground; she knew that right away. Miho had never seen the Ground, but her father had told her about it, and this looked nothing like those stories. She must still be in the city. It was dark, and she couldn't see much, but she recognized the sounds of the engines in the distance, and the walls nearby looked like dirtier versions of what she knew. She must be in the lower levels, maybe even the lowest levels of the city. Those were supposedly filled with murderers and monsters. But then again, she had just fallen because she was being chased by a murderer and a monster, so it wasn't like things were worse.

"You have a very logical brain," her mother had said to her once. "It will take you very far in life, no matter what you do or where you go." Mother was always so wise. At the thought of her, Miho reached instinctively for the little tin near her heart. She winced and cried out as white, sharp pain shot through her whole arm and shoulder. This wasn't normal pain, she knew; it hurt way too much. Something was wrong. It hurt so much she felt like she might get sick. She stopped moving and focused on breathing through the pain. It faded and her mind cleared.

'It must be broken,' she decided. Using her other hand, she felt her injured arm. It hurt to touch it, but it wasn't at a weird angle, or bones sticking out, or anything gross, but there was an odd lump where none had been before.

She used her non-broken arm to reach for the tin. Its tiny, lumpy form comforted her. 'Still there,' she thought to herself and felt comfort. 'Now what?'

Miho was trying to decide what to do when she felt something moving nearby. She could just barely hear a little noise of movement, but she jerked in alarm. Her broken arm hurt so much she felt waves of nausea, but she tried to look and see if it was "Him." It wasn't. It was a rat moving about nearby, the biggest rat she had ever seen. Her instincts screamed at her to get away from where she was. "He" would look for her. She needed to move.

When she got up, she ached all over. The broken air vent that she must have fallen through was above her, casting a gloomy light down. She tried to walk, but her ankle couldn't support her weight, so she started limping. She was in some sort of room. The only light was coming from the air vent, so she really couldn't see much. There was no way to judge how big the room was, but she guessed not too large. Limping forward, she tried to find a wall. She groped around for only a minute before finding a vertical surface. She felt along for anything that might be a door or a light switch, hoping she wouldn't find the rat, or worse.

She started to feel afraid. It was dark, and she was alone. Now that Father was gone, she was totally by herself in the world, and would always be alone. Warm tears began to fall down her cheeks. She was completely alone, lost, hurt and feeling around in the dark, hoping she wouldn't get eaten by monsters, bitten by rats, or found by "Him."

A feeling of complete sorrow and anguish overwhelmed her, and she felt so tired. She slid down the wall and let her feelings explode out of her. This wasn't like when Mother died. Those tears had been silent. She always tried to stop those from falling. She felt she wanted Mother's tears to stay inside, as if she was losing pieces of Mother when she cried. She still cried about losing Mother, but she always tried to stop quickly.

This explosion wasn't like that. She didn't care anymore. Nothing mattered. Father was gone, Mother was dead. She screamed from fear and loss, and she didn't care. Her tears fell like a rainstorm. They went on and on, and she made noises like a wounded animal. She didn't care if "He" found her. She didn't care about anything. She felt like giving up. She didn't care if she died. She cried in the dark until nothing more came out. After she sat sniffing for a while, she realized she was hungry. It was then that she heard her father's voice in a memory: she remembered one time when she was hurt and upset, overwhelmed and wanting to give up. They had been going at the swords for over an hour. Her father insisted she learn. Miho hated it.

Nobody used swords. It was useless to know. She had never seen a sword carried by anyone except during the ceremonies. Father insisted, though, and he rarely insisted on things. She had tried to learn the swords because it meant so much to him. This particular day, he had gotten in several good hits. She was sore, and battered and angry that she had let him get so many hits in against her. She sat right down on the floor and silently cried, anger bubbling near the surface. Father came over and knelt beside her. "What is it, little bird?" he'd asked softly. "Are you hurt?"

"Yes," she'd said, with as much venom as her burning soul could muster. "Ah," he'd said patiently. "And do you want to give up?"

"Yes," she'd said louder, close to an explosion. She had wanted to explode. She had wanted to tell him how stupid it all was, in these modern times of airships and cities in the sky. People used black powder muskets now, not swords and knives in combat fighting, but she didn't want to insult Father. She remembered he sat down on the ground beside her, and bowed his head as if understanding her thoughts. "Yes," he'd said calmly and quietly, "Life will often hurt us. We walk through each day and we risk getting hurt. Some days it hurts so much that we want to give up. This is natural. Everyone feels this. From the Queen down to every single person in this city."

She'd looked up into his face, no longer bubbling with anger. That had burned off, but she was still teeming with emotion. There were lines around his soft brown eyes. His eyes slanted like hers, and like her mother's. Everyone she knew looked the same, except for her family. They were taller, heavier, pale in skin, with round eyes of different colors. Her mother and father had come from Japan, far away, they said. Miho had heard hundreds of stories of their homeland, but had never seen it herself. All she knew was this city where she grew up. She'd looked into her father's eyes and saw wisdom and patience. Just looking into them was like looking into the night sky, as if they went on forever. His smile was sad and sincere.

"We all feel like this at one time or another, little bird, but we must find a way to move past the pain, move past the sadness, for there is so much to be done. It is acceptable to take a little time to feel what you feel, but don't spend too long there. Otherwise, you will get blown every which way, like a leaf in a strong wind. You must be the tree, with deep roots. Don't be the leaf, be the tree."

Miho never understood how her father could make her feel better, but he always did. "Don't be the leaf," she said through gritted teeth as she stood up in the dark, smelly room. "Be the tree." Her father was gone now, thanks to that monster up there. She could stay here and let the monster get her too, or she could keep moving. There was so much to be done. She wanted to get that monster for what he did, and she couldn't get him lying in the dark crying. She started feeling along the wall until her hand found a handle, and with a deep breath of relief, she twisted it to open the door.

The door was locked. For a split-second, Miho felt a rush of panic, gripped with fear at the thought of being trapped. She felt for a lock lever on this side of the door. It was there. She clicked it and tried again. A pale, dim light crept into the room from the hallway, blinding her in the darkness. She took a deep breath, trying to drink the light into her. There was no noise from the hall. She stuck her head out to take a quick look. The hall stretched on in both directions with no noticeable change or landmark. It was endless in its shabby sameness, musty, smelling of dankness and a hint of urine. There were no sounds of people or anything else, except the distant rumble of the city engines.

Miho looked at the plaque outside the door. It read "Storage" and was followed by a long list of numbers and letters. A quick look back into the room revealed a lever on the wall for the light. She turned the knob and lowered the striker and the gaslight bloomed into brightness. With a quick word of thanks in her head, she quietly closed the door again. She needed to think. Boxes and crates filled the room. It looked like no one had been in here for years. There was a thick layer of dust and rat droppings everywhere. She could clearly see the broken ventilation duct that she had fallen into the room from, high in the ceiling in the far corner.

She felt the sudden urge to move. "He" would be looking for her, and it was best to move, but her leg still couldn't support her weight. She looked around for a stick or something she could use. It appeared most of the crates contained some kind of machine parts. She found a hunk of metal that she could use as a knife, but it wasn't very sharp. She tucked it into her clothes just in case. After a few more minutes of searching, she decided there wasn't much that would work well, so she pulled a board from a box lid and attempted a make-shift crutch.

She flicked off the light and made her way out into the hallway. She couldn't lock the door from the outside without a key, but she closed it and noted the room number "Storage T2319." With a deep breath to steady herself, she tried to decide which direction to go. She chose the one away from the ventilation ducts where she had fallen. After hobbling along for what seemed like forever, she came to an intersection. She couldn't tell one path from another, so she headed in the direction she thought smelled slightly better. After a while, another intersection and another guess. She started hearing sounds of people far off. At first, she was frightened by the sounds of running and screaming. Miho imagined some twelve-foot rat-like creature hunting people through the hallways, but as she continued on slowly, she realized these were the sounds of life, children and adults moving and living. As she struggled with her wounded leg and her broken arm, she realized the board was digging into her armpit and that now hurt too.

Then, suddenly, three children appeared out of nowhere. They were running as fast as they could and screaming at the top of their lungs. Miho's heart sank into her stomach as she imagined the rat monster behind them. None of these strange children seemed to notice her until they were right on top of her. She struggled to get out of the way as they came to a sudden halt, staring at her just as she was staring at them. The middle boy was shorter than Miho, who was small for her age. He had a grubby face and thick glasses that were far too big for him. His hair was a ruddy brown and looked unwashed. His nose was round and red, and when he spoke, it sounded like he had a cold.

"Who are you?" he asked. He didn't sound mean, just curious.

"What's wrong with her eyes?" asked the blonde-haired girl on the boy's left, pointing with her dirt covered hand. Miho stepped back and winced with pain.

"Nothing's wrong with them. Some people look like that is all," said the boy knowingly. "She is from far away."

"What is she doing here?" asked the tallest boy on the right. He looked at Miho like she was a spy. Miho reached slowly for her make-shift knife.

"I dunno, do I?" said the middle boy.

"THERE YOU ARE!" said a loud voice from behind the children as two hands grabbed the outside kids. "You three are going to have to deal with me for sure!"

Everyone looked terrified. Miho looked up into the face of an older girl. She had shoulder-length, brown hair that was windblown. She had a thin face with large green eyes. The eyes showed intelligence and determination. This was not a girl to go against, and she looked mad. Miho guessed she was 16, a few years older than herself. She was thin and looked like she had recently grown a few inches. She was slightly awkward with her movements, like she wasn't used to this bigger body. The three children looked as if the older girl was going to eat them.

"Arty, Sam, Mika. Today is wash day, and I don't want to hear another word. You get to the tubs right this minute," the teenager said sternly.

10

"We found thomeone," said the middle boy with the glasses and the stuffy nose, pointing at Miho.

The older girl noticed Miho and her face became quizzical as she stepped around the other children.

"Hello, there," she said, not unkindly, "I don't think I've seen you before."

Miho felt her hand wrap around her knife. She couldn't go back. "He" was looking for her. There was no one to trust. She had to run; she had to get away. As she shifted her weight to run, a pain shot up her leg that made her tense her wounded arm. Everything hurt all at once.

"Hey, you alright?" asked the teenage girl, reaching out her hands. Miho reacted in a second. She drew her knife and tried to back away, but she couldn't move easily with her wounded leg.

The teenage girl gave a half smile. She didn't seem afraid at all. It was as if she had knives drawn on her a few times a day. She stopped moving and glanced at the knife.

"Hey, I'm not going to cause you any trouble, alright? I would like to help if I can. Your right arm looks broken, and you look like you have been through a furnace, and I don't mean that as a good thing." She smiled as she said this, but her eyes were taking in every detail.

Miho's hand shook. Her strength was leaving her. She was tired, hurt, scared, and exhausted.

"You want me to get help?" asked the boy with the cold.

"No. No, we don't need help. Arty, you get yourself to the tub. You two go with him. No more fussing. I'm going to help our new friend here."

They started shuffling off with many backwards glances. "Do you have a name?" she asked, looking at Miho. Miho shook her head slowly. The last of her strength was leaving her like blood flowing from a wound. She didn't want to say her name. She didn't want to say anything that might help "Him" find her.

"Alright, dear, you don't have to say your name. You hang onto that, okay?" she said, pointing at the knife as she put an arm around Miho to steady her. "My name is Jen, and I'm going to help you."

CHAPTER TWO

The girl was younger than Jen, and from the far east by the looks of her face and skin. She looked like a dirty little doll. A broken, dirty little doll. Her arm was obviously giving her a lot of trouble, and she looked like she had fallen down every level of the City and hit each one. She was shorter than Jen, and now that she really looked her over, Jen could see that the girl was breathtakingly beautiful. She had shoulder-length, raven black hair that was currently dirty with grime and who knows what else.

The girl's grimy clothes were actually beautiful robes of pale purple. At her waist was an elaborate and ornate sash, and Jen noticed that her skin was perfect, with no scars or blemishes. Everything about this girl gave off an air of privilege. She had hands that were small and bore no signs of calluses. Her teeth were all white and present. Her eyes were a beautiful shape, like almonds, and the several shades of brown shone brightly with intelligence – and with pain. This young girl was in distress, and Jen was going to help her.

"Right," she felt herself say out loud as she decided what to do. "Let's get you in here and look at you."

She led the girl around the corner to the entrances to the baths. Every few weeks, Jen would round up every child she could find and drag them to the tubs. Strictly speaking, the part of the city they were in was not supposed to have people living in it. The Underbelly is what everyone called this place. When trash is dropped anywhere in the city, it either falls off the city or it rolls to the Underbelly. That included a good number of people and any detritus from the citizens above. Still, the people in the Underbelly were needed. It's just that no one wanted to admit it.

Jen had insisted on their baths, and so she had these rooms converted to boys' and girls' wash rooms. She had to work with city workers, engineers and, of course, the criminals to get everything she needed. They had to redirect rain water, find ways to heat it, fashion the tubs and make sure no one stole or destroyed anything, arrange for drainage; and most importantly, she had to work with the various groups to ensure that no one "owned" this area. It had been exhausting, but soon enough, more and more people started using the baths, and now they were just part of the Underbelly.

She led the girl into the girls' wash room and undressed her. At first the girl resisted, but Jen insisted. "We have to know what's wrong before we know how to make it better."

The room was large with three small make-shift tubs in the middle. There were stools all around for scrubbing and smaller tools for after. Electric light bulbs hummed in the corner. Jen quickly assessed that only her girls were in the room. The other girls, in various stages of undress, gathered around with questions, like birds all chirping together.

"Who's she?" asked scrawny Ashly, a young girl with grimy hair half covered with soap bubbles.

"Is she hurt?" chimed in tiny Hattie, who was five or six. She still had the round plumpness of a baby, but on her head was a beautiful crown of brown curls that were accented by her huge brown eyes.

"What's going on, Jen?" asked Mabel, who was slightly younger than Jen. Mabel was struggling with the curly-haired Hattie, trying to get her undressed for scrubbing, but the little girl wasn't helping. She was just staring around at everything in the room, disinterested.

"Ladies, this girl needs our help," Jen explained, gesturing toward Miho and assuming her usual commanding tone: "Ashly, keep an eye out for anyone coming while I look her over, please. Everyone else, please give us some space and get back to washing."

She could tell the girl was shy and uncomfortable. To help calm her, Jen insisted she keep her makeshift knife in one hand, and assured her she would not undress her all the way. Being slow and methodical, Jen untied her sash and slipped the robes off the girl. It was obvious her right arm was badly broken, but the bone wasn't sticking through the skin (thank goodness). The girl had a gash on her left leg that was still bleeding, and it appeared she had a bad sprain to her left ankle.

"All-in-all, not too bad. Let's see if we can get you patched up," Jen said, using the motherly voice she had learned from Sister Amelia back in the monastery. Amelia could calm anyone down with that voice, and not for the first time Jen was thankful she had learned it herself.

Jen took in the scrawny girl from toe to tip. She looked at the well-made small clothes the girl wore under her robes, the girl's frame, and her general development. Jen guessed the girl was about twelve. She gently washed some of the filth off the girl, used some clean cloth to bind her gash and brace her ankle enough so she could bear the weight of walking. All the while, the girl's broken arm was foremost in her mind.

If she were honest with herself, the broken arm could kill this girl. The upper bone in her arm was broken so badly that there was a bump where the bones didn't line up properly any longer. Jen knew that even if this girl didn't die from infection, once those bones fused, that arm would be useless and painful for the rest of her life. They had to get a doctor to set the arm. Jen knew that most doctors would prefer taking the arm off, because it was cheaper than setting the bone and the following treatment to stave off fever. Most people in the Underbelly needed to work every day just to scrape by a living. Jen didn't want to see this girl have to lose her arm for such a senseless reason as that it was just faster to cut it off than to treat it.

There might be a way to get her some real help, but it would be costly. The payment was one she was saving in case one of the children in her care needed it, and this girl was unknown to her.

But Jen knew she was the only one who could help this girl, and that her decision to help would affect the girl's whole life. She knew she would help this girl. The payment was ready, but wouldn't be available for long. For all Jen knew, this was meant to happen.

She took a deep sigh. It was time to act.

"Listen, I won't lie to you," she said, looking at the half-dressed girl in front of her. "We need to get that arm taken care of, or it will mean trouble for you, and bad."

The almond-shaped eyes were staring fixedly at her. Jen continued, "I'm guessing you don't have any money to pay a doctor." The other girl shook her head slowly. "Right, I have something we should be able to use as payment. I want you to wait with Arty and this lot and I'll go get it and come back here…"

She stopped when the girl was shaking her head again. She looked like she was about to panic, and cry, and run—all at the same time. "Look, where I'm going ain't gonna be easy to get to, and with that arm, you might not make it."

Still, the girl stared at her and shook her head. She began to put her robe back on. It was clear to Jen that she would not leave her side.

Jen sighed again. She couldn't really blame her. "Alright, dear. Let's get going then. Stay close, and be mindful."

CHAPTER THREE

Miho kept her mouth clamped shut, because she was sure if she opened it at all, the pain would make her throw up. The girl Jen helped her get her kimono back on and issued a few orders to some of the older children. After that, they set off. They left the damp air of the baths behind and started down a dimly lit corridor. Miho gripped her knife and stared into the gloom, expecting giant rats, or monsters - or worse, "Him" - in every dark shadow.

Miho had lived in this city for as long as she could remember. She hadn't been born here, but this was still her home. She had never seen parts of the city like this, though. It was unkept and ugly, dark and forgotten. There was an air of neglect everywhere around her. She had to imagine that it affected the people who lived here. She thought about her home and how beautiful and warm it was. How could both places exist in the same city?

Miho remembered going to the park with Father. Sometimes Mother would get to come too, but her position was so important that she was often away, defending the city. More often than not, it was just Miho and Father. They would leave their house and step outside into the quiet bustle of the street. The horse-drawn carriages would carry people or goods around the stone streets, and the well-dressed citizens would walk up and down their street, saying their hellos to those they passed.

Miho loved the days when they could see the sun. Usually, the clouds made everything a dull color, but on sunny days, the colors would be vibrant and alive. The little trees would sway and dance in the breeze, while their leaves would rustle and talk. At the end of the short front walkway was a simple iron gate that would creak and moan at being used, but Miho always thought the sound was happy, like an old man who makes a noise when he moves but is still glad that he can.

Her family dressed in the fashion of Japan. They all wore Komon in their daily lives and had different styles of kimono, depending on the events they attended. They often attracted looks from people passing in their dark western suits or dresses. Miho loved the bonnets and bowler hats, as her family rarely wore anything on their heads. She didn't know any other Japanese people in the city, so she wasn't sure if it was just her family or all Japanese that didn't wear hats.

Father and she would often go to the little park at the end of their street. It wasn't enormous, but the trees were thicker and it had a couple of wide-open spaces. Father had said they were lucky to live in a part of the city where you could see the sky, and not everyone had this just outside their door. Miho had never understood that before, but it was apparent to her now. She remembered the times she and Father would fly a kite, or stroll around the small open spaces looking at the bugs or birds and talking about the world. Sometimes, and these were some of Miho's most favorite memories, Father would seem to time their visit to match a special occasion. They would often stop in the middle of the green space (it wasn't big enough to call a field), and they would look up past the high city walls and buildings to see the swirling clouds. Miho loved those times, because she knew what was coming. She would scan the walls of grey clouds looking and waiting.

On the sunnier days, shafts of light would push through the clouds and trace the buildings and trees. Then above the clip-clop of the horses' hooves, and the chittering of the people, she would hear the "Voosh-Voosh" that meant an airship was approaching. In truth, she often couldn't hear the aircraft above the city, but she liked to pretend she could. Usually there were two airships, one slightly ahead of the other. They would fly low, and Miho could see all the details of their intricate designs. Their bulbous fronts with many windows looking like the eyes of a dragonfly, their slowly flapping wings giving off that distinct sound, their long, sleek bodies that seemed to emit trails of steam from various joints and connection points - the airships were a jumble of wood, brass and silver molded together into an artful design.

Once or twice, Miho could make out the form of the pilots as they turned their ships on the sides. Her mother flew a smaller, open craft and would wave to them as she flew by. Miho's heart would always swell with pride and excitement at seeing her mother, and Father had a warm smile that was both sad and joyous. Miho knew he was worried about Mother's safety. The sounds of city life, mixed with the animals and trees, always seemed to fill Miho's heart. She would close her eyes and let the sounds, smells, and breeze flow through her.

Miho opened her eyes and saw the gloom of the place she was now, while trying to keep the memory of her old life close in her heart, but she knew they couldn't both exist at the same time. She awkwardly limped behind the girl named Jen, feeling the shafts of sunlight and cool breezes from her memory being replaced by the dark and stale air around her. The dank, rusty corridor seemed endless as they trod along. The shadows seemed to cling to her, like a living animal trying to smother her and weigh her down.

"I'm guessing you've never had the pleasure of visiting the Underbelly before?" Jen asked in an overly warm tone to imply sarcasm.

Miho shook her head slowly as the darkness reached the edges of her heart. They turned a corner and she could see an opening just ahead. The room beyond was brighter. She could hear sounds of people coming down the corridor.

"Well, I know it's very different from other parts of the city above, but I think you'll find we're every bit as vibrant and thriving a community as you will find elsewhere." They walked through the opening into the biggest single room Miho had ever seen. It was massive. On the floor of the room was a collection of tents and ramshackle structures. Light shone through an opening high above her and Miho noticed green plants among the structures. It was like a market mixed with a shanty town, and this market was alive with hundreds of people. Some people were walking through, some were inside their stalls or tents working or shouting across the open space. Ropes and chains hung from all sides of the vast area where lanterns and brightly colored cloth hung. It was so bright in the room that Miho had to squint her eyes while they adjusted to the light.

All along the walls of the massive room were dozens of other doors leading to many more corridors and even more people were coming and going. The people were calling to others below or walking along catwalks to gantries, ladders or stairs. Children ran and played all around, while adults shopped and congregated. Miho noticed none of the fancy dark suits or dresses from above in the city. Here, people wore more colors and many styles. It was impossible to make out what any one person was saying at this distance, but the overall feeling was life, thriving.

"Welcome to the heart of the Underbelly," said Jen as she looked at Miho's expression. She let the newcomer soak it all in for a moment and said, "Well, we can do a proper tour soon, but we had best be off."

They set off around the edges of the vast room. They were not at the ground level, but one floor above. Miho counted five stories of catwalks around the edges of this space.

"Oi, Jen, come look at the pretty lace I just got in!" one lady below called up to Jen when she spotted her.

"Hello Molly, I'll come by a bit later. I'm in a rush presently."

They continued around the room. Jen replied to many more people who greeted or called to her. Miho limped along, and for a time forgot all about her fear and pain. She felt mesmerized by the constant flow of people and energy going on around her. She heard snippets of other languages, like French and German—some were languages she didn't know, which excited her. It was not unlike an ant hill she had seen in the park near her house. Hundreds of people crawling all around, talking and doing, but somehow it all seemed to be part of one system. This wasn't chaos, but a practiced and well-worn life of the people in this area.

They left the great expanse of life behind as they turned off into a corridor. The light and life of the marketplace died almost at once and they returned to the dark network of passages that connected all parts of the Underbelly. They had taken a few turns and walked for another couple of minutes. Miho wasn't sure she could remember the way back if they got separated. All these corridors looked the same to her. They came upon one rusty old door and Jen stopped. Miho looked up and down the corridor, but no one and nothing was around them. She heard a dripping coming from somewhere in the gloom, but other than that, there were no sounds.

Miho looked at the door before them. It was an ordinary door, just like countless others they had passed. She couldn't tell, but it looked like it was rusted shut. This door, like many they had passed, had a strap of old and battered metal that was secured across the opening to show no one used it any longer. Jen looked at Miho and seemed to size her up. Finally, she spoke.

"I'd appreciate it if you could keep what you are about to see between you and me," Jen said firmly, looking into Miho's eyes.

This made Miho very uncomfortable. No one ever looked into her eyes. Her parents only did it a few times she could remember. It felt like this Jen was invading her mind or her space. Miho wanted to take a step back, or to look away, but she didn't. She took a deep breath and tried to imagine what this girl in front of her was feeling, and what she was thinking.

This girl, Jen, was helping her when she was just a total stranger, Miho thought. She knew she didn't look like everyone else in this place, so there was that too. She knew Jen was taking her somewhere important, and important to those children she seemed to take care of. Miho looked at Jen and took in all she could see. Jen was taller and older than Miho. She kept pushing her hair behind her ears, which revealed a pretty face with high cheekbones. Her eyes were green, like jade or gemstones. She had a few light freckles on her cheeks and still looked like a young maiden—except for her eyes. They were a woman's eyes. There was a maternal air about her, and her body gave off the impression that she'd had to grow up faster than she should.

Miho kept Jen's gaze and nodded her head. She would keep anything this girl asked her to keep a secret. After all, Miho could be in this gloomy, dark abyss all by herself.

"Right then," Jen said with a half-smile. She reached down and flicked a small piece of metal about a foot up from the bottom of the door. It was to stop the door from moving, but now that she flicked it around, the door opened noiselessly on its hinges. Miho just had time to admire the door lock when a roaring gush of fresh air buffeted her and she heard the roar from the other side of the door.

They ducked under the metal strap that was used to block the door, and Jen closed it and spun the makeshift lock. They stood in a short hall, about ten feet long, and at the end of the hall was a wall of clouds that moved in an unending churn. Miho inched toward the end of the hall and saw a narrow catwalk that stretched off around the metal structure they had just left. Miho had read about mountains. Enormous pieces of rock and earth that filled your complete vision. She had never seen a mountain, just like she had never seen the ground. Not even living in this city for almost her whole life had prepared her for a sight like this.

She thought of a mountain because behind her was the city. The city she had always known, but she had never seen it like this. It stretched up and away from her so far as to be lost in the constant churning clouds. The wind roared and buffeted her, and she thought she would lose her balance. She put her hand on the wall near her and looked from the great expanse of steel and stone above her, and craning her neck to peer over the catwalk's handrail she saw nothing but churning clouds below. There wasn't much of the city beneath where they were now, and that made Miho uneasy. Miho tried to cling to the wall, but her other arm hurt when she even thought about moving it.

"Try not to look too far up or down, dear," Jen called over the roar. "Just focus on where your feet are now. Do you still want to come with me? I can leave you here. It won't take long."

Miho sucked in her lower lip and nodded. Jen smiled, and she set off down the catwalk. Miho followed, holding on for dear life in case a gust of wind should pick her up and throw her into the swirling clouds below.

CHAPTER FOUR

Dr. Elizabeth Porter took a slow, steadying breath. She was tired and cross, and she needed to keep her composure. She was struggling with her patience.

"My patience with my patients," she mused as she smiled inwardly. The smile never reached her face; a physician should always appear serious. "My patience with my patients, for Patience," she thought, furthering her idle thoughts.

She stopped those thoughts with an iron will honed by years of study and discipline. "Patience," she said out loud. "What are we looking for?"

Her youngest daughter lowered her notes and gazed at the man on the table. He was naked below the waist, his legs spread wide, exposing his genitals. Elizabeth was looking at her daughter.
Patience was looking at the man.

"Signs of movement in the scrotum that would indicate that the Sickness has progressed to stage two," Patience said in a flat, monotonous voice.

The man did not look at the two doctors. He stared at the clinic's ceiling with a look of uncomfortable embarrassment on his face.

That was common, Elizabeth thought. People are always uncomfortable in this situation. What was unusual was that his wife wasn't in the room with him. She guessed the wife had to mind the store, or stall, or whatever these people did for a living.

"What other indicators do we have for the Sickness?" Elizabeth asked her daughter. Patience was smart, and coming along well in her studies. She didn't have her oldest sister's gifts, but she also didn't have her oldest sister's bull-headed ideals and wild musings. Patience was steady, a hard worker. The youngest of Elizabeth's three daughters, she showed the most promise of becoming a fine physician.

'God only knows what will become of Chastity,' Elizabeth thought. 'That girl will be the death of me.' She took another steadying breath.

"Typical banding of the epidermis is a sign of inherited Sickness from a parent," Patience began. "The patient doesn't show a distended belly, but complains of swollen glands along his body. If we see movement in the scrotum, it's probable the Sickness has progressed."

"Mr..." Elizabeth began, but broke off when she didn't remember the patient's name. "Mr. Jones," Patience interjected.

"Mr. Jones," Elizabeth started again. "Have you had any extra itching between your legs? Front or back?"

"Front or back, mum?" asked the man, bewildered. "Your cock or your bum," Elizabeth explained.

"Oh, pardon mum," said Mr. Jones. "No, mum. No extra itching. Is that good, mum? A good sign, I mean?" he added nervously.

"I think so, Mr. Jones. Is your wife here with you?"

"No, mum," Mr. Jones said. "She couldn't leave the shop, and said to tell you..." He took a steadying gulp. "She said 'If Dr. Porter needs to take your stones, you tell her she has my permission.' But I'm hoping it won't come to that, mum."

"I don't think we are quite there yet, Mr. Jones. You may get dressed now."

Elizabeth turned to her daughter. "The patient does not exhibit signs of elevated Sickness. The swelling could be from the type of work he does. Sometimes working around farm animals, or certain chemicals, can lead to swollen glands. It could also be the beginnings of an ague, or other communicable infection. Give him herbs to calm the inflammation and instruct him to return if any symptoms get worse," Elizabeth rattled off.

Her teaching of Patience would have to continue at another time; she had too much to do right away. Elizabeth and Faith had been up most of the night working on observation and cataloging samples from three other districts. She looked at the man getting dressed. His wife had been brave to send him here, she thought. She wouldn't let her husband within 100 meters of her clinic, but this man's wife couldn't afford to lose her husband to the worm, and she understood that.

Patience was making her notes when the door opened and Chastity entered. Elizabeth's hair stood up on the back of her neck.

"Dr. Porter," Chastity said in a quiet tone that solidified Elizabeth's misgivings. "May I have a moment?" This could mean nothing good.

With a glance at her youngest daughter to make sure she had everything in order, Elizabeth stepped into the hallway with her oldest, not quite feeling ready to face whatever tempest Chastity was about to bring down on her. She looked at her daughter. Chastity was 17 now, so nearly a woman. Her long blonde hair was plaited down the back and capped with a simple fabric that kept it out of her way, and showed her proper upbringing. Still, Elizabeth always felt the wild electricity emanating from her daughter. 'She's like a living thunderstorm,' she thought.

"What are you up to now?" Elizabeth began, in an icy voice. Chastity never called her "Dr. Porter" unless she wanted something she knew only too well that her mother would never agree to easily.

"Mother, I have a patient in the back that I require your assistance with," Chastity said firmly but softly.

"Humbleness is something I don't see on you often," Elizabeth said to her daughter. "I must admit, I'm interested."

Chastity wisely ignored this comment and walked toward the back of the clinic. "The patient is of unusual background. I have never worked with someone like her, plus her break is rather severe."

"Oh god, Chastity," Elizabeth said in a tired voice. "What stray dog are you trying to rescue now?"

They walked past the laboratory door and Elizabeth saw Faith writing out a report next to the microscope. She stopped to call, "You are supposed to be resting, Faith."

Faith didn't even look up. "As are you, Mother, but we both have a lot of work to do. The sample from Dr. Stevens is showing positive signs of his suspicions. The patient has an increased infection rate."

Elizabeth nodded. "You were right to send the sample to test. That nobleman will have to address the infection's increased level." She contemplated all that implied: Dr. Stevens was old, but an excellent physician. Many of the nobles of the city trusted too many of the quacks that practiced more superstition than actual medicine or science. It was also important that Dr. Stevens understood that the Porter laboratory was the best in the city.

Elizabeth followed Chastity again, glancing at the portrait of her great-grandmother on the wall near the laboratory entrance. Her great-grandmother was the first healer in the city when it rose. Her family had been physicians in this district now for more than 150 years, each generation building upon the legacy of the last.

Elizabeth took great pride in that fact. Everyone knew they were a well-to-do family and respectable. Her heart sank a little as they walked back to her least favorite section of the clinic. Her grandmother had opened their back door to the urchins and unwanted of the city, and like fleas to an unclean bed, they had flocked to the rear door. Elizabeth's mother had an even softer heart, like Chastity. Elizabeth would have been more than happy to close that back door forever, but it sometimes had its rewards.

Plus, it soothed her soul somewhat to know that they did a little good for the extremely less fortunate, but kindness needs to have its limits, she thought, '...otherwise, the Urchins would overtake us.' The wife of the man she had just seen had most likely saved for a week, or even a month, to pay for a visit to this clinic, and here Chastity was wasting her talents and time on trading for chickens or cloth. It was exasperating in the extreme.

"The patient is just in here," Chastity said, directing them into the back room. Elizabeth could see a line of filthy men and women out the back door. The sight almost made her stomach turn. She averted her eyes and stepped into the room.

There, on the rickety little table, was a disgustingly dirty girl in a heap, with another thin girl standing over her. As Elizabeth got closer, she recognized the "Urchin Queen," as Elizabeth liked to call her. She did not know what the little tramp's name was, and couldn't care less what it was. She was always in here with one child or another. God knows how many were actually hers. She looked little older than Patience, but she must have been breeding like a rat down in the city's Underbelly.

The girl on the table was something else altogether. She looked like a doll that had been dragged through the mud. She was from the far East, Elizabeth was sure of that. That would be what Chastity wasn't sure of about her appearance.

'We don't see many Asians here,' she thought. The girl was small and delicate looking, maybe 12 or 13 years old. Besides her filthy appearance, she looked feverish and clearly in pain. Someone had splinted her right arm.

"Who bound this arm? This isn't your work," Elizabeth said to Chastity.

"I did," the Urchin Queen said. The little tramp stared at Elizabeth, and it unnerved her. The girl clearly didn't know her place, or was being rude out of spite, she thought, tensing and getting more and more agitated.

"It is a decent attempt," she said flatly. She looked at Chastity.

"Well?"

"The arm is severely broken, and I'm afraid of infection from the internal bleeding," Chastity said. "I wanted your experience with this."

"So, lop it off and get on with your day," Elizabeth said harshly. "They only need one arm to push the wheels." The little girl on the table seemed to growl, like a wild animal. Elizabeth took a step back. "I need you to save her arm," the Urchin Queen said, over Chastity's protests.

Elizabeth stared at the girl and then at her daughter. They both wore expressions that showed they were ready for a long, drawn-out fight. Elizabeth collapsed under the idea of it all.

"Fine," she said, too exhausted to care.

"Nurse!" she called, and the pug-faced man scurried into the room with a courteous, "Yes doctor." "Get some bandages and a cheap splint, and…"

"No," interrupted the Urchin Queen. "The good stuff, and medicine. I'll pay for the pain relief and whatever is needed to fight infection."

Elizabeth raised her eyebrows. "Oh, will you?" she said, in an oily tone. She'd had just about enough of this whole situation. "Did you bring me a whole chicken, or perhaps your best blanket?" she asked, with as much acid as she could project–and she had quite a lot of acid within her, it seemed.

The Urchin Queen just smiled as she looked at her. "No, with these." She held open a bag full of fresh plums. There were dozens of them. Their sweet scent filled the room and everyone but the injured girl seemed on edge. "These are the finest plums in the city. You can't find better in any market or shop."

Elizabeth had to admit, picking one of the fruit out of the top, the girl was right. The plums were huge and fresh. She might have picked them today. Elizabeth stared into the Urchin Queen's eyes for a moment, thinking.

"Stolen?" she asked in a low voice.

"Of course not. I have a secret grove. I save them for special occasions," the girl said pleasantly. "These could make a fine wine, or a succulent dessert."

Elizabeth noted the girl had tried to adjust her accent to sound more proper. Her accent wasn't local. London, perhaps? Certainly not High London. They continued to stare into each other's eyes for a minute. "Very well," Elizabeth said. It really didn't matter if they were stolen or not, the bag's contents were an unheard of treasure.

"Nurse, get the necessities. Chastity, unbind the arm, we need to reset the bone." The pug nosed man left to gather the items. Once the binding was off, it was clear that Chastity was correct, the bone was indeed badly broken. There might be significant internal bleeding. Elizabeth adjusted the arm, taking in all the details, and the patient let out a hiss and a hushed "futuo." Elizabeth shot a glance at her. It was so faint that she wasn't sure she had heard it. She looked at the others, but no one else had seemed to hear it. This changed everything. No one from the Underbelly cursed in Latin.

"I'm doubting this one is one of yours," Elizabeth said conversationally.

"I don't know her," the Urchin Queen said, looking at the girl. "She appeared out of nowhere and needed help."

"How noble," Elizabeth said, thinking hard. The sound of the nurse returning with all the supplies shifted her attention back to the task at hand. Now she really knew she must save this girl. Not just for the plums, but because she might just be someone important.

CHAPTER FIVE

Miho woke with her arm aching. Even though it had been weeks since the doctor set it, it still hurt if she slept in an odd position. She didn't sleep well in the first place, but her sleep, like her arm, was getting better. She lay in the quiet dark, listening and thinking. In the dim light, she could barely make out her surroundings. Her space was tiny, but it was clean, and she was feeling like it was a home, of sorts.

The sheer panic she had felt when she first arrived in the Underbelly had subsided. She still had dreams about Him finding her, but they were just dreams. She hated dreams. They were always the same: her mother leaving, her father falling through the clouds, Him looking at her with that hungry expression.

Miho shifted in her bed. It wasn't good to lie with these thoughts. It was better to get moving. She sat up and started pulling on her clothes and gathering her possessions for the day, the first of which was her favorite knife. She always tucked it under her pillow as she fell asleep.

Sometimes she would fall asleep holding onto it, and wake the next morning, having never let it go. She pulled it out of its spot and looked it over.

Jen had given it to her shortly after they returned from the doctor. She had made it for her. Miho loved this knife. It was perfect in every way. It was a small, thin blade no wider than her thumb, and the edge was a little longer than her outstretched hand. The handle was thin and wrapped in different colors of wire and string. The many colors formed a vast array of patterns and designs. Miho would stare at them for long stretches of time while she thought. She remembered when Jen gave it to her.

"This is for you," Jen had said simply after breakfast one day, about a week after the doctor's visit.

Miho had said nothing, she just took the item.

"The one you were carrying looked a bit like an impromptu weapon, so I made you this."

Miho had inspected it in silence. She never spoke at that point. She looked up at Jen, wondering if the older girl had some other motive. Was she in debt to her now? Wasn't she already in Jen's debt? The fruit Jen had used to pay for her doctor was worth a lot of money. Miho dropped her gaze in shame. She didn't enjoy owing this girl even more. She handed the knife back.

"Take it," Jen said flatly. "Down here, you may need it. You should practice with it every day, until it feels like a part of you. I made it pretty balanced, so you should be able to throw it, but don't. Don't throw it unless you absolutely have to. When you throw a knife, all you are doing is getting rid of your weapon, and maybe giving one to someone else."

Miho looked up at the girl, wondering why she was being kind. Miho had not had very many friends. Most people stayed away from her because she looked different. It hadn't bothered her so much when she had Mother and Father. They had always been her company, but they were gone now. One thing they had taught her was that kindness was a rare and valuable thing.

"Thank you," Miho whispered.

Jen's entire face lit up as her eyebrows shot up. "She speaks!"

Miho felt her cheeks blush as she looked down again. Her splint hurt, she was hungry, and she wasn't in the mood to be teased. They might have just finished eating, but her belly was by no means full.

"I was wondering when you would ever speak to me." Jen said brightly. "Does this mean I get to know your name?"

Miho shook her head slowly. She didn't want anyone to know anything about her. If He ever found out... if He ever found her... She shook her head a little more firmly. This was best.

"No name, huh?" Jen asked, with a slight frown. "Well, I have to call you something. We can't just call you 'almond eyes' or 'broken arm.' I mean, the arm will heal for one thing. We have to call you something. Have you ever had a nickname?"

"My father used to call me 'little bird,'" Miho replied quietly, still looking down. She hadn't spoken about her father since the day she lost him. Her throat started tightening, and her eyes stung at the corners. She refused to cry here, in front of this girl, even if she was being kind to her.

"Little bird, huh?" Jen murmured, either not noticing Miho's emotions, or being kind enough not to mention it. "Well, you only ever talk at night when you're asleep."

Miho's eyes shot up to Jen with shock. She didn't know she had been talking in her sleep. What had she been saying? She started thinking about her dreams as her stomach turned to stone.

"So I can call you Nightingale for now, or how about just Gale?" Jen asked, with a soft smile.

And so, Miho was called Gale by everyone from that point on. She tucked her favorite knife with its simple metal sheath into her belt and tucked in the other two small blades that Jen had made her in their spots. She picked up her mother's tin, which she kept always on her, and the small bits and bobs that were all she now owned. They were put in safe places when she lay down at night, and she put them on her body and carried them during the day. Jen had suggested this.

"You may find a great place to sleep, but there's no guarantee it will be there the next time you lie down," she'd said one time when Miho was still new. "Best to carry with you all that you care about and find a hiding spot for the rest."

With all of her possessions on her, Miho pulled on her shoes and started to get ready to leave her special spot for the day. The Underbelly was alive with people. These people constantly moved around. While many of the people had carved out their living spaces, or made their claim on a favorite spot, these changed a lot because of fighting between the large groups. Nothing in the Underbelly was certain but the unrelenting dirt.

Dust, all kinds of dust, coated everything: coal dust, dirt from the upper decks, from the machines and furnaces and from the dusty, dirty people. Miho always kept her sleeping spot clean. It might be the cleanest spot in the entire Underbelly, she thought, mostly because she couldn't stand lying down in filth, and because there weren't many people who could reach it.

The first few days she was down here, she couldn't sleep for more than a few minutes at a time. She was terrified of Him finding her, of the loud and smelly people and the unfamiliar sounds. She tried various places to sleep, and at last found her spot. It was an opening between a tall stretch of pipes and the back of a heat exchange for a large boiler that took up most of this room.

The opening was a little less than a meter wide, a little more than two meters deep, and about one and-a-half meters high, but the pipes blocked the entrance. In fact, because she was so small, Miho could squeeze through the pipes that blocked the entrance and crawl about a meter before there was a turn, so her space was well hidden. No one who looked through the tiny gap in the pipes could even see where she slept.

It amazed Jen that she found it. The light from the boiler that ran day and night was soft and came from above in her sleeping area. Jen couldn't get through the gap when Miho had tried to show her, but then she figured out that the big pipe that most impeded her wasn't used anymore, so she disconnected a fitting nearby and swung the pipe out of the way. She then crawled on her hands and knees to see.

"Wow! This is amazing!" Jen had said when she finally reached it and could stretch out. "Really excellent find. This is yours now, but try not to get too attached. Things always change in the Underbelly."

She had looked around, taking it all in, and then said, "But I think you may have found a spot you can call home." Jen had given Miho a wad of brightly colored string not long after. "Take this to add some color to where you sleep. String is dead useful. You can tie back your hair with it, fix things that are broken, bind things together. The possibilities are endless."

'That's Jen,' Miho had thought to herself. The girl was always finding uses for things. She could make or fix anything, and she was surrogate mother to dozens of children in the Underbelly.

Everyone knew who Jen was, and because Miho followed Jen everywhere, most people knew "Gale" too.

Food was always on everyone's mind in the Underbelly. Jen had taken Miho into her care, but she also had collected around a dozen children that she looked out for as well. It was up to the older children to take care of the younger ones. Everyone had jobs to do. The youngest helped as they could with sewing and washing, the older children worked Jen's "gardens" outside, or went on raiding parties for food from above. Both jobs were dangerous. Outside, someone could fall through the clouds to die, and above, if caught, an even worse fate might await.

Miho had wanted to join the raiding parties as soon as she could. She felt she owed Jen for her kindness, but Jen wouldn't allow it. "Nothin' doing with your arm in that state," Jen had said. "You can help in other ways while you heal. Don't fuss, you'll be joining me and Arty soon enough."

Arty was Jen's right hand. The boy was loyal and had a good mind, despite his appearance. Miho always thought Arty had a vacant look in his watery eyes that was magnified by his thick, mismatched lenses. Perhaps it was his different sized eyes, or the slightly pudgy way he lumbered about, but Miho just assumed him a simpleton at first. Arty, as it turned out, had a very sharp mind. Perhaps he hadn't grown into his mind yet, she wondered? That was something her father had said once.

"Children grow at different rates," Father had told her. "Some minds grow faster than bodies, some bodies grow faster than minds. Childhood can be very uncomfortable, and it is all too easy for those of us adults who have gone through it to forget how uncomfortable it was." Miho felt that aching sadness she always felt when she missed her parents. She could no longer sit still in this spot. She had to move away and hopefully leave the shadows of her parents here to guard her space.

Miho picked her way out from her sleeping spot, thinking about Jen and the past few weeks. She tightened the pipe that Jen had found. At night she loosened it, so anyone who tried to come to where she slept would knock it loose and wake her. Then she crawled out into the room and stood up. It was time to start her day.

CHAPTER SIX

Jen yawned so big she heard her jaw crack. She had gotten little sleep. The Benton twins both had ear aches, and had woken her several times in the night. She stretched her long, lank form and looked over at the sleeping girls. They were both sleeping soundly. She considered being grumpy over the fact that they could sleep now, but she had to start her day. But the thought was gone in an instant. The twins were never any trouble, and they worked hard.

Jen rearranged her skirts and layers and pulled on a moldy boot. It stank. Perhaps she should boil them? She was considering this and making plans for her day when she felt Gale come close. The girl never made a sound. It was eerie how she could do that; Jen hadn't even heard the door to the room open. Gale was her little shadow, the mysterious visitor from who knows where. Jen kept expecting her to disappear as fast as she had appeared, but every morning the girl came back.

Gale had changed a lot since first arriving in the Underbelly. Jen knew she was from up above, and she knew Gale was running from something–or someone. It didn't matter now. Little Gale was one of them, and never said a word. She just did everything Jen told her to. It had been strange at first, when Gale had followed her everywhere, but then she got used to having her around. Gale was always so helpful. It didn't matter if she needed to fetch something, hold a pipe while Jen mended it, or even once or twice threaten someone who tried to do Jen wrong.

The first time was outside the market, Jen remembered the altercation as she cleaned her teeth. Jen had traded bread and meat for some wire and a few spare parts when a big brute tried to take her food. Jen had her hands full and couldn't reach for her knife, when all of sudden Gale gave the man a prick and he screamed. He had stood his ground, and before Jen could say anything, the man's hand was badly cut. He dropped his own knife and ran. 'I swear if I hadn't calmed Gale down, she would have chased that bloke and done him in,' she'd thought with a smile.

The other time, Jen was bartering for rice. The man had stolen it from above and was trying to get rid of it quickly, but he and Jen didn't agree on a fair rate. He got angry and was about to lay hands on her when, quick as a flash, he had a knife to his throat. Gale was small, but she was quick. The man calmed down and they made a good deal after that.

Jen looked over at Gale. She looked like a little doll, her perfect brown skin, her big brown eyes, that beautiful raven black hair. She was pretty, and thin ... and deadly,' Jen thought.

Gale was shorter than Jen, and a couple of years younger. The short pants she wore, which were rolled at the legs and waist to fit her, swallowed the girl. Several shirts that were too large for her made layers to cover her torso. She refused to wear a dress. The robe they had found her in was gone now. It was filthy and Gale had seemed to want it gone. She could have cleaned it, Jen was sure, but the girl had thrown it off of the city as soon as she had the chance. Jen could still see it falling through the clouds.

She smiled at the memory of Gale's face when she had learned they were as far down in the city as you could go.

"What do you mean 'below,' dear?" Jen had said to Gale once when she had mentioned heading to a lower deck to flee the stink of the Underbelly. "Why, there isn't anything below you but ground," she'd said teasingly.

The effect on Gale had been like watching children realize it was bath day. Gale's eyes got as big as apples and she started side walking to the wall with her arms outstretched. Jen had almost screamed with laughter. "Well, them walls aren't gonna stop you from falling any more than the floor is dear." She snorted and wiped tears from her eyes. "Them floors have held us for hundreds of years, and I reckon they've got a few more years left to 'em."

Like most everything, the information had shocked Gale, but she quickly recovered. When she asked to see the clouds, Jen had taken her to one of her make-shift gardens. The outskirts of the Underbelly had broken and fallen through the years. With the Kaisers, the Danes and the Prussians attacking every few years, plus the normal rust and wear over time, the Underbelly had lost a lot of what it used to be, and of course nobody above cared to fix it.

Jen had found a few places she could get outside and set up some simple gardens in the sunlight. Give a plant some access to the sun, a little water and some attention, and she proved to have a knack for making things grow. She had set up several small gardens where nobody could easily see them, and nobody would find them unless they were really looking. It gave her an excellent source of food for the kids, and some trading items to boot.

She had taken Gale to one after she had requested this of Jen. The girl brought a few items, including her robe, and tossed them into the clouds below. "May the ground receive them and make them anew," Jen had said out of sheer habit. They had stared at the sky for a bit, and then returned. Gale had seemed scared then, but now they went together to her gardens every few days – all except for Jen's most secret place. That was still for her alone.

It hadn't come up yet, but Jen supposed she would have to give Gale something to do so she could visit her special place alone. She considered showing it to Gale. Perhaps.

Someone opening the door to her room pulled her out of these thoughts. Several of the children nearest the door shuffled and jumped in surprise. The familiar face of Jessie poked his head in. His wiry face, with its patches of stubble, split into a half grin. Several of his teeth were missing. "Morning, Miss Jen. Pikeys spotted about a click out. Thought you'd want first 'ello."

Jen lit up with a smile. She silently thanked the fact that she still had all of her teeth. "Thank you, Jessie! I would." Jessie closed the door as he headed off.

Jen looked at Gale, who looked confused.

"Pikeys," she said, looking at Gale. Gale still looked like she didn't understand. "Traders. Traveling merchants. Sometimes called Gypsies."

She could tell the girl didn't know what to make of this information. "Come on, we'll greet them before they get overrun. It's always a big to-do when we get visitors." Jen started grabbing what she needed and folding up what she didn't into her bed bundle. She nudged the nearby sleeping Arty and whispered loudly, "Arty, get up, I have to go. You need to watch over everyone and get them started on their chores. The Benton twins are still with an earache, so let them sleep. Otter, Amelia and Marcus go to the wheel today. The others will need to do as much as they can."

Unintelligible mumbling came from the lump where Arty slept. Jen pulled on her other boot and started for the door. "Arty, you get all that?" she asked in a louder whisper.

"Yes, Miss Jen," came a sleepy voice.

Gale followed Jen as they wound their way through the Underbelly. Section after section was beginning to stir. The young kids were always the first out into the common areas. Jen couldn't call them 'streets' or 'squares,' but they were close to those things.

"You ever see a Pikey?" she asked Gale as they made their way past a chicken coop. Soft cooing could be heard inside the coop, and it radiated heat as they passed.

Gale shook her head.

"They come and go as they please in big cities like High London or Yorkshire, but here we don't get as many. Most of the time, they come to us when they're about to cross the channel, on their way to High Paris, Brussels, or God knows where."

They made their way out of the Underbelly proper to the ruins of the outskirts. There were usually only a few places the Pikeys liked to dock, and you couldn't move in or out of the docks without running into Dane Alice's crew.

Like the summoning of an evil spirit, two such specters were on the path ahead of them. One Jen knew, the other she was glad that she didn't. Tommy was a large beefy man, who was slow and stupid, but he liked Jen, so he was often kind to her. Jen knew all too well what his hungry looks at her meant. She kept a civil tongue, though, and made sure to stay just out of reach. Tommy's companion was the largest woman Jen had ever seen. It wasn't muscle, although she had some of that to be sure, but her bulk was also reflected in her gluttonous eyes. They looked Jen and Gale over with a hungry gaze.

"Morning, Tommy," Jen said brightly. "How's your little sister?" Jen always liked to start with this. It reminded him she had once done him a favor, and also that she looked out for the children.

"Morning, Miss Jen," Tommy said thickly. "Little Sarah is well, thank you. Are you here for the new arrivals?"

"I am. I'm the welcoming party," Jen said with as much sweetness as she could muster given the overwhelming smell coming from these two.

The big woman sneered, "Bet you'd like to do some business that no one else knows about, wouldn't you?" Her voice was deep and nasal.

"Now, Minnie," Tommy reproached, "Miss Jen is a respectable citizen."

Minnie looked less than convinced. Jen could feel Gale tense and hoped she wouldn't do anything.

"They's arriving in the old South dock number 10, I suspect, Miss Jen."

"You are a dear, thank you, Tommy," said Jen as she made her way quickly away from the pair.

As they made their way to the big door leading to South Dock number 10, Jen could see the dock workers prepping line and unloading pallets. The door swung open, and their ears were filled with the sound of wind and the roar of engines. Jen caught a glance at Gale's eyes as they got as big as apples again. Jen giggled.

The sight beyond the door was always one that Jen loved. A vast opening of the city, which revealed a huge opening to the clouds below. The caravan slowly hovered and maneuvered as it made its way to the key. The vastness of the City lay all around them as they stepped out onto the key. All around them was the gray and rust covered metal of her home. The clouds rushed and flowed under it all like the waves of a vast sea.

The caravan had five multi-colored cars with large wagon wheels. The wings, large sails, and flapping tail of the makeshift propulsion all pulsated and wriggled. It made the caravan pivot and turn, looking like a giant, living dragon. On top of the front most car, operating the controls, were three familiar faces, Ma and Da McCowan and their daughter Rose. They worked like one person with six arms, each doing their job exactly in time with the others. The caravan touched down with a deep, soft groan and all the moving parts came to stillness as steam hissed from multiple joints. The dock workers came to tie the caravan down as Ma and Pa McCowan shouted orders to their own workers. Jen only had eyes for Rose. Rose spotted Jen, and they started for each other.

Jen beamed at the family and said, "Welcome, all of you, to High Hastings. Please mind your step."

CHAPTER SEVEN

Miho was aware of all the movement and strange sights going on around her, but she couldn't take her eyes off the clouds. The gaping maw that was the opening in the city to the outside seemed to breathe in with a loud, drawing groan. Miho even imagined the various iron girders and poles that jutted out as the teeth in the open mouth. But the clouds, the movement was hypnotic. She saw them rippling past the opening with a constant churning speed. Still, she gazed. She felt, somehow, the clouds pulling at her, welcoming her. She consciously thought to herself that she mustn't heed them.

Men and women bustled around her, tying down the colorful collection of wagons and carts. They cleared the wide flat landing site of excess ropes, sacks, barrels and debris. The people of the caravan were dismounting and talking and working with the dock workers to unpack. Miho paid them all little mind.

From the corner of her eye, she could make out Jen's form with her hands on her hips, calling loudly and fondly to the people at the caravan's front. Still, Miho listened and stared at the clouds. She remembered her father disappearing in the swirling mist and her heart tightened to stab her insides like one of her knives. She wondered where he was now. Could he have survived the fall? The Grounding ceremony wasn't supposed to kill you; Father had told her this. It was supposed to give you a chance at a life where you knew what you had lost. You were supposed to live knowing what they had taken from you. Miho stared into the clouds, remembering.

"Anytime a city, or castle, or even an airship uses skystone to fly, there is always mist," her father had told her long ago. "The great cities of Europe are so large, they have clouds around them constantly. They say those big cities pull the very water from the sea, and lakes and rivers. In the Emperor's palace of our homeland, the clouds turn the color of a thousand fires when the sun sets and rises. If you are near a skystone, you will be in the clouds."

Miho had loved the sound of her father's voice. His voice was slow and soft as a worn tree, but powerful as an iron beam. Father had taught her so much. He taught her about the engines of the city, and how some airships, like her mother's, used that mist in their engines. He had been an engineer in this rusty city, so far from where they had all been born, and they had sent him to the Ground.

Miho remembered the day of the Grounding. She remembered all the people on the platform, some in the fancy clothes of the upper levels, some in workers' clothes. Everyone was so serious. She remembered their whispers and stolen looks at her father. She remembered how he stood, his face like a carved mask. He never looked afraid, and at one point, he looked right at her with an expression she could not read. He didn't stop looking at her while the men read from their papers.

Then the fancy men stopped reading, and a priest came forward. She couldn't remember what that woman had said, but Miho called out to her father. Her father's expression broke then, and in his eyes she saw the pain and the fear. She had tried to run to him, but a pair of enormous hands had seized her and held her in place.

Then "He" whispered to her, "Now, now." And His breath stank of decay and beer. His stink of sweat and grease didn't even faze her as she reached out to her father.

There were men strapping Father to a cross with leather straps, and they were fitting a cover above his head that blocked his eyes. Miho called louder, and "He" tightened his grip on her shoulders.

"Nate, hold her," "He" had said to one of his crew, and smaller but still powerful hands replaced His as He went to her father. Was he going to save Father? she had stupidly thought. Her heart had actually grown lighter for a split second.

"Watch it!" said a man on the dock in front of the caravan as he passed in front of Miho. "Move your arse, Urchin!" Miho stepped back, and her thoughts drifted back to the day of the Grounding.

"He" had approached her father and whispered something to him. Her father moved his head and looked at Him.

"Traitor!" her father had shouted in Japanese. Father and Mother only spoke the language when they were at home. She had never heard either of them speak it outside.

"Murderer!" he shouted, again in their language. Nobody was startled but Miho, because nobody knew what he was saying. Father must have said this so she could hear and understand. "You will never lay your hands on my daughter, you liar! You scoundrel! It was you, you killed them and framed it on me!"

They were dragging father to the edge of the platform, strapped to the large cross. While tilted back, he locked eyes on Miho.

"He" was walking back to where Miho and His crew were standing.

"Miho!" her father shouted. "Run! Don't let Him get you! Don't trust any of them!"

Miho's heart froze. With a couple of soft words from the priest, they pushed her father overboard. Miho screamed, and her father screamed, "Run!" as he and the cross disappeared through the clouds. She turned her gaze to Him as He was getting closer, and she saw the hunger in His eyes. On his face, she saw joy and rapture.

Miho twisted hard in Nate's grip and punched him in the balls as hard as she could. The man had yelped and reached instinctively for his privates, and Miho ran without a look back. She had heard the steps, the calls, but she never slowed down.

That was more than a month ago. Had it been two months yet? She seemed to come back to herself, she had been away with her thoughts and memories. She was again standing on the dock, and she heard Jen calling to her.

"Gale!" came Jen's voice. "Hey Gale, come here. I want you to meet some people."

Miho took a calming breath and turned to Jen. She turned away from the giant open mouth of the monster; turned away from the memory of her father. Her eyes found Jen, and the people gathered near her, but then looked beyond the small group across the dock with its teeming mass of workers and visitors, all dressed the same in shades of brown. Up on a catwalk was a man dressed in the blue coveralls of an engineer. He was walking with his toolbox. It was Nate. Nate, the worker on "His" crew. Nate, whose balls she had punched to get away.

Fear and fury washed over Miho like a bucket of cold water from above. Nate wasn't looking at her. He was walking along, not noticing anything but where he was going. Without thinking, Miho reached for her knife in her belt. She had a burning coal of murder in her heart. Her healing arm throbbed, and she walked towards him.

Just then, Jen stepped right in front of her. "Hey, are you alright?"

Miho pulled her eyes off the man just long enough to look at Jen and say, "I must go." And with that, she went.

CHAPTER EIGHT

It was getting late, and Jen was getting worried. She had gone about her day and accomplished several of the more pressing tasks on her unending list of things that needed to get done, but all day she wondered where Gale was. Why had she looked so startling when she left, and where had she gone? These thoughts had chased through her mind like a dog after its own tail. She had gotten used to Gale always being by her side. To have her gone today felt strange.

Once she had settled and welcomed the McCowans, they had made plans to sup tonight. She had bartered some spare parts for some clothes in the Underbelly's market. Arty was dutifully getting "The Brood" about their daily chores when she finally made it back to their current sleeping area. The twins and their ear aches, the twisted ankle of little Becka, a crushed hand from Tom Liston, who was working on the wheel this week—but she kept turning and expecting Gale to be there. It disturbed her how much the absence affected her.

If Jen was honest with herself, she shouldn't be too worried about Gale getting hurt or in trouble. These past weeks had hardened Gale. Jen knew that the small girl could fight if pressed. She'd seen some of the bigger kids try to bully her, and before Jen could say a word, Gale put them down flat every time. Some of them were almost adults. Then creeping doubt pushed the pride she felt off the edge of a cliff. Jen knew that if a full-sized man caught hold of the girl, there was nothing she could do to help herself.

Jen's surroundings went dark and her heart felt like a ball of sharp ice in her chest. Yes, she knew all too well how strong a man could be, and how forceful. An acid rose in her throat as flashes of memory and emotion stung her like a raging hornet. She could smell the sweat and stink of the man, the rot in his breath, and Jen thought she might get sick. Her breath was shallow and her heart was racing as she saw images of the red-shirted man flash before her.

She remembered the last time a man had tried to force himself upon her. Her hands were sweaty as she gripped the shirt she had been folding. The pounding in her ears was so loud she could hear nothing else. He had come at her late one night. He must have been watching her for a while, because he was waiting out of sight along one of the well-worn paths she used to walk.

'He's the reason I don't walk the same routes anymore. I always take a different path now. I can't be predictable,' she thought. At least she had learned something, and as long as she was learning, she was improving. She had tried to scream, but he had punched her so hard that all the air had left her lungs. That red shirt was all she could see, but she'd felt the powerful arms pull at her clothes, the weight of his dirty body pressed up against her. She'd felt him pinning her wrist so she couldn't claw at him. Jen smiled a mirthless smile. 'That was his mistake,' she thought. 'He couldn't pin both my arms and pull down his britches too.' Jen tried to swallow, but her throat didn't work. She remembered reaching for her knife and remembered her hand becoming warm and sticky with his blood. She saw the surprised look in his eyes as she pushed it deeper and deeper between his ribs, so deep she lost the blade. His weight doubled, and she thought he would crush her, but she had wiggled herself free. His stupid red shirt. She hated that red shirt and she hated that man she didn't know. Most of all, she hated herself for being stupid.

Why had she been forced to do what she did? Why had he tried to force himself on her? She didn't want that, and asked no one for that. She just wanted to live and help her kids. Jen had just wanted to be more like her own sister, and less like herself.

'But men are men,' she thought with acid in her mind. 'They act like animals. They are animals.'

"Not all men are the same." She heard the Mother Superior's

voice in her mind, "and not all women are either. This world has sinners and saints, and neither of them looks like you expect."

Jen's venom subsided a little. She hadn't thought about the Mother Superior in a long time. She wondered if the Mother Superior would condemn her to Hell for killing the man in the red shirt. She snorted, not knowing if she was the sinner for killing the man, or he was the sinner for trying to force himself on her. Perhaps she was a holy warrior, like the Church's warrior nuns? Jen's darkness lifted at that thought. That little knife she carried had saved her from being raped, maybe even saved her life.

The thought of blades turned her mind to Gale. Jen had seen her tuck metal shivs into folds in her clothes, and hide makeshift knives down her sleeves. It was impossible to say how many sharp bits she kept on her, but one thing was certain: Gale knew how to use them.

Jen had seen her practice throwing different blades every day. She didn't mind. It was good for her to work that wounded arm. It was impressive how well Gale could hit her targets. The little girl could hit a cockroach ten feet away. Not always, but usually, and she was getting better. She only hoped Gale would never have to use a knife as she had. She hoped there was no red-shirted animal waiting in the shadows for Gale.

Then, about an hour before she was to go have supper with the McCowans, Jen was sorting through some clothes and thinking how to keep everyone in something to wear. She turned to pick up a pile of socks and Gale was standing right behind her. Jen screamed and jumped at the fright. Then a rush of anger rose up through her like a teapot about to boil. After looking for her all day, to be so frightened when Gale finally turned up infuriated her.

"Jesus, Mary and the Holy Saints!" Jen barked. "Where the bleeding hell have you been all day?" Gale didn't flinch or even laugh. She just looked at Jen, bemused. Her expression was always so hard to read. Jen knew that the girl always kept her emotions down deep. The little girl always reminded her of a doll. Usually, it was nearly impossible to read her, but Jen thought that sometimes Gale's emotion would creep into her eyes. They might change, but only for an instant.

In this moment, Jen could almost imagine Gale half smiling at having scared her. She was quiet when she moved. 'I think she prides herself on being sneaky,' she thought.

"I had something to do," was all Gale said quietly.

"What'cha have to do?" pressed Jen.

Gale thought for a moment before answering slowly, "Nothing that would cause trouble for you, or the children."

Jen had to smirk at that comment. Gale knew that the kids, and any added trouble for herself and them, were the most important thing to her. It was a well-played non-answer.

"What about trouble for you then?" Jen poked.

Gale hesitated, but her eyes remained focused. "I don't think so," was all she said.

Jen snorted. "Well, help me put these up, and set these aside for one of the girls to mend tomorrow," she said, gathering up the clothes. Gale fell right into line helping. "We have guests, and we'll eat with them tonight." Gale started loading up her arms.

"The McCowans go to all the high cities in the U.K., and some abroad. They know everything goin' on everywhere. They might even know some of your people. You have family in any other cities?"

Gale shook her head slowly, as a darkness fell behind her eyes. Jen stopped and looked at the girl. "No one? No family?"

Gale's shadow seemed to grow slowly. "No. My mother died on a mission several months ago." Gale's hand reached to her chest absently. "She was a pilot for the city guard. My father... was Grounded... the day I met you." Gale said this last part, turning her eyes upon Jen. The empty void behind her eyes made Jen want to cry, but she didn't. She reached out a hand to the younger girl. She had seen so much pain and loss and was still so young.

"They must have been important people," Jen said, and meant it. "If some wretch from the Underbelly got tossed off the city, nobody would care two shits. They don't ground people from the Underbelly. They just disappear them, or work them to death, or worse and make them an example to others. Skystones don't get wasted on people like us." Jen was about to spout some empty words about how they must have loved her and been wonderful parents, but she knew nothing about them, or Gale. She didn't even know Gale's real name.

"I'm sure you miss them," was the only thing she could think of to say. And so she said it, and it helped about as much as she thought it would. Jen grew frustrated not knowing what to say, so she just said what she felt deep inside. "None of us knows when we will lose the ones we care about, or how, but that doesn't mean we should stop caring about people. Maybe your mom and dad were great to you, I dunno, and maybe they were horrible. I'm guessing by the way you look, you loved them and you miss them. I'm sorry they are gone, then. But you can find other people to care for, and who care for you. I missed you today, and I was worried. I care for you."

Gale smiled, the first of her smiles Jen had ever seen. It was like the sun coming through the clouds on a warm day. Her entire face seemed brighter. "Thank you," Gale said and put her hand on Jen in return.

"Right, let's get to it," said Jen, as tears stung the edges of her eyes.

CHAPTER NINE

Miho thought the McCowans smelled funny, but not enough to lure her thoughts away from Nate, the man she had followed all day. He haunted her thoughts. She felt uneasy, and she wanted to know where he was every minute. Miho wanted him to pay for what he did to her father. The memory of her father's face as they tossed him off the ledge kept flashing in her mind. The image of his terror and madness in his expression were vivid.

She could remember the feeling of the warm sunbeams that played around the platform that morning, and she could see the faceless people lined up in their fancy clothes. Memories of the ruffles in the ladies' dresses, and the pressed greys and blacks of the men's suits haunted her. She felt the hand on her, Nate's hand, keeping her from running to her father's aid. The memory filled her with such passion and hatred that it was hard to breathe.

Miho remembered her father's breathing lessons. She burned with guilt at the harsh thoughts and things she had said to him. How pointless were breathing lessons? People breathed, they didn't even have to think about it. It just happened.

"Hm, yes, you can breathe without conscious thought, Miho, but when you bend your mind to the act of breathing, you can change your entire universe," her father had said patiently. He was always so patient with her. He loved her with every breath he took. Mother too. Miho felt she had been so lucky, so amazingly fortunate. In her weeks in the Underbelly, she had heard so many stories from the kids. They all were so sad.

It was an amazing thing, but if you don't talk, people think you must want to listen. Miho never wanted people to talk to her. She just wanted to be alone with her loss and grief, but Jen's children kept telling her she was so easy to talk to, that she was a good friend. Every story broke her heart. These children had never known love, never had plenty of food or lessons in culture and history. They didn't know how to read and write in four languages. Miho felt blessed with good fortune.

She felt her heart harden at the thought of Him, and Nate, and the other one–those three men who had taken it all away. Was it better to have known love and a good life, and lose it all, or to have never known it all? She thought that loss was worse than wanting, but it really didn't matter if one was worse than the other. This was all she had. She took a slow deep breath and remembered her father's teachings about "letting go of the things you cannot change." Her heart still pounded in her ears, and she must have had a very serious look on her face because she heard Jen stop mid-sentence when she caught sight of her.

"You alright, hun?" Jen looked into Miho's face, concerned. "Mm," Miho grunted curtly with a quick head bow as she assumed her place at Jen's side.

"Jen, you haven't introduced us to your friend," Mister McCowan's wife said, with an appraising glance at Miho. Mrs. McCowan had an unusual elegance about her. She was a taller woman, and thin, but while some of her attributes, like her hips, were curvy and strong, others like her cheekbones were tight and high. She had ink-black hair with streaks of grey and almond-shaped eyes of a jade green. Her accent was something Miho couldn't place. Spanish perhaps, or somewhere in the middle Europe countries?

Miho knew little about those countries except what her father had taught her. Her nanny, Machiko-san, wasn't as educated as her parents, but Machiko knew countless stories and legends. Miho had loved Machiko's stories.

"Well, I haven't had proper time, have I?" said Jen, in her thick London-town accent, a little stung. "She don't talk all that much, but our Gale is amazing. All the kids love her. She's been with us about a month, I'd say."

Mrs. McCowan walked over to Miho and took both hands in her own. This made Miho very uncomfortable. The older woman stared into Miho's eyes, and while she stared back for a while, Miho had to look away, breaking eye contact.

"Welcome to you Gale," Mrs. McCowan said warmly. Miho bowed her head.

"You see that a lot in the people of the East," said the large, slow-moving form of Mr. McCowan as he came closer. Mr. McCowan had a slow, deep voice with a thick English accent Miho couldn't place.

"Nǐ huì shuō," he said slowly and the strange words sounded stranger for his accent. Miho just stared at him, wondering what he had just said.

"Hmmmm, no?" said Mr. McCowan, sitting by a small cook fire and reaching for some herbs. "Hangug-eohaseyo?" he tried again.

Miho couldn't help but lighten her mood. What in the world was this strange man doing? Mrs. McCowan took the herbs out of her husband's hands before he could add them to the cook pot and replaced them with a cup. Mr. McCowan didn't seem to notice, as he switched again. "Nihongo wakatamaska?"

Miho's eyes widened as she heard this. How was he able to speak Japanese? She wasn't conscious of her stuttered, "H...Hai?" Mr. McCowan lit up like a beacon as he looked around the group, saying loudly, "Well now, she's Japanese!" He seemed very pleased with himself. Everyone around them made sounds of interest as he looked down at his hands, confused by what he saw there, but then took a sip.

"Blimy, I didn't know that, Gale," Jen said, looking at Miho. Miho felt very out of sorts to see this large English man speak what she had only ever heard her mother, father and nanny speak before. She nodded at Jen in acknowledgment.

"Do you speak English?" Mr. McCowan asked in Japanese. While Miho could understand him, he was obviously not comfortable speaking Japanese.

"Yes, I speak English," Miho answered in a quiet voice.

"Well, that makes things easier," said Mr. McCowan warmly, in English, and took another sip from his cup.

"Oh yeah, she can speak, but she doesn't do it often," said Jen, sitting down next to the fire to help with some veggies that Mrs. McCowan had been cutting up.

They were back in the bay where the caravan had docked. The massive doors outside had been closed and the vast room was dimly lit. None of the dock workers were present now. A few people walked around on the catwalks, either carrying out business or doing some simple security. The McCowans' caravan was home to a lot more people than Miho would have guessed. There were about six fires in the bay, and all of them had some number of people around them – Miho guessed about 20 in all. At the fire where she was, were Mr. and Mrs.

McCowan, their two sons, their daughter Rose, Jen and herself. The McCowan boys were younger than Rose, who appeared about Jen's age. Miho guessed they were younger than herself, so perhaps nine and 11?

"Wow, how many languages of the East do you speak, Papa?" asked one boy. He had his mother's almond-shaped eyes and her whipcord build. He was the youngest boy, Philip. The older boy, Thomas, looked more like his father. He had tufty brown hair and a stocky build. The older son was helping with the vegetables as well.

"Oh, I wouldn't say I speak any that well, son," Mr. McCowan replied to his youngest as he picked up a small pile of greens and began sifting through them. "I've met a few people from that area, though, and picked up a few things. I spent two years taking the high road to the silk traders of the orient. It was dangerous travel, and I saw many things that were strange to me." Mr. McCowan had sifted through the green leaves but not found anything inside, but before he could ask his wife, his son had excitedly asked, "Tell me about the silk, Papa? Did you meet pirates?" Mr. McCowan launched into a tale that sounded to Miho as well-practiced and most likely had grown larger than life. Rose came out of the shadows and asked Jen to help her unload some dinner things from the caravan, and they slipped away. Mrs. McCowan turned her jade-green gaze upon Miho and Miho felt ensnared like a water bird in a net.

"So, young Gale," Mrs. McCowan asked in her thick, unusual accent, "What kinds of foods do you enjoy?"

CHAPTER 10

Rose's lips were as soft as Jen remembered. In the darkness, Jen let her hands reach out and find the form she had spent countless nights thinking about. Rose kissed her back, slow and soft at first, but with each withdrawal, she came back hungrier and harder. Jen's mind was empty and her heart was racing as the two bodies stood intertwined, hands reaching and caressing anything they could find. Jen's hands couldn't stop moving. She couldn't think about her hands because the lips were back, and what could be more important than those lips, but then her hands would find something worthy of attention and Jen's mind hissed like a wet log tossed into a raging fire.

"I have thought of nothing else but this since I saw you standing on the docks," Rose murmured between kisses.

Jen could smell the oils Rose used, bergamot and myrrh, mixed with a faint scent of her sweat from the day. Jen gave in and knew nothing for a few more minutes.

"My God, I've missed you so much," Jen gasped heavily, as emotion and lust swelled inside her.

It felt like a spring of water that sprung from her heart. It tightened her throat as it headed toward her eyes. She could feel the emotion gathering as tears in the corners as her eyes stung. "I love you so much."

"I love you." Rose stopped kissing her with passion and placed both her hands on either side of Jen's face.

Jen could barely make out her shape in the dim light, but she could tell Rose was looking right into her eyes. Rose kissed her forehead softly and slowly, and Jen's knees buckled and wobbled.

"Rose!" the whip-like sound of her mother's voice cut the darkness, and both girls jumped. Rose leaned over and picked up the bundle she had dropped when they could fight off their feelings no more.

"Soon," Rose whispered as she moved off, but turned back to Jen and quickly stole a kiss. Jen could tell Rose was smiling in the dark when she did so. Rose's long, beautiful form slunk back to the fire and Jen let out a deep breath before picking up her own bundle and starting after her. Jen stumbled with her bundle of dishes and utensils. She made her way around the fire to an open spot across from Rose. She could still smell her and it drove her wild. Mrs. McCowan was still talking to Gale. Gale wasn't saying much. The others were in their own discussions.

"Ah good, Jen. I have a gift for you," said Mr. McCowan, as Jen started organizing things. Mr. McCowan reached inside his coat pocket and pulled out a small parcel and handed it to Jen. She took it and unwrapped it to see a collection of seeds.

"Satsuma oranges," Mr. McCowan explained. "I know your fondness for the citrus plants. These won't do well in the northern U.K., but we are far enough south that you might get them to grow."

"Oh Jacob, these are brilliant. Thank you!" Jen exclaimed, as she looked at the seeds like they were gold and jewels.

"I have something for you two as well," Jen said, reaching inside her rucksack to pull out a small bag of lemons. "They are growing great this year! I have quite a haul."

"My word, would you look at that?" Jacob said with a smile. "These are amazing. You are amazing, Jen. However do you do it? I'm convinced you can grow anything."

Jen beamed at them as Mr. and Mrs. McCowan coveted the lemons. Miho had never seen one before, so she looked on with interest. Miho wondered just how many gardens Jen had hidden outside on the city walls.

"I've got some dried herbs for trade, and I'm hoping you got some dirt. I'm running outta space to plant things."

"I believe we have a barrel set aside for you already. We can work out the details tomorrow," said Jacob, and he stood up. "Gale, I just remembered that I have something for you."

Gale's eyes grew wide. She looked at Jen, not knowing what to do. Jen smiled at the girl and nodded.

A short time later, Jacob came to sit beside Gale and pulled out a tiny item that looked like a comb of sorts. Jen had seen nothing like it. He handed it to the tiny girl, and she reached out a delicate-looking hand slowly. It only had four teeth, and was very narrow, but at the top it had a fan shape. It gleamed like gold, but didn't appear to be metal. The fan had three long white birds with long necks painted on it. The birds seem to be in an endless circle, as if they were dancing or chasing each other. Above the fan were white beads that were arrayed using string or wire. It was exquisite, and very delicate looking, and tiny. It reminded Jen of Gale. "I am told that the women use these as ornamentation in their hair," Jacob was saying to her slowly in his warm, calm voice. Jen always loved hearing him talk. "They wax their hair and put it into shapes with sticks and ribbon."

He was moving his hands about his head as if to show her. Jen smiled widely at the sight. "... and they put one of these atop."

Gale stared at the comb and looked up at Jacob. "I cannot accept such a gift." She whispered. Jen noticed Gale looked shy. It was adorable.

"Nonsense!" Jacob exclaimed, "I insist." He looked her in the eyes as he closed his hands around hers.

Gale dropped her gaze. "I have nothing to give you as a gift, and you have all been so kind to me," she said, looking down.

"Ah-Ho, well, that may not be exactly true," Jacob replied warmly. Gale looked up at his broad form and bushy mustache. "Did anyone in your family happen to tell you any stories from where you are from?" His face lit up at the last word.

Jen knew it was coming, and Gale's face was exactly what she thought it would be. Jen had to hold back from laughing.

"Yes," Gale answered quietly.

"Wonderful!" Jacob said, elated. "After dinner, please let me hear one of your favorite stories. I collect them, you see. We travel the world, and I love a good story."

Gale blushed. Jen knew Gale hated to talk, but she also knew that she would want to repay Jacob's kindness. Gale reached into her overlarge shirts and pulled out a small cloth that Jen knew she kept close to her heart at all times. Gale unwrapped the shiny cloth. It was a pale green with darker greens like leaves on a tree, and it had gold stitching that she couldn't really see from where she was. Inside the cloth was a small tin. It was small enough to fit into her palm. The tin was very thin too. Whatever was in it had to be tiny indeed. Gale treated each movement with reverence as she unwrapped the tin and laid her new comb on top.

Gale looked up at Jacob before wrapping the tin and the comb back up in the shiny cloth. Jacob seemed to know exactly what the tin was. He had a very serious look upon his face as he said softly, "I'm very sorry for your loss." Gale looked at him for a long moment and bowed her head. She wrapped up her bundle and tucked it back inside her shirts.

"Mina, dear, are we ready to eat yet?" Jacob asked sweetly of his wife, and like a clock ready to chime, everything happened at once. Plates, cups, dishes swung into place and everyone was moving. Jen had seen this many times. She didn't really understand why it worked like this, but Mina McCowan waited for her husband to announce when they ate. Jen was sure that everything had been ready for a while now, and Mina had everything taken care of, but she waited 'til her husband was ready before they ate. Jen was more confused every time she thought about it, but she also loved it. Whatever the reason, Jen knew it had something to do with love.

They ate until Jen thought they would burst. Everyone talked during dinner, everyone but Gale, of course. They shared stories and gossip and news. Jacob told them about the midland cities having to drift to find resources, and the grumbling from the other cities for them to stay in their space. Word was that the Parisians were having trouble with Italy along France's southern borders, and the Kaisers were growing more aggressive throughout the region. The Catholic Church was pushing into the Middle East, while the Muslims and the Central Church of Europe were trying to keep them out. Pretty much, it was the same stories as always.

After dinner, everyone was sleepy and slow. Rose caught Jen's eye, and they felt an electric charge between them. "Mother, Jen and I will do the first load of dishes."

"Oh, will you?" Mina said with a cocked an eyebrow at them both. "Yes, I suppose you two have much catching up you'd like to do."

And like an unfettered skystone racing for the stars, the girls shot off.

CHAPTER 11

Miho rose to help clean up, but Mrs. McCowan put a hand on her shoulder and gently pushed her back down. "No dear, I think you have something else you need to do," she said, and with a smile she looked toward Jacob. Miho felt her heart sink. She was going to have to talk, and more than that, she had to tell this man a story. Her heart started racing as the large, friendly man settled down for his payment.

Machiko-san's voice came back to Miho clearly, warm and soft. Her voice flowed through Miho's veins. It was a part of her makeup. Machiko's voice was like a piece of rough wood: it had character and spirit. Miho had loved the old woman. Her image lived inside Miho's heart. She was short, and her wrinkles had wrinkles. She was missing teeth and always kept her dry grey hair up in a bun. Her weathered hands had been soft, and she loved to laugh and talk.

Machiko had been with them when her mother, father and Miho had fled Japan. Miho was only a couple of weeks old, so she remembered nothing about Japan, but Machiko spoke about her homeland constantly. Machiko had been connected to Miho's mother, Kana, but Miho couldn't remember how. Where Mother went, Machiko went. It was as simple as that. Machiko had doted on Miho.

"Ah, Miho-chan," she would say in her soft voice that could turn stone hard in an instant if she wanted it to. "You are so lovely and wise. You will become a beautiful woman of great power."

Machiko had died three years ago. Miho had never known loss before then. "We will cut her hair short for the funeral," her mother had said. "The braid will go into our shrine until one of us can take it home to Japan." Miho remembered seeing her mother carefully put the braid of dry, silver hair gently into a small compartment in the wooden prayer shrine in the corner of the largest room of their home.

Miho had cried and cried when Machiko died. Her father had tried to comfort her, saying, "She died peacefully in her sleep, Miho-chan. Love surrounded her. We all must die one day. Not all of us will be that lucky." Miho understood what that meant now. She remembered the anguish on her father's face as they threw the cross of metal they had bound him to off the city. Her mind flitted to Nate, and "Him," and those who had lied about her father, and she tensed and grew dark, but then she took a couple of deep breaths and looked up to Jacob, who was sitting peacefully across from her.

Miho steadied herself and remembered the various stories Machiko used to tell. The tale of The Crane Wife came into her mind. It wasn't her favorite, but it would do for her needs. She remembered Machiko's calm voice, and she tried to sound like her when she spoke. "Long ago," she began, slowly but firmly. It seemed like most of Machiko's stories began with "long ago," Miho thought. She had asked the old lady about that: "Why do all your stories begin with 'long ago?'" she had asked in bed one night before sleep.

"Ah yes, well, that is because it sets your mind to be ready for what comes next. It's like the first course of a good meal. It should be small, easy to digest, but get the taste in your mouth for yummy food that is to come!"

Miho smiled inside her mind at the memory and said a thank you to Machiko for all her wonderful stories.

"Long ago, there was a very poor man who lived near the water," Miho told the tale while looking into the fire. She could speak if she didn't look at Jacob, or Mrs. McCowan, or anyone around them. She pretended to be talking to Machiko, telling the story slowly, to remember all the important points. Miho wasn't used to hearing the story in English, so she spoke carefully, in order to translate in her head. Thankfully, The Crane Wife wasn't a long tale, and soon she was at the end.

"…and the man cried and asked that she stop hurting herself, because he thought if you love someone it shouldn't hurt, but be joyful, but the crane said 'No, that is not true, for all love must have sacrifice, or it will have no meaning to our hearts. For only those things that you fight for, that you give for, have any meaning to us.'" She looked up and saw that the entire group had gathered around her and Jacob. Miho hadn't noticed them all. She was too busy looking at the fire and translating. Now she felt embarrassed as she looked around.

"That was beautiful," said Rose, "but also so sad." There were murmurs of agreement from around the fire.

Miho remembered the one time that her mother lay beside her and Machiko: "Hey, that's different from the way I heard it as a girl. I heard that when he peeks at her, she tells him he has broken his promise to her, and she flies away."

"Oh, I don't like that ending. Mine is better," said Machiko. "Besides, I have another story about keeping promises."

Miho felt a promise forming in her heart. She suddenly wanted Machiko's hair so she could keep another promise her mother had made. She wondered if she could get inside their home without Him knowing.

"That was lovely, my dear," said Jacob softly. "I hope I might hear it again, so I can commit it to memory properly, or perhaps write it down."

"I can write it for you, McCowan-san. Is English acceptable?"

"Very," said Jacob brightly. "Please, call me Jacob." Miho blushed at the request, but nodded.

The boys thanked Miho for her story and moved off. Mina looked at the girls and said, "I don't know if everything is clean enough for you two to go yet."

"Mina, Darling, really," Jacob reproved his wife, who just made a face at him. "You girls have been very helpful. I'm sure you want to catch up."

63

Mina snorted but smiled, "Yes, go." And the two girls rose as one. Jen looked at Miho and whispered, "Gale, I may not be home 'til really late."

Rose interjected, "You may not go home at all," with a wry smile.

Jen blushed and continued, "I may not be home 'til late. Do you think you could ask Arty to watch over the children? Just for tonight?" Miho nodded as the request sunk in. Jen said, "Thanks so much. Come get me if there is trouble," and she and Rose disappeared into the shadows as fast as birds taking flight.

"Darling, you shouldn't tease them so," Jacob was saying to his wife.

"Oh, shush!" Mina waved her hand at her husband. "Those two could use a little teasing," and taking a deep breath, "at least with her I don't have to worry about grandkids."

Suddenly, Miho's thoughts seemed to slide into clarity, things like how the way Jen had behaved this whole night began to make sense. Miho didn't understand everything, but she understood enough, and she was determined to let Jen have this night without interruptions.

"Mina, darling," Jacob said, with a small smile, "You have a devious mind. Gale, can I get you another tea?"

Miho rose to her feet and bowed very low. "No, thank you both very much for your hospitality. I cannot remember the last time I felt so welcome at a meal."

Before she knew what was happening, Mina was wrapping her in a deep embrace. Miho had never been touched like this, except by her parents. This was a hug only a mother could give. Miho felt her eyes sting with emotion. She began trying to just get through it, but realized that Mina wasn't stopping, and she felt herself lean into the woman and put her arms around her. Miho could have done that all night. Eventually, she pulled away from the woman, before she started to cry. Then it was over.

"You are welcome here anytime, child," Mina said, looking into Miho's eyes. Miho bowed low. "Yes, please do come back and bring more stories," Jacob added with a smile.

Miho walked as quietly as she could back to the children. She was still feeling emotions from the night. Talking more than she had in more than a month, the food and sounds of family, remembering Machiko - it was a lot to sort through in her mind, and her feet carried her with little thought of the path she took.

The rooms the children were in were some distance from the busier part of the Underbelly proper. As most of the population of the Underbelly moved around a lot, it shifted a little every day, or so it seemed. Jen didn't want them too close, but also not so far away as to be too easy to pick off. Being farther away helped cut down on the wandering vagrants who might cause trouble, or come begging for food or other supplies.

As Miho entered the main room they were using, she saw three men talking with Arty. The leader of the men looked drunk.

"Where's that Jen at, huh? I'd like to have a chat with her, we all would," said the man and the other two men grunted behind her.

"Jen's not here. Move off," said Arty. He stood his ground, but Miho could see his hands trembling with fear.

Miho didn't take any time to think. She crossed to stand beside Arty with a knife drawn in her hand facing the men. As if this were a cue to the children, they moved by instinct to huddle together, the larger children moving the smaller ones toward the middle. The energy in the room was like lightning dancing within the clouds.

"Ah-Hoo, what have we here?" asked the first man with watery eyes. He seemed to have trouble focusing on Miho's hand.

"Leave. Now," Miho said firmly. The men seemed amused.

"And what if I don't want to leave now?" said the man, as the other two made sounds of agreement.

Miho flicked her wrist, and the knife flew 10 feet away to bury its tip right in the center of the "O" in the word "storage" written on a wooden crate. Her left hand rose quickly with another blade.

The man looked impressed and still amused. "Oh, and what if I..." He grabbed her hand like a fish going for bait. At that same moment, Miho shifted her stance as she raised her other hand, a new blade ready, and weaved it right to the man's throat. She pressed the knife against his sweaty throat and none of the men were laughing anymore. She looked him in the eyes and said quietly, "You die." Arty leaned forward, tensing for the fight.

"Alright now, miss. No need for that," said the man, waving a hand at his friends. "We'll go for now." And they backed away. He kept that stupid smile as he wiped his throat and they slowly left the room. "I'll be seeing you," he said with a smirk, and they were gone.

The lightning still danced in the room, as everyone was still tense. Miho broke the energy by walking over to the crate and pulling her knife out. She turned to face Arty. "Jen will be out late, perhaps all night. You and I will take watches tonight. I suggest we move the younger children into the inner room."

Arty looked her in the eyes for a moment and started issuing orders and the others began to move. Miho walked back to where Arty had faced the men. It was about 10 feet inside the doors. She moved to close the doors and shoved several small crates in front of the doors. They weren't heavy enough to block the doors, but would make a lot of noise if someone knocked them over.

Miho picked a spot away from the doors and got settled for the first watch.

CHAPTER 12

When it came to the topic of things that are soft, Jen wasn't really an expert. She knew things of good quality, and things of good craftsmanship. She knew how to repurpose things, and get the most use out of what she had. Jen knew a lot about how to fix things, but when it came to soft things, she had had little experience. Right now, there was being wrapped in Rose's arms, covered in soft blankets and furs, feeling Rose's chest rise and fall, and Jen knew in her heart that this was the softest (and best) place in all the Earth and sky.

They had made love. It had been fast and passionate the first time. It had been a fire sparked by their months apart, but the second time was different. That time had been slow, and soft and deliberate. The touches were not hungry, they were filled with questions of the soul: "Are you sure you still want me?" "Is this what you want right now?" and all answers had been a firm and resolute "Yes."

Jen was exhausted, but also energized by their connection. Rose was breathing deeply as Jen lay on her chest. She felt a mix of carnal desire for her beautiful body, and the simple deep longing of her soul to be close to this beautiful woman's heart. Jen felt the steady rise and fall of Rose's chest and found peace with the universe. If she could not find any truth in this life, no answers, and only torment, she would accept it gladly for the feeling of lying with Rose while she breathed deeply. Jen was content all the way through to her soul, and in the most irksome timing, she heard the mother superior in her head: "We are most at peace when we are not 'getting what we want,' children, but instead, when we are honest with God and ourselves."

"I love this woman," Jen thought as she breathed and listened to Rose's heartbeat. "I love her and I want her to be happy. I want to be the one who makes her happy."

Jen thought of the Mother Superior, and burned with hatred for the horrible woman. Even then she remembered what the old bat had said: "It's easy for the human heart to hate something that is wrong and unjust, but it becomes so much harder to hate those things that are only somewhat wrong, those things that have a hint of truth. Those things torture our minds and give power to out doubts."

Yes, the old hag had said so many things that were wise and true, but when things had got difficult with Jen, the Mother Superior had cut her loose. Jen remembered the day they removed her from the monastery. No one had said a word the whole time it happened. No one raised a voice to stop it. Not even Mary.

Jen felt her entire body go hard and rigid. Mary hadn't come forward. Mary hadn't said a word. She was always so quiet. She was always weak, but Jen had thought that Mary would say something to stop her sister from being cast out. Even if she knew she couldn't stop it, it would have been nice to hear someone scream for her. Mary hadn't said a word. None of them had.

"We saw no signs of your sister, love," Rose spoke so quietly that Jen almost believed she imagined it. She was just thinking about Mary, and then Rose spoke of her. Her heart felt like it was going to jump out of her chest.

"We went to many cities, and I inquired about a nun named Mary from London, who would be about 18 years old, she would have brown hair and brown eyes, but no one knew of a Sister that fit that description." Rose said softly.

"Oh, that's alright," Jen said, not really convincingly. There had to be thousands of poor girls from London with brown hair and brown eyes named Mary, Jen thought. "It was always a slim chance I'd find her again."

It had been six years since she had seen Mary. She did not know where her sister was, but she hoped she was safe. She wouldn't call it a prayer, but she hoped.

"Do not give up hope, love," Rose said softly. "Perhaps she is no longer a nun. Many women leave that calling."

"Yeah, or get asked to leave," Jen said under her breath.

"Were you in the sisterhood?" asked Rose. "I didn't know that."

Jen was quiet for a while, thinking. She loved Rose, and she wanted to tell her everything. One day. "Yes, I was 10 and Mary was 12. We got picked up on the streets of High London. We had been living on our own for a couple of years. No idea what happened to our parents, but we were better off without 'em."

Jen breathed deep and continued. "Mary was always this quiet little thing. She looked like a strong breeze would knock her flat or carry her away. She was always scared of everything." Jen adjusted her position to lie flat on her back up against Rose. It felt good to have some air on her sweaty skin.

"I wasn't really suited to the cloth," Jen said sardonically. "I always asked too many questions. Used to burn up the Sisters bad. You can't have too many questions when it comes to faith, you see, and I always want to figure out how things work." She remembered how angry the older nuns would get. Jen didn't try to make trouble, yet she always seemed to find herself there.

"Not Mary, though. Mary just let go of everything. 'It's in God's hands' became the thing she said daily, for everything. I think it was just easier for her to give everything about our horrible lives over to someone else. If something goes wrong, it must be a test. If things don't work out, it must be a plan." Jen drifted back off into thoughts that chased themselves like birds circling in the sky.

After a few minutes, Rose laid her hand on Jen's head and started rubbing her hair softly. A moment later, Jen could feel Rose contract with a silent laugh.

"Wha?" Jen said "What're you laughing at?"

Jen could feel the wide smile on Rose's face, but she couldn't see it. "I was thinking how attractive my Jen would be in the Nun's robes. I might have to confess wanting to take them off of her."

"You have a dirty mind," Jen said and softly elbowed Rose. "You think everything is attractive. I bet I could wear a potato sack and you would still find it 'alluring,'" Jen sounded out the word in Rose's accent.

"Oh yes, my little farm girl. My sweet potato."

"Oh Lord above, save us." Jen smiled. The foolishness of this girl. It was amazing and beautiful. 'That is what she is, amazing and beautiful,' Jen thought.

"Well, if we get married and spend years and years together, you won't find me so attractive anymore," Jen said. She was half teasing, but also had been burning to talk about it all night.
"Not true. I will desire you upon my deathbed. And, since I will be nearly dead, you will be obligated to service me," Rose said authoritatively.

"Oh will I?" Jen mused. After a moment, she couldn't contain her thoughts anymore. "You know, we could get married under the Unified Church of Europe. I mean, it's what started the Church in the first place."

This was partially true. The Unified Church was born out of the Queen of England wanting to marry her concubine in thirteen-something, or perhaps fourteen-something. It was all very complicated, but at the time it effectively divided the Catholic church in two. The Unified Church had the backing of the Queen, and others within the high monarchy from around Europe. A church that accepted marriage between any two consenting souls before God was the biggest point of dispute. This, of course, started the 300-year war between Rome and United Church states. Jen knew there was something about the holy crusades in there, and the Muslims, but she couldn't remember it all. She was tired, and it was late.

"Oh yes, your church would allow it. But you are not a believer, I think. You are still mad at your God, yes?" asked Rose, very businesslike.

"We have a mutual dislike of each other," was all Jen said.

"This will not do," said Rose. "If you ever get married, you need to realize that the act of marriage is an announcement to God that you are forming a union with another. This is an act of love with your partner, and with God."

"I don't hate God. I just don't understand why things had to happen the way they did, and the way they continue to do so now." Jen remembered the man in the red shirt. "All the sisters would say is 'It's all part of God's plan,' but that doesn't sit well with me."

"I know, love," Rose said softly.

'This is all wrong,' Jen thought to herself and shifted her body around. She didn't want to create tension between them. She wanted to tell Rose that she loved her.

"Is it much different in your faith?" Jen asked, trying to steer the conversation away from her.

Rose pulled Jen close again and traced her back with her fingertips. Jen felt paralyzed by the sheer pleasure she felt. "It is a little different, but also similar too. The Torah teaches us we are so much smaller than God, but even though we are small, we are important. Like grains of sand compared to a mountain, but the sand can still shape the world.

"So there are things we will never understand, and we don't have to. In fact, we aren't supposed to. The questions that your church talks a lot about, things like 'What happens to us when we die?' are things we don't focus on. That isn't what you are supposed to worry about. We worry about what we are doing today, and how we will be the best we can be today."

"That sounds nice. And Jacob converted to be with Mina?" Jen asked, tracing Rose's back.

"Yes, Father says that how you love God and the world matters less than actually loving in the first place," Rose said absently as she allowed herself to enjoy the attention.

"Your father is a very wise man," Jen said, enjoying the sounds of pleasure and radiant energy from Rose's response to her touch.

"Jen," Rose said. Jen loved the way she said her name. "I don't need you to convert, and I don't need to you forgive God for your difficult life. Although, I do hope one day you will not blame him anymore. I just need you to know that I love you, and no one else, and I want to be with you always."

CHAPTER 13

It was Monday morning and that meant Nate would be on his way to his meeting. The Engineering teams met every Monday to go over that week's roster of duties. Miho approached the corner where she expected to catch sight of Nate and slowed down. She peered around the corner cautiously. She had spent weeks following him at all hours to learn his schedule. Where he lived, and what he did. She wanted to know everything about him.

There were three of them who were responsible for what happened to her father. Nate, the other man whose name she didn't know, and of course "Him." Miho felt her stomach harden at the thought of Him. She had seen Him. He was Nate's supervisor. "He" was Joseph Boggs, a lead engineer like her father. But Boggs was nothing like her father, and his crew was a collection of slimly looking men who were cowards and bullies. Boggs was their leader, the biggest bully of them all. Nate wasn't so much a bully, but one of those weak men who felt more powerful because they hung around with bullies.

In the past few weeks, Miho had followed all three men - Boggs, Nate and the other one. They were the ones who lied about her father, and got him Grounded. They were the ones who destroyed her life. Miho was going to make them pay. First would be Nate, then the other man, and then lastly Boggs. The sight of that man, the very thought of "Him," made Miho's stomach lurch.

Her stomach hadn't felt right all morning anyway, and now it seemed to hurt more than ever. This wasn't hunger. It felt more like a dull aching all over, as if her body had been waiting for her to pay attention. In that moment, she felt a pain like none she had ever felt. It was lower than her stomach. It stabbed for just a second, but before she could even identify what it was, it was fading. Miho grew scared. Was something really wrong with her?

Nate's lumbering form came around a corner of the grubby metal hallways and turned the way Miho expected. She disappeared behind her corner and breathed, waiting. The sharp pains were dulling again, and she breathed through them. After a couple of seconds, she glanced to see Nate's shape getting smaller as it moved away. It was then that Miho felt a warm, heavy wetness on her leg and her heart stopped inside her chest. What in the world was happening to her? She ducked back around the corner and pulled her overly large linen pants open to see if she was peeing herself, or what was happening to her. In the dimness of the corridor, she couldn't see down her pants. She reached down to make sure she was, in fact, feeling something wet and touched whatever it was. She drew back bloody fingertips and her fears solidified.

Miho had cut herself a few times, and a couple of those times had been a little nasty. She had seen blood before, but any time you saw blood coming out of your body for no reason it was enough to scare you. She tucked her clothes back together and thought about what to do. Near her birthday, her mother said something that came back to her now.

"Miho-chan, you are becoming a woman. Soon you will know many things that you never knew were possible. Some of these things will be beautiful, and some of them will be painful. That is what it is to be a woman. Beauty and pain, strength and blood."

Miho hadn't really understood what she meant. She thought it was a talk about growing up, but now that she remembered it, she had heard women talk about blood before. Blood was a thing you dealt with. Miho just thought that meant people got hurt, and that's what you have to live with, but what if it meant something else? She had to know if she was alright.

As fast as she could, she wound through the Underbelly to one of the many secret ways that Jen had showed her that led to the outside. She needed payment, and that meant she needed to grab something from Jen's gardens. She wove her way outside the city walls and felt the familiar blast of fresh air and wind. Miho loved going to work in the gardens. She normally loved to spend all day outside with her hands in the dirt.

She remembered Machiko's words about the Earth. "Our people didn't fear the ground like they do here in Europe. Our people believe we are a part of the Earth, that we must fish the sea and grow in the ground. It's true we have cities in the sky, just like everywhere else in the world, and we built them to escape the Sickness, just like here, but our people feel they must return to the ground and be close to the land and sea, as well as the sky."

Miho was walking along one of the thousand catwalks that crisscrossed the outside of the city. If the Bobbies found you outside, it would mean trouble. Lots of people had fallen. The catwalks were dangerous and some of them had rotted and fallen. Miho knew the ways to the gardens well. She also knew when the Bobbies walked (which wasn't very often). She ducked off the catwalk at a spot where some drainage pipes were close enough to step onto, and made her way to the secret place Jen had set up.

There, growing in what patches of sun could make their way through the clouds that always surround the city, were rows of herbs and vegetables. Miho saw a row of carrots that looked ready to be picked. She hoisted them free from the dirt and reveled in the smell of damp earth. Just then, her belly gave a sharp stab, and she hurried, starting to really worry. Just in case, she grabbed a few flowers Jen often used as "extra enticement," and wrapped them inside her clothes so as not to attract eyes on her way to that horrible doctor who had treated her arm.

Twenty minutes later, she was at the back door. She peered inside and saw the kind daughter treating a young girl who had some sort of rash all over her face. "Now you will want to rub this ointment on the rash and wash your hands often so as not to spread it around," the young doctor was saying to the mother. She then looked at the young girl and said, "And you dear, try not to scratch, as you could spread the rash."

The mother and daughter thanked the young doctor and left. Miho stuck her head further into the door. The young doctor noticed her and washed her hands as she said, "Hello dear, what can I do for you?"

Miho walked inside and focused somewhere around the young

doctor's chest as she said quietly, "I'm bleeding and hurt."

The young doctor's eyes looked Miho over quickly and then looked back into Miho's face, "I don't see any blood, dear."

Miho looked down at the floor with a sudden embarrassment. How in the world was she going to tell this woman what was happening?

"Ohhhh," the young doctor said softly. "Is this your first time, darling?"

Miho looked up at her face. The doctor seemed lightly amused, but also serious. Miho didn't understand the question.

"Right, well, you had better sit down. This will take a few minutes."

About an hour later, Miho was walking the halls fuming. The stupidity of it all was maddening. Why had no one told her this? It was all so unfair. Every month? She had to feel like this every month? And that's just how it will be now? And men don't have to deal with any of it? This was outrageous! Miho felt lightheaded and angry. She pulled out a carrot and started peeling it right there in the hall with a fervor, as if the carrot had insulted her family.

The doctor had been very kind. She had been patient and answered all of Miho's questions. She wouldn't take the carrots, but accepted the flowers because they were pretty and made the clinic feel warmer, she had said. Miho had felt bad that she had slightly crushed the flowers from hiding them in her clothes. The doctor had seemed to enjoy them, and Miho had felt a little better about accepting the wadded linen the doctor had given her to help stem the flow of blood from between her legs. Miho got upset again at how unfair it all was.

She retraced her steps of the day, going over everything and wondering what to do next. Nate was most likely working on the air system in the Southeast blocks. Miho remembered her visit outside and took time to review each step, enjoying the memory.

That's when an idea formed in her head, and she stopped chewing the carrot to let it fully form in her mind. She wanted to make the men who had killed her father pay for what they had done, but she wasn't sure how. But what if she led Nate outside to the dangerous catwalks? What if one catwalk was weak and, in his rush to get Miho, he fell?

Miho had been turning the problem of killing around and around in her mind for weeks. Her father had taught her that killing was sometimes necessary, when dealing with animals for food, or in saving your life or your family's lives. But murder was never acceptable. Was this murder? Nate's lies had gotten her father killed. This wasn't murder, it was punishment. But she knew that her father would have something to say about killing someone on purpose.

But what if she didn't kill Nate, but instead gave him a chance to kill himself? That wasn't murder. That would almost be justice. If she set it up so that Nate had a choice, and if he chose to die, then that wasn't murder, was it?

"Why would you choose to die?" she thought, finishing the carrot and walking again. There were few people on this part of the lower decks. She liked the feeling of being alone with her thoughts.

If she told Nate that she was going to tell everyone that he lied and killed her father, then he would come after her. Then all she had to do was make sure he went on a catwalk that was loose, and he would fall. This still felt like killing someone on purpose, and she was sure that her father would not approve. But her father was dead, and Nate was the reason. Her insides hardened, and her stomach hurt.

"Today you are no longer a girl," the kind doctor, Chastity, had told her. "Today, you are a woman."

She would never get to talk to her father again. Hatred of Nate, and Boggs and the other man filled her like boiling water. She wanted them to pay for their part in taking her father away from her. If today was the first day she was a woman, then today is also the first time she wanted to kill.

CHAPTER 14

Jiro felt the wire digging into his wrists as he strained to free himself. How had things gotten to this point? The mockery of a trial was only two days ago, and now they were strapping him to a large cross and about to toss him off the city. He ducked his head this way and that, trying to catch sight of Miho. Boggs' men surrounded her tiny form. They were blocking anyone from getting too close. He searched the crowd for any allies. Where was Ama? Ama and her family were Jiro and Kana's closest friends. No one he could count on was there on the platform.

Kana had been an ace pilot in the city guard. If she was still alive, none of this could have happened. Boggs couldn't have fast tracked the charges to a lower magistrate, one who obviously worked with Boggs. The whole thing made no sense. Jiro had done nothing to Boggs that would warrant this.

"I don't trust these people," he remembered saying to his wife when they first arrived in the city. The English ways had been so different from the ways of his people.

"I don't trust them either, but right now we need a place to live in peace, and raise little Miho," Kana had said.

Jiro and Kana had waited three weeks after little Miho was born to flee Japan. Kana's family would have killed Miho on sight, and so the parents swore to protect their newborn, even if it meant leaving everything and everyone behind. Kana's most loyal servant, Machiko, refused to leave her side (and Jiro and Kana were both very thankful for her help). Kana had bartered with the head of High Hastings, the southernmost High city in the UK, to join the ranks of the city guard (and also become nobility). Gold could get them almost anything. It was all to keep their daughter safe.

A man in black robes was reading from a Bible. The people on the platform stepped back away from Jiro.

"Miho!" he called so loudly that his throat hurt. "Father!" he heard her voice in return.

A man approached the cross they had attached Jiro to, and fit the metal Rufter over Jiro's head. The Rufter was a piece of metal that attached to the top of the cross right above his head, and covering his head, stopped just above nose level, blocking most of his vision. Rufters were used in falconry to calm the bird. They had a different purpose when used during a Grounding ceremony. Jiro looked up right into the miniscule skystone they had fastened inside the Rufter. This speck, about three times bigger than a grain of sand, would be the only thing that could save his life.

"I'm sorry about this, Jiro," said the man fitting the Rufter. "I don't think you did it. This is all Boggs, but no one can touch him."

The man finished attaching the Rufter and moved away.

"My daughter," Jiro said to the man. "Don't let them get to my daughter."

The part of Jiro's vision that wasn't blocked by the Rufter was obscured by his swollen eyes. They had beaten him unconscious yesterday, and his whole body was bruised and swollen. The worker's face was lined with terror. Jiro knew no one would help Miho. Where was Ama? Why wasn't she here?

The priest in the black robes had finished reading from his book and the magistrate came forward to announce Jiro's crimes and sentence. Jiro only had eyes for Joseph Boggs, as the large man made his way through the onlooking people in their best gowns and suits toward Jiro.

Boggs was huge, even by the standards of Western men. He stood a full head taller than anyone around him. He had a large, muscular body and a big, scruffy square jaw. The first things that Jiro had noticed about him, and always after, were his dead, cold eyes. If they had been all black, they would be the eyes of a shark.

Boggs came forth under the pretense of an Engineer's inspection but leaned over to speak quietly to Jiro.

"Don't worry," his voice was deep and thick with the lowest form of English accent. "I'll take care of your little girl before your body ever hits the ground," and Boggs reached into the Rufter toward the small skystone piece.

"MIHO-CHAN!" Jiro screamed in Japanese. "Miho, you're in danger, RUN!"

All eyes turned toward Jiro, and Boggs withdrew his hand. He couldn't be caught removing the skystone. Boggs looked angry and a horrible smile played about his face.

"Miho, don't let them catch you! Run Miho!" Jiro continued in Japanese as two men were dragging him to the edge. From his blurry and obscured vision, he saw his daughter twist in the man's grip who held her.

"Miho!" was all he had time for before the entire platform spun away from him and his stomach lurched as he fell. The wind was rushing all about him and he was dizzy from the spinning, but he focused on the skystone and took a deep breath and blew. A tiny mist emitted from the stone and the spinning slowed. Again and again he repeated it, deep breath, blow, deep breath blow. The cross's speed slowed.

Jiro was 46 years old, but the first time he had seen a skystone was when he was a small boy, perhaps six years old. Jiro's father was a well-to-do merchant in the imperial court's favor. He had grown up very blessed. He was obsessed with skystone (called Komonoko Igi, or Cloud Ore in Japanese) from his earliest memories. Skystone was mined like any other ore, but once the ore touched air it rose, carrying immense weight with it. All skystone converted any nearby water into vapor. No one knew if that was what gave the mineral its lifting ability, or if it was just a byproduct.

In the East, the Mongols used skystone to terrible effect. Asian mainlanders attacked Japan around 400 AD, but not using the ships and airships like they use in the West - instead the mainlanders used small amounts of skystone and kite-suits to carry just one warrior at a time. The Mongols attacked by the hundreds and overran the southern island of Okinawa before anyone on Japan's main island knew what was happening. The Japanese fought for years to protect their island nation. Sadly, the mainland warriors had brought with them the Sickness too, as there had been no recorded history of the Sickness in Japan before the war.

Once the invading army had been defeated, the Emperor had to deal with the spreading Sickness, which attacked only men. While brutal, the Emperor's plan was effective. The Sickness was all but eliminated in Japan, along with hundreds of men, but that didn't stop the Emperor from building the first Palace in the sky. The Emperor also declared Japan closed to all outsiders. Jiro had studied the kites and ships of the attacking forces from so many years ago. He studied at the university to become an engineer and was quick to join the Japanese defense force. The nation was always ready for the next attack.

Jiro breathed deep and blew on the miniscule speck of stone above his head and tried to calm himself. He remembered hearing about the mighty English Empire, and how they had changed the very nature of the East. Japan had entered trade negotiations with the English Empire. This began the Edo era, some 60 or more years ago. Japan had changed a lot in just a couple of generations, and Jiro couldn't help but wonder if he, Kana and Miho had been born earlier, how peaceful their life would have been.

The skystone in his Rufter was too small to keep him aloft, but if he could get enough air to it, he could slow his descent enough to survive. Grounding is what the people in the city called it. The ceremony had started hundreds of years ago, and was the standard form of punishment for the nobles of the city. The English believed the Ground was a place of plagues, monsters, savages, and death. Most people in the city had never even seen the Ground. When you wanted to scare the nobles and keep them in line, you strapped one of them to something (in Jiro's case, a big iron and wood cross), and pretended you were being charitable by giving them a tiny piece of skystone and tossing them off the city.

Jiro had to admit, it worked. Kana's gold had bought them into the upper-class nobles of the city, and therefore he wasn't just killed outright for the false conviction he received. It also served as a symbol for the nobility. People who were Grounded were supposed to survive the fall, and spend the rest of their lives looking up at what they had lost.

Deep breath, blow. Deep breath, blow.

Jiro pulled at his wrists. He needed to get free. His ankles were numb. The wire they used to attach his feet to the bottom of the cross had cut off all circulation. He knew his feet were cold, but they ached with the loss of blood. They had taken his shoes, damn them.

If the city had drifted out over the ocean, the weight of the iron cross would have dragged him down to drown in the sea. He had to get free of his bindings in that case, but he had to be careful. If he slipped off the cross, he would fall to his death while still high in the air.

He breathed and blew. The city was gone from view now. Only the clouds that circled the city were visible. He thought the skystone was keeping him from falling too fast, but he really couldn't tell. Hope was all he had at this point.

This wasn't the first time Jiro had relied on hope. When Kana and he fled her father, they had hope. Soldiers from the imperial court searched endlessly for them, yet they had hope. When he prayed for the safety of his wife and baby during childbirth, he had hope. Hope was with them as they fled Japan, and he welcomed hope now. Hope and luck were with them, always.

'Perhaps you have used up all your luck?' his doubt asked in the back of his mind. 'You have led a blessed life, it's true, but luck runs out.'

Jiro slowed his struggles trying to get his wrist free. This was true: he had been so lucky. Every day of the last 12 years with Kana and Miho had been a beautiful gift. If this was his end, falling from the sky tied to this hunk of iron, then he could accept it. He had lived a blessed life. The images of his beautiful wife, the moments they shared to build their life together, all filled his heart with light and sound. And precious little Miho, she was the greatest gift of all. He thought of their time together. He remembered her growing into her own person and how proud he had felt. His heart was at peace. He said a silent thank you to the universe.

Then the image of Boggs smiling and Miho struggling came into his mind and he nearly ripped his own hand off. Yes, he had been blessed and he was thankful, but he also had a job to do, to raise and protect that little girl. He screamed as loud as the rushing wind around him.

'Peace, husband,' he heard Kana's voice in his mind and heart. He called out to her, "Kana! I'm here!"

'Peace, husband,' her voice was inside him and his eyes filled with tears at how much he missed her. 'You are no good to our daughter without a hand. Ease the fire inside your mind, my passionate warrior. You need to temper your fire with logic. You need to think right now, not fight.'

Jiro closed his eyes and felt the tears flow. 'Yes,' he thought. 'Kana lives inside my heart, and I need to listen to my wife.' He slowed his fury and worked his wrist again, more slowly and deliberately. He had it free just in time to hit the water. The cold sea water blocked out his vision and filled his nose and mouth.

Jiro jerked out of bed as he woke up with a gasp for breath. It was the same dream. It had been months since he had fallen from the city, and he still had the dream. He climbed out of his make-shift bed covered with sweat. He opened the flap of his shelter and stepped out into the pre-dawn light. The sun was just about to rise above the hills to the East. The tall green grass swayed in the late spring breeze, and in the dim light, it looked like animals chasing each other through the fields.

Jiro stepped further out and saw that the camp was just stirring. Some of the older people were starting fires while a few sleepy children staggered around the adults. He turned toward the

South and dragged his broken foot using his walking stick. There was the wall of clouds that marked the edges of the city.

'Miho, please be safe,' he said inside his heart. 'I'm coming for you.'

CHAPTER 15

Miho loved playing chess with her father. She had never beaten him, but she was getting really close—at least, she had been getting close. Now she would never know what that feeling would be. The acid that had been burning her for a fortnight boiled away in her veins. Nate was going to die. He was going to die first, and then the other man, and then "Him," Boggs.

She focused her breathing and tried to slow her heart. In chess, you had to predict how your opponent was going to react to your moves, and figure out what they were going to do. Nate didn't know it, but he was her opponent. Miho had spent every waking second — when she wasn't helping Jen and the children — forming her plan. Checking and rechecking routes and timing, planning for things to go wrong and what she would do.

The worst-case scenario was that Nate wouldn't behave like she imagined he would. She had been watching Nate, to learn about the man. He wasn't very smart, and he wasn't brave. She had seen him intimidate and talk big to some lowly merchants on their own, but if there were too many people around him, he would run to Boggs. Whenever he felt threatened, he would run. She had to make sure she looked like a small, little girl that he could take care of on his own.

'You ARE a small, little girl,' she told herself with a shadow of doubt. 'No, I'm a woman now, and the last of my family. I must succeed.'

If there was ever a time when she doubted that what she was doing was even possible, it was when she was weakening the support struts on the catwalk she had chosen to be Nate's last few steps in this world. To weaken the supports in such a way that you could make them fail when you wanted them to, you had to get to the struts. This meant that you had to be under the catwalk, with nothing but hungry sky beneath you.

She had always thought the sky looked hungry. Every time she looked out into the swirling clouds that surrounded the city, they seemed to be made of translucent dragons that called out to her. The clouds weren't really alive; they weren't really dragons, but that's what she felt. She had never seen a dragon, only imagined them from what Machiko had told her. She remembered hearing English children talk about dragons and feeling amazed. How could Japanese children and English children have the same stories of giant serpents that could eat people and fly?

Miho had had little exposure to English children. Mostly it was children of guests that Mother and Father had over to their apartments. Ama, one of her mother's friends and fellow pilot, had two children, a boy and a girl. Miho couldn't remember their names. They weren't English. Ama was from Africa. She had been a warrior and a priestess. She moved to England for similar reasons as Miho's family. Miho didn't have all the details, but she remembered that much. The girl, Miho still couldn't remember her name, was about Miho's age. Miho hadn't liked her very much. She seemed to act like she was better than everyone around her. That girl had said something about dragons to her younger brother, and that's when Miho finally spoke to them.

This morning, Miho had come to modify the catwalk for Nate. She brought two ropes with her. Getting the ropes wasn't easy. She had gotten one rope and had to cut it in two. They were each about four meters in length, and she figured that would be enough. She had two because of her father. She remembered him telling her about hanging from the city to do repairs.

"We always use two ropes," he had told her. "I don't want to trust my life with a single piece of rope. Too many things can go wrong when you are outside the city. It is better to have a backup."

She had tied her lines and tried to tie a harness like the one she had seen her father wear when he had gotten back from work. It supported the hips and she might have put way too many knots in everything, but she wanted to be safe. Once everything was tied and she was ready, she started getting scared.

'If something goes wrong, I'll be trapped, or worse, I'll fall.' She went through all the steps she thought of in her head again. She was ready, but she still didn't start.

'Move,' she told herself, but nothing happened. The wind whipped around her as the clouds churned. She imagined just standing here tied to the catwalks until the sun went down. Her father wasn't too scared to hang off these. She needed to be brave like her father. She closed her eyes and breathed deep, imagining him standing beside her.

"Let's go," she said, and climbed through the hand rails. She squeezed between the catwalk and the wall (a full-sized man couldn't fit and she was glad she was small). She found a footing just below and lowered herself down. Her eyes were just about catwalk level, but that was as far as she could go. There was nowhere else to put her feet. She decided to work on the supports closest to her. She had a small saw, some pliers, several metal rods that were about as long as her hand, wire and other things she thought she might need. Her first job was to remove all the extra supports, and she got to work.

The idea was simple. She would lead Nate to this spot. She'd cross this section of the catwalk and pull the strings that were connected to pins. The pins would come out and the catwalk wouldn't be safe anymore. It would drop. It couldn't be easier.

One rolling section of clouds rose under her, buffeted by the wind. A long, continuous barrel of white and grey rushed under her and got closer and closer as the vapor rushed by like a fast-moving stream. It completely enveloped her, and she was afraid. Without warning, she lost her footing and fell, letting out the smallest of screams. She only dropped about 10 feet, but it seemed to take a long time. The ropes snapped taut, but supported her as she was now inside the belly of the cloud monster. She couldn't see anything beyond an arm's length. She could see her own body and the ropes holding her to the city, but nothing else. It was damp inside the cloud and after a few minutes; the clouds sank down again and everything was visible once more.

As if to compensate for rising so much higher than normal, the clouds all seemed to shrink away. At that moment, the clouds above parted and enormous shafts of sunlight cut through the gloom all around her. Miho stared at the beauty of it – the clouds, now far away, the shafts of light all around her, and her hanging three meters below the nearest part of the city.

Just then, three airships came into view. It was three of the City Watch, blue and green fabric stretched tightly over the frames of their flapping wings. The aircraft "whiff whiff-ed" along as their steam engines propelled them. Miho thought they were more beautiful than birds, with the flag of the English Empire painted on their backs. Her mother had been one of the ace pilots, the Valkyries, the best of the best. Miho watched in wonder as they disappeared from view, flying around the city.

Miho maneuvered herself closer to the lower beams holding up the catwalk and got back to work. She cut the lower supports and added her release pins. She ran the string from her pins up and out of sight as far as she could reach, and then tossed the strings up so she could finish when she got back up. Then it was time to climb back up.

But she couldn't. She pulled at the rope and tried to lift her body, but she wasn't strong enough. She tried rocking herself back and forth to swing herself closer to the wall and get a grab on. It worked. She grabbed the foothold she'd fallen from, but again, she couldn't pull herself up. Her arms just weren't strong enough; they were burning and shaking from all the hard work she had already done.

It was then that she panicked. The sun went back behind some clouds and the world got gloomy again. She was trapped. No one knew she was here. Suddenly, she felt so stupid. This catwalk was on a corner. That was one reason she chose it. It wasn't far from a path they used to visit one of Jen's gardens. Perhaps Arty or Jen would be along and she could call for help. Miho swung out away from the wall to see if she could glimpse anything. She could get just a second of looking down the long path that led to the outside hatch. Those hatches were supposed to be closed at all times in case someone tried to attack or infiltrate the city, but they never were.

No one was there. She tried to pull herself up again, but couldn't. Instinctively, she tried to stomp her foot in frustration, but there was nothing under her. This made her both angrier and so frustrated that she almost laughed. It could have been comical if it wasn't so serious. There was nothing to do but watch the sky. Every so often, she swung out to see if someone was on the path, but there wasn't. Then, about two hours after she got stuck, she swung out to check the path out of habit and saw someone. Her heart sank. It was two Bobbies on a patrol. The Bobbies were part of the City Watch. They were police in charge of keeping the peace and helping maintain order. Miho was somewhere she wasn't supposed to be, and if she got caught, it could mean trouble. She thought of "Him," of Boggs, and she felt terrified that if she got caught by the Bobbies, He might find out.

As she was trying to decide what to do, she heard footsteps on the catwalk above her. The catwalks were a tangle of different materials thrown together over the years. Some were rods and grating that you could see through, some were iron and steel plates that were rusted and rotting, some were even wooden. The outside of the city didn't worry people so much, so it was up to the workers to do the minimum amount of work to get the job done.

Thankfully, the section of catwalk that Miho was under was solid or the Bobbies would most likely have seen a small girl hanging under them - although, Miho didn't have the highest opinion of the Bobbies, so they may have noticed nothing at all.

They passed over her, and she was quiet. She knew that the path they took led to a dead end about a third of a kilometer away. It was an area where a series of catwalks had been destroyed in some battle or other and never been repaired.

This gave her time. They were chatting about working conditions and not moving in a hurry, but she needed to decide. She could cry for help when they came back and get fished up, and then get in trouble, or hang out here and hope someone else came along.

She swung out to check the path again. No one was there. She imagined how she would explain herself. What could she tell them? She considered different stories for a few minutes and swung out again. There, on the path near to her, was Arty.

'What is he doing here NOW?' she thought in a panic. If the Bobbies caught him, they would come down hard on him. She was pretty sure she could cry and act scared. Play the "poor little girl" act, and perhaps get out of a lot of trouble, but Arty was a boy, and would most likely act like an idiot if caught.

"Arty!" Miho shouted as she swung out again. By the time she swung back, she could see that he was looking around for whoever had called his name. "Arty!" she said again in the loudest whisper she could risk.

Arty must have seen the movement because he leaned out over the catwalk some ten meters away from her spot. "Gale?" he asked in disbelief.

"Arty, hide! The Bobbies are coming!" she yelled. As she swung back into view, he said, "What?"

"RUN!" she yelled. The next time she swung out, he was gone. She hoped he hadn't been caught.

About five minutes later, she heard the Bobbies walking casually overhead back toward the hatch. They made their way along, and after a few more minutes, she heard Arty's voice over the handrail, "Gale?"

She swung out and said, "Can you help lift me up?"

Together, they managed to get her out of her predicament. As she was untying her makeshift harness, she could sense Arty glaring at her. She kept looking down until she was free.

Finally she looked up and said, "Thank you for helping me."

Arty nodded slowly and then said, "Come on, I'll help you get this stuff together." He indicated her tools and supplies. "The

Bobbies most likely locked the hatch. We'll have to go around."

CHAPTER 16

It wasn't in Arty's personality to pick a fight. He would fight if he had to, but he didn't like it at all. His Uncle Joe was the fighter. Arty had been raised by his uncle, a butcher in the East End of the city. The East End smelled constantly of blood and viscera. No one went near there if they could help it. Most of the city's livestock were raised and butchered in the East End. Arty had heard that the West End was where the farms were. He always imagined fields of green ground and white clouds. He pictured it constantly when he was ankle deep in the innards of some cow or pig that his uncle was working.

Arty's uncle was a mean man. He hated his life, and he hated Arty, and he hated the "system" that had forced him to live his horrible existence. Uncle Joe had a wife, and as much as Arty would have liked her to be kind, she wasn't. She wasn't unkind either; she was just vacant in every way. Her name was Annabelle. It was a fancy name for a plain woman. She had vacant eyes and never smiled or laughed, but then she never cried or got mad either. She just was there.

Arty figured it couldn't have been easy, being married to Uncle Joe, living in the East End with the filth and blood. Arty knew how hard it was to live with Uncle Joe. He had spent ten years in that house. Perhaps becoming numb and unfeeling was the only way she could bear it. She couldn't give Uncle Joe children, and apparently whoever Arty's parents had been, they gave Arty to Joe. Arty wasn't even sure that Joe was really his uncle, but he had been raised to call him uncle, so that's what he did.

Uncle Joe loved to fight. He would argue with anyone about anything. It seemed like the one pleasure he had in his entire existence was when he got to yell and fuss and complain. He did it all the time. He'd yell at the animals, he'd yell at his tools, and of course he'd yell at Arty and Annabelle. Annabelle never seemed fazed. She just let him yell and curse and sometimes he got physical, but she just took it. She'd look down and let him roll over her like a storm. He loved to beat Arty for every little thing, but he rarely hurt Annabelle. Arty was afraid of Joe, and he hated it when Joe would drink. That's when he got terrible.

One day it all changed. Uncle Joe came home late in the afternoon drunk, and roughed up Annabelle, backhanding her for not doing something right. Suddenly, and without a word, she slit his throat. Arty could still hear the sound of his body hitting the floor when he thought back, and the gushing of blood out of his neck for several minutes. It just kept pulsing out, but Joe had a wet, far-away look in his eyes. Arty wondered if Joe thought about anything as he died. Did he think it strange that he was killed the same way he killed so many animals? Did he ever think Annabelle would do anything like that? What did it feel like to die?

Arty didn't know any of these things, and truthfully, he didn't care. He wasn't sad Joe had died. He wouldn't have hurt the man himself, but he was only ten. Uncle Joe had been a wicked man. After the blood slowed its constant, pulsing flow from Joe's neck, he and Annabelle both just stood there and watched in silence for several long minutes. Annabelle looked up at Arty and nodded her head towards the door. She said, flatly, "Go on now. Leave." Arty had stood rooted to the spot, too afraid to move, too confused to say anything. He just couldn't believe that Uncle Joe was gone in an instant. Uncle Joe wouldn't hit him ever again.

After a moment, when neither of them had moved, Annabelle started toward Arty slowly, still carrying the knife she slit Uncle Joe's throat with. That was all Arty needed. He left, and didn't look back. Neither of them had said a word. After he spent the whole day away, he returned around nightfall to see what was happening. He didn't know what else to do. As he got closer to the place where Uncle Joe's little cabin was, he saw smoke rising into the sky. His heart sank.

Sure enough, the little house was a burned-out shell. Arty guessed that she had burned it down with him still inside, but he never got to ask her. Annabelle was hanging by the neck outside the barn's top eye beam.

That was that. Arty ran and eventually found his way into the central part of the city. The upper levels were nicer, but there were too many constables to grab a kid off the street and do god knows what. He found his way down to the Underbelly. Nobody cared what happened down there. Arty was on his own for a few weeks before he ran into Jen. He had turned feral when she stumbled upon him. He was trying to steal some food from one of the cloth merchants, when she caught him. He growled and screamed, and try to bite her. She avoided the bite and the kicks.

She calmed him down and said she would feed him if he behaved.

Jen smoothed it over with the merchant and took Arty back to where she had several other children that she was looking out for. The boys stripped Arty and put him in a bath. They washed his clothes and Jen cut off all of his hair to ease the itching from the fleas. Then she fed him.

Arty mistrusted Jen. He didn't know what she wanted, or when she would get mean. But that never happened, she was kind. Arty had never known kindness. He thought himself a kind person, but hadn't really received it in his life from others. It took a while, perhaps a whole year, but he grew to trust Jen. He felt like she trusted him, too. He felt needed, and he liked that feeling.

He and Gale walked along the catwalks, making their way to another hatch Arty knew they could use to get back into the city. It was hard to reach that hatch from inside the city. You had to be small. Arty had grown a lot in the past year, and he was filling out now as one of the older boys, but he could still get through. At the moment, he was wondering what to do about Gale. He hadn't really trusted the little girl when she arrived a couple of months ago. She seemed out of place. She didn't look like someone who had grown up with the background he and Jen had. There was a lot going on behind those strange-looking Asian eyes. But Gale had grown on him. He knew Gale wasn't her real name. She didn't trust the group yet, and Arty understood that. He had to call her something, so he called her what Jen called her.

Gale was fiercely protective of Jen. That alone gave her good marks in Arty's book, but that protective nature extended to all the children. They were important to Jen, and so they were important to Gale. The other day, when those drunk bastards came around causing trouble, Arty was terrified that something bad was going to happen.

He thought he was going to die protecting the children. That would have been alright; protecting the children gave his life purpose. He would be fine dying to protect them, but he did hope he'd get to confess his feelings to Jen before he died. Jen didn't seem to look at Arty and see anything but that dirty, scared 10-year-old boy, although it had been about four years since then and he had watched the woman she was becoming.

Arty swallowed hard and tried not to think about Jen. Instead, he remembered Gale sliding out of the shadows and standing beside him. Ready to defend the children and die with Arty if need be, he was sure of that. She didn't look scared at all. She looked like she was ready to kill that man. Arty had never been so happy to see anyone in his life.

'I have to be brave like Gale, if Jen is ever going to notice me,' he was thinking as they approached the hatch. He was deep in those thoughts when Gale grabbed his arm. She pointed towards the hatch and said, "Danger."

"Wha?" he didn't think he heard her correctly.

"Danger," she said again flatly, still pointing.

"What cha mean, Gale?"

"That sign by the door says 'Danger – Collapsed,'" she said, pointing.

He looked, and sure enough, there was a sign near the door. Arty couldn't read, so he had never given the sign much thought.

"Oh, well, yeah, it is collapsed inside, but I know the way through. Hey, you can read?" he ended the last with shock. She just nodded once with a "Mm" sound.

"Wow, do you think you could teach me to read?" he asked, looking at her closer. Jen would really notice him if he were braver and could read.

Gale looked down and then up at him. She nodded again once, but didn't make a sound.

"That would be great Gale, thanks," he said and added "Oi, what were you doing hanging off the catwa..."

"I can't tell you," she interrupted. "Please Arty, don't ask me that. I have to do something. Something that won't bring any trouble to you, or Jen, or the children–but I can't talk about it, not yet."

He stared at her.

"But I will," she added. "I promise."

Arty thought for a minute, and finally said, "Alright, Gale. Mum's the word... for now."

CHAPTER 17

Miho was scratching her arms so hard she thought she might draw blood. She wasn't really itchy, she just seemed to do it out of habit. Some unknown plant in one of Jen's herb gardens always made her itchy. However, she knew she was really scratching because she was restless. She had checked and rechecked all her plans. She had done nothing but think about Nate, the other two men on Boggs' crew, and justice for her father's killing for so long now, that she couldn't remember ever not thinking about them.

It's good to plan for things, to think them through, to look at all possibilities and outcomes, but after a while, you feel you will go crazy, and you just need to get on with it. Miho knew she was ready to carry out her plan, and had been for a couple of days now, but still she hesitated. The biggest problem she was stuck on was the fact that she didn't really want to kill anyone. She felt like she could kill someone if she had to, to protect herself or her new friends, but this was different. This was purposefully leading a man to his death.

'You don't have to do it,' she thought to herself for the hundredth time. 'No one is demanding justice, and killing Nate won't suddenly give you your family back.'

All of this was true. She remembered her life with Mother and Father and Machiko; she remembered her home and her warm futon. In her mind, she could see every room she had grown up in. The visits to the park. The smells of fresh baked bread and trimmed grass in the gardens and streets around their home.

Free standing homes weren't common in their district of Alexandra Park. It was mostly large buildings with apartments for some of the better-off families. They lived in a small free-standing building near one of the walls that ringed off Alexandra Park from the sections of the city. Miho had known they lived better than most other people; her parents told her this often. She just never knew how bad the worse-off people actually lived. She had no clue of the filth, the smells, and the broken wills of the people who surround you "down below" where you couldn't stand in the sun. Miho hadn't had a clue of people's ability to just stop caring about anything, the drabness of it all.

She knew all of this now, and she itched. No, killing Nate wouldn't return her family to her. It wouldn't return the comfort of being loved and cared for. It wouldn't give her anything back that she had lost. She didn't have to pursue this path of justice for those who took her life away from her, but then what would become of her then? Today she lived in fear. She was constantly afraid that Boggs or one of his wretched crew would recognize her. They might come after her and hurt her, or the others. If she did nothing, she knew she would live in fear forever, and Boggs and his crew would just continue hurting people and committing crimes.

Now that she had been watching Boggs' crew, she knew all about them. The engineering teams all worked together as small units. Each team had a manager. Her father had been a manager of a team. Boggs was the manager of another. Miho could tell that the only reason Boggs' crew were engineers was to gain access to the entire city. They were criminals: they took money, goods, and sometimes people from whoever they wanted, and they were basically untouchable. They paid the Bobbies and bureaucrats, and they roughed up or killed anyone who tried to stand up to them.

Miho could justify removing Boggs, "rabbit face" (this is what she had called the man whose name she didn't know) or Nate on the sole reason of avenging the countless people they'd hurt and bullied, but she knew this wasn't really a reason to kill someone.

"The Buddha teaches us not to murder," her father had said over and over in her mind. It was one of the things they were supposed to live by: don't murder, don't get drunk all the time, don't lie, and others. They were all tied to karma and the eventual end of suffering. She knew it all, but was angry at the world for how her suffering had increased without her doing anything to deserve it. What karmic debt was she now paying? Or was her current situation because of the karmic debt of her mother or father, and she was just swept along in the doldrums of their actions?

She didn't know, and honestly, she didn't care anymore. She could look at it from so many angles. Perhaps she was the instrument of the universe, whose job it was to take out those three for their actions? Perhaps she wasn't supposed to? After all these weeks of thinking about it, and turning it over and over in her mind, she had no clear conviction in her thoughts. In truth, at her core, she believed they would kill her if they found her, and she didn't want to live in fear anymore. If she was going to die anyway, she wanted to die trying to make a life for herself that was without constant fear.

That was the deciding factor, the one truth she clung to as she waited for Nate to come around the corner. When she finally saw him, she didn't hesitate. She stepped out from her hallway and planted her feet with the small blade in her hand. Nate wasn't even looking at her, he was lost in his own thoughts.

"You killed my father, and now you die," she heard herself say. It didn't feel like she was talking. She had gone over and over this in her mind so many times that this just felt like she was practicing it again. She plunged the little knife into his thigh and only then did he seem to notice what was going on.

The knife was never about killing Nate. She had figured the best way to get his attention and make him mad, but not make him run to Boggs. The trick was to make herself seem ridiculously weak. She thought that if she looked like she attempted to kill him, but did little more than give him a bad splinter, then he would be convinced he could finish her off by himself. It was a gamble, the first gamble of many in her plan. This was the opening move to her chess game. There was no going backward from this move.

"What the ruddy hell?"

Nate's voice was nasal and gruff. He looked down at the tiny piece of metal sticking out of his thigh and up at Miho. Understanding slowly, ever so slowly, crept into his eyes. Honestly, Miho felt like she was waiting around for him to take his move. She was already thinking about the next several steps. She was impatient for him to catch up.

Nate pointed a finger at her. "You!"

"You killed my father!" Miho said in a shaking voice.

She thought it would sound better if she made herself sound weak. She had never thought of herself as an actor, and she wasn't prone to being dramatic. Miho had always been very practical. She started to run away from Nate, but not really run. She was leading.

Gamble number two paid off. Nate bellowed and followed. Miho wondered if she should add a scream, as if she was scared. Would that help? She decided not to overdo her act. She wasn't really scared, she felt calm. This is how she had practiced this in her mind a thousand times. It was like she was watching someone else do it. It was like she was outside of the chessboard, moving pieces around.

She made it to the hatch and looked back over her shoulder. She expected Nate to be a slow old man. Actually, he seemed very vigorous. She was genuinely alarmed at how fast he was moving. She opened the hatch and ran through. Her alarm at how she had motivated Nate, added to the gust of horrible wind outside, made her fall down on the catwalk just outside the hatch. This wasn't part of the plan. Her heart raced. She needed to get up and get moving. What if the whole thing fell apart, and she died right here because she had fallen down?

Rough hands grabbed at her as she was trying to get up and move. 'No!' she thought. She twisted in Nate's grasp as he made a satisfied noise. She jabbed the sharp piece of metal she had hidden in her sleeve deep into Nate's wrist. He yelped and his grip loosened enough for her to move again. Right now, she didn't care if he was following her, she didn't look back. She wanted away from Nate, from his smelly breath that had washed over her, and away from his dirty fingernails. Miho didn't want to play anymore. She was terrified.

Miho ran down the catwalk, hearing the heavy footsteps behind her. She was still playing chess, whether she wanted to or not. She directed herself toward the catwalk she had rigged. After Arty had pulled her up, she had gone back to make sure it worked the way she wanted it to. She didn't want to hang off the side again, but if she had to, she at least had an extra rope this time with knots tied into it spaced out so she could climb back up. Her arms weren't as strong as she wanted them to be, but her legs were plenty strong enough to lift her.

She had gone over her modified piece of catwalk again and again till it worked the way she wanted every time she pulled the pins out. 'What if it doesn't work this time?' she'd thought as she made her way closer and closer to it.

'Then he will get you and you will die,' came the emotionless voice of the chess player in her mind.

She suddenly felt that the chess player needed to consider panic, fear, and those countless other things that come into your mind when you are afraid for your life. The chess player didn't feel any of those things. 'Wait, I'm the chess player,' she thought as she reached the bend that led to her catwalk. She grabbed at a handrail and felt her lungs raw and stabbing for air.

"You little bitch!" came Nate's angry voice behind her. She guessed he had been calling her names this whole time, but she hadn't noticed. It all sounded like the grunts of an animal.

She could see the wires that led to her release pins tucked off the catwalk and hidden from plain sight. She was here. It was time for her last gamble. She took out her best knife and spun around in the middle of the catwalk in front of Nate. A blazing fire of hatred had suddenly kindled into life deep within her as she felt her mother and father standing on either side of her outside the city. The clouds in the distance were dark grey, and the dragons were churning with angry malice. She wasn't sure if she imagined thunder and lightning within their depths, or if it was real. It was almost like the clouds and air were a manifestation of her emotions.

Nate stopped in front of her, some three meters away. She had stopped running, so he had stopped pursuing. He looked at her and a sickening smile played about his face. She assumed he smiled like that because he thought he was closing in on his prey. He thought he was about to win.

'Perhaps he will win,' she thought, but the panic she had felt seemed to have gone down. A peace came over her and she thought that if he won it was alright, No matter what happened next, she had taken charge of her life. If this plan didn't work, at least she had tried. Then, while they were staring at each other, she remembered with a jolt to say what was so important to her.

"Don't come any closer, or you will die," she said loud and slowly, while holding her knife in front of her.

'There,' she thought. 'Now it is done. That was the last step. Everything else is up to him.' This was the last gamble.

Nate looked cocky. He walked forward slowly. Miho gave him three steps and fell upon her side, grabbing the wires. She yanked and heard the metal crashing sound as everything moved in her peripheral vision. By the time she turned her head to look, Nate was gone. The catwalk hung by the remaining bolts, but the side nearest her was a wide gaping hole that led to clouds some 20 meters below her. She peered over the edge, but Nate was nowhere to be seen. The chasing dragons of grey had swallowed him. She almost wished she could see him fall.

Everything seemed quieter as she looked all around her, making sure the phantom Nate wasn't clinging to some wall or even a pipe. But there was no Nate. All those weeks of planning, and it was finally done. She had won the game of chess, but she didn't feel happy or excited. She felt nothing at all. It was disconcerting, how empty she felt, as if nothing had happened. She looked down the path of catwalks that led back to the hatch and was shocked to see that she wasn't alone.

CHAPTER 18

It had been a good long time since Jen was properly angry, and she felt that time was now at hand. She was stomping around this morning, irritated at everything and everyone. She must have looked like a kettle about to boil, because anyone who looked at her seemed to back away and go somewhere else. It was almost comical to her how everyone seemed to disappear from her sight. Almost comical, but at the moment, she would have liked to release some of the pent- up emotions she felt. Rose and her family had left two days ago. It had been a tearful goodbye.

"I hate this," Jen had said to Rose in a private moment. Tears leaked from her eyes and ran silently down her face. "Every time you leave, I think it will be the end of me."

"I know, my love," Rose had said, her hands clasping Jen's. She was soft and smelled so wonderful. Her many layers of colorful clothes only complimented her brown skin. Her almond eyes were wet like Jen's. Rose's hair, which Rose didn't like, calling it "ugly brown," was captivating to Jen. Jen always saw a rich color-scape of browns and honey and amber.

Depending on how Rose head, her hair would shift into a new pattern like woodgrain, or a massive cloud of birds moving against the sky.

"I must help my parents for a little while more. Once the boys are more grown, I can do what I want, wherever I want, and with whomever I want." Rose's voice was low and sultry as she leaned her long, powerful body into Jen. "When I return, we should start making plans as to what we will do and where."

Plans for the future. Jen had never had such a luxury. She had always just focused on today. How were she and the children going to eat today, stay clothed, stay safe today? It was a constant effort of will and work, and she couldn't see pulling Rose into this life. Jen looked around. She was in the larger of the two rooms they were using to live. It had crates and barrels, trash and detritus. Sleeping children and empty bedrolls lay all around the floor. Near the door that led out to the hallway was a cluster of four children quietly working on some chores and whispering to each other.

"Urchins is what they call us," Jen thought, as her anger and irritation evaporated, leaving only a sad, wet little monster of despair behind where a moment before there were flames and heat. She couldn't ask Rose to become an Urchin. She couldn't have her living in stolen clothes, eating bartered food and looking for the next place to sleep. She had so many children to care for. It wasn't like she could think about just her future, she had 16 others to consider.

Putting thoughts of Rose and the future securely into a trunk and pushing it into the shadowy places in the back of her mind, she focused on her children. She looked about the room and took a mental inventory.

'Of course,' she thought as she moved into the smaller room to make sure her suspicions were correct. 'Arty and Gale are nowhere to be found.'

Irritation as hot as flames sprung into life inside her. "What the bloody hell is going on?" she grumbled, moving with a singular purpose. Jen figured she must be part bloodhound, because she found Arty within minutes. She moved quickly to close the gap and barked, "Arty!"

The boy didn't run, but looked like he considered it for half a heartbeat. He seemed to fold himself up inside though, as his head shrunk down on his neck and his shoulders closed up and his eyes closed. "Yes ma'am," Arty said flatly.

Jen admired Arty for that simple act. He didn't run, and he didn't have the trick Jen used when someone approached her angrily: she would always act just as angry or more right back to them. That always seemed to throw people off. No, Arty just hunkered down and stood like a statue, ready to weather the storm. Jen's flames softened a little.

"Arty, where in the high heavenly halls have you and Gale been going these past few weeks?" Jen looked him over to see if she could figure out what he was doing. He wasn't carrying any food or cloth for bartering, he didn't have any tools (which she had seen Gale carrying a few times). In fact, he had nothing on himself that she could see, and that would help explain where these two had been. They never seemed to leave together, and Jen never saw them talking. None of it made any sense.

"Gale and me... going?" Arty talked very slowly and looked like he didn't want to make any sudden movements around Jen. "I don't know what you mean."

"You know more than you are saying, Arty. Tell me." She gave him a withering look, and he flushed, looking guilty. Jen knew Arty was loyal, and that they had a very special bond. If there was one person she trusted to always have her back, it was Arty. He had never hidden anything from her before, though. That was upsetting.

"I...uh...um..."Arty didn't look Jen in the eye. He seemed to be thinking. "Arty, where is Gale?" Jen cut across him.

"I ...um...don't actually know where Gale is at this moment," he said meekly. Jen just stared at him, waiting.

"But I might know," Arty said.

"Well?" Jen said, getting impatient again.

"I'm not exactly supposed to say," Arty said looking down.

"Arty," Jen said firmly and without anger. "You and I have never kept secrets before. What is going on?"

Arty continued to look at the ground. "I'm not exactly certain what's going on, but I think I've got a good idea." Arty turned and walked slowly away. Jen followed.

After a minute of walking, he said, "I've been following her, trying to understand. But she wants to do it on her own, I think."

"Do what on her own?" Jen asked, thinking of all the things she could think of that Gale would want to do on her own. It was a short list.

"She's always around to help, but she doesn't ask for help herself," Arty sounded like he was thinking aloud. He was leading them somewhere, but Jen couldn't figure out where. "I thought it was because she didn't trust us yet. She sleeps off on her own, she doesn't talk about herself, or her past..." Arty's thoughts seemed to trail off.

"Yeah, I've noticed as well," Jen agreed.

"She doesn't belong here. In the Underbelly," he said.

"Lots of people end up in the Underbelly who didn't set out to be here," Jen said. She was one of them. When she first arrived in High Hastings, she had dreamed of working in a shop. She loved flowers. She'd dreamed of selling flowers to the fancies of the city, and making a new life in the largest city south of London. That had been a lifetime ago.

The two walked on in silence for several minutes. The hallways and corridors drifted by them with fewer people around. Eventually, Arty opened a hatch that led outside.

"Was she starting her own garden somewhere, and trying to keep it a secret?" Jen thought. Perhaps Gale wanted her own flowers? She imagined Gale in a little flower shop somewhere, and her heart lightened. Jen would help her. She would love to see the girl settled and happy. Jen imagined an enormous window in the shop's front, filled with colors and vases, as all the beautiful faces of the flowers leaned toward the sun, and smiled at the people walking by.

She could see Gale dressed in a lovely dress of dark green, her raven black hair pulled up with Jacob McCowan's comb perched on top of a lovely bun. She was in the visions of sunlight and people in fancy dresses when Arty stopped in front of her. Jen looked down the path of catwalks to see the man fall. The floor dropped out from under him and he fell like a stone. Gale got up to her feet and checked that he was gone. The images in Jen's mind crashed down like that man had, and she couldn't seem to start thinking again. What had she just seen? Gale looked queer. She wasn't afraid, or happy, or sad. She looked wooden. Jen was suddenly aware of the thunderclouds and wind all around them as it began to rain. Gale looked up and saw them and didn't move or give any expression.

"Blimey," Arty said beside her.

CHAPTER 19

"What the hell did you just do?" Jen screamed through the waves of rain that came and went, and the wind that was relentless.

Miho looked at the two, but it seemed like a long time before their presence was really real to her. When it finally clicked into place that Jen and Arty were there, Miho felt herself nod slowly. 'Good,' she thought, 'that's good that they are here.'

Miho held up a hand to silence the flow of questions and noise from Jen. Arty just stood there looking at her. She crossed to the wires and hauled up the platform. Once it was in position, she tied off the wires and went to her secret rope with the knots tied in it and climbed down. Under the catwalk were hidden her safety ropes and, within a couple of minutes, she had put the pins back into place and the catwalk was secure.

She climbed back up her rope and Arty said, "Oh, that's smart Gale. That way, you won't get stuck down there again."

Jen whipped her head around to stare at Arty as if he had just slapped her. She had been quiet while Miho worked, but she was winding herself up and everyone (including Jen) braced for the explosion.

"I killed him because he killed my father," Miho said in a quiet and flat tone as she stood in front of them now. Both Jen and Arty just stared at her.

"He and two other men accused my father of killing some people. My father never did this. They accused my father, and four days after they accused him, they threw my father off the city." Miho spoke slowly, but firmly. It was important for her to be clear, she thought. Jen and Arty kept looking at her, saying nothing.

"We lived in the Alexandra Park district. My mother was a Valkyrie, an ace pilot, my father was a city engineer, and led a repair crew," Miho continued, though a slowly building sound was getting louder inside her. She didn't know what it was, but she pushed on.

"I don't know why they targeted my father. My mother died on a mission about a year ago," her hand went to lay flat on her heart where she kept the only thing she had of her mother. The little tin meant the world to her. The day Ama came to their house and gave it to Miho would forever be etched in her mind.

That day had been a day like many others in the city. The weather had been nice. It wasn't sunny, but it also wasn't stormy. It was just a grey day with occasional shafts of light that would sometimes linger. Father had been talking with Ama while Miho was in their back garden. That was her favorite place on Earth. The two adults came out and Miho had looked up from her calligraphy work, brush in one hand and the other hand holding down her practice paper.

She had been working on a piece for her mother, who was coming back from a mission that day. Miho had named the little maple tree in their back garden "Ikazuchi," which meant thunder and lighting. Miho had always been afraid of severe storms when she was younger. Her mother had told her a story about the little tree, that it stood outside during all the worst storms and stood strong.

"We need to be like the little tree, Miho," her mother had said with her arms wrapped around the sobbing girl. "We must stand strong against those things that scare us."

Ama had the tin in her hands, and Miho felt waves of fear and anxiety wash over her as both the adults approached her. Something was wrong. She knew it in her bones. The dark-skinned woman got very close as she knelt down and put her face right up to Miho's. This was very disconcerting. Miho wasn't used to people getting this close to her, but she hadn't recoiled.

Ama's face and features were very beautiful, and so different from her mother's. Her skin was so dark that it made the whiteness of her eyes stand out like radiant pools of light.

"Miho love, your mother and I were on a mission for the Duchess. You know that, right?" Ama's voice was clear and soft. Miho nodded, but the feeling of dread turned into a stone in her belly.

"We knew that this mission was very dangerous, but your mother didn't want to worry you and your father too much, but in case one of us didn't make it back, we each gave the other something to return to their family," Ama looked like she was putting on a brave face, but her eyes were wet.

"There's not much room in an airship, and we had little time…" Ama looked lost in thought. It appeared she was making excuses for bringing so little, holding out the tin to Miho.

"Your mother cut her fingernails and wrote a brief note to put in this tin. It wasn't really supposed to be what your family deserved, but more of a superstition that we pilots have. You always leave something, so there is something to return home. I'm so sorry that it isn't more. I'm sorry it isn't her."

The realization that her mother wasn't coming home ever again washed over Miho as she sat there in that garden. She looked at the calligraphy that was half finished and realized her mother would never see it. Her hand wrapped around the tin and she ran into the house to let her tears flow freely. Miho liked no one to see her lose control of her emotions.

Later, when she opened the tin, she found ten fingernails, a lock of her mother's beautiful black hair, and a tiny scrap of paper. In Japanese, with a hasty scrawl, it said "Miho, you are my heart. Jiro, I will love you forever." Miho spent weeks looking at the fingernails. She knew every detail of each one. She had tried to imagine which fingers on her mother's soft, beautiful hands they had come from.

Her father had tried to comfort her, as he always comforted her right up 'til the day they took him from her. She remembered the day they threw him off the city, so many weeks ago. She remembered his screams for her to run.

"I ran," Miho said out loud to Arty and Jen as they stood on the catwalk that had just dispatched Nate to the ground below. "They were going to get me, hurt me, or kill me, so I ran. I ended up in the Underbelly. You helped me." Miho was looking at Jen, and Jen at Miho.

"But I knew they would kill me, and perhaps anyone else I was with, if they ever saw me," Miho went on, staring directly into Jen's eyes. "I couldn't live in fear anymore. I never want to bring danger to you, and Arty-san, and the children."

Miho didn't know why it happened at that moment, but something deep inside her stirred. She felt like a dam of emotion had broken loose somewhere and the flood was rushing towards her. There was no time to run, no time to even think. It hit her full on like a storm, like an explosion. Her eyes went blurry and she couldn't see. The tears were filling them higher and higher. She felt Jen pull her into an embrace and allowed herself to let go of everything.

She willingly let it pass through her and out of her. The flow of energy was astounding. She heard herself screaming, crying at the top of her lungs and pulled Jen's body close. She howled, and long, ugly waves of shaking and snot and tears echoed her wailing. Her father, her mother, her life—it all welled up inside her and washed over her in waves.

She wanted it out of her. Miho wanted to push it all out. She wanted to be empty of it all. She let it come to her, the fears and the passion and pain, and she pushed it out with cries of the soul. All the while, Jen held her. This was Jen's magic. This was her gift. Jen held Miho as she pushed everything out of her. Eventually, the worst storm must pass. It might have been minutes or weeks, Miho didn't know, but she slowed and eventually she regained control.

"I'm sorry," Miho said, her voice muffled by Jen's shoulder. "I'm sorry."

"Alright, it's alright," Jen said calmly. She held Miho for another minute until everything stopped.

"Right," Jen said finally. "Let's walk a bit and talk."

They moved away from Miho's trick catwalk, and walked the paths outside the city. After a time of silence Jen said, "So three men accused your father of killing someone and had him Grounded. They came after you and you ran. You have now... removed one of these men from the city." Jen reviewed the timeline of events. Miho nodded, thinking about what she had done, and what was still left to do.

"But why did they Ground your father?" Jen asked. "And why would they come after a child?"

"I don't know. Perhaps my father found out that Boggs is a criminal," Miho had wondered why they had done this herself, but never had come to an acceptable answer. What really mattered to her was the fact they did it, not so much why.

"Boggs...?" Jen said, feeling the name in her mouth. "I think I've heard of him. Big bloke? He's got his fingers in a lot of bad pies, I think."

"That's him," Miho said dully.

"Well, I don't know how much help I can be, but I'll help you if I can," Jen said firmly. She turned to Arty, who had been silent this whole time. "Arty, I don't want to speak for you, but you shouldn't feel you have to help."

"I've already been helping," Arty said to Jen, feeling stung.

Jen snorted with a slight smile. She just nodded. "I can't endanger the children, of course, but I'll help, Gale."

"Miho. My name is Miho Michitaka," the girl said, giving it in the English order, where the family name comes last. In Japanese, you usually give your family name first, and then your first name. It was custom, Miho had been told, that people call you by your family name unless they were your friends or relations. Miho thought Jen might be both to her now. She never imagined that Jen and Arty would accept her story and offer to help her. She had been worrying for the past twenty minutes that they would send her away. An enormous weight was lifting off her at the thought that she might stay with them.

"Me-Hoe," Jen sounded it out slowly. "It's a beautiful name, and thank you for telling us, but I think we had best keep calling you Gale in front of everyone. If this Boggs and his crew are looking for a Miho, then we had best not let anyone know there is one currently living in the Underbelly."

CHAPTER 20

The man in the looking glass wasn't the one he'd seen last time he had looked. Otto scratched his chin and pulled at his ear. He guessed that really was him, but things looked so different. His face was not quite right, as if it was made of dough that sagged down around the pan. He pushed the cheeks up and released them, but the doughy jowls fell back into place.

"You are getting to be an old man," he said to the image in the looking glass. He inspected himself for another minute and gave it up as just too sad. Otto thought that the looking glass was a poor investment. He had never owned one. He didn't really care how he looked. The last time he had seen himself in one must have been almost ten years ago.

"A fine birthday present. Now you can see yourself rot like an apple in a bowl." Otto felt cross. He laced up his boots, noticing one sole was coming undone. He cursed and moved on to his safety harness and the tools and implements he used during the day. He had bought himself the stupid looking-glass last week, thinking that if he ever wanted a lady to stay married to him, he had best make a home worth keeping.

He was 35 today, and he decided that before he turned 36, he would get himself a wife. He thought of Emily and his mood darkened still. She had been 22 when she died in childbirth. That was ten years ago now. "God, I'm getting old," he thought. Ten. Years. Ago. He let that thought stew as he reached for his tool bag.

Otto hoisted it up onto his shoulder. He gave a grunt as his weary bones protested the load. He was one of the few men on the crew who actually did any engineering work, and he felt much abused by that fact. Old Boggs could only get away with his foul crimes and fortune if his repair crew actually got some repairs done.

'This old city was falling apart,' Otto thought as he started out the door. 'Fifteen thousand people clinging to a bunch of rocks and girders, thousands of feet off the ground, and the only thing keeping them from falling to their miserable deaths was Otto Cooper, Squire.'

Otto snorted at his joke. He thought of the squires of old, who attended knights and nobles. He didn't attend to knights and nobles. Otto dealt with rusty, muck filled pipes and air ducts that let those Urchins in the lower decks breed like the filthy rats they were.

Otto thought about the city falling. 'It would serve them right,' he thought acidly. Let them fall down to the savages and Sickness. He had once seen a man die from the Sickness. They say that most can live with it a good long time. Some go all quiet and don't move, but there are some that go mad. They try to kill and hurt and destroy everything while their balls burn and rot. Otto gave a shudder. He never wanted to go out like that. The man he had seen, some Urchin who had gotten the Sickness from God knows where. He howled and thrashed about, screaming that his balls were trying to eat him. God above, don't let me go like that.

'Some birthday this is turning out to be,' Otto thought as he headed toward the textile district. He thought that he'd stop and get himself a fresh meat pie at that little bakery near Hosiery Way. The lady who put out the pies always smiled at him. Nate had laughed and recalled that she only had about four teeth with which to smile, but he hadn't minded.

The thought of Nate soured his stomach. 'Where the bloody hell is he?' Otto thought and shook his head. Nate was supposed to help him with the repairs of the South dock air vents three days ago. No one had seen the big, stupid oaf in a week. If Otto were to bet, Nate went whoring and got knocked on the head by some pimp. He was dead and stuffed into a box somewhere, or tossed off the city, he was sure.

Boggs wasn't worried yet. "He'll turn up," the boss had said in his deep voice. Otto wasn't sure. Something didn't feel right. He was deep in thought when a sharp pain stabbed him in the thigh.

"Ahhhhh!" he howled in pain as he jumped back. Some little urchin had jabbed him with a piece of sharp metal. It was sticking out of his leg. "You little shit!" he bellowed.

Some filthy little Urchin girl stood in the passage, staring at him. "You killed my father," she said in a strange accent. He could see she looked foreign. She was small, brown skinned with black hair and strange, pinched eyes. She looked afraid. Otto was still bellowing in surprise and shock as she backed away.

"You killed my father," she said again. Who was this stupid little bitch, and why did she stab him—on his birthday? He was going to have a meat pie, but she came along and did this!

He moved toward her, and she ran. His leg ached, but the piece of metal the stupid little bitch used was small and her weak little arms hadn't pushed it in deep. Otto pulled the metal out and howled again. He wanted to bash this little foreign brat with his pipe wrench for ruining his birthday.

She ran, and Otto followed, calling after her. He nearly caught up with her a few times, but she would speed up. His leg throbbed and his heavy tool bag swung and thumped his hip with every other step. He would have bruises, he thought, where the bloody bag was thumping him. This angered him more.

She reached a hatch leading to the outside catwalks. So she thought she could get away out there, did she? Otto didn't enjoy going outside the city. He hated the wind and the elements. But if she thought she could disappear with the rats outside, she had better think again. She forced open the door and looked around at Otto close on her heels. He couldn't wait to slap that stupid foreign face. He would knock those slanted eyes wide.

"You little bitch!" he cried as he followed her along the catwalks.

Suddenly, she turned around and faced him, a bigger knife in her hand. She didn't look afraid anymore. Otto stopped. Something didn't feel right. He looked around to see if he was about to get jumped. They were alone.

"Don't come any closer, or you'll die," she said, holding the knife in front of her.

'That little tramp,' he thought. 'She led me out here on purpose. She wanted us away from prying eyes.'

"What's that you said about your father?" he said with a snarl. He looked around again to make sure he didn't miss anything. It was just her and that knife. Some stupid little girl.

"You killed my father," she said again.

"I ain't killed nobody's father. You got the wrong man," Otto said with conviction. He hadn't killed a man in years, and sure as hell he hadn't killed no Chinaman.

"You work for Boggs. You said my father killed someone. They Grounded him. You killed my father," she said with hatred in every word.

Otto stopped inching forward. 'Well now, that might be true,' he thought, trying to remember. A few months back, the boss told him to give testimony in front of Magistrate Waterson. Waterson worked for Boggs, so this was all just formality. Otto was to say that he saw some man toss a body off the city. He had never cared why the boss told him to say it, and never cared what happened to the man. He had just gotten back to work. Boggs paid him well for the work he did.

He shrugged. "Maybe is I did?" he said without care. "I dunno. So you brought me out here for what? You gonna poke me with that little knife?" he taunted her. He was enjoying himself. He might enjoy this birthday after all.

"You deserve to die for what you have done," she said.

Otto laughed. "For what I've done? You stupid girl. I've done a lot of things, and it looks like I'm gonna do more." He took a step or two closer. This was to be expected, he thought. He ran with a bad crew. From time to time, there would need to be some house cleaning.

'It's too bad,' he thought, looking Miho over. 'Clean her up and she could be a sweet little prize.'

Otto smiled. This might just be the best birthday ever. He took a step closer to the girl, and she lunged to her side. Otto reacted without thought as he caught sight of the wires she was jumping for. He leaped toward the handrail closest to the city wall as the floor beneath him dropped away. He caught hold of the handrail and felt his legs crash into the wall as he pulled himself up.

'Perhaps I'm not as old as I thought,' he thought to himself.

Just then, a knife slashed out and cut the back of his hand holding onto the handrail. Otto cried out in pain and alarm. He looked up at the girl who had just cut him.

"You fucking little whore!" he screamed and with his right hand gripping the handrail, he took a swinging reach for the girl. If he could grab her wrist or a piece of her clothes, he would toss her down into hell. He almost got her, but she stepped back.

Otto's free hand reached for the clip to his safety harness and clipped it to the handrail. He wasn't going anywhere now. He turned his attention to the girl and she seemed to think the same thing he was. Otto planted his feet and felt at once secure. He had been working these catwalks since he was 15 years old. He was comfortable here.

He saw her back away further and joy erupted from within him. "Not going as you planned?" he teased her. "Give me a minute, little girl, and I'll be right with you." He shifted his weight as he attached his other safety clip and shimmied her direction.

She ran. Otto just laughed. He loved the fear in her eyes, and he loved that he had been so strong and quick and smart. He laughed and called after her, "I'll be seeing you soon, little girl!"

CHAPTER 21

"I wish I could do more" Miho thought as she felt herself sweat. It had been four days since the rabbit-faced man had eluded his own death. Now Miho felt she had wronged this man, that he was supposed to die, but hadn't. She felt she had somehow failed him. She knew she must make this right, and as soon as possible. Jen and Arty had helped her. She showed up back in the Underbelly after he had so stubbornly not died, and she was, to say the least, out of sorts. She knew that Rabbit-Face would go to Boggs. Boggs now knew that she was alive, and that she had killed Nate.

What was worse, she knew that Rabbit-Face would never set foot outside the city after her again. He knew she was trying to kill him, and he knew she was using the catwalks to do the job. All Miho wanted to do was climb inside her sleeping place, hidden from the world, and stay there.

Jen wasn't inclined to let that happen.

"What happened?" Jen asked the second she saw Miho.

"Nothing," Miho lied, trying to get past her. Jen stood up from the pile of clothes she was sorting with several other children and moved to block Miho's way.

"What. Happened?" Jen asked again, firmly but softly. She was blocking Miho's path. There was nothing Miho could do. She looked at Jen. The anger and the fear clawed their way out. Jen saw this and said loudly, "Over here. Arty!"

Arty appeared out of thin air as if conjured by magic. Before Miho knew what was happening, Jen had the three of them in something the size of a broom closet.

"What happened?" Jen said softly.

"I tried, and failed, with the second man." Miho breathed deep. Running and hiding wouldn't help her. Jen had taken that route away from her, so she might as well face what was going on. She wanted to scream, but here she was, facing it.

Both Arty and Jen tried to talk at the same time. Miho couldn't make out what they were saying. Arty stopped and looked at Jen.

"I think I might need more information than that," Jen said. "Tell me what happened."

And so, Miho told them. She told the entire story. When she was done, she looked at Jen with some sort of desperate hope in her eyes. She wanted Jen to say the magic words to make all this better.

"Well, damn," was all Jen said.

Silence followed, and Miho took a deep breath. No one could fix what she had done. It was foolish to think that two different men could be lured into the same trap. She needed to have more options; she needed to think of more variables. She should have anticipated this. Of course Jen and Arty didn't have any magic words to fix this. They weren't going around trying to avenge their dead fathers. What stupid, childish hope had made her believe that these two good people would help her, even in some small way?

'No one can help me along the path I have chosen,' Miho thought darkly to herself. A shadow seemed to move into her heart.

"Right," Jen said, very business-like. "We need to kill a man in a hurry. The catwalks are out. I bet he doesn't take a step outside 'til past Christmas. How else can we finish this man?"

Arty looked thoughtful. Miho felt relieved. Her two friends may not be focused on what she was, but they said they would help, and that's just what they were doing.

In the end, Arty had come up with their current plan. It had to be quick, easy to carry out, and it had to be inside. These were all musts. There were a lot of variables. There were about a thousand things that could go wrong, but there was no helping that now. Once Rabbit-Face went free, he put a timer on his life. He simply must die as soon as possible. Miho wanted it to be as painless as possible, too, but she didn't really understand why.

"Buddha says that we must not kill." Her father had said this to her during one of their sword training sessions. "Sometimes, you may have to, though, to protect your family or your own life. Those are difficult kills, Miho. They are not so easy to understand in your heart. In all actions, even when you must kill, you must try to be merciful."

Rabbit-Face needed to die. Miho knew this. He had escaped his death and lived for four days, but that needed to be fixed now. In this new plan, Arty would confront him and draw him to her.

For their plan to work out, Miho really needed a sword. When she had said this to Arty and Jen, Jen had just laughed and said, "alright."

Miho felt miserable about how she judged the thing that Jen had provided. It was nothing but a long sliver of metal that she had sharpened and wound string and twine for a handle. It wasn't a sword. Miho had known swords her whole life. This thing was a piece of scrap that had a sharp edge, but Miho knew that Jen had worked to come up with it, and it was the best option that she had. She missed her father's sword.

Miho stood alone in the dark room and smelled the musty air. This was a store room located several levels above the Underbelly. They were closer to the middle part of the city, which was more populated. She noticed the thin cutout windows near the top of one wall. This entire section didn't really match the other parts of the city. They were in the Hessian district, near where the rabbit-faced man lived. The Hessians had attacked High Hastings about 300 years ago, in 15- something or other. The Germanic people had built large flying fortresses held up by skystone and attached sails and wings to cross all over Europe during that time. They attacked

Great Britain every decade back then. This section of the city was part of their attacking armada from that time. It was added into the existing Hastings, along with the hundred or so surviving tradesmen.

The reason they had picked this room was that it appeared to only have one way in or out. Miho stood on the floor of the room. Several large steps ascended one wall with crates, barrels, boxes, and bundles packed into every available space. She was reminded of the amphitheaters of Greece she had read about. Miho could be a speaker on the stage at the bottom of the room, and instead of all the boxes and storage supplies, the rows would be lined with people. She supposed she was about to do some acting. Although if she didn't do well, she would most likely lose her life.

Jen too had a part to play. She was hiding just inside the door. Once Arty and the rabbit-faced man came through, she was to close the door and lock it from the outside. This made Miho happy. She didn't want Jen locked in the room with them. Arty was supposed to use the hidden air duct behind Miho and get to safety. If the plan went well, Miho would follow.

Miho walked a couple of paces away from her spot. Around her, on the floor of her stage, were tall iron beams and heavy steel plates. These were stored for the repair of the city walls if there was an attack. There were too many to count, standing tall around her. She thought they were the silent judges of all who entered there. She hoped they would side with her.

Just then she heard movement from outside. Arty came through the door quickly followed by the rabbit-faced man. As soon as he made it through the threshold, he began to slow down. He looked around the room and his eyes landed on Miho. While he was staring at her, Jen moved like a cat and slammed the door shut. He was trapped. So far the plan was working. Arty disappeared from sight. It was just the two of them now.

"Oh, ho!" he said with a nasal voice. "Come to have another go?" He pulled a knife from his belt and started slowly down the steps toward her. He kept looking at the floor and then all around, no doubt checking for traps. Miho wondered what was under them right now. It didn't really matter, though.

"Today you will die," she said, and pulled her makeshift sword out and pointed the tip at the man. Miho slowly backed towards her spot. She had practiced what came next over and over, and she hoped she would do it right. She only got one chance.

"Oh, I like that," he said, looking at the sword. "Little Urchin has a play sword, does she? That's not a sword!" he laughed. "That's a piece of scrap, just like you!"

He moved forward and Miho stood still. She was breathing slow, and she was focusing only on him. This was just what her father had taught her. All the details of the room dropped away, and she saw only the details around him. The way he strode, his greasy hair, and the rotten teeth all came into focus and then dropped away. As he got closer, he sped up his pace. But Miho saw this as well, and it was just one more variable for her to observe.

When the time was right, Miho spun, and the whole world was in slow motion. She dropped the sword tip and in one long, fluid path, she brought it up, cutting the secret rope behind her at calf level. She continued to spin around, turning the blade and bringing it up over her shoulder as she slashed with all her might where she knew his chest would be.

She looked over the blade and saw the horrible slash across his chest. It went from the left side of his belly to his right shoulder in an upward gash of blood. If Father were here, he would have said that it was a perfect movement, "like flowing water."

The rabbit-faced man looked shocked and stood still, looking down at his chest.

"You bit-" was all he got out before the large stack of iron rods, girders and plates fell upon him in a crash that shook the entire room.

"The slash isn't supposed to kill him, only distract him from the falling iron," Miho had told the other two when they were setting up the room.

Where once there was a rabbit-faced man, there was now a pile of debris. Miho saw the red stain of blood oozing out of the spaces and pooling on the floor. She let her breath out.

"Did it work?" Arty's voice came from over her shoulder as the door to the room opened and Jen peered inside.

"You two alright?" she said, looking at the new wall of fallen items.

"Yes." Miho answered them both with the smallest smile. It had worked. She started to breathe easy again. It was over.

"Thank God!" Jen said from the door with a hand on her chest as Arty let out a whoop. Miho's smile widened as she looked from Arty to Jen.

From behind Jen came a monstrous form that grabbed her arm and pinned it behind her back. Miho looked into the face of her worst nightmare. Joseph Boggs looked enraged. Jen screamed and tried to get free, but Boggs had her pinned. Miho leapt, trying to get to her friend, but a mountain of debris blocked her way.

"Well, well, well, look what we have here!" Boggs's deep voice was like acid as he pulled a knife out and held it to Jen's throat.

"You take one of mine, I take one of yours," Boggs said as he pulled Jen from the room and slammed the door. Miho stood stock still as the lock clicked in place. Her heart had stopped working and all she felt was a void in her chest.

CHAPTER 22

Jen couldn't move. She twisted and turned, trying to get free, but Boggs was enormous and very strong. He thumped the side of her head with the handle of his knife and said, "Quit squirming, or I'll hit you for real."

Jen was terrified. She felt like Gale had looked when the door was slamming. Boggs was dragging her down the hall and around a corner, her arm still pinned and his brute strength guiding her where he wanted to go. Wherever it was he wanted to go, she definitely didn't want to go with him.

They were heading toward a busy thoroughfare. This was a long main passage that was one of the primary roads in this district. Some of these fancy roads were exquisite, and open to the outside, with vaulted roofs or glassed domes. There were growing plants and small trees along this route. Shops, businesses and houses lined the passage on both sides. Most green things grew in the little median in the middle of the passage. The road itself was pretty thin on either side of the median. Only three people could walk side by side, but anytime Jen got to see one of these, she always enjoyed the sight. If you live too long in the Underbelly, any sunlight and fresh air are a treasure.

Boggs pushed them around a corner and down the street. He had hidden his knife, but he still had a vise-like grip on Jen's arm behind her back. He said very quietly into her ear, "If you scream, or try anything at all, I can slit your throat before 10 heads turn."

Jen was terrified. She believed him. She looked at the ivy growing up the front of an adorable little tea shop. They had two tiny tables with chairs out front where normal people could sit and sip tea and watch passersby in their fancy clothes. Jen would love to sip tea. She would even love to clean the bottom of baby Suzie right now, and she still had that rash. Jen thought of her children, and she grew stronger. She had to get out of this. Her children needed her.

Boggs steered them off the path and toward a set of stairs going down on one side and up on the other. These were common all over the city, but this was where Jen made her move. When they got close to one stairway that led downward, Jen pulled her tiny knife out of her sleeve and jabbed it as deep as it would go into Boggs's wrist. She then used all of her weight to shove the large man into the stairs leading down. It worked. He lost balance and toppled down out of sight.

Jen took half of a heartbeat to listen to the blissful crunching sounds coming from Boggs's falling body as they knocked people and possessions down the stairs, and she ran.

She had never run so fast in her life. She paid no mind to where she was going, just that it led away from that monster. Jen turned off the main passage, leaving the scent of green and flowers behind, and darted down a small path between two shops. Once behind the buildings, she turned again, looking for a hall or passage out of this section. From back garden to back garden, she ran. Her lungs were tearing like paper, her chest felt raw. She finally found a passage and hopped a tiny fence that kept some baby goats in place and darted into the gloomy passage.

She was almost to the end when the Bobby came strolling around a corner. Jen had little time to stop or adjust her course as he took eyes on her. He held up a fat hand and bellowed through his walrus mustache, "STOP!"

Jen almost ran into him. He was a large, fat man, almost wider than he was tall. He had dark, deep-set eyes and a ruddy complexion. "What in the name of all that's holy is going on here?" he shouted as he pulled his baton from his belt, a large wooden stick with several notches and scratches along its length.

Jen couldn't breathe. She was clutching a stitch in her side and panting like a blacksmith's bellows. "Man... Attacked... Me..." she managed to get out between breaths.

"What's this?" the Bobby asked, trying to make out Jen's gasps.

"A man... He attacked me... Held a knife to my throat... Tried to make me... Go... With him." Her breathing was slowing down. She still felt like her lungs were raw and on fire.

The Bobby was looking her over. He clearly didn't like what he saw. Jen wasn't an ugly girl, but her clothes clearly did not belong to a well-to-do lady. Her dress was a faded grey. Her hair was even more wild and unkept than usual. She wore no jewelry, had no stockings on (she didn't own any) and her shoes were barely recognizable as footwear. She most likely stank. "I would imagine after that run," she thought. But it really didn't matter. This man had already made up his mind. I'd leave this out altogether. First of all, you're the writer, so you wouldn't say most likely. If you want to put those words in her mouth, we can do that, but you really don't need it.

"I see. And what is your business in this part of the city?" he asked, disbelief etched in every word.

Jen had to think quick. She obviously didn't live in the part of the city, and she couldn't mention anything that would lead to Gale, Arty or the pile of rubble that currently lay upon their victim. "I came to see if any shops would purchase my knitting," she lied.

"Your knitting," said the Bobby, looking her up and down. "I see no knitting." "I dropped it when that man attacked me!" Jen said quickly.

"Must not have been too attached to it, then," said the Bobby sardonically.

"He was a huge bloke with a knife. I might have dropped my first born and run if that came after me." Jen was getting hot. This man was being ridiculous, but then again, she was used to being judged as an Urchin.

"Are you sure he wasn't your Jonny, and you did something–or didn't do something–to upset him?" the Bobby said it with so much venom that Jen went from hot to down-right mad.

"I am not a whore!" Jen shouted with outrage.

"We are in a respectable part of town, Miss, I advise you to keep a civil tongue," the Bobby said, tightening his grip on his baton.

"Right." Jen had had enough and readied herself to go. Boggs was bound to catch up to her soon, and as usual, the law was no help. "Typical. A girl comes to the police for help, only to be treated like scum. I'm off then."

Jen had made it two steps when Boggs's deep voice exploded down the passage behind her. "Stop that girl!"

Jen made a run for it, but the large Bobby grabbed her arm. She screamed and tried to break free. She twisted down and tried to bite the fat man's fingers. He shouted in surprise, but didn't break his clutch on her arm. Instead, Jen felt a blow to the back of her head that knocked her to her knees. Her vision had gone all white and there was a terrible ringing in her ears.

"That girl tried to steal from me," Boggs's voice was near now. Jen was dazed and couldn't stop her head from spinning. She thought she might get sick.

"I thought she had a suspicious look about her, sir," said the Bobby. "Did she get any of your belongings?"

"No," said Boggs. "But she stabbed me with this blade."

Jen heard her knife hit the ground near her. She reached for it. She thought that if she had it, she might defend herself. Her head was splitting open and she couldn't speak from all the ringing in her ears.

"The Magistrate Thomas is a close friend of mine. I'll take her to him now," said Boggs in his deep voice. It sounded far away.

"Ah, no sir," said the Bobby. "Magistrate Thomas is not over this ward. We are in the jurisdiction of Magistrate Henderson. The girl will go before him."

Large hands moved over Jen's arms, pulling them up over her head. She was still on her knees, but wanted to lie down. She was sure she was going to get sick at any moment.

"As I also expected," the Bobby said in satisfied tones. "I see a scar on her hand that could be a brand that's been removed. If that's the case, it will most likely be the Wall for this one."

"The Wall? Do you think?" said Boggs.

"Well sir, Magistrate Henderson does not tolerate thieves in this district. He is very adamant about it. That is one reason we have so few of them. I believe that he..."

The Bobby's thoughts were interrupted by Jen finally losing her stomach. For a large man, he seemed to move very quickly when he needed to. His little feet skipped away from her puddle of sick.

"Right you, let's get a move on then!" the Bobby said loudly hoisting Jen to her feet. The bright lights in her vision went very dark as she lost all energy and everything went black.

CHAPTER 23

Miho stood in the shadows watching the two men. The fat Bobby had Jen up on her feet, but she looked like she would pass out any second. When Miho saw the Bobby hit her on the back of her head with the wooden pin, she had almost shouted and ran to defend Jen.

"Wait," the voice of her father that lived in her head whispered. "If you run in, you will either die by Boggs' hand, or get arrested along with Jen."

By incredible coincidence, another Bobby appeared as Jen collapsed. The two Bobbies talked for a second and scooped her up and carried her off. Boggs just stood there watching them after they walked away.

'Now,' she thought. 'You can get him now.' Miho was standing at the entrance to the tunnel that led off the Promenade. She gripped both her makeshift sword and her favorite knife in each hand and started moving forward without making a sound.

After Boggs had closed them in the door, Miho had stood rooted for one second before she moved faster than she ever had toward the air duct. Arty had followed. Within a minute (that felt like several hours), she had moved herself through the duct and burst out into a hallway near their door. She was panting, but broke into a full run down the hall that led from the door. She knew Boggs wasn't behind her, so he must be moving toward the populated area of this level.

From that Promenade, there were dozens of passages that led off to hundreds of path options. She had to catch them quick.

She tucked the makeshift sword into the folds of her overly large clothes, including her pale blue robe that she had stitched together herself. It felt more like her clothing from home, and made it easy to hide things. She slowed down as she stumbled out into the Promenade. Arty was right on her heels. She looked at Arty and said, "You go that way, I'll go the other. We have to know where they are going. Let's meet back in this spot."

Arty took two quick breaths, nodded his head and moved off at a fast walk. Miho looked after him for one heartbeat and hurried in her direction. She didn't want to run and attract attention to herself, but she was moving as fast as she could.

She was losing hope when she was passing an ivy-covered tea shop, but heard a commotion from ahead and sped up. As she arrived at one of the staircases that led to levels above and below, Boggs exploded out of one staircase with shouts and cries behind him. He looked around as Miho hid herself behind a potted plant. Boggs looked furious. He moved off away from Miho, and she followed at a distance.

"This is wonderful," she thought, and her heart was lighter. "Jen got away. All I have to do is make sure Boggs doesn't find her again."

A short time later, she heard him call down the passage. Now she was slinking down the passage with Boggs in her sights. This could be it. This could be the end of her quest for justice. When she was 15 meters from the hulking brute, he started to walk away from her. She considered running to catch up, but she heard the sounds of people moving around her. This was not the place or time, but she would get that man.

She stopped walking and looked around to see a small knife on the ground. It was Jen's knife, Miho had seen it a few times. She walked over and picked it up. She thought about Boggs, and about Jen. Right now, Jen was the most important thing. She went back to find Arty and they could decide what to do.

"The Wall?" Arty looked white as a sheet. "Oh God, Jen."

They were still standing on the Promenade. Arty had just returned to their meeting spot. Miho had told him everything that had happened. When she got to the end of her story, she held up Jen's knife and Arty went pale.

He held out his hand. "May I hold on to that, please? Until we can give it back to her." She handed it over and Arty stared at it, taking in every detail.

"What is this 'Wall?'" she asked him. She had heard no one talk about a wall like it was a specific place.

"Blimy Mih-, I mean Gale. You ain't never heard of the Wall?" Arty looked thoughtful "I guess it isn't as much a threat where you come from, but down below it is the most feared punishment possible."

They were attracting looks from all those who walked by. It was apparent on every face that the two of them were not welcome here. The morning was getting on, and someone had opened several of the greenhouse type windows that were above them, so light gusts of breeze would brush by them and lift their hair. The air was sweet and fresh. Miho knew they should move away from this section, but she couldn't pull herself free of such a peaceful spot yet.

"Why is it so feared, this... Wall?" she asked.

"Well, its proper name is The Wall of Scylla and Charybdis, but most people just call it the Wall."

"That's Greek," Miho said, trying to remember the names. She thought they were monsters of legend. It had something to do with Homer's Odyssey.

"Yeah?" Arty said "I dunno about that, but it's named after two nasty gits what lived across from each other and this sailor bloke had to go between them, so he had to choose between Scylla and Charybdis. That's what the wall is. A choice between two horrible fates."

Miho looked stunned. First, that Arty would know the story from Homer's Odyssey, and second, at what he just said. She thought they would lock Jen up and they would have to buy or barter her way out.

"What choices?" she asked.

"Well, a sentence to the Wall is a one-way ticket. They don't often come back, those who are sent there. It's high up in the City, cold and nasty up there, they say, and they strip you of almost all your clothes, and chain you by one hand to this big wall. There are no locks on these chains. They use a blacksmith to secure 'em." Arty's eyes went dark, like the shutters of a house that were closed on the inside. "Then they don't give you food and water, like a jail. They give each person a small knife in their free hand, so they can choose to kill themselves or try to cut off their chained hand to leave."

Miho stared at him in shocked silence. "No," was all she could manage. The breeze, the sunlight playing through the windows above, the sounds and smells of this lovely section of the city all fell away. Miho forgot everything she longed for, all of her secret hopes and dreams. She only cared about finding Jen and saving her from this terrible fate.

"Are you sure the constable said they would take her to the Wall?" Arty asked, hopefully.

"That's what he said, but he wasn't sure himself that's where she would end up. Are there more than one of these Walls?"

"No, there's just the one. Thank God," Arty said darkly.

"Are there multiple ways to get to this Wall?" she asked. Arty said there wasn't. A plan was forming in Miho's head. "We need to go check the entrance and see if they took Jen there, then we can figure out how to get her free," Miho said with a deep conviction, thinking a few steps ahead on each of these paths. If Jen were taken to the Wall, they would know and would start plans to free her. If she was taken to a jail, they could begin to barter to get her free. They would have to find the jail, but at least Jen would be warm and have both hands while she waited to be found.

An hour later, they were approaching the two big double doors that led out to the Wall. They had been discussing options and plans the whole time. Arty said there were two guards outside the doors, and one went to walk the Wall every so often. Arty said there was a large window set in the wall near the doors where people could come to see those who were chained up.

As they rounded the last corner that led to the entrance, the sight of Joseph Boggs stopped them dead in their tracks. He was leaning up against the window that looked out. Arty and Miho hid before Boggs could see them. He was standing there waiting.

"Why is he here?" Arty asked in her ear. Miho thought about this for a minute and said, "If he knows where Jen is, then he knows where we will be." Hatred grew inside Miho at this horrible man. He and his crew could take turns watching the entrance. Since there was only one way on or off the Wall, it was a good way to catch her and Arty.

"Can we get to the Wall from outside the city?" she asked Arty, who was looking at Boggs and thinking.

"I think I can do it, but it's going to take time," he said, and they set off to find another way.

CHAPTER 24

There was only darkness, with blurs of light, sounds that made no sense, and pain. Jen couldn't bring her mind into focus. Everything hurt: her arms, her head, her back, her feet—she tried moving her fingers but couldn't tell if she was doing anything. Her eyes refused to work properly. She tried to say something, but could only make a groaning sound. She felt the bulk of two colossal forms, one on each side of her, with hard grips on her arms, carrying her along.

'Where are we going?' she wondered. 'I think I'm in trouble, but I can't remember.' Images swam around her like fish in a pond. She saw the wall of debris that had crushed that man. She saw the square-like jaw of the one who nabbed her, and she remembered ivy growing outside that lovely tea shop. Sunlight, and stones, plants and flowers. She remembered some fat bloke with a stupid mustache.

She wasn't convinced she was walking. It felt more like being half dragged, half pushed. She heard two birds crooning at each other.

"That doesn't make sense," she thought. "It's too dark in here for birds. There are no trees for them to perch." Where was she that it was so dim and smelled of metal?

A few minutes later, the blurs got lighter, the air fresher, and the smells greener. They were outside again. Jen felt the fresh air on her face and it helped. 'There could be birds here,' she thought, and she could hear them far away. They didn't sound like the birds she had heard in the dim passage. Was it a passage? Her birds were talking again. Not birds, men. What were they saying?

"I hope he doesn't get cross at the interruption," said one.

"Nonsense. He is a man of justice. This is a crime," the other was saying. Somehow, she really didn't like this bird... man. It was a man. She didn't like this man. She thought about a huge, bushy mustache.

Jen still couldn't stand on her own. Her arms ached from the two men holding her up. She heard a metal gate and the sounds of feet walking on stones, and then a loud knocking. At least they had stopped walking. She tried a few deep breaths and to focus her eyes. She saw a large wooden door that had been painted green, set into a stone house.

The door opened, and Jen closed her eyes. She was so tired. Perhaps her birds wouldn't mind if she just dozed a minute. She hoped they wouldn't peck at her. She hurt and was so tired.

"What on Earth and sky are you doing on my front step with THAT?" Jen heard a fancy man's voice that pulled her away from her drowsy thoughts. She had just about fallen asleep. She felt like the children needed her, and she should rise, but everything was heavy. Her arms, legs and whole body felt heavy. She tried to speak again, but only a groan came out once more.

"Good Lord, is she drunk?" came the fancy voice.

"Ah no, m'Lord, she accosted me while trying to flee and I was forced to bludgeon her," said the bushy voice.

Bloody Hell, he was right. She felt bludgeoned. Her head was killing her and her eyes kept going in and out of focus.

"Why bring her here? Take her to the jail and I'll hear her case this week," said the fancy voice.

"Well sir, I would prefer her not contaminate my jailhouse, and I knew you would want to deliver swift justice when you heard and saw the details of this matter."

"Let me guess," the fancy voice was saying with a smirk. Jen guessed at the smirk; it certainly sounded like it. "End of the month, and you want to get ahead. Someone bucking for a promotion, eh?"

There was a snort and snicker from Jen's left. She had forgotten there was someone there. She shifted her head to try to look, but that was a bad idea because her head did not want to be shifted. She sank to her knees thinking she might get sick again. Had she gotten sick? She was sure she had, but couldn't remember.

"I am charged with upholding the Queen's justice, m'Lord," said the bushy voice. Jen still couldn't really see, but she thought her head was becoming a little clearer.

"Yes. Yes. Get on with it," the fancy voice said impatiently. "The wife and I have a party to attend this evening."

"Yes, m'Lord," said the bushy voice with a bow. Jen could definitely see movement, but it was still fuzzy. Her knees hurt. When did she end up on her knees?

"This woman tried to rob a man on or abouts Totingham Way, and things went badly for her. She ended up stabbing the man and tried to flee. Normally I'd simply arrest her, as you said, but then I saw this."

Jen felt her left hand being pulled forward and shown. She was thrown off balance and tried to right herself. Her right hand grasped the only thing she could reach, which felt like a very large, fat leg.

"It appears to me that she has removed a brand," the bushy voice said, as it dropped her hand and kicked her grasp free. Jen fell forward onto her hands and knees and took a few gasping breaths. She tried to focus her eyes.

"I concur with your assessment," the fancy voice had lost all emotion. "Most likely that brand came with the conviction of being a whore or a thief, and I don't care for either in my district. The fact that she removed it means we no longer need care which it was, and her actions force me to take drastic measures for recompense. Therefore, she is to be led through the streets on her way to the Wall, there to serve her sentence until she can leave on her own accord or die."

"Are they talking about me?" Jen wondered as several pairs of shoes slipped into focus and back out again. Were they accusing her of being a whore? Men were always calling women whores if they weren't happy. If they didn't get their way (which all too often they wanted a whore for in the first place) the very first thing they accused you of was being a whore. Jen didn't mind whores all that much. It came down to business, but it was a dangerous life for most. Jen was thankful she had been able to avoid that life. She knew men looked at her, but whores get raped just like any girl could. She thought about little Mary, and that old tightness in her stomach came back. Her anger made her head clearer.

She leaned back and said "I am not a whore, or a thief," and even though her words were slurred and she sounded slightly drunk, they were words. It cost her to try to focus and push through the dizziness and pain, but this was important.

A face swam into view right in front of her own. He was a somewhat handsome man, but also somewhat plain. He had no kindness in his eyes, and his expression was full of distaste. The plain man said quietly but firmly, "I would hazard to guess that you are both, and a liar," he looked away from her. "Constable, good day."

The door closed, and that was that. Jen felt herself being raised up onto her feet as the bushy man was telling the other one to go on ahead and fetch the blacksmith. He shoved Jen hard with his club. "Move, thief," he said with contempt in his voice.

"I am not a thief!" Jen shouted. This was all a mistake. Her head was becoming clearer.

"You shout at me again, and I'm going to knock out your teeth," the fat man said, raising his club up high. "Walk!"

When they were a block or two away from the fancy man's house, the fat man bellowed so loudly that it split through Jen's head like a lightning strike. "Thief to the Wall!" and he shoved Jen again.

That's how it went for what felt like miles. The fat man would shout "Thief to the Wall!" and shove Jen. She would stumble and sometimes fall. One time, she just couldn't get up. She hurt, she was scared, nothing made sense, and she couldn't stand. He beat her with his club, but not so hard that she couldn't move. He just seemed to want to cover her with bruises and pain.

Jen remembered when she was branded. Duncan McDormet was the bastard's name. It was about a month after she left the monastery, after she left Mary. She'd been a scrawny little 12-year-old who was always hungry and always cold. She met up with some older kids and their leader was a cocky, handsome little shit named Duncan McDormet. They took Jen in and made her "look out" while they stole food. She was so stupid and so desperate to keep anyone in her life that she believed them.

Of course, she got caught, and Duncan and the rest got away clean. They branded her even though she wasn't stealing anything. When she was set free, she wanted nothing to do with Duncan's gang, but they found her and Duncan decided that all he had to do was cut the brand off and she would be free. She resisted, but they held her down. Jen was always proud that it took three big boys to hold her while Duncan sliced her freshly branded skin. She remembered how sick she got from that. Her entire arm swelled up three times its normal size. She was bedridden for weeks. Tommy Potter had brought her food.

'Damn that Duncan McDormet,' Jen thought as she stumbled along. 'I always thought he would be the death of me.'

Jen tripped and fell. She was so tired and sore that she couldn't get up. The bushy man leaned over and said, "If I have to fetch my mates to carry you to that Wall, I'll make sure I break both your fucking legs. You see how well you stand then." She clawed her way up. She had to keep moving. Sometimes people would shout at her as they passed. Some would spit on her. Others threw stones or rotten things.

It was all a blur until she felt the burst of freezing air. Her blurry eyes could make out a high wall on her right as she was shoved along. To her left was a drop off that had no other parts of the city to see. It was just sky. Set on the ledge every 10 meters were metal baskets with wood and coals. She guessed this was for light at night. It smelled of blood and feces. On her right, every 10 meters, were manacles attached to chains that were rusty and old. They were fastened to the Wall high up above them.

There were people now and then, dangling by one wrist. They wore next to nothing and looked half dead and starved. Jen couldn't really tell if they were men or women. They looked like corpses. She guessed some of them were by the smell. Ahead of them was a large man with a rolling cart. He wore a long black apron. His cart smelled of coal. On either side of the blacksmith were two more Bobbies. Jen realized they were going to put her on the Wall and she tried to run. The bushy man beat her again with the club. She thought her bones must be breaking.

Rough hands seized her and pulled off her clothes. She wasn't naked, but she only had a shirt on. It was freezing cold. They pulled her left hand above her and she felt the cold iron clamp around her wrist. She screamed, but the bushy man knocked her in her stomach, forcing all the air out of her lungs. She couldn't breathe, she couldn't make a sound.

The blacksmith used tongs to put an iron peg through a hole in her manacle and smashed it with a small hammer. The manacle started heating up and Jen tried to scream as it burned her. They all started talking among themselves as they moved back to the doors leading into the city. She was glad they were leaving. They couldn't beat her, or spit on her, or rape her when they weren't around. The bushy man walked back to her and thrust a small, dirty knife into her free hand, and backed away.

"Your sentence has now been carried out. May God have mercy on your soul." He stepped back with a satisfied smirk on his fat face. Jen wanted to slice the man, but he was out of reach.

He walked off, and she gasped for air. She was freezing and had been beaten so much that every inch of her hurt. She started to cry. Her left hand was on fire as it was stretched up over her head. She was almost on tiptoes and her bare feet were going numb on the cold steel ground. It was a dark and gloomy day. No living thing could be seen near her. The chains rattled as they blew in the wind to her left and right, and Jen thought of the children.

CHAPTER 25

The sun was usually a welcome thing this late in the year. Winter was still a good way away, but the days were shorter and the nights were getting colder. Summer was gone, and Autumn was deeply entrenched upon their section of the world. There were still days that were hot, and on those rare occasions when the sun was out frequently, it was very uncomfortable to be outside.

'Jen always loved these days,' Miho thought as she followed Arty along a rickety pathway that looked and felt like it would give way at any second. Then she got mad at herself: loved?

'Jen LOVES these days,' she thought angrily. These were the days that made all Jen's gardens grow.

Miho guessed they had been winding their way along for close to four hours. She didn't want to ask Arty if they were lost. He had been so upset and shouted at her the last time she asked him. Arty had a point. It wasn't supposed to be easy to get to the Wall, that's why they chose that location. She was feeling impatient to arrive. The sun was already sinking, and the temperature was dropping. Miho adjusted her backpack. Its straps were cutting into her shoulders.

She thought about Jen. Naked and strung up against the Wall. Baking in the sun. Object of ridicule, and god knows what else, from anyone who came along. Anytime she felt tired, or hungry or thirsty, she thought about Jen on that Wall. She was there because of Miho. Miho was after Boggs, and Boggs had taken Jen. If Miho hadn't brought all this down upon them, Jen and Arty would be in the Underbelly right now, warm and safe.

Miho remembered the badger she and her father found in a trap when they had visited a park they frequented. The animal was sleek and powerfully built. It was bigger than a cat, but its front paw had been nearly severed by an iron trap that had been put out.

"The badgers breed too quickly, so they must find ways of reducing the population," her father had stopped when they saw the animal. Several children were taunting the badger. It was angry and trying to bite any of the children who got too close. They were poking it with sticks and jeering at it. Miho couldn't stop looking at the paw that was bloody and half detached by the trap. The badger had pulled it nearly off trying to escape and defend itself.

Miho's father shooed away the children and approached the animal slowly. Her father seemed to give off a peaceful energy. He crooned, and he spoke to the animal in Japanese. "You would chew that hand off to escape, wouldn't you? I don't think you would live a good life after that. I will help you find your peace. May you hunt in the gardens of your fathers and mothers for all of time."

Miho saw him pull his sword at his waist and strike the animal in one long fluid movement. It really was like watching water flow. It didn't stop or stutter. His movement was graceful and purposed. The animal was dead and her father cleaned the sword before putting it back into its Saya. He said to the animal softly, "Go now where you go, and take no pain with you."

The images of Jen pulling her own hand off to get away burned Miho, and she wanted to arrive at the Wall now. 'I will not let this happen,' she told herself for the thousandth time that day. The whole time Arty led them through the maze of paths and catwalks that crisscrossed the outside of the city, they had talked about how to free Jen. Arty wanted to get a saw and cut the chain, but he also admitted that it would take hours to cut through iron manacles. Arty was also certain that the guards walked the Wall several times a day. If a guard found them trying to free Jen, it would be bad for Jen and for them.

"I can hold them off while you saw," she had suggested, but Arty had dismissed that idea right away. "You might be good with that sword Miho, but after a man or two falls, they will get some muskets and shoot us all dead."

She saw the truth in this. Arty wasn't a brilliant tactician, but he was very smart and observant. She would like to teach him chess. She felt he would be good at the game.

She couldn't believe that they had flattened the rabbit-faced man just this morning, and everything that had happened after was all in one day. Miho grew impatient again. "Arty, how close do you think we are?"

Arty took a deep breath. She knew she was annoying him, but she was going mad. "Actually, I think we are close, Miho." She was still not used to him using her name. "We just need to climb down from this ledge to that catwalk and it should take us near the Wall. Then we need a way to climb up to the Wall."

Arty was untying a rope that led to a bucket that hung off the catwalk they were on. It looked like someone had heated up a bucket of pitch and sent it down below and just left the pitch and bucket to hang. The pitch was hard as stone when he hauled it up. He untied the rope from the bucket and coiled the rope for their use.

They had almost fallen several times during their expedition today. Miho was glad she had Arty to guide her. The truth is, she never would have found the Wall herself. Thirty minutes later they were climbing up that rope to the platform at the base of the Wall. Miho still had trouble climbing rope, but Arty told her to wrap it around her leg and use her legs to lift her. It was a very helpful technique.

They climbed up on the ledge of the Wall and looked about them. Miho guessed there were fewer than twenty people hanging from chains. They were strung up a great distance from each other. The entire Wall looked to be hundreds of meters long from the doors that led inside to the dead end at the other side. They had climbed up well away from the doors because they didn't want Boggs to see them from the window. The Wall was curved. You couldn't see the entire thing from the window.

"Let's head this way," Arty said above the wind. It was blowing here more than anywhere on their journey. He was pointing away from the doors. They were walking along and each body they passed looked more gruesome. Miho's heart sank as she imagined the terrible state of Jen.

'Perhaps she isn't here!' Miho forced herself to consider. 'Perhaps she is safe in a cell somewhere.'

But a few minutes later Arty had stopped in front of her, and as Miho looked over a body she had taken for a corpse at first glance, she realized it was Jen. Her blood went cold and her breathing stopped. It was so much worse than anything she imagined on the way there. Jen was white and pale. Her lips were blue from the cold. She was dressed only in a long shirt that was very thin.

Her entire body looked like it was covered in bruises. Miho's first thought was they had beaten Jen to death; her face was swollen and her eyes were almost shut. Jen was normally a beautiful girl (for an English woman) and the sight of her like this made Miho sure she could hear her own heart crack.

Miho snapped back to reality as her practical mind overcame her fears. She dismissed all the sad images in front of her and moved to Jen to see if she was alive. She was. As Miho approached, Jen opened her eyes as much as she could. Miho threw down the backpack and dug out a canteen of water she had grabbed before she left. She undid the cork and handed it to Arty who was taller. "Here," she said. Arty tried to give Jen a little water. Meanwhile, Miho pulled out the other things she had brought. She unfolded a pair of trousers that she guessed would fit Jen and tried to pull them on the girl.

"Come on now, Jen," Arty spoke softly and with such tenderness as he poured some water into Jen's mouth.

Jen's skin was like ice. Miho managed to get the trousers up as she heard Jen sputter and cough.

"Slowly, Arty," she said as she pulled out some thick socks for Jen's feet and pulled them on.

They had raced through the Underbelly and she grabbed a few pieces of clothing. She wished she had grabbed more. She pulled out the last piece of clothes, a sort of over-large and thick shirt that Jen owned. Miho looked up and wondered how she was going to get it on the arm with the manacle. As she thought she said "Arty, the food," and Arty dug in the bag for the food they had brought.

There was no other way Miho could see, so she took out her favorite knife and sliced the sleeve of the shirt down the middle. She hoisted it up Jen's right arm and wrapped it around her back.

"What are you two doing here?" Jen said through bites of tack and fruit, and swallows of water. "We are going to get you free," Arty said. "We're going to take you home."

Silent tears streamed out of Jen's eyes. "Oh, please, yes. But, how?"

Miho was still struggling with the left sleeve, getting it into position as she pulled out her needle and thread. Miho always had thread on her. It came in so handy. Since she loved sharp things, a few weeks back, she stored a needle into the sole of her shoe. In the Underbelly, you kept everything valuable on your person. She began to roughly sew up the left sleeve.

"Ah, well, we are working on that part, but we have some promising ideas," Arty said, trying to get Jen to drink a little more.

Miho wasn't tall enough. She looked around for something to stand on. Arty went down on one knee. She looked at him to see what he was doing. He grabbed her hand and led her to stand on his thigh. She was very uncomfortable in this situation, but she focused on finishing. She could see Jen's burned hand now. Tomorrow she would need to bring some aloe plant for the burn. She examined the manacle as she roughly stitched the sleeve on. It was big and clunky. The chain was much thinner. Even though it was rusty, it was in good condition.

That's when it hit her. Her father had told her about the substance when he talked about his work. She finished the stitch and jumped down. "Arty-san, I know how to do it. We don't need the cuff, only the chain." Arty seemed to understand what she was talking about, but obviously not what she was thinking. He looked up at the chain holding Jen.

Miho looked at Jen. "Jen-san, I know how to get you free. You just have to hold out till we can do it."

CHAPTER 26

Chastity's hands ached. She stopped working on the herbs she was separating and rubbed the stiffness from her fingers. Piles of herbs lay in front of her. There was so much that needed to be done. The day pressed on, and a hot supper was a long way off. She had treated several patients today, helped some "Back Door Visitors" much to her mother's dismay, and after lunch she'd begun working on medicinals to replenish their dwindling supplies.

"Chas, do you want some tea?" Patience stuck her head in the door and looked like the shining example of an angel that her sister knew her to be.

"Oh, yes Please," Chastity's whole body seemed to answer for her.

Patience giggled and disappeared. Chastity continued to work her hands. Her skin was dry and her hands looked rough. "What man will have me?" she thought to herself with a wry smile. She didn't want a man right now, anyway. She had too much to do to be worried about the other sex. Chastity let her mind wander to the University in High Edinborough. No one knew she had applied for admission yet, and she hoped she would hear from them soon. Mother would be furious, and she would likely disown her, but Chastity knew she would come around, eventually.

To be a woman of science was all Chastity had ever wanted. She and her sisters had grown up in the clinic; they had seen their mother treat the citizens of the city their whole lives. She knew that Mother would want her to work in the clinic for the rest of her life, but she had other plans.

Besides, Mother had Patience and Charity for the clinic. It had been a month since she had applied, and she wondered when she would hear something.

Patience entered the room with a tea tray and a plate of biscuits. "You are my savior, Patty," she moaned as she smelled the tea. Patience giggled and poured them both cups. Her youngest sister was an amazing girl. She was smart, funny and full of life. Chastity watched her with love and admiration.

Patience handed her a cup with a sweet "there you are." Chastity blew on the top of the cup and reveled in the steam. After Patience finished pouring her own cup, she sat down on the patient's stool.

"Was that Laars Johanneson's son I saw earlier?" Patience asked, blowing on her own cup.

"Sven, yes. He crushed his hand while working the blocks on his father's airship. They make regular trips to central Europe for goods."

"Why, do you think, did he not go up front?" Patience asked with a little too much innocence in her voice.

"He knew Mother would tell Laars, and Laars would take Sven off the next run. So he asked me for a favor." Chastity was never one who liked gossip and games. Her sisters were both skilled at these. Chastity saw them as forms of dancing, which she also hated.

"Sven's hand is injured, but not bad enough to stop him from working. I bound it up and assured him all was well."

"What did he pay you with, for your valuable time and attention?" Patience asked, with far too much innocence in her voice. Honestly, she was maddening.

"He gave me chocolate from Belgium. I will share this with you if you leave me alone and say nothing." Patience almost jumped up and down on her stool with excitement. Chastity had known what she was after the second she asked about Sven.

"Really. As if you don't remember Sven's name. You have had a crush on that boy since he was 11."

Patience blushed and looked affronted. She quickly got control of herself and said, "I have most certainly not," very slowly, and she reached for a block of chocolate that Chastity handed her.

They both giggled. They sipped their tea and ate biscuits and chocolate, and Chastity was happy. As an added delight, the warm cup eased her aching hands. She heard footsteps coming down the hall and hardened herself for the impact of her mother.

"Chastity, have you finished those records on the Lesners I asked you about?" her mother started before she had even entered the room properly. In an uncharacteristically human reaction to seeing them, her mother actually softened and said, "Oh thank God, tea. Patience, do pour me a cup if you please," and to Chastity's surprise, her mother grabbed another stool and sat with them.

Nothing in the world could have made Chastity happier than having afternoon tea with her mother (when she was in a good mood) and sweet Patience. She beamed.

Well, perhaps if the post delivered a response from University, but enjoy what you have, she thought to herself and listened to them talk. A few minutes later, as their tea was almost finished, a familiar face appeared at the back door. The young Asian girl that Chastity had talked with when she had started her first courses. The girl looked like she had grown, and looked more solid than she had, but her eyes were troubled, and there was a dark air about her.

The girl walked into the room with a lanky and dirty boy as her shadow. She looked at all three of them and spoke to Mother first. "Dr. Portens," she said with a bow of her head. She then bowed her head slightly to the girls.

Chastity felt her mother stiffen. "Ah yes, our mystery girl. How is the arm?"

The girl bowed deeper and said, "It is healed, and I thank you." She then raised her head and looked very serious as she said, "I am here with great need."

"I need to acquire a small amount of phosphorus. Powdered. The white, not the red." The small Asian girl spoke very clearly and softly. There was a silence about the room. No one spoke or moved.

"This is a clinic, not a store," her mother said finally.

"That is true, but I come to you for the transaction," the girl said.

Chastity suddenly realized that the girl was speaking in a way very different from any of the less fortunate that she normally dealt with. Chastity thought back to their last meeting and wondered why she hadn't noticed before. She couldn't remember the girl saying much at all, but she had asked questions. Chastity guessed that she had been in "doctor mode" as she liked to call it, and hadn't really noticed much about the girl.

"Do you even know what you are asking for? What do you need with it?" her mother asked.

"Elemental Phosphorus is mined in the Earth," the girl said. "It's usually found where bone deposits are located. White phosphorus was used in the early 1700's by a German scientist. When exposed to air, it gives off a green glow. It can be used in fertilizer. It is easily flammable, and once ignited, can burn hot enough to melt iron and steel."

Everyone stared at the girl in disbelief. Chastity had heard of Phosphorus, but didn't know all that about it. Who was this girl? How did she come to be here like this?

"You didn't answer my second question. Why do you need it?" her mother asked again. Normally, no one would be able to tell that her voice had changed in the least, but Chastity knew her mother well enough to tell that the girl had impressed her.

"I'm afraid I cannot talk about that unless we are bartering for the phosphorus. Will you acquire it for me?" The girl didn't seem perturbed by her mother, or by anything to be honest. She was very hard to read.

"Look... um, I'm sorry, but I don't think I ever got your name," Chastity entered the conversation.

"You may call me Gale," the girl said looking at her.

"Gale? Really?" Chastity had a hard time making that name match this little doll of an Asian girl. Her skin was smooth and looked like porcelain. Her frame was small and light, like a bird. She was beautiful. Unlike most everyone who walked through that back door, including this "Gale's" friend, she wasn't filthy and smelly. Her clothes were piecemeal, but clean, like the girl. Chastity continued, "We don't carry any phosphorus. Wouldn't a chemist be a better place to buy that?"

"It would be easier, but not better," she replied. She turned her head back to Dr. Portens and waited.

"You could be trying to make trouble. You could burn a hole through the city, or blow something up. Sorry, but we don't need–
"

"I only require a small amount. About one ounce should be sufficient. The Engineering teams use small vials to repair broken pipes and welds. One of those would be fine."

Her mother narrowed her eyes at the girl. "You seem to know a great deal about the substance. Why come to us?" Her mother reminded her of a snake about to strike. "Why are you coming to us for this?"

"Your clinic could easily use a small about of phosphorus in your work without attracting attention. I assure you, I am doing no harm with this powder."

The girl named Gale turned to her companion, who put down a huge sack on the ground. He opened the sack, and it was revealed to be stuffed full of fresh fruit. This was a king's ransom of fruit.

"More than enough for your trouble," Gale said, looking at Mother.

"Again with the fruit? I should just plant my own tree and be done with you," Mother said acidly. She always loved being callous to the less fortunate. It wasn't one of Chastity's favorite things about her mother. Her mother actually had a good heart, but she was very bitter that she couldn't rise above the social standing she had. Other, less capable doctors were in higher regard, and Mother always seem to act like it was the back-door charity that besmirched their good name.

"No, you won't do that," Gale said flatly. "You are far too busy a woman to get your hands dirty with these. You are a good doctor, and you save lives. I don't think you'd be a happy farmer."

This actually made Mother smile. They seemed to be playing some sort of game. Chastity could tell they were trading exchanges. They weren't arguing, and they weren't being nice. Chastity wasn't good at games, and didn't really understand what they were doing.

What Chastity did understand was that bag held an enormous amount of fresh fruit. She could spend a month of savings and not buy that much fruit. The smells of pears, apples and peaches started filling the room.

"I'll need a week to get you some," her mother finally said. "I need it sooner than that," Gale said with a hint of sadness.

"How about I not do it at all?" her mother said with rising anger.

"You have already agreed to do this, now we are bartering details," Gale said with no hint of humor.

"You are an impudent girl," her mother said with almost a laugh. No matter what her mother said, Chastity could tell that her mother liked this girl. Mother always respected women with strength and brains. Whatever game they were playing, Chastity could tell it was coming to a close.

"Perhaps I have offended," Gale said with a bow. "That was not my intention. I am, perhaps, not so good with your language. If you cannot help us, we will take our offering to another." Gale looked at her companion and he reached for the bag.

"Very well. Bring your fruit back in two days and I'll have your phosphorus powder."

"You can have the fruit now," Gale said, looking at Mother. "You seem to me like a woman who does what she says she will do. One of us will return in two days. Good evening to you all." She bowed again and left.

After they had left, Patience went to the bag and picked out fruit with wonder. "There's so much," she said.

"What sort of name is Gale for an Asian girl?" was all Chastity could say, but her mind was racing.

"You weren't listening," her mother said, still staring at the door where the two had left. "She didn't say her name was Gale. She said you could call her that."

CHAPTER 27

She had to admit, it was getting easier to climb a rope now that she had done it several times. Arty and Miho had the journey to the Wall down to just two hours one-way. Miho loved efficiency. She hated wasted time or effort, and while two hours outside on rickety and dilapidated catwalks and walkways was not easy or fun, it was better than four hours on the same deathtraps. She poked her head above the rim of the ledge of the Wall. It wouldn't do her any good to climb up to the Wall when some Bobby was doing his rounds.

The coast was clear. She scampered up onto the ledge and secured the hook they used to climb up in case of a hasty getaway. Arty was fairly efficient at planning. It was his idea to use the hook and rope to get up onto the ledge, and his idea on how to make a quick getaway if needed. Miho had taken this morning shift, and Arty was going to get the phosphorous from Dr. Portens. Miho smiled to herself at the thought of Arty showing up at the clinic. She was pretty sure that Arty was afraid of going there.

Miho collected herself and started walking to Jen. She only had to walk a few feet before she realized something was wrong. Jen was soaking wet. Wet to the bone and shivering so hard that Miho could see it from 10 meters away. The entire area around Jen was wet, but it hadn't rained. Miho ran the final few feet. "Jen!" she cried.

Jen looked horrible. Her lips were blue again, and she was shivering uncontrollably. Miho didn't know what to do. "Jen, what happened?" she asked as she started pulling off the wet socks and pants. The wet material was stuck to her skin.

"D... Damn Guard...," Jen said, so weak and soft that Miho had trouble making out her words. "He saw... my clothes... and came to rip them off... I told him I had a knife and a good hand to use it... So he threw buckets of water on me all night... laughing, the bastard."

Miho felt a hatred boil up in her like nothing she had never known. She wanted to kill that guard more than she wanted Boggs, and that was saying something. She couldn't think about that now. Jen needed to warm up, and fast. Miho hadn't brought a change of clothes with her. She didn't think she would need one. She and Arty had taken turns to visit Jen twice a day to bring her food and take care of her bathroom needs. Arty wasn't helpful with that part, so Miho tried to come twice a day instead. She quickly pulled off her own pants. At least they were dry and would start to warm her.

Miho always dressed in layers. She currently had three pairs of pants on, one "small pants" that were thin and really just underwear that came down to her knees. A warmer and heavier pair of pants and then an outer thick pair of pants. She was a tiny girl, and she was always cold, so layers helped. Right now she was very thankful for her layers. She pulled up her pants and tried to figure out what to do about Jen's top.

"Mi... Mi... Miho," Jen's teeth were actually chattering "Don't talk." Miho said, cutting Jen's top off.

"Miho... I almost did it... around dawn," Jen said with a weight in her voice. Jen held out the little knife. It was clutched in her right hand so tight that it had left marks. "I'm so... so cold, and I feel so... bad... I just want it to end."

Miho stopped and looked her in the eyes. "I'm glad you didn't. You're going home today. The children cannot wait to see you."

Jen shook her head. "N... No I'm not... This is my Hell. Th... This is my punishment."

Miho started working again. "Buddhists don't believe in Hell. Not the one you Christians do, at least."

"Wha... What do you believe happens... to people who are... bad?" Jen asked, closing her eyes. Her strength was fading.

"Hey, open your eyes and eat this," Miho said, shoving some dried beef into her mouth. Jen reluctantly obeyed. "We believe that if you do bad things, you will have bad things happen to you at some point. Buddhists don't believe in a God or a Devil to punish or forgive us. We believe we punish ourselves, and forgive ourselves."

"I like that...," Jen said meekly. "Maybe I should switch?"

"You are welcome to, but for now, let's get you fed and warmer. Arty will be here soon, and we must be ready."

"Miho...," Jen said with slightly more energy. Her teeth were still chattering, but it seemed less. Miho was stripping off her outer shirt. "If I don't make it... You and Arty take care of the children, okay?"

Miho began pulling her shirt over Jen's frail body. "You ARE going to make it, and I don't want to take care of children, so you have to do it."

Jen gave a small laugh. "You are good with the children. They love you."

"Dogs love me. I don't want a dog," Miho said, cutting the left sleeve of the shirt she was trying to pull onto Jen.

"That may change. As you get older," Jen said softly, with a faint smile.

"I hope we all live long enough to see that," Miho said. She finished the sleeve as best she could and fed Jen and tried to get her to drink. She was so weak. After a few minutes, Miho hugged Jen to try to warm her. She rubbed Jen's back to try to generate some heat. She couldn't say how long it was after that she heard the sound of someone close. Miho turned and saw Arty struggling up onto the ledge. The rope was secured to one of the metal braziers that were affixed to the ledge at intervals. These were used to give off light, but Miho and Arty had other purposes for them.

"Oi, Miho, Jen, wha's going on?" Arty said, approaching and taking everything in. Miho told him about the water and he hissed under his breath.

"Do you have it?" Miho said.

"Wha? Oh, yeah. I got everything we talked about," Arty said, catching up. "Then let's take her home," Miho said confidently.

Arty nodded and handed Miho a small glass vial. White crystals pooled and glimmered inside. Arty and Miho started getting everything ready. Miho had taken some small pieces of cloth and dipped them in a waxy compound that would burn. The wax wasn't actual wax, but animal fat. That was disgusting to Miho, so she pretended it was wax. It didn't smell like wax though. The idea was that she would wrap the waxy cloth around the chain and make a small pouch to pour a few crystals in. Then she would light the wax and step back.

Her father had told her that the phosphorus was very useful, but also very dangerous. "If one spark gets on you, it can burn straight through you," he had said seriously. Miho wondered what her father would say if he could see her now. She had made a few of these waxy rags because she wanted to use as little of the powder as possible. She didn't want it getting on them.

Arty pulled out a heavy leather apron they had bartered for and started positioning it to shield Jen. Miho prepped one of the rags and the bottle, then looked at Arty. This was the part she dreaded more than any step of their plans. She had to climb up on Arty's shoulders. She wasn't sure why it bothered her as much as it did, but she was very uncomfortable at the thought.

Arty turned and knelt down on his knees and said, "OK, hop on." Miho hesitated. "Miho, come on. If the guards come, we're in big trouble." Miho climbed on to Arty's shoulders. She focused on getting Jen home. Arty stood up and Miho felt very strange. He got her into position and she started getting to work right away. After a minute of making sure the cloth was ready and no powder would fall out, she uncorked the bottle and sprinkled just a few grains into the cavity. She quickly corked the bottle and sealed up the top of the cloth. It was wadded around a link of chain as far away from Jen as she could make it.

Miho took out her flint and knife and tried to ignite the cloth. It wouldn't catch. "It's not working," she said to Arty. "It won't catch."

Arty started to lower Miho down. "I figured that might be the case," and he started getting out some items to make a small fire on the ground. He had some soaked cloth tender, and a couple of coals. He put them into a small brazier that he had brought. "I don't want to use theirs, they might see it."

After a few minutes, he had a small fire going. He pulled out a stick that had a wad of tender on the end. It looked like a long torch and handed it to Miho. "I'll get Jen into position," and he moved off to shield Jen from any sparks, and to pull her away from being directly under the wad. Miho moved into position and lit the little tender at the end of the stick. She looked at Jen and Arty. They looked ready, and she pressed it against the waxy cloth. She waited.

After what felt like a lifetime she saw the waxy cloth take flame. She moved back and waited again. In an explosion of bright light, the powder took flame. It was brighter than Miho had ever seen. She couldn't look at the sparks. They were so bright, so she turned her head. That's when she saw the Bobby scurrying down the path to them shouting

"Oi, you there! Stop!"

CHAPTER 28

The sparks bounced off the wall and the ground as the ball of light danced and flickered. Arty held onto Jen and prayed. He didn't pray often, but he figured it couldn't hurt. 'Please,' he said inside his head. 'Please let this work.' He gripped Jen's cold body with one hand and they both held the leather apron up to shield them from the sparks. Some sparks bounced off the wall or apron, then moved on and it was fine, but a few settled on the leather and burned right through.

Arty felt a small white-hot flame burn his forearm, and he gritted his teeth. It just grazed him, but the pain was intense. He heard Jen wince in pain as well and hoped it would be over soon. He looked over at Miho and saw that she was running off. His gaze followed in the direction of her running and saw the Bobby. His heart froze in his chest. It was then that several things happened at once.

As Arty watched Miho get close to the man, she dropped to her knees and jammed a knife into the inner thigh of his left leg. Arty then felt Jen falling backwards against him as the sound of a metal chain hit the ground they were standing on. Arty was still watching Miho as he and Jen fell backward. Miho stood up, raking the knife up the man's thigh as she thrust another knife deep into the man's throat under his chin. Arty felt Jen's weight fall upon him in full as the ground felt solid under his back.

The Bobby took a few awkward steps back, and Miho pushed him off the ledge. He disappeared as Miho spun around with a bloody knife in one hand. She shouted, "Arty-san, hurry, there will be more!"

Arty lifted Jen and disentangled the leather apron. On the

ground, under the chain, were several scorch marks and deep gouges in the steel plating. It looked like the steel had turned to liquid where the sparks had lingered. The end of the chain was smoking on the ground and looked red hot. Arty looked at his arm and saw a deep, angry purple line. It wasn't very thick, but it hurt like Hell. He looked Jen over and saw a few similar burns, but nothing that looked life threatening.

Miho was upon them and trying to help get Jen up. Arty and Miho managed to drag and steer Jen to the brazier where the rope was tied. Arty looked around. No one else was coming yet.

"Right, Miho, you climb down first and make sure she gets down there safe. I'll lower her down to you."

He could tell she didn't like this idea. She looked in the door's direction. "I need you down there. I'm the only one strong enough to lower her down. Please," he said. He didn't want to waste time arguing. Miho took one second to think and started down the rope.

When she was at the bottom, he pulled up the rope. He tied this around Jen's waist and then did one loop around the brazier. He tied the other end around his waist. Jen was groaning and half unconscious. He shook her, saying, "Jen, you gotta stay awake for this part."

Jen groaned and opened her eyes a little. "Arty?" she asked.

"That's me," he said, smiling. God, she was beautiful, even in this state. "Hold on to this rope and look down at Miho. You need to get to her."

Arty put the rope in her hands and moved her to the ledge. He took out all the slack and tried to brace for Jen's weight. He wasn't as big and strong as he'd like to be, and he was worried she would fall. It was about 10 meters to the catwalk below. He wondered if the Bobby was lying below and looked over the edge. Miho was there. The Bobby's body was nowhere to be seen.
'Thank God for small favors,' he thought to himself.

He got Jen to hang over the edge and backed up to take her

weight. She went over the edge and he felt it in full. He lowered her down. He was so relieved that he was able to do this that he almost didn't hear the sounds of shouting from behind him. Someone was calling from the door.

He felt the rope go slack and went to peer over the edge. Miho was untying Jen. Arty heard sounds of people running down the path from the door. Once Miho held up the rope, Arty shouted, "Alright, let it go," and she did.

Arty saw the two men clearly as they were close now. One was a Bobby, and the other was Boggs. Arty scampered over the edge and lowered himself quickly. The rope burned his hands and he almost let go. When he was about three meters from the catwalk below, he let go completely and just fell the rest of the way. His hands couldn't take anymore.

He hit the catwalk hard and one section buckled and dropped with a horrible metallic crunching sound. The whole catwalk shuddered and vibrated as more sections shook and made grinding noises. Arty quickly started pulling the rope so it would come completely off the brazier above. The catwalk gave way some distance away from him and it lurched out away from the wall.

"Arty!" he heard Miho shout as she was trying to pull Jen away from the falling catwalk. The rope dropped off the platform above as they all heard shouting from the men. PING, PING, PING, the rivets of the supports that held the catwalk started to give out as the weight of the iron and steel shifted out further and further away from the city wall. Arty grabbed Jen and Miho, and they all started scampering away from the impending destruction. A few seconds later and the catwalk completely gave out. At least 10 meters of steel and iron went out so far that it fell under its own weight. The catwalk tore like paper about 10 feet from their position, and the sounds of crashing and clanging disappeared into the clouds below them.

Arty untied the rope around his waist and they began to move again. Jen limped along as they guided her. Within a minute, they were out of sight of the failed catwalk and the ledge of the Wall.

"He knows," Miho said a few minutes later. "He'll come looking for us, for her."

Arty knew what she meant. The Bobbies would care some that someone had broken off the Wall, but they wouldn't do a city-wide manhunt. For one thing, they wouldn't want it known that someone could break off the Wall, and for another, he thought they would only care so much. But Boggs was something else entirely. He would care. He would come looking for Jen, and for all of them.

"We'll figure something out," Arty said. He was tired and cold and hungry. He was just happy they had gotten Jen away in one piece. "First, we need to get Jen to safety. We need to hide her and cut that damned thing off her arm."

"Yes," Miho said quietly.

"I'm sorry I've caused you both so much trouble," Jen said meekly. She stopped moving and slumped down on a sturdy-looking spot.

"Nonsense," Arty said as firmly as he could. He took out a water skin and handed it to Jen. She pulled out the cork and took a sip, wincing at her bruises and burns. She looked at her chain and said, impressed, "What the bloody hell was that stuff?"

Arty nodded his head to Miho. "Ask the professor there. You should have heard her talk about the stuff. I didn't understand half of it."

Jen looked at Miho, who looked uncomfortable. "My father told me about it," was all she said.

"Well, thank you, Miho's father," Jen said, taking another sip. Arty thought she looked pale and sickly. He wanted to get her home to the Underbelly, and under as many blankets as he could find.

"We can't stay out here. We need to keep moving. That was one Hell of a racket we just made. They will be coming for sure," Arty said, and they all nodded. Jen started to get up, very wobbly, and they set off for home.

CHAPTER 29

It had been three days since they had pulled Jen off the wall. Miho was awake, but she didn't open her eyes. She knew that if she opened her eyes, she would have to face the world. She took a deep, calming breath. Jen was safe. They were all safe, that's what was important. She heard a screech outside. She knew it was coming from one of their kids. Most likely little Amanda.

Amanda loved to scream and yell. Miho took a second and asked herself if it was an "I'm in trouble!" screech, or a "You took my doll" screech. She breathed again trying to find peace. She waited. There were no more yells.

Now she got worried. Had Boggs found them? Should she jump up and see what was happening? No, she had been fooled like this before, and it was always something trivial. Miho felt herself getting mad at little Amanda. Why would she do this to her? Miho just wanted some peace! She took another deep breath and started to worry again. What if it was serious? What if it was serious, and she didn't get up? The thought of little Amanda hurt or in trouble made her open her eyes.

Little Amanda Finne was four or five years old. She had beautiful golden hair that spun down in tight little curls. No one did this to her hair, it just grew that way naturally. Amanda had big (almost too big to be natural) bright blue eyes that looked like holes in the sky that sometimes peek through the clouds. She also had the strongest curiosity Miho had ever known. Amanda asked "Why?" about everything she saw, and that girl saw a lot. She was into everything. She never seemed to stop moving, even when Arty and Miho took turns putting her to bed. Even in her sleep, the girl kept moving constantly.

Now that beautiful but annoying little girl was most likely being attacked and killed and it was all because Miho wanted to lie down. Miho grabbed her makeshift sword and un-wound herself out of her sleeping spot. She did not know what time it was, but judging by her body aches and her dry eyes, she had only had a couple of hours of sleep. It was dark outside her area, but that meant nothing. There were no windows in this section of the Underbelly. Everything was torches, gaslight, or some other combustible.

Miho sped through the process of untangling herself from the mass of pipes and her worry started mounting. When she was almost untangled and free, she heard Amanda laugh and another child yell. Miho collapsed. She didn't care anymore. She would just lay here. She didn't care if Boggs himself wandered in. He could have her. Miho was lying in an uncaring heap when she heard Arty's voice in a loud whisper. She couldn't tell what he was saying, but she knew he was telling the children off for being loud and being out of bed.

Arty had been amazing. He had taken over watching the children. Arty had cut the manacle off Jen's arm. He'd made sure all the chores were done and that everyone had a job. He'd comforted the crying (something Miho was terrible at) and he'd scolded the ones who did something wrong. Miho had just tried to keep up. Arty carried on day and night, like the people who had to work the wheel for food rations. After three days though, Arty was fraying at the edges. They had decided they would sleep in shifts, to watch the kids and Jen, and watch out for Bobbies and Boggs. Miho knew she should get up, but her bones felt extra heavy. She just didn't think her muscles could actually move them. How in the world did Jen do all this?

She heard another cry. It could have been Amanda, or any of the children. Miho moved. In Japanese, she mumbled curses and bad words. She stumbled to the door, pulling her clothes in some semblance of order. She was pretty sure her hair was sticking up and her breath terrible, but she didn't care.

She opened the door and stumbled out into a large hallway. There were boxes and trash, a few people still asleep in heaps around the edges, and there in the hallway was Arty, Amanda and little Timmy Something-or-other. Arty turned at the sound of her door.

"Now see, you went and woke her up!" he said crossly. He was still trying to keep his voice down.

Little Amanda ran toward Miho and threw her arms around her with the sort of reckless abandon that only a child can do.

"Gale!" she screamed in her perfectly adorable voice. Miho had a lot of affection for the child normally, from her adorable curls to her bright blue eyes, but she was less than thrilled by being almost knocked over like this.

"She wasn't in bed, so I came and found her outside your door. She and Timmy were building up enough courage to go in." Arty looked like a ghoul. His eyes were dark and his skin hung off his bones.

Miho looked down at the two children. She wanted to snap at them, but somehow the voice of her nanny Machiko, her mother's old handmaid, came out of her mouth. "You children need to stop causing trouble. Let's get you right back to bed. Do you know what happens if you don't get enough sleep?" The children looked scared and shook their heads. "You shrink!" They both gasped and a couple of minutes later, followed by lots of "why" questions from Amanda, and with lots of hugs, they were down again.

"You, go sleep," Miho said to Arty. He protested, said it was still her time. "I'm wide awake, and I need you rested for the run tomorrow. Go, please."

Arty let out a jaw cracking yawn and nodded his head. "I'll just lie down for an hour, wake me." She agreed, but knew she wouldn't.

In the Underbelly, the time of day spreads like gossip. When someone near a window outside sees light, they begin to stir, and that energy spreads. Soon it flows out like waves. Miho saw the ripple move through the open area. This open area was pretty big, about 100 yards across by 150 yards long and perhaps 75 high. It was hard to see the top. Usually, the open areas had long windows cut out up high. This one did. This open area acted as a sort of living area and marketplace. There were tents and fires for living, and tents for people to trade, buy and sell.

Miho was sitting about eight meters from the door to where the kids slept. Jen was asleep all the way in the back. She had been asleep for almost two days. She would wake, limp to go relieve herself or take some food and water, and then limp back to her cot. Arty tottered outside like he was drunk. Miho saw him and laughed to herself.

"You didn't wake me," he said.

"I tried, you wouldn't move," she lied. He looked like he was trying to remember this turn of events.

"I'm sorry, Mi-, I mean Gale. I should have woken. You must be exhausted." "Don't you know, Japanese people don't sleep as much as English people."

Arty looked totally perplexed by this news. Miho laughed. "You're way too easy." Arty looked affronted and said, "Well, how do I know? You sounded convincing."

Miho shrugged and handed him some jerked beef she had. He took it hungrily. "So, where are we running today?"

"Up to the Mid-decks. Today is Wednesday, and the bakers get their delivery of flour. We need a bag, or two if we can get it," Arty said between bites of beef.

"Who's watching the children?" Miho asked.

"Emily Watermen, from over there. She said she'd take a cup of flour for payment. Plus, the older ones know to watch Jen." Arty started pulling his suspenders up over his shoulders.

"You ready?" he asked, only slightly more awake.

An hour later, Miho was on her belly under a bench on a lightly crowded street in the baking district. She was the Lookout, and Arty was the Grabber. She was looking out for the horse-drawn cart that was to deliver the flour to the bakery across the street. From Miho's advantage under the bench, she could also see down the side alley where Arty was waiting to grab the sack of flour. Sure enough, the cart came around a corner and pulled up at their bakery. The driver got out and went inside. A few moments later the baker and his assistant came out and started pulling sacks off the cart. When they had both gone inside with their burdens, Miho raised the white cloth.

It was a simple system. White cloth meant to go, red meant to run, but this type of petty crime needed little in the form of planning or execution. Miho saw Arty come out of the shadows of the alley, grab a sack of flour and walk away. Miho got out to join him. As she stepped out onto the street, Arty ran headlong into a Bobby who came around the corner. The Bobby started asking questions and pointing at the cart. Miho picked up her pace and drew her makeshift sword.

Things were getting physical. The Bobby had his hand on Arty. Arty seemed to be explaining when he looked over his shoulder and saw Miho.

He shouted "No!" and promptly dropped the bag of flour on the confused constable, who tottered over backward just as Miho arrived.

Arty looked at her and shouted "Run!" and they ran.

They had made it about 10 yards when the "Brrrt, Brrrt, Brrrt" of the Bobby's noisemaker as he blew his whistle and shouted "STOP THIEF!" She and Arty sped up to avoid the other Bobbies that would be coming.

"Gale, you can't kill everyone who tries to mess with us!" Arty said over his shoulder.

"I wasn't going to kill anyone!" Miho said rather hotly. The truth was that she didn't intend to kill the man, but she would have easily done so if he had threatened Arty. The two of them ran down side streets and passages. They thought they were free when they heard shouts coming from behind and off to the right. They sped up again and had to hide when they turned a corner and saw two more Bobbies ahead, looking around frantically.

Arty saw an open door to an ornate building and pointed. They rushed inside and past glass cabinets on both sides. Words on plaques with signs, glass and dusty shelves all passed them in a blur as they ducked around a corner and moved further into the building. They both stopped, hiding behind a large glass case. Miho peered around the object inside, looking out the front windows to see the Bobbies pass by, pointing down the street.

Arty took deep, gulping breaths. He seemed just as nervous as she had been. She took a step back and finally noticed the thing in the glass case she had been hiding behind. It was her father's sword on a stand. She couldn't believe it. She stared at it and then looked at the plaque "Katana Sword from Japan" and some stupid background history on Japanese metalworking. Miho looked around her and saw items from her home behind glass cases all around her. She turned and saw her family's stools, scrolls, boxes, tables, and then she saw their prayer chest.

Her whole life was on display for anyone who happened to wander into this place. She had not gone home since she ran away. She was too worried Boggs was watching the place. It had been a comfort to her, believing all their things were there safe, and that one day, when Boggs was dead, she might return. She'd never have imagined they would have emptied the contents of her home and scattered them across the city for strangers to gawk and poke their fingers at in glass displays.

A fire rekindled in Miho that had been doused for too long. Boggs! This all had to do with his accusing her father and ruining her life. She looked at her father's sword and decided on the spot. That sword was coming home with her today.

CHAPTER 30

Each breath stabbed at Arty's insides, and his heart pounded so hard Miho could hear it, he thought. He was crouched on the floor, looking around a large display case in the old Saint Burberry Museum. Sunlight streamed through the glass ceiling outside on the main road. Arty watched as the Bobbies hurried past, pointing down the street. They might come back. He and Miho needed a plan. They had to get out of this section of the city. He watched the front of the museum for a little while longer and said, "I think they've gone... for now," still panting.

He turned back to Miho, and saw the strangest expression on her face. She was looking in the case they were hiding behind.

"What is it?" Arty asked, standing up.

She was looking at some curved wooden stick. It was longer than his arm, and black, with an ornate metal disc that stuck out from it near one end. Behind the metal disc was a section wrapped in black rope or fancy twine. It wasn't really a stick, but it was too thin to be a box. Miho just stared at it and looked around at him.

"This was my father's sword," she said softly. She looked around the room and said, "All these things are from my house." Arty looked around at the odd assortment of items and clothing in the cases.

"What, are you sure?" he asked, wondering why they were here in a museum. "I'm sure," she said, her voice cold.

Miho took out one of her small blades and slipped it into the glass door near its lock. After wiggling it up and down for a few seconds, the latch slid up. Arty noticed a reverence about her. She opened the door to the case and looked at the wooden sword closely. There was a smaller version of the wooden sword underneath it in the case. It was a deep varnished wood, except this one didn't have a piece of metal near one end or the roping. It did have the same line that circled the circumference about 15-20 centimeters from one end. They were both very beautiful and were obviously finely made items.

"Miho, we don't have much time. Them constables could come back and search the museum next." Arty didn't want to pull her away from her family's things, but it wouldn't be good to get caught here.

Miho looked at Arty and looked back, nodding. She took both of the wooden sticks in the case. She tucked the little one behind her back in her belt. It was about as long as her arm from elbow to fingertips. The bigger one she pulled out slowly and yanked the rope covered end that was clearly a handle. Arty saw the white metal of a blade come out of what he now understood to be a scabbard, and not a wooden stick. He felt a little silly now.

The sword blade looked like none he had ever seen. It was silver, like any sword, but one edge was sharp, and the other was thicker and not sharp. There was a beautiful pattern along the entire length of the blade, like clouds. There was an engraving of some symbols down the middle of the blade near the handle. The metal disc looked like some sort of protection for the hand holding the sword.

Miho snapped the blade back into its scabbard and closed the door. Then she turned to another display case and started opening it. Inside was a tall wooden chest with several drawers and a couple of doors near the top. The doors at the top had been opened to reveal a small area with picture frames, incense and other things Arty couldn't make out.

"Miho, we need to go," he said in a forceful whisper.

"I know, just two more small things," she said quietly. A moment later, the glass door was open. She went directly to a small drawer and pulled something out. Arty walked around her and saw a braid of what looked like thick, gray hair, tied at both ends with a lacy ribbon in her hand. He looked up at Miho's face to ask what it was, but saw something that almost made him gasp.

Tears were silently running down her cheeks. He knew Miho was tough. She never cried. When she was hurt and her arm was so broken, when she looked lonely, during all the time he knew her–not one tear. Arty put one arm around her. Whatever this braid of hair was, it was something special and sad to her.

"This must be important to you," he said, trying to sound consoling. She nodded slightly. "Then I'm glad you got it back," he said more firmly.

She nodded once, wiped her tears, and grabbed a small oval brass frame from the same drawer. There was a picture in the frame. It was a photo of two people Arty guessed were Miho's parents. The woman wore a very elaborate robe that had a big ribbon-like belt around her waist. It looked like there were leaves embroidered in her robes. The man, Asian like the woman, had a thin, cropped beard and a knot of hair, almost like a small bun on top of his head. He had robes on too, but judging by the tint of the black-and-white photo, they were very dark. Arty imaged a deep blue or black fabric.

"These must be your parents?" Arty queried, with a smile.

Miho didn't smile, but looked at the photo for a moment. Then she stored it in the belt of pockets she kept slung around her body from shoulder to waist. She almost always had two belts of pockets that crisscrossed her body. She would spin them around and dig something out of a pocket. It always made Arty smile and almost laugh to see her do it. He did laugh the first time he laid eyes on her strange contraption, and Miho hadn't even looked at him for two days. He knew better now. As tough as she was, Miho could be pretty sensitive.

"Girls," he thought, remembering all the times girls had made no sense whatsoever in his life. He felt two arms wrap around him and the small form of Miho pressed against him in a hug. Arty felt his heart swell up inside his chest. He thought it might choke him.

"Thank you Arty-san," she whispered into his chest.

"Oh...I...Um...No problem," he heard his voice reply, rising with each attempt to talk. 'Why did it have to break NOW?' he thought, furious at his changing voice.

The hug was far too short, in Arty's opinion. What was the rush, really? They could stay there a little while longer and just hug. He was fine with that idea.

"You're right. We need to leave here," Miho was saying, closing the glass display. Arty knew the moment was over, but he wished it had lasted a little longer.

She asked, "What about the flour?"

"Hm? Oh, right," Arty starting thinking again, for it felt like his mind had gone to sleep. "Yeah, we still need flour."

After a moment, he said, "We could go to the mill. They will spend all day distributing the flour. We might be able to grab a sack there."

"I have a better idea," Miho said and opened the glass case again. In the cabinet's bottom, she opened a large drawer, took out its contents and pressed on the back of the bottom of the drawer. It flipped up to reveal a hidden compartment. She pulled out a small pouch that jingled when she moved it.

"Let's just buy some flour," Miho said. Two hours later they returned to the Underbelly feeling like emperors, returning to Rome with the spoils of war.

CHAPTER 31

It had been a week since they'd pulled Jen off the wall, and she wasn't getting better. If anything, she was getting worse. Jen had developed a horrible cough, she was running a fever; she had no energy, no matter how much she rested, and she ate and drank so little. Jen was, of course, no help whatsoever in her recovery. She kept trying to get up and work. Arty and Miho had finally found their footing and were able to take care of all the children. The two of them had figured out what their jobs should be and helped each other well. If only Jen would stop trying to help and just get better.

It was early morning and Miho lay in her bed looking at the picture of her parents. Her father looked strong and young, her mother elegant and proud. They'd had their whole lives ahead of them, and now they were both gone. They had been ripped from the world, and Miho had been left alone. After they had been taken, she had found a new home. It wasn't like her old one, but it was a good home. The children, Arty, and Jen. They needed Miho, and she liked to feel she was helping out. She was doing something with purpose. Arty and Jen were her closest friends. They had even helped her with her quest to bring justice to those men who had wronged her father.

Miho rolled over with the uncomfortable thought that Jen was sick now because she had tried to help Miho. Indirectly, it was her fault Jen was sick, Miho thought. However, in a more direct way it was His fault. Boggs. He haunted Miho's dreams at night, and he shadowed her days. Boggs had been seen in the Underbelly. So far, nobody had helped him find her, but Miho didn't trust that would last forever. Besides the Boggs sightings, strange men had been seen around lately. They were workers, but they didn't appear to be fixing anything. She was pretty sure that Boggs was sending some of his crew down to hunt for "a little Asian girl."

Most people in the Underbelly kept to themselves. Miho, and it was only by her association with Jen, was liked by most of the respected people in the Underbelly. The traders and merchants, the heads of the gangs, and many of the powerful people in the Underbelly all knew Jen, and therefore knew "Gale." Jen was neutral in the Underbelly. She looked out for the children and stayed out of the turf wars. People liked Jen. So far, no one had mentioned where Jen was, or that Miho was in the Underbelly. It only took one person to talk, though, and this whole thing would come crashing down.

Miho heard the door to her room open. The mechanical room that was her secret hiding spot was loud to most people, but Miho found the constant hum of the pipes and slowly turning machine parts that moved air relaxing. Miho sprang up quietly, grabbing her father's sword and tucking the small portrait away.

"Gale," the whisper was just a little louder than the hum in the room. "Don't come out. There are men looking for you. Rough-looking men. Arty says to stay put for now."

This must be one of the older children, but Miho couldn't make out which one by the whisper alone. She was just about to ask what the men looked like when she heard a deep voice that she knew from her nightmares out in the hall.

"You there, boy," Boggs said.

From the hall outside her door she heard Arty's voice say "Wha?" He sounded afraid but defiant. "You know her. I saw you with her," Boggs said.

Miho felt trapped. She couldn't run to Arty's side. It took effort to get out from behind her hiding spot. All the pipes and air ducts made her twist into odd angles to get in and out. For the first time, she cursed her hiding spot. She gripped the handle of her sword.

"I dunno what you are on about. I'm gathering these children to get off the passages. Come on now, Molly," Arty said.

Boggs sounded menacing. "Tell me where she is."

"No idea, and that's the truth," Arty said.

Miho felt like a powder keg about to go off. She couldn't shout, she couldn't move. How dare this man come to her home and threaten her friends? She felt her blood boiling.

"If you are lying to me, I'll slit your throat," Boggs said simply.

After a long moment, there came some other voice. "Oi Boggs, nuttin 'ere that we can see. Suppose we head to the docks?" came the other man's voice.

A long moment passed with no sounds. Miho couldn't tell what was happening. Then she heard movement and the exhale of breath. The tension seemed to fade.

"I think he's getting desperate, or he's still angry we got Jen off the wall," Arty's voice came out of the silence. Miho started making her way out of her hiding spot. "You should stay back there Gale," he said and Molly was agreeing.

"No, I can't stay hiding," Miho said. "I have an idea. While I know he's here in the Underbelly, I can go above. Arty-san, will you be okay if I leave for a while?"

An hour later, Miho was standing outside of an apartment building called Mulberry Arch. These apartments were common for middle-class citizens. Everyone from merchants to the governmental staff who helped run the city lived in them. Miho thought they looked like the worst, soulless places on Earth or in the sky.

Each building had several apartments per floor, and every apartment and every floor looked the same. Miho looked up from the ground she was standing on and lost count of all the floors, and that was just in the building she was in front of. The way this part of the city was designed put the backs of several buildings all facing a common open area. They made a sort of ring. This open area was truly open on both ends, skyward and downward.

This allowed light in from above, which filtered into all the windows in the back of each apartment building, and also allowed for a giant open hole below that all the apartments' backs faced. The contents of chamber pots, garbage, and God knows what else could (and did) get thrown out of the back of these apartments down to the swirling clouds below the city. This is where Miho had to go. In the weeks that she'd sought out the three men responsible for her father's death, she'd followed each of the men home. This grey, dull, soulless apartment building on the edge of some forgotten part of the city was the home of Joseph Boggs. Since Boggs had burst into her home, she decided it was only fair to return the favor.

Miho counted up the seven stories to Boggs' apartment. She knew better than to try the front door, so she snuck down a walkway that led to the back of the building. She quickly leapt over a small wrought-iron gate that was one of those gates that exists to protect the government when some idiot stumbles somewhere they shouldn't and dies. They can say, "But there was a gate for people's safety," and everyone nods and says it's a mystery why that person died. No one questions that the government did all it could to protect the people.

Miho made it to the back of the building and the smell almost made her drop to her knees and empty her stomach right there.

The back of this building, and all others in this "ring" of building backs, was covered in garbage, entrails, feces and urine, and so many other things that had been tossed out the back of an apartment. Miho tried to breathe through her mouth, and focus on the seven stories she had to climb.

'People in groups could really live like animals,' she thought.

She got to work trying to scale the building. The funny thing about the middle class, no one will ask you anything if they can avoid any interaction at all. Once or twice, people came out of the back of an apartment to toss something into the clouds below. They may have seen Miho, but no one stopped her or made any sign that something was wrong. Miho wondered if they just didn't want to be involved, or if she was that amazing at not being seen. She decided it was their apathy, rather than her own skill.

The seventh floor finally came. Miho knew now why the upper apartments cost more than the lower ones. Boggs had an apartment less than halfway up the building, and so the back of his apartment was covered by many questionable things. Miho tried not to gag as she found hand- and footholds to climb along the length of Boggs apartment, testing each window.

She finally found one unlocked and slightly cracked. Miho shoved it open and climbed through as fast as she could to get away from the mess. She lay panting on the floor of a small dressing room. She checked herself and the surrounding walls and window for anything disgusting she might have dragged in with her.

Once she had tidied up, she made her way into the apartment. She drew her wakizashi from behind her back. The little sword in the set she reclaimed from the museum was ever so useful. Her father had told her all the history and uses behind the weapon, but Miho couldn't deny it was special to her. Somehow, it just felt right in her hand. She opened the door and stepped out into the hall.

The apartment wasn't overly large, and it wasn't overly furnished, either. Miho looked into a great room; off that was a kitchen and what she guessed was the front door. Behind her was a hall that led into three doors. Once she decided there were no attack dogs, or any ghoulish thugs in the shadows, she set about searching the apartment.

She searched for half an hour, looking everywhere she could think of, but she couldn't deny that the apartment just seemed barren. The more she looked around, the more barren it appeared. It had furnishings, but no memories. There were no photographs, or drawings, there were no paintings on the walls, and nothing that looked like it reflected the personality of its owner.

After a week of sleeping in her hiding spot in the Underbelly, Miho had added simple things to make her space more personal. Strings of bright colors, dried flowers from outside, bits and bobs from her daily life. This place had none of that.

As she gave the only bedroom, with an unmade bed, another look around, she decided this place was just for show. She had found women's clothes in the wardrobes. Not to show a woman lived here, it was like a collection of left behind articles. She walked to the head of the bed. On the nightstand was an oil lamp, water jug, an ashtray with a stinky cigar in it, and a bowl full of change, scraps of paper and what she guessed were the accumulated contents of pockets.

Miho knelt down and felt under the pillow and then the mattress. Her hand found something hard under the mattress. She pulled out a pistol that looked old, but well taken care of. It wasn't very large, but it was heavy. It had writing on it that looked German. Along with the pistol was a letter. Miho opened it and read:

"The next shipment will arrive on the 9th of August. I'll have it taken to my usual warehouse in the Southeast block, Building 8 after 11:00 p.m. Move the goods before the 15th. The fact that you still haven't found the girl is troubling. Clean up your mess."

It was signed "S.C." Miho stared at the page. It seemed the game of chess she was playing was larger than she imagined, and there was yet another player.

CHAPTER 32

Jen coughed so hard she thought she would pass out. It was another rolling wave of coughing. Once it came on, it wouldn't stop. God above, she wished it would stop. It hurt so much. Her chest hurt, her lungs hurt, her head hurt. She couldn't catch her breath. She thought an iron box must be sitting on her chest. And to make everything worse, she was cold. No matter how many clothes she piled on, or how many blankets she lay under, she was freezing all the time. She was thankful to be alive, but she was miserable.

She honestly remembered very little about the last week. She had flashes in her mind, but mostly she remembered feelings. The emotions were clear and sharp, but everything else was fuzzy. Jen closed her eyes and tried to think clearly. She knew she'd been chained to the Wall, but she couldn't see the complete picture in her head.

She definitely remembered her wrist hurting so much. She flashed on it, pulled so high above her head. The memory of a clanking chain, and her wrist burning so much that she cried, echoed in her mind.

Jen sat up. She couldn't lie down any longer. That would make her cough, and she would do anything not to cough any more. She looked around her. Gale and Arty had her hidden in a tiny little space. She smiled to herself that she called Miho "Gale" first in her mind. She was on a cot and an oil lamp was burning low beside her, resting on a box. That was about as much as could fit in this little closet. Jen's bladder wanted her attention. She knew they had left a bucket under the cot, but there was no way in high heaven above the clouds that she was going to pee in a bucket so someone could take it away. That was simply not going to happen.

She knew that there were boxes and crates stacked up outside the door to hide it from view. Arty had said that strange men were walking through the Underbelly looking for Miho and for herself. Jen shivered more and pulled the blanket around herself tighter. The memory of her teeth chattering, and the feeling of being soaked through and so cold, a cold down to her bones, flashed in her mind. She shivered harder.

She wasn't like that anymore. She was home and free, and she needed to get herself together. Jen stuck out her right arm and looked at the fresh scars that ran down it. She remembered the burning embers of Miho's fire. It had freed her, but also marked her forever. The little lines were bright red against her pale skin.

A sadness spread through her. She wondered if Rose would think them ugly. Jen knew Rose wouldn't care, and that Rose would just want her safe and whole, but she still thought about Rose thinking her scars were ugly. She held up the other hand and looked at the brand that had been cut away without her consent. All of her scars had been given to her without her consent. A gloomy mood seemed to darken the room.

'Well, that's just stupid,' she thought, almost with a small smile. 'Who in their right mind would consent to getting scars? Don't you think all scars happened without the person really wanting them to happen?'

She looked at her scars and thought that she had been through some difficult times in her life. "... and if I can get through them times, I can make it through this one," she tried to tell herself so she would be more confident. The truth was, she was afraid of how sick she was. Her body started crumpling, as what little energy she had ebbed away. Jen felt herself lean back onto her pillow. It was wet with sweat. How could she be sweating when she was so cold? She drifted off into blackness, wondering.

Some time later, she woke to the sound of the boxes being moved outside her door and then the door opening. She hadn't realized how hot it must be in the little closet until the wave of fresh air ran over her from outside. It smelled less stale, and she welcomed the movement of air over her exposed skin. Her gown was stuck to her with sweat, but she was still so cold. Arty stood in the doorway outlined by the light outside.

"Oh God, you look horrible," Arty said in a low voice.

"Oh, well, thank you very much for that." Jen tried to sound sarcastic, but her voice came out frail and weak. She tried to sit up, but it was more of an effort than she had guessed.

"Sorry Jen," Arty said sitting down on the edge of her cot. He had a bowl of broth in his hand. She could barely smell an earthy scent coming from the bowl.

"Where did you get mushrooms?" Jen asked.

"Mi-Gale bought some with a little money she had. I've tried to grow them. I found a quiet, dark spot in one of the boiler rooms." She could hear the pride in his voice and she tried to smile. "You'll have to come see when you're back on your feet."

Jen took the warm bowl in both hands and tried a small sip. It felt wonderful on her sore throat. She was tired, but so happy for the company. She honestly felt like her skin could fall off her bones right now, and perhaps that wouldn't be so bad.

"Arty, you need to be prepared in case I don't make it." She said this quietly, and between sips. She wasn't trying to scare him, but it was obvious that they all were worried about her. They were all thinking the same thing.

"Don't talk like that Jen. It will be alright. You just need rest."

"Arty, I'm trying to get better. I'm resting, but I feel worse. I'm not saying I'm going to leave you and the children, but it could happen, and you need to be ready if it does."

"No," he whispered.

"Arty…" She wanted him to stop being so stubborn, but she was too tired to fight. "You and Gale have been so wonderful taking care of the children. I've always been able to count on you. Thank you."

"I'll always be there for you Jen. I... I...," he shifted and got very tense.

"I know," she said simply and let her head fall heavily onto his shoulder. They were a family. The best kind of family. The family you choose as opposed to the one you are forced into being with. He seemed to relax a little. She could feel another coughing fit trying to claw its way out of her lungs. She handed him the bowl just in time for her to move away from him and start exploding.

After a minute, she was gasping for breath. "It feels like porridge is in my lungs," she said miserably.

"It sounds like porridge is in your lungs," he said.

She laughed, but had to stop before she started coughing again. "Right." She started to stand and said "I'm going to the street," feeling the fullness of her bladder.

"Jen, you can't go out there," came Arty's familiar argument. "Try and stop me," Jen said, rising in both temper and body. "I am, you goose," he said dryly.

"Arty, this is not a discussion. I am going." And she made for the door. Arty protested outside and all the way to the open toilets that most everyone used in the Underbelly. "Arty, we're here. Give me some peace." She had been leaning on his arm, but went on in private. The small stall was welcome respite from the constant bellyaching of Arty.

"Bless him," Jen said as she sat on the makeshift throne and felt the bliss of release. The howling wind outside was actually welcome on her backside. She must be feverish, she thought as she rested her head upon the divider wall beside her. When the deed was done, she pulled her dress together and made her way outside the stall to Arty. He began speaking as soon as she reappeared.

"We need to get back right now. This isn't safe." He looked so serious. She just smiled.

"What is she doing out here?" came the familiar voice of little Gale.

She really should start calling her Miho in her head, she thought as Arty got defensive. Jen just smiled wider, looking at Miho. She had changed so much in the past few months. This wasn't the little, frail doll that Jen had found on wash day. That girl had been broken, afraid, and unsure of everything. She looked at the wild, strong, confident young woman in front of her and felt proud.

"I'm going back," Jen said weakly.

This brief excursion had sapped her of every ounce of energy she had. She honestly wanted to climb back into her little cot and sleep till Christmas. Arty and Miho bickered like an old married couple. It was adorable. Jen felt a coughing fit coming on and reached out for something to support her. The coughing gripped her lungs and blackness started creeping in from the sides of her vision. It was like the room was getting dark. Still, she coughed. She felt her knees give out, and she ended up falling onto them, coughing.

"Jen!" Arty shouted, and she felt a hand on her arm.

"Jen-san," came Miho's voice, and she felt her warm grasp on her other arm.

Jen coughed and coughed as the room got darker and darker. A rushing sound was loud in her ears and Jen knew no more as she passed out.

CHAPTER 33

Miho ran to her hiding place as fast as she could. She jumped over bodies lying in the halls and almost knocked over a little old man who stopped in front of her without warning. She bolted down the hallway that led to her sleeping spot, stopped in the hall long enough to see she wasn't being followed, and wrenched open the door to her room. After closing the door, she made her way to the air vent in the corner opposite her sleeping spot. Within seconds, she had the vent cover off and was shoulder deep to retrieve her money bag. There wasn't a lot left, but she knew it would do. Another few minutes later and she was in front of Jen's hiding spot. Arty was moving boxes back into position.

"Otter has the watch. I'm going with you," he said, putting the last piece in place.

"I'm going to hurry," she said.

"My legs are longer than yours. I won't slow you down. Let's stop talking and go."

Miho looked up into Arty's eyes. She almost never looked at someone in the eyes. She knew the English did it often, and usually felt disconcerted if you didn't look at them in the eye when you talked, but her parents and Machiko never looked at each other in the eyes unless it was really important.

"How is she?" she asked, deciding this was very important.

"She's still breathing, but she's still passed out. We need to do something. Whatever this is, it isn't going away."

They moved at once as they set out. Miho looked down the hall toward where the children were and saw Otter sticking his head out the door. The boy gave a somber wave. Miho nodded at him and waved back. She knew this would work. They had to help Jen. The journey from the Underbelly to the clinic of Dr. Elizabeth Portens was a twisting, turning path that wound its way up the nine levels to what they called "City Proper." City Proper was the middle levels of the city. It comprised the widest parts of the city that incorporated the outside city sections, like the butcher district and the growing farms.

Miho had heard that one of the city Noble's bought his way into the upper families of the city by donating the tracts of land they used to grow crops. This smaller island was attached to the city and made part of the City Proper, and another noble family was added to the upper echelons of the city elite.

Everything above City Proper belonged to the wealthiest families, and was built on top of ground held up by skystone. Everything below City Proper was hung off that ground and considered the lowest of the low. The Underbelly was actually the bottom three to five levels of the city. The lowest of the lowest of the low.

Most of the bigger cities in England, and all over the world actually, were made up of lots of smaller sections of earth and buildings, each supported by their own skystone. Most wars fought among the sky dwellers were fought for resources (especially skystone itself). In the earliest days of sky history, people built castles and forts in the sky to escape the Sickness and to rise above the teeming masses of the poor and the savage. Once aloft, these moving sky castles would raid other castles and forts and absorb them into larger and larger collections that became the largest sky cities. Of course, nobody really cared what happened on the ground. Miho remembered her mother saying that most of high society refused to even talk about the ground, as it was literally and figuratively beneath them.

For all of his boasting about long legs, Arty stopped running about the same time she did. That was about halfway up to City Proper. They went from running to walking as fast as they could and after a while of that, Miho's feet hurt and her side had a stitch.

She continued to think about the layout of the city. She remembered her lessons about the history of High Hastings. High Hastings was the southern-most sky city in England. The Duchess who ruled from the top most castle was responsible for everything south of London, which was the next and largest of all the sky cities in England. Miho remembered something about a war with France, somewhere in the 1300s, in which Hastings had actually crossed the English Channel and captured a castle and grounds in an enormous battle. The French weren't thrilled by this and had often ventured across the Channel during the last 500 years to get it back.

Miho and Arty passed an opening in one of the City Proper Promenades and she looked up at the many castles that made up the Upper City. It was all so silly, but it was a part of life. Her mother had taken her out in an airship a couple of years back, to fly around and see the entire city. It hadn't been really possible with all the swirling clouds, but Miho still loved it. In a lot of ways, the under portions of the city hung off the City Proper in the same way the castles rose above it. It wasn't all one big Underbelly, but lots and lots of buildings and spires that were interconnected. Miho wished she could go flying with mother again.

At last, they arrived outside the clinic. They had slowed to a respectable pace when they entered this section of the city, as they didn't want to arrive panting and out of breath. Arty started off in a direction that would take them down the alleys and around to the back of the clinic. Miho reached out and tugged at his sleeve. "No," she said simply. "This way."

Arty stared at her. "Wha?" he said in disbelief. "We can't do that." He stared at her like she was mental. This actually irritated her more than anything else.

"We are paying customers. We use the front." And she set off without a backward glance. Miho was so fired up by Arty's accepting that the two of them were some sort of lower-class people who didn't belong using things like front doors. She didn't understand why she was so mad, but the thought made her fume with anger.

She stomped up the steps to the little brownstone and rapped a little louder than she had intended on the front door. She noticed the glass looked like it was about to break under her knuckles and took a moment to breathe.

Arty was as good a man as she had ever known. It wasn't his fault that he had been born into the lowest levels of the city. It wasn't his fault that he hadn't been given any education or love. By all accounts he should be a low-life pic-pocket, murderous scum like so many who saw him assumed he was, but he wasn't. He was a kind young man, with a gentle nature and enormous heart. Despite all his hardships, he was a good person, and it angered Miho that he accepted the role that society had just thrust upon him. She then remembered that she hadn't done any more reading lessons with him. They had started the English alphabet, but only made it to the letter E. She vowed to teach him the rest as soon as they helped Jen get better.

As the door was opening, Dr. Portens was saying "Good afternoon, do you require medical..." and she stopped talking as soon as she saw who was on her doorstep.

Dr. Portens, who had fixed a warm smile upon her face as she opened her door, dropped the warmth and hissed, "What are you doing here?"

"I am a paying customer and have an emergency that requires your treatment," Miho said flatly, in an attempt to keep her emotions under check.

"I have an appointment in a few minutes," Dr. Portens said quickly. "You'll have to come back another-"

"Now. This is life and death." Miho cut her off.

Dr. Portent's face grew very stony. "What are you paying with, little girl? Fruit, chickens..."

Miho pulled out her purse and thrust it into the woman's hands. The woman took a moment and weighed the small sack in her hands. Then she looked up and down the street and opened the door to admit them. Miho stepped onto the landing and saw Arty slink in behind her. It was like Arty was trying to be small and unnoticeable. Miho shook her head ever so slightly.

Dr. Portens didn't even close the door all the way behind her. She spun on Miho and said, "Quickly and succinctly tell me what is wrong."

Miho ignored her curt manner and explained the conditions that had led Jen to feel the way she did and the symptoms she was experiencing. She also said what they had done to try to help Jen recover.

"Patience," Dr. Portens said loudly.

"We have been patient," Miho said quickly. "It's been a week. We need treatment to help her with the coughing."

Dr. Portens smiled, looking at Miho as a young woman entered the parlor. "Ah Patience, I need you to gather some opium, mustard plasters, the eucalyptus leaves, and the necessaries to treat an intense ague or bronchi inflammation."

Miho felt stupid. She tried not to show it, as she knew Dr. Portens would enjoy it too much. The young lady moved off with a "Yes, Doctor" but before she had left the room, Arty spoke up.

"Also miss, if you have something to treat small but nasty burns," he asked and the young lady looked at him and said "Burns? What kind of burns?"

Arty pulled up his sleeve revealing several nasty, deep red lines several centimeters long that ran the length of his arm. "They are just like these, but not on me, of course."

The young girl took Arty's arm into her hands, gently saying, "Oh my, those are nasty." And Arty flushed to a deep red color in the face. Miho didn't hear their next few remarks as Dr. Portens' head snapped from Arty's arm to Miho with a knowing look.

"Those appear to be phosphorus burns," Dr. Portens said slowly, while attempting to bore a hole through Miho with her eyes.

"They are," Miho said flatly.

"That is not something I would expect a child to play with," Dr. Portens said acidly.

"A child didn't play with it," Miho said again flatly.

Dr. Portens breathed deeply through her nose and said, "I don't... want to know. Patience, get the salve and some dressings."

Within a few minutes, Patience returned with a small bag full of vials, dressings, and several other items Miho didn't recognize. The young lady pulled out a small sheet and said to Arty, "I've written everything down so you know about how much and when to give it to the person. I need some information..."

Arty was looking uncomfortable.

"Do you not know how to read, sir?" she asked him kindly.

"No mum, but I have a very good memory. If you tell me, I'll remember," Arty said firmly.

Patience smiled and said, "I can help" and they moved over to a small table and she began to explain everything.

"Is it stolen?" Dr. Portens asked quietly. "The money," she added, holding up the bag. The question did not surprise Miho. "No. It was my money to give."

Dr. Portens poured it out into her hand looking the coins over. "You know nothing about money, do you, girl?"

Miho stared at the woman. "I know some, but I haven't had a calling to use it, so the types of coins are confusing to me." Miho felt it was better to be honest than to appear to be cunning and fall short.

Dr. Portens took three of the smaller coins and put the rest in the bag. She handed the bag to Miho and said, "Learn."

Miho bowed her head. The woman could have had the contents of the bag. Miho didn't care, but she was trying to help Miho and she appreciated kindness wherever it came from.

Patience and Arty were coming across the room. Patience was still talking and holding Arty's bandaged arm as they walked. "Now you must change these dressings every day and keep the burns clean." Arty was as red as an apple and stammered "Y... Yes mum"

Miho couldn't help but smile. "Thank you, doctor. We will..."

"Miho!?!" A voice came from the direction of the front door. Miho didn't turn, but her insides seemed to solidify. In the space of a single heartbeat, she knew what must be done.

"Arty, run!" She looked directly at Arty, who looked confused. He opened his mouth to protest, but Miho cut him off. "Get the medicine to Jen. Go now!" and she nodded her head at the door leading to the back of the house. She spun around, putting her hands on her sword and her knife.

There in the door stood Ama, her mother's friend and ace pilot for the City Watch. Ama was tall and slender with the darkest skin Miho had ever seen. Her eyes were sharp and exquisite. She was dressed in a soft dress of Amber and looked as radiant and glamorous as ever. Miho would not allow any emotion on her face. She had considered trying to find Ama during the past few months, but always hesitated because she didn't know where the woman's loyalties lay. Her father had shouted for Ama before they threw him off the city. Miho had often wondered why this woman had not been there? Why hadn't she saved her father? Why hadn't she saved her mother? Miho just didn't know.

Ama threw up her arms and was genuinely overcome with emotion at the sight of Miho. "Oh my God, it is you!" she said as she started walking toward Miho with her arms outstretched.

"I've looked for you for so long. Where have you been?" She knelt down and embraced Miho deeply and then held her at arms-length, looking at her as if to see every detail. Miho heard the door close behind her and felt a comfort that Arty was away. She didn't know what was about to happen.

"Lady Ba," Dr. Portens asked in a wooden tone. "Do you know this young girl?"

"Know her, I'm her godmother," Ama said, not taking her eyes off Miho.

Miho didn't know what a "godmother" was, but she knew that she would remember the look of abject shock on Dr. Portens' face till the day she died.

CHAPTER 34

The little girl that Ama remembered wasn't looking up at her now. This was no woman, but she was close. Too close for one who was still so young. But did that matter? The past several months had been a blur of grief, worry, and anger. It had driven a knife in Ama's heart that she had not been able to honor Kana's wishes, but now the long nights of stress and anxiety were over. Little Miho was safe, healthy and whole. Ama felt years younger, as a tension left her chest. She was so relieved. She knew this girl had been through hell, and they would both have to deal with that, but for right now, Ama felt whole for the first time in a long time.

"Miho, I can't tell you how happy I am to have found you," Ama said. "Dr. Portens, have you been caring for this girl?"

The doctor seemed to jump out of her own thoughts at being addressed directly. "I, eh, treated the child for a broken arm several months ago." Miho looked at the doctor with a curious expression.

"You treated her without knowing who she was, without compensation?" Ama asked. This seemed out of place from what she knew of this woman. Dr. Portens was known as a capable physician in the city, and one of the foremost experts at dealing with the Sickness. Her clientele were mostly middle-class men, as far as Ama knew.

The doctor looked very uncomfortable. "Well, we operate a separate clinic for the less fortunate of the city. It was a charitable clinic begun by my grandmother."

"But you were compensated," Miho said flatly to the woman. It appeared that the girl didn't like the doctor. Dr. Portens returned

Miho's look with one that bordered on contempt. They appeared to mutually dislike each other.

Ama was confused. "Miho, how did you compensate her?" She knew the girl had disappeared the day of the grounding with nothing more than the clothes on her back. Ama had checked everywhere she could think of for her. The other engineers had volunteered to help look for her, too. Ama went routinely to their house to see if the girl had returned. She was worried now about just what the girl had done to survive. Ama had heard that some of the lower levels of the city were very dangerous and shady.

"My friend bartered for her services. The doctor wasn't confident my arm could be saved," and the girl raised her arm and looked at Dr. Portens. "It is a testament to her skill that I fully recovered."

Dr. Portens looked like she had swallowed something vile, but managed a thin smile. "Obviously, you are made from sterner stock than most, dear girl." She said this through the smallest opening in her mouth Ama had ever seen.

Ama was now thoroughly confused. These two looked like they hated each other, and now they were complimenting each other, although it looked like it pained them both. "Well, goodness knows I'm glad you didn't lose your arm," Ama said, but was thinking fast. Obviously, there was more going on here than she knew. It was best to isolate the issues and tackle them one at a time. She knelt down to address Miho.

"Miho, I'm very glad that you are safe. I can tell that you've been through a lot. Right now, I'm going to need you to come home with me. Will you do that?"

The girl looked at her for a full six seconds before saying, "yes" in a flat tone. That was enough. Ama stood up and addressed the doctor.

"Doctor, I'm very glad that you could treat Miho. The reason I made an appointment with you today is because of my son, Henry. I want to have an initial evaluation regarding the Sickness."

Dr. Portens raised an eyebrow and fixed a doctorly look of distant interest on her face. "Of course, Lady Ba," she said to Ama. "Would you like the girl to wait outside while we talk about this matter?"

There was no way Ama was letting Miho out of her sight now that she just found her. "No, Miho is a part of my family now, and I trust her to keep these matters private." She looked at Miho, who nodded at her with slightly wider eyes.

"Very well," the doctor went on. "How old is the boy? Has he exhibited any symptoms?"

"Henry is 10 years old," Ama answered. "He hasn't that I know of, but his father carried the Sickness from his own father, who had it in Africa."

"While the Sickness can pass from parent to child, it is more rare than most would imagine. However, some symptoms arise in children of those who were infected, but they do not carry the Sickness itself. Banding of skin, swelling of the male genitalia, and other genetic... complications can all be passed down to the children without the Sickness itself."

"I see," said Ama.

"May I suggest a thorough examination of your son, Lady Ba? I assure you I am both capable and discreet. There need be no added stress to your family," the doctor said with a bow.

"So there is a chance that Henry has it?" Ama asked point blank, the question foremost in her mind.

"It is extremely unlikely," the doctor said, "but it is better to know these things early."

"Very well," Ama said. "I will write to you to inquire about a time."

The doctor gave a bow and said, "My clinic will adjust our schedule to fit any day or time that you suggest, Lady Ba."

"I thank you," Ama said, bringing the conversation to a close. "Miho, are you ready?"

The girl bowed to Ama, turned to Dr. Portens and said, "Thank you doctor, for all your assistance."

"Of course..." the doctor said and added, "... miss Ba."

Ama smiled. She looked at Miho, who looked startled. They made their way outside into the sunlit streets of the city. Ama signaled her coachman, who was waiting at a pull off in the middle of the road some way away. Ama and Miho walked to the pickup as the coach clipped- clopped down and began its swing to pick them up.

"Miho, I don't know what you have been through these past few months, but I want to hear the entire story," Ama spoke clearly, trying to start a conversation.

"Why weren't you on the platform when they Grounded my father?" the girl asked flatly.

Ama stopped dead and looked at Miho. The girl had gone straight to the point. Ama's heart hurt, as it always hurt when she thought about Kana's family and what happened.

"Miho, I'm sorry I wasn't there. I had been sent on a mission two weeks before. I didn't return until three days after it happened. By that time they had arrested, tried and convicted Jiro-san, and carried out his sentence." Ama's blood still boiled when she thought about it.

"I made inquiries to the Magistrate who convicted your father. I couldn't believe such a serious miscarriage of justice had transpired, but all my attempts were blocked. It was like he was being protected. I never stopped looking for you, Miho," Ama said, kneeling down again to look the girl in the face. "Please believe me, I would have fought with all my might to protect you and Jiro-san."

Miho looked her in the eyes for a few seconds and nodded. The girl seemed to soften a little at what Ama had said. This made Ama feel a little better.

"Direct honesty," is what she and Kana had talked about all those years ago. "Honesty is like an onion," Kana had said to Ama. "It has many layers to it. Japanese people are not directly honest very often. Direct honesty can have powerful side effects, so we use it very sparingly."

Ama missed her friend, as she had so often since the day she was taken.

CHAPTER 35

Miho shivered, clutching the towel around her, the remains of her bath dripping on the floor, as she looked around the room. This one room was bigger than the area where all the children slept in the Underbelly. Its opulence was only matched by its size. Oil lamps burned on tables as the gaslight fixtures burned on the walls. The room was bright and warm, with rich, ornate wallpaper that was broken by oil paintings of flower gardens and rich browns of sandy deserts. Carved masks hung in alcoves and sconces. Everywhere Miho looked, there was a sign of wealth and status. Ama's African background influenced colors and motifs, just as her own home had had a very Japanese motif so long ago.

'I slept in my room, with its rice paper walls and tatami flooring, and it wasn't much smaller than this,' she thought as she pictured it in her mind. It didn't feel as opulent as this room, but she had also grown up in an elegant home. The Japanese kept things pretty simple and free of clutter, preferring this simple decorative harmony to excess and opulence. Her family had beautiful hangings on the walls too, but it all felt like a lifetime ago, not the six months it had actually been.

'Six months,' she thought in disbelief. She turned to the bed where she had stripped off her clothes and all of her worldly possessions. Ama had insisted that her maid take Miho's clothes to be laundered, but the bed held an intricate spread of knives, sharpened bits of metal, wire, ribbons, string, pins, and all the other things that she kept either tucked in her clothes, or in one of her belt of pockets. She hadn't unloaded her two belts of pockets because they held the handwritten note from S.C. and the gun— both of which she stole from Boggs' apartment. She instantly noticed an item missing from the way she had laid it all out. Her eyes shot around the room and found the portrait of her mother and father on the table near the head of the bed. Ama must have placed it there.

"My God, they just keep coming," Ama had said when Miho had begun to lay it all out. Miho hadn't wanted to take a bath right away, but she knew she must be filthy and admitted she must smell. When she lay out the portrait, Ama gasped.

Ama gently picked it up to examine it. "I had no idea this even existed," she said with watery eyes. "I'm so glad that you have it."

When the maid announced the bath was ready, Miho had trouble leaving all of her possessions somewhere she couldn't reach out and touch them.

"I promise you Miho, no one will touch your belongings while you bathe," Ama said seriously to her. "This is your home now."

Miho stared into her face, but still couldn't find trust in her heart. She had a plan, though, and being near Ama would help her with that plan. In the end, she nodded and only took her swords with her. The bath was amazing.

Now she looked around herself and felt out of place. She felt exposed somehow, even though she reminded herself that she was safe here. Exhaustion crept over her, and she wondered how Jen was doing. Did Arty make it back with the medicine? Was she going to be alright? Thoughts of the children and of her friends filled her mind as she dressed in the robes that had been provided for her.

"You should rest tonight," came Ama's soft voice from the door with a large platter of food. "A soft bed will do you good."

After checking if Miho needed anything, Ama gave her a hug and left for the night. Miho's thoughts were getting slower. The bath had muddled her mind. She picked at the platter of food and collected her things off the bed. When everything was put away, she stared at the bed. It didn't feel right; it didn't look right. She felt exposed again, and her anxious feelings started staving off sleep. That wouldn't last, though. In the end, she put some blankets on the floor of the closet, made a dummy body out of more blankets that she put under the covers in case anyone looked in at her. She slid the closet door shut and wedged her daito, her longer sword, to insure no one could open it without her knowing. She fell asleep that night with her shorter shoto in her hands and her parents' portrait beside her head.

Two days had passed and Miho had barely left her room. She'd declined to attend meals with the family so far. Late into the night, after the house had gone to bed, she dressed herself in her clothes and made to creep out of the house. It was August 9th, and S.C.'s shipment was arriving after 11:00 p.m. Miho had reviewed the note she had found in Boggs' apartment at least a hundred times over the past week, and she needed to see what was S.C. smuggling, and perhaps who S.C. was.

Miho made her way toward the front door as quietly as she could. She was pleased with how quietly she could move. The house was enormous, and the front door was a suitable distance from the living quarters. The closer she got to the door, the less she was concerned about making noise. As she approached the front hall, she noticed a dim light flickering out of the room. Her chest grew tight as she walked into the room to see a few lanterns set around the room. They cast long shadows all around. It was very dim, but she could easily see a man sitting with his eyes closed on a low stool near the middle of the room. She crept slowly into the space, watching to see if he moved.

"You move very quietly," he said softly, with his eyes still closed. He was a thin African man, with dark skin, high cheekbones and shocks of white in his thin cut beard, moustache and hair. His voice was deep, but not so deep it was scary. It sounded soft and slightly amused.

"I have to go out," Miho said quietly. He still didn't open his eyes, and she found it unnerving. "Am I allowed to leave?"

The man smiled softly and said, "That depends on where you are going," still without opening his eyes. His accent wasn't British, but instead he spoke English with the pronunciation of someone who was used to speaking a different tongue.

Miho crept a little further into the room. She remembered reading about the large black panthers, large cats that would stay very still and then pounce. She felt like he might pounce at any minute, but he hadn't moved or even looked at her. "I have business to attend to," she said, so softly that even she had trouble hearing it.

"Hmmm," he let out a panther-like purr that seemed to indicate that he was thinking, or agreeing, or she did not know. This was unnerving. Miho looked at the large wooden stick that he had across his lap. She thought it was a walking stick at first, but it was very long.

"My wife worries you may leave and not come back," he said again with his eyes closed. "And while I would worry about a young lady out on the streets alone, I think it's also wise to worry about you leaving and what you may bring back." He opened his eyes and stared directly into Miho's eyes. His eyes were the most vivid pale blue. They were the most beautiful eyes she had ever seen. Wisdom, strength, and honor all seemed to radiate from him.

"I will bring nothing back," Miho said softly. She felt like this was a test.

"Mmmm," he said again, but sounding like it had thoughts behind it. "I remember Jiro saying you were getting very good with the sword. How about we spar?"

Miho's hand instinctively lay upon her sword hilt. She didn't understand what was going on.

"No, not with your father's sword. Try one of those," he said, pointing at the back wall near where she had come in. Several wooden practice swords were standing out from an umbrella stand.

"You knew my father?" she asked, moving toward the collection of practice swords and selecting one. She turned around to see him standing.

"He was a good man, and a good friend," he said, smiling. "And I never once beat him at chess."

"I didn't either," Miho said, moving toward the older man. A clock chimed from somewhere inside the house. She didn't know why he wanted to spar at 10 o'clock at night, but she was restless and could use the experience to let go of some anxiety. Miho didn't want to hurt the old man, though. She held the sword aloft in front of her, wondering how she should try to attack a man with a long stick.

Clack. Whoosh. He had knocked her sword aside and swung up the bottom of his stick so fast, and with so much force, that the wind from it parted her hair. She felt the power from the swing through her whole body. He had missed on purpose. This was just to establish that he knew what he was doing.

"Do you spar with your children?" she asked, and tried a few testing swings to see if he could block them. He did, easily.

"My children will spar with me, but neither put much heart into it," he said lightly as he spun and twisted in a series of swings and blows that Miho could barely keep up with. He was fast. Very fast. "My son is a farmer in his heart, and my daughter is a diplomat."

Crack. Crack. Crack. Miho could block his attacks, but she could tell that he was just gauging her experience.

"And what are you, in your heart?" he asked as he swung wide and she deflected, but felt the power of his blow through her arms.

She didn't really think about the question. She was focused on his fighting style. He didn't fight like a swordsman. Miho wasn't used to this at all. "I am a sword," she heard herself say.

Crack. Crack. Crack. The duel was ramping up. Each was adding attacks into the act of defense. Attack, defend, counter attack and feints. The motions were getting faster. They were beginning to duel in earnest.

"A sword is a tool that is used by another," he said softly, while his arms and stick moved in a blur. "Are you being used by another?"

"No," Miho said, getting upset. She began to deep breathe. Father once told her that warriors will use words to make their opponents off balance. She must keep her cool. "I am a warrior."

"To be a warrior, you must have a war. Do you have a war?"

"Of sorts," she said with doubt.

'Am I fighting a war?' she wondered to herself. 'If this is a war, what are the sides? How do I win?' Her thinking felt deep and slightly dark. What she wanted was justice for her father.

"That isn't a war," she concluded.

Whack. Whack. Whack. "I do not fight a war, but I fight for justice and for my friends. I fight to protect, and to honor." She defended against his attacks, but not well. Her hands were numb and her lungs raw from the workout. A sweat made all of her clothes heavy and she suddenly felt like a child being toyed with.

With a sudden and fierce blow, he knocked her sword out of her hands and it clattered away as he brought the end of the stick level with her face in what would have been a finishing move. She had lost completely. Her heart sank at her defeat.

"It is good to defend your friends and protect the ones you love. But don't let your whole life be fighting, or you could end up losing what you are fighting for in the first place." He lowered the stick and met her face to face. "You fight very well."

"I lost my sword. You defeated me easily." She didn't want his pity or to be patronized. A thunderstorm was brewing around inside her.

"You have never fought someone with a Bo staff, have you?" he asked, smiling.

"No." she responded with a scowl.

"Yet I sparred with your father hundreds of times," he said, almost cheerily. "I had the advantage in this duel. You will be better next time, and I will be in trouble."

"There isn't always a next time in battle," she said, but the grumpy storm was blowing away before it really set in.

"This is why we train," he said simply. He stuck out his hand. "I am Abe. Abe Ba, husband to Ama, and father to Henry and Adana. I am happy to meet you."

Miho suddenly felt a rush of liking and respect for this man. He could have hurt her easily. He could have put her on the floor or knocked her around the room, but he didn't. He never landed a blow and still taught her. He was patient and kind, and he had let her into his home. She shook his hand and then bowed very low and said, "I'm Miho Michitake. Thank you for taking me into your home, and for teaching me."

He bowed in return and said, "Konbanwa, Miho-san." His Japanese was pretty good, and he smiled with brilliant white teeth. "Be careful out there and be careful what you bring home with you."

Three hours later, as the flames of the warehouse lit up the entire area surrounding the Southeast block, Miho wondered at all the different meanings of his last statement.

CHAPTER 36

In the entire world, there was nothing better than that time of being half asleep and waking up slowly. Dreams felt like they were real, and all the troubles of the day had no hold over him. Arty was slowly waking up and imagining his head being rubbed. It was so soft, and the gentle strokes felt like waves of tiny bliss. He felt himself moan in pleasure. No one needed him.

Everyone he cared about was safe. His body wasn't sore from all the days and nights of taking care of Jen and children, working and cleaning, mending and worrying. He felt so light, and his hair being played with was like an anchor to this peaceful moment, and also like wings that tried to carry him away. He felt another low moan rumble as he smiled.

"You would make a wonderful dog, Arty," came Jen's voice teasingly.

Arty's eyes shot open in surprise. He tried to pick apart which parts had been real, and which dream. His body ached, and of all those aches, the top of the list was his neck. He had fallen asleep beside Jen's cot. He was sitting on the floor and his head had fallen backward onto Jen's cot. She was still rubbing his head. It felt just as good as it had in his dream, but shock and embarrassment forced him to move. His back and neck gave immediate spasms of protest.

"Ugh, Jen! What's going on?" he managed to get out, grabbing various hurting spots.

"Nothing Arty, relax. I woke up and found you asleep. You shouldn't sit there like that. Why don't you go have a lie down for a while? I've got the children."

"What, no. You need your rest. I'll get up." Arty tried to move, but his leg had pins and needles and he started massaging it with a grunt.

"Arty, it's been 10 days since you brought me that medicine. It's almost all gone now, and I'm feeling much better. I still get tired more easily than I used to, but everything else is gone. The cough, the chills, the feeling like muck. I'm on the mend!"

"Well, you aren't there yet. I'll rest when you're better," Arty replied, and with that he stood up. He thought he was making audible creaking noises and spoke a little louder than necessary. "You stay here and rest. I'll check on the children and bring you some food."

And before she could protest, he was off. The truth was that Arty was running on pure adrenaline at this point. He couldn't think straight. His body, mind and soul were pushed well past exhaustion. It was true that Jen was looking and feeling better. They were over the hump, and he could start leaning on her more and more. As much as he was looking forward to not being constantly awake and working, there was a small part of him that was going to miss taking care of Jen. She had been so sick, so weak, and they had been very close this past week. Perhaps now, finally, she would see him in a new light.

Arty's heart swelled at the thought of Jen being grateful to him. Images sprang into his exhausted imagination. Jen thanking him for taking care of everyone. Jen wanting private time to thank him for taking care of her. Jen rubbing his head and saying, 'There, there, you rest now. You've earned it. My Arty is so strong, and he took care of everyone all by himself.'

"Why are you smiling like that?" Otter asked him as he walked into the area where the children slept.

"Huh?" Arty turned slowly as his mind was pulled out of warm visions of an angelic Jen folding him into her arms.

"Arty, you look like 'ell." Otter was as crass as ever. Otter was one of the older children. He, Victoria and Thomas were the eldest under Arty. They would all be moving on soon, Arty thought. Once the children got to be around 13 or so, they could find a job or an apprenticeship. Arty felt like he would miss Otter the most. He was headstrong, with big ideas and infectious energy, but also very level-headed and loyal.

"Thank you," Arty said dryly. "How are things?"

"Well, the twins are starting a ruckus with Basil, Little Jim wet his bed, and Peter won't stop picking at his scabs, so his bed looks like a murder scene. I've got most everyone up now, though, and Mary has started laundry. How's Jen?"

"She's doing better. I'll get her some food and we'll go for our walk. Then I'll come help."

"You need a couple hours' rest. Any word about Gale yet?" Otter asked cautiously.

"No. No word," Arty said darkly. He had not stopped worrying about Gale, Miho, for 10 straight days. Where was she, and what was happening? It was because of Miho that Jen recovered, and he was so thankful for that, but he was going to give the girl an earful when he saw her again.

He looked at Otter, who, despite his rough exterior, looked concerned. He was worried too. All they could do was wait. The men who were looking for her (and he guessed Jen, too) were still wandering around the Underbelly. A guilty part of Arty was a little thankful that Miho wasn't around. It was easier to take care of Jen and the children and not have to worry about Miho being in danger. A dark cloud passed over Arty. How could he think like that? Miho had always been a good friend and they had been through so much together. It wasn't her fault that Boggs and his crew were searching for her.

"She'll be ok, Otter. She's stronger than any of us," he clapped the boy on his shoulder and set off to find food.

A little while later, after he and Jen had gotten some porridge in them, they set off for Jen's walk. Jen wanted to walk a little every day if she could, but she always ran out of energy. Arty loved it when she would put her arm on his and use him to help her along. It made him feel special, and he loved her touch.

"Did you hear about that bad fire out in the Southeast block?" Arty asked as they made their way toward an outside door. Jen liked the fresh air, and sometimes they would visit one of her secret gardens.

"I heard something," Jen said, moving slowly and holding Arty's arm for support. "Something about it burning down an entire block of warehouses?"

Arty felt electric under her touch. "Yeah, I heard it wasn't an accident. Someone set it on purpose. They found two guards knocked out. They say they saw nothing. It's lucky that those buildings weren't inside the city, but had only open sky above them. Remember the stories about that fire in 1820? They said the smoke killed more people than the fire did."

"I've heard," Jen said, putting out her other hand to a corner intersection of several corridors so she could rest.

They were close to an outside door. Arty guessed they were going to try to make it out to a garden after all. Glancing behind them, he felt uneasy. He couldn't help but feel they were being watched. He had felt that way for the past quarter hour. There were people coming and going, but no one looked out of place. He scanned each corridor in the intersection. That's when he spotted her. Miho was walking down a corridor that led to the upper decks. She hadn't seen them yet. She looked healthy and clean, and moved with quiet purpose. One hand rested on the sword at her waist.

She was wearing her usual many layers of clothing, a collection of pale blues and rusty browns. Her light brown cloak, over wide pants looked almost like a long skirt. She wore a pale blue shirt that had patches all over and was sewn in multiple colored threads. Her belts of pockets crossed her chest. Her raven black hair was tied back and out of her way. Only a few strands swept her small, round face. Arty's heart swelled so large it almost choked him as he pointed down the corridor to show Jen. Miho spotted them and a smile lit up her face.

Then many things happened all at once. Miho's face switched to one of shock as Jen screamed while falling to the ground. Arty turned to face behind him but someone grabbed his hair and almost pulled him off the ground as a large heavy body came up behind him.

"I told you what I would do," came the deep voice in his ear.

Arty felt the hard metal rake across his throat as a sharp pain pushed everything else out of his mind. He tried to call out, but only a sick, gurgling noise erupted from him. Hot, sticky blood flowed down his front as he saw Miho running toward them, her face full of shock. He lost sight of Miho as he fell to the floor. Jen was screaming and there was a rushing sound in his ears. Everything was happening so slowly.

Jen pulled him into her lap as he flipped over to tell her. He had to tell her. He might not get another chance.

"Jen...," he tried to say, but only a sick gurgle emerged.

"Oh God, Arty!" Jen was crying and yelling. She was putting her hands on his throat and looking about her.

"Jen... I love... I love...," it was no good. Nothing was working. Arty was cold, but he didn't mind so much. He felt peaceful. He was near Jen, and that was good. It was all going to be okay.

CHAPTER 37

Miho ran with every ounce of energy she had. She willed herself to move faster, as fast as a lightning flash, but Arty's body fell in a bloody heap beside Jen. Boggs raised his knife to meet Miho, and she was still five meters from him. She knew she couldn't draw her long sword while running, so she grabbed two knives and lunged at the hulking man. Everything moved so slowly, and yet the world around her was a blur. In her mind, only one thought had any space, 'Boggs. Must. Die.'

In the hour that it felt she was lunging at Boggs, she had time to consider if Arty was still alive, if Boggs' men were nearby so she would have to fight more than one opponent. She thought Jen had looked more healthy before Boggs had shoved her to the ground. All these things dropped like flower petals from her mind as she had a singular focus on Boggs.

He swung his knife at her, but she twisted in midair to avoid it. She raked one of her blades down his forearm as she aimed the other at his chest. Miho knew that if she hit a rib, the knife wouldn't kill him, but if she could slide the knife between the ribs, then this fight was over as soon as it started. She felt the blade stop hard and knew she hit a rib.

Before she could move, though, Boggs had grabbed her with his left arm and swung her into a nearby wall. She was bringing up her second knife as all the air exited her lungs. As the full force of Boggs' blow was following the impact of her body with the wall, she brought up her knife without seeing where it was going. The blade went straight through his forearm.

Stars erupted into her vision as she gasped for air. A small part of her brain noticed that this knife had slid neatly between the two bones in his arm, a smaller gap than the ribs. How unfair. Sadly, there wasn't time to continue her thinking as the back of her head was letting her know it had hit the wall hard.

Boggs pulled his knife-skewered arm away, dropping Miho as he let out an animalistic roar of pain and shock. Miho dropped like a sack to the floor, reaching for another blade. Her vision was blurry as she made out that Boggs was rearing back to kick her in the head. Dodging his kick, she raked the blade along his leg. She would give him a thousand cuts before she killed him. She would take him a piece at a time, like he took her life and the people that she loved.

Boggs still had a knife in his right hand, the knife he slit Arty's throat with. His left arm was out of commission from her blade, that was still sticking through it about 20 centimeters behind the wrist. He thrust his right hand down to impale her. Boggs was strong, but much slower than Miho. She pushed herself off the wall to avoid his powerful blow. She rolled a couple of feet away and sprung up with her blades at the ready.

"I'll fucking kill you," Boggs said through gritted teeth.

Miho just looked at him, thinking about their next moves. She took a moment to absorb everything that was going on around them. A horrible gurgling noise was coming from the place Jen was sobbing a few feet away. A small crowd of people had gathered around them at a distance. No one was approaching though, so she took heart in that. Still, Miho and Boggs stared into each other's eyes. She knew something would happen any second. One of them would make their move.

"Boggs!" came a man's voice from behind Miho. She could tell that the man was some distance from her. She wanted to look, but the second she took her eyes off Boggs, he would lunge for her. "There's people, run for the Bobbies. We gotta beat it!"

"Grab the girl!" Boggs barked, gesturing at Miho with his knife hand. He was holding the left arm up and away from himself.

She felt lumbering footsteps close in behind her. Without taking her eyes off Boggs, she pulled her wakizashi from her waist, aimed it pointing backwards, and pushed with her legs backwards while generally aiming through her cloak, all while keeping Boggs' eyes.

"Look ou-!" Boggs shouted at his man, taking his eyes off her.

She had connected, and thrust the blade backwards with her left hand, while shifting her weight to spring at Boggs. She heard a high-pitched scream as she knew her blade had found flesh.

"My Bingy!" the man wailed with a squeal. Miho spun in a complete circle. As she swung around, she saw the man doubled over, holding his crotch. She sliced his throat easily and was facing Boggs again when his body hit the ground. She heard gasps from the onlookers. Boggs stared at her in shock and anger. He bared his teeth like an animal.

Then he ran. Miho stood transfixed at the space he had taken up a second before. She couldn't believe her eyes. The man she had feared all this time. The man who haunted her nightmares, and kept her stomach in knots, her specter, her phantom–and he ran from her. Miho felt a bubbling anger rise from her lowest depths and she started to chase him.

She only made it one step before she heard Jen's anguished cry, "Miho!"

Miho stopped and turned around to face Jen. The scene before her was so brutal and heartbreaking, but it also had a kind of beauty to it. Arty lay with his head in Jen's lap. His blood was everywhere around them, like a dark pool. Miho smelled iron and could taste something metallic in the air. Jen was crying over him, but he looked so peaceful.

Miho didn't want to see his eyes not blink. If she saw that, then she would be broken in mind and soul. This boy, this beautiful soul, who had always been there for everyone. He was as close to being a brother as Miho had ever felt. The seconds stretched into years as she looked at his pale face, and then, like the falling of a flower pedal, he blinked, looking only at Jen. Miho's world snapped back into its rightful speed. She looked around them at the crowd and spotted two large dock workers staring dumbly at the scene.

"You two!" she snapped at the men while reaching into her pockets. "This boy and girl need help. Carry them to Dr. Portens' office on Cherry Blossom Way, in the south side."

Miho walked to the two men. Everyone in the crowd backed away from her. Miho held out two coins and barked, "Quickly!"

Whether they moved out of fear of the small Asian girl who just killed a man without looking at him, or for the two large coins shining in the corridor's light, she couldn't tell, but it didn't matter.

"Whirrrrrrr, Whirrrrrrr, Whirrrrrrr" came the soft sounds of a Bobby's noise maker from some distance away. Miho knew she didn't have long. She turned to Jen and thrust her money pouch into Jen's hands, saying, "Jen, help him, save him."

Jen looked at her with a broken expression of pain and misery, etched on every line of her face. "What about you?"

"I'm going after Boggs," Miho said with a stone in her heart. "This ends today."

CHAPTER 38

His leg throbbed where the little bitch had cut him down his thigh. He felt at the stab wound on his chest where she had poked him with her stupid knife. It wasn't bleeding that much, but that didn't mean it didn't hurt.

"Damnit!" was all he could say through gritted teeth as he looked at the metal that went through his left arm.

The little bitch was fast. She was like a feral cat with sharp metal claws. He did a quick inventory of what was bleeding, what was hurting, and what he could ignore. All he needed was to land one good hit on her. She was still a child and weighed less than a bag of stone. If he could just whack her a good one, that would stun her enough for him to finish the job.

'The job,' he thought, as he paused his running long enough to grab the makeshift knife and pull it out. How had it all gone so wrong? The girl wasn't part of the job. She wasn't a factor in any of the plans. She was a useless child. No one even considered her. He pulled the last of the metal out and used her knife to cut a piece of his shirt off to wrap around his injured left arm. He dropped her makeshift blade and thought of his options.

He stumbled forward, knowing she would most likely be coming behind. He needed a plan. Either he could get away and regroup, or he needed to kill the feral cat here and now. He wanted her dead. This thorn in his side, this black mark against all that he had built. His reputation, his little empire, was all at stake because of one slant-eyed little bitch. With each step he took toward the outside hatch, a plan formed in his mind. He knew what he must do.

He burst through the hatch and turned around. He made sure he could see the blade he had left behind and the drops of blood on the ground. A perfect little trail to follow. He looked around wildly for what he sought. Within 100 yards of the hatch, he found it. A pipe, a little longer than a meter. It wasn't too rusty, or too thick to use. He might have been able to shove his thumb into it, but he didn't want to try. It was the perfect thing. He used his strength to detach it from the City Wall.

The next part was play acting. He rested one end of the pipe on his foot and started to limp badly, as if she had done serious damage. He held the pipe close to his body, running up one leg. This would prevent it from being seen from behind. Then he started limping down the narrow catwalk away from the hatch that he had come out of. As the clouds swirled and danced, the howling winds whipped around the outside of the city. The sky was a stone grey. The morning was chilly. He limped along, feeling excited. Now he just had to wait for the sound of her footsteps.

Through the howling winds, he heard the hatch open behind him. Slowly, he hobbled along. He smiled at his show. He waited. She was small and light, but he would hear as she got close. He remembered the bloodlust in her eyes back in the corridor during their fight. She was dead set on killing him, and he knew that being so focused makes people miss things. He limped along and closed his eyes. The breeze felt wonderful. Refreshing. He opened his eyes again when he heard the running footsteps behind him.

"Wait," he told himself. "Make sure she is close."

It was in that moment that he felt so uncomfortable. He didn't enjoy having his back to something so dangerous. This little cat with her metal claws. Well, he was a big, bad bulldog, and he was about to bite. When he knew she was close enough, he swung himself around, swinging up the pipe with his strong right hand.

He put all his force into the swing and crashed it into her hand, bashing the knife out of her grip. It shot off in a high arc, like a bird taking flight. She looked horror-stricken as he brought the pipe down with all his weight. She tried to dodge, but he had the reach now. His blow landed on her leg with a satisfying jolt that rippled through his arm. If he hadn't broken her thigh bone, he had at least knocked the shit out of her. She crumpled to the grating beneath her and he smiled, sensing victory.

"Sweet fucking God, I can't wait to kill you," he said with joy in his heart.

It was finally going to be done. He had hunted this girl for months, tied up his crew, gotten so many people involved. It had been messy. He hated messy. He liked things to be clean. Neat and clean. That's why he loved working outside the city walls so much. It was so easy to get rid of anything you didn't want. Got a body to clean up, toss it. Evidence of wrongdoing, toss it. It made all his problems go away, so neatly. No mess. Of course, her slant-eyed father hadn't gone as smoothly as he'd wanted. That's what started it all.

"You know, it's too bad it has to go down like this." He was standing over her as she held her injured hand, crouching on the grating like a little wounded animal. "You're a pretty good killer. I could have used talent like you," he smiled at the thought. The idea of having his own little cat to be part of his crew made him laugh once to himself. "Oh well, you're all out for revenge for dear old daddy."

"Why did you do it?" she asked through gritted teeth. "Why did you kill my father?" His smile grew to a full grin.

"Your father was a pain in my ass, and I got paid to do it. It was win-win."

"Paid by who?" she asked quietly, as the swirling wind grew louder and then softer again. He leaned over to get closer to her. "Like I'd really tell you."

Her eyes were dark brown and burning with rage. She sprung up like a firework and sliced his face as he tried to pull away. She lunged at his right eye. He reacted instinctively by throwing out both arms. He couldn't see her, but she was close. His wild swing collided with her as she was trying to move around him and he saw her fly into a handrail. She limped heavily away as fast as she could. His left arm had shooting pains from him moving it so much. He felt his eye that she had slashed, but it was fine. Another few centimeters and she would have taken the eye out, the little bitch.

Boggs hadn't noticed in the exchange, but he now found another shiv sticking out of the back of his right hand. He felt like a pincushion. He used his injured left hand to pull the shiv out.

"God damn her and all these pieces of metal," fury spiked inside him.

He was mad at himself for talking with her, and he was mad at her for continuing to fight when there was no way she was going to live through this encounter. Now she was the one running. Clenching his fist, he watched the blood ooze out of the wound on the back of his hand. He considered picking up the pipe, but honestly, he wanted to beat this girl to death with his fists. Boggs took a deep, calming breath. He willed his anger to ebb away from him. She wasn't that far ahead of him. He moved to catch up.

He didn't hurry. There was no need. He knew where the path they were on was going. There was no place for her to escape. He saw her supporting her wounded leg as she started up some steps. It didn't matter. The higher she climbed meant the farther she would fall when he threw her off the city. Now the only decision was to beat her to death and strangle the life out of her before he threw her off, or to toss her off alive and let her fall screaming for a few minutes. Honestly, either would be fine for him, but at this moment, he thought beating her to death would give him the most satisfaction.

He started climbing the steps. The day was perfect. A perfect day to finish what he had started more than a year ago. He remembered the little brat's mother. Now that had been a fine-looking woman. She was a bitch, too. The way she always looked down on everyone, and how she would walk about like she was surrounded by the scum of the earth. She acted like some princess in the clouds.

"You know I hated your mother too," he called up the steps as he took them one at a time. The cuts and jabs were catching up with him. He would take a couple of days off after this. "She was easy on the eyes, but she was a hateful bitch. Always thinking she was better than everyone. Bitch."

He neared the top of the steps. The path took an immediate right turn at the top. It was a perfect view. He thought about all the trouble this little cat-girl had caused him. He thought about the fine-looking mother and considered maybe having some fun with her before he finished her off. After all, she wasn't that young. A primal energy stirred near his crotch. Why not? He'd earned a little fun.

"You know, I figure you owe me for that warehouse you burned down," he said, reaching the top of the stairs. Knowing she had little space to run, he turned, saying, "Might be I take some payment befor—"

She was sitting on the path, pointing a pistol at him. He thought the pistol looked familiar as it went off. A cloud of white smoke exploded out of the barrel as he felt something rip into his stomach. The force of the blow knocked him backward, and he hit the railing, which promptly gave way under his weight.

He lost balance all together and reached out to grab something, anything, but nothing was around. He fell and saw the catwalks disappear into swirling clouds as he wondered what the hell had just happened.

CHAPTER 39

Miho sat upon the decking in a crumpled heap. She ached everywhere. She drew long, painful breaths. Her arms twitched and quivered where a moment before they screamed with the pain of the shock wave that had exploded from the gun in her hands. She sat looking at the place where Boggs had fallen off the catwalk. She stared, waiting. This wasn't the end of it. It couldn't be over. She felt the cold wind shift and cut through her as her body ached. Legs, arms, torso– everything hurt. The swirling clouds chased themselves in their endless dance and her eyes moved away to follow their movement.

The sun cut through the swirling mass and shafts of light played like a many-legged creature that was trying to touch the city. Behind her, solid and familiar, the city rose and was swallowed by other clouds. The light from the sun and the swirling dragons she imagined in the clouds made her focus slip, and her mind buzzed with a sleepy numbness. Everything was so beautiful. She slowly shifted her head around her to take it all in. The rusty catwalks stretched on endlessly around the city. She thought about the paths and stairs and dead ends, and she doubted any one person knew them all. She and Arty had gone on quite a few. Her mind drifted to Arty.

Had Jen and Arty made it to Dr. Portens' clinic in time? Should she have gone with them? She had made her choice, and she could only hope that Arty was going to be okay. Her eyes drifted back to the spot Boggs had gone over. She looked at the broken handrail. She hadn't known it was faulty. Almost all the outside of the city felt like it could just give way and fall at any time. You just sort of got used to it as a shabby, hodge-podge collection. She looked around at the collection of scrap that had been welded and fused together to make this section of catwalks. The entire area seemed rickety, even by normal standards of the city's outside.

She took an assessment of her body and state of mind. The brute had badly beaten her leg and hand, but they still seemed to work, albeit under protest. The rest of her was bruised and battered, but still whole. It was while she was checking her fingers to see if he had broken any that she noticed the movement out of the corner of her eye. She looked up to see an image of her nightmares made flesh. Joseph Boggs was rising above the catwalk. He looked totally odd, and her brain refused to put all the pieces together. Finally, she made herself start from the beginning and say inside her mind what she was seeing.

She wasn't crazy, Boggs was floating in midair in front of her. He hung, suspended by one wrist, around which a leather strap was tied. That leather strap was attached at the other end to a small leather pouch. A bag that was smaller than her fist, and inside that pouch was sewn a small piece of skystone. She saw the wisps of vaper escape the bag. She had never actually seen skystone before. It was more valuable than gold or jewels. Some believed it was the most valuable substance in the world. Wars were fought over it. Kingdoms had risen and fallen over the ore.

The entire city that she now stood outside of was suspended in the clouds by skystone, and her mother had been an ace pilot of airships that used skystone. Even though all their lives had revolved around the precious and rare material, Miho had never actually seen any before now. It was the size of a small pebble, about the size of a pea. The pouch Boggs was using had a cinch of wire that would close the bag off, cutting the amount of air reaching the skystone. It was a simple design. If you opened the bag you would allow air to hit the stone and it would rise, taking you with it. Closing the bag would decrease the air and you would fall.

"Did you think I was gone?" Boggs shouted in a terrible voice.

Boggs hung in the air a few meters from the catwalks he had just fallen from. Blood stained the front of his shirt and trousers from the fresh gunshot wound, and it also oozed from his face and multiple stab wounds that she had given him. Yet despite all his wounds, his eyes blazed with fury and triumph.

"This is my insurance policy," he called to her.

The clouds swirled and danced behind him, giving him an even more sinister look. Miho rose. Somehow, when he had fallen, she didn't think it was over. She hadn't expected this, though. Her body ached, and her mind was buzzing. She took inventory of how many blades she had left. She thought about how she was going to finish this once and for all. Amazingly, she wasn't afraid. They were both injured, but she knew she could take him.

Boggs rose a little too high in the air. He reached up with his finger to the end of the wire that closed the bag. Slipping his fingertip into the loop, he closed the bag just a little. He started dropping ever so slowly.

"I guess I owe your bitch mother for this," he said, looking up at the pouch with the skystone sewn inside. "I stole this from her airship before we sent her on her last mission." He looked back at Miho with murder in his smile.

"You stole that from my mother's ship?" Miho felt her blood heat.

"I knew she wasn't coming back. Why let the stone go to waste? I made sure my crew was in the hangar for pre-flight. These stones are only used if a pilot has to abandon ship, and I knew we didn't want her coming back."

"Why have you killed my family?" Miho shouted.

Boggs' smile widened into an evil grin. "I told you," he said in a low voice. "I was paid to."

Miho whipped her wrist and one of her throwing knives flew through the air in a flash and sank into Boggs' left shoulder. He howled in pain. She flicked her wrist again, and another buried itself into his right thigh.

"You fucking bitch!" he roared.

"You've made yourself an easy target," she said. "I have plenty more knives."

She threw another, but Boggs batted it away with his free left hand. His left arm, where she had stabbed through the arm, was bleeding freely through his makeshift bandage. It hurt him to knock the knife away. He bellowed again in pain and frustration.

"I'm going to fucking kill you!" he screamed.

"I'm right here!" Miho shouted back. "Who paid you to kill my family?"

She took out another knife and started eyeing where to throw this one. Boggs was furious. He started to swing his legs towards her and away. Then when his body was swinging towards her again, he closed the pouch and soared half the distance to the city before opening it up again. He was just out of sword reach. He couldn't do anything but shout at her. She threw the knife and it sunk into his other thigh.

"Ahhhhhhh!" he screamed and then snapped his gaze to Miho's eyes. "I'm going to murder you slowly," he said as he started swinging again. "I'm going to carve you up and throw the pieces off the city!"

Miho had heard enough. She felt like her mother and father were there beside her on the catwalks. Feeling no fear or anger, she only knew that it was time to finish this. She calculated his swing and threw a knife that buried itself into the neck of Joseph Boggs. His broken right hand scratched at the knife as he twitched and jerked in mid-air. After a minute of gurgling and grunting, he stopped moving all together. His body hung limp, and blank eyes stared openly at the unending clouds that swirled away around them.

Miho stared at Boggs' body as it twisted in the wind. After a few moments, she decided to send him to her father. She took out one of her last throwing knives and, with a quick flick, she severed the leather strap that tied his body to the skystone pouch. Boggs' body fell like the piece of trash that it was and disappeared into the clouds below. The little pouch flapped and fluttered in the air above her. Without Boggs controlling the opening, it opened and shut in the fluttering wind, and then landed with a small thump a few feet away on the catwalk.

Miho picked up the pouch and stared at the dark blue ore. It had lines of silver, like little veins, that seemed to run around its surface. When she opened the pouch to look at the stone, it gave off small wisps of vapor and she felt it rise from her hand. She flicked the pouch shut and pocketed it. It was her mother's, after all. She looked at the place where Boggs' body had disappeared once more and started limping slowly on the path that led back into the city. Her leg wouldn't take her full weight. Everything hurt. She felt numb inside, but also like she had reached some major milestone.

"You can rest now, Mother. Be at peace, Father. It is done," she said to the clouds as she made her way slowly down the steps. She wanted to sleep, and she wanted a hot bath. Thoughts of sleeping in her soft bed for the first time were presenting appealing images in her mind, but there was something she needed to do first. She needed to know Arty's fate.

CHAPTER 40

Jiro scratched his beard to give himself time to think. It had been half a year or more since he was thrown off the city. Every time his mind returned to Miho, his beautiful sunbeam, his heart rose in his chest as if to choke him. He had no way of getting back to her, not yet, at least. He had spent countless nights hoping and praying that Ama had found her that day, that Miho was in a good home. Most nights, he forced himself to focus on those visions, and not on that demon who had gotten him thrown off unjustly. Bile rose in his in throat. He was a man of peace, but he wanted nothing more than to kill the brute Joseph Boggs.

Jiro pushed Boggs, his thoughts of revenge and his lovely Miho out of his mind. Right now, he needed to focus on what was in front of him. It had been weeks of chasing rumors and secrets. Weeks of dead ends and wasted time. Just when he thought he had ended up with nothing for his efforts, now he looked at a pocked face man who might give him the information he so desperately needed.

"You-a understand English?" the pocked-faced man said slowly and deliberately through his thick cockney accent.

"Yes," Jiro answered with a quick snap of his head. "My English isn't the problem. I don't understand your request."

The weeks of searching for anyone connected to skystone had been like the search for a mythological monster. He might have asked people about finding dragons or fairy folk. Jiro loved the old stories of monsters and legends. When they had first arrived in England, he had researched as much as he could, for no other reason than his own love of old stories. He liked the stories of fairy folk. Japanese had similar types of stories, but they were mostly accredited to spirits or demons.

Most people who lived on the ground just didn't think too much about the people in the sky. There were not large gatherings under the sky cities. The clouds blocked most of the light, you never knew what was going to be dropped from above. There was the chance of a rare find, but most likely you would get a shower of the contents of a chamber pot. People just stayed away and lived their lives. They knew they were there, but as long as they stayed up in the sky, nobody seemed to mind.

Jiro needed more skystone. The little speck that had slowed his fall off the city wasn't enough to lift him back up again. He removed it from the cross they had strapped him to, and even now it was tucked into his clothes and away from the air. That is what made the pocked-face man's statement so unnerving. Jiro asked if he was the contact he had been sent to seek out, a Mr. Jamison. As soon as Jiro had asked, the squat little man with a hunched shoulder asked to see his stone.

"Your stones," the bulky little fellow bellowed. No one in the pub seemed to pay them any attention, but Jiro felt disturbed by this strange conversation. Perhaps this fellow was mad?

"If you want to talk to me, I need to see your stones," the man continued, looking resolute.

Jiro still didn't understand. Did this man know he had a skystone? How could he? Jiro had shown no one the stone.

"I came to talk to you about skystone. I don't have any," he lied.

The man looked sour. "Not those stones! Your bullocks. Your balls." Jiro looked shocked. This man was insane.

"Those sky-pigs send spies to find people out. They gather all sorts of information to keep us down 'ere on the ground. I don't talk about them cities or skystones with any women, most of the people they send are women, but if it's a man, they usually don't got their bullocks. So, if you wanna talk to me, mate, you gotta show me what's between your legs."

Jiro could see the logic, however odd, in what the man was

saying. He knew that the sky cities sent raiding parties to the surface, as well as trading parties, and intelligence gathering missions. Still though, the thought of pulling out one's privates in public was just unsettling.

To buy himself time, Jiro said, "You first."

The pocked-face Mr. Jamison looked completely stunned at his response, and after a moment's thought, broke out into an explosion of laughter. "Well, that is a first, I must say!" the little man bellowed.

"Good for the goose and the gander, eh?" and without a second's hesitation, he stood up (which didn't make him rise all that much from his sitting position) and pulled down the front of his britches.

Jiro looked quickly. The banding of blue lines around the genitals was common of any man who lived on the ground and was exposed to the Sickness. Jiro didn't look longer than a second. He didn't care about this man's privates, but now it was his turn. He did the deed as fast as could be managed.

The barkeep barked, "Oi! Take that outside, if you please!"

Jiro sat back down, holding up his hand in apology. He was deeply uncomfortable, but he had important business. He had to get back to Miho.

"Right, now that the formalities are out of the way, let's drink and talk business," Mr. Jamison said, warmer than he had before.

So they drank. Jiro had a decent amount of coin on him. There was always work for a man who knew machines and how to fix them. He easily found odd jobs in every village he had visited. The first few months after being Grounded, he had a lot of trouble while his ankle and foot recovered. Now it hardly bothered him at all. Sometimes it would ache right before a big rain, but Jiro thought this a blessing. He almost never got caught in the rain.

"Nah. I know no one who has any skystone in England. Most of our efforts are in finding the spies they send down to hide among us," Mr. Jamison said after their fourth round of ale. "What you need to do is head to Paris."

"Paris?" Jiro asked, perplexed.

"Let me ask you sommen first, before I go on about lovely Par-re," his face was getting redder and redder with each passing drink. "Why do you want to go up?" He looked Jiro dead in the eyes, and even though his eyes were glossy and wet, they were hard as stones.

Jiro felt a flood of responses come into his mind. He tried to keep his face still in front of the rush of emotions he felt. He was sure that if Mr. Jamison knew he was from a sky city, their conversation would be over now. Finally he decided on a form of the truth.

"They took my daughter," he said while trying to move his mouth as little as possible. If he saw Miho in his mind, he might be torn asunder right here and now with the flood of emotion that he kept back. He guessed some of that showed on his face. As Mr. Jamison's gaze lingered on Jiro, he had a fire that kindled behind his eyes.

"Those soulless bastards," Mr. Jamison said flatly. He nodded his head slowly, as if he were making up his mind about something. "What is her name?" he asked finally.

Jiro felt his throat contract. He hadn't said her name out loud since his Grounding, unless you counted when he woke up screaming it at night. He took a deep breath and said, "Miho" through gritted teeth.

Mr. Jamison nodded and then said, "Paris. Man by the name of Rene Lerox is leading 'Le Resistance' against the whole sky. All the cities. They say that his efforts are what brought down New Paris a few years back." Mr. Jamison hunched his shoulders so high they almost collided with his ears with a "who knows, it might be true" expression on his face. "I'm not saying he did, but he is 'ell bent on bringing them sons-a-bitches down." He pointed a stubby little finger skyward before taking a deep drink.

"How does this help me?" Jiro said, trying to connect the dots.

Mr. Jamison took a sober moment before saying, "Well, to bring the cities down, you gotta go up to knock 'em down, don't ya?" He took another drink. "Rene has skystone," he added bluntly.

Jiro understood now and nodded. He had to get to Paris, which means he needed a boat. "How will I find him?" This task seemed larger than the past few weeks he had spent getting this far.

"No worries," Mr. Jamison said, putting down his mug. "I'll tell you how to find him, and I'll write you a letter of introduction, shall I?"

Jiro took a deep drink of his ale. He finally felt like he was making progress.

CHAPTER 41

Miho had sat in the bath so long that steam was no longer rising from its surface. She pulled her legs up to her chest and wrapped her arms around her knees, lost in thought. Once again, for the thousandth time, she felt the deep, painful bruise on her thigh and winced. She looked at the huge, black mark that ran most of the length of her thigh. After a week, some edges where it wrapped around her leg were changing from purple to green.

It was healing, very, very slowly. She saw the body of Boggs hanging limp by his wrist and her expression hardened. Words her father had said during training echoed once again through her mind: "Life is precious. All life. The people we interact with are precious. Some of those people we will love, and some we will not like at all. Hopefully, you will never let yourself hate anyone. The animals we share the world with are precious, even the insects and trees."

Miho had heard these words over and over in her mind. She hadn't really thought about their meaning when he had said them, but she had never taken a life then. Now she had taken several lives, and those words weighed on her.

"Sadly, we must end life. Sometimes it is to survive. Sometimes it is to save something or someone we cherish," her father had explained.

"What matters most is why we do what we do. What are your intentions behind your actions? This is what separates someone who has to kill, from someone who commits murder. Murder is killing not for defense, and not to protect yourself. It is planned. It's intentional. Murder is killing when you don't need to kill."

"I'm a murderer," Miho said quietly to her knees. It was the circle that had been chasing itself around in her mind for hours. She always started with the fact that she wasn't sad that Boggs was dead. He was a cruel and hateful man. He would have killed her, or worse, of that she was sure. She had watched him slit Arty's throat, and she'd rushed in to help, but did she have to kill him? She could have run away weeks ago. She could have hidden from him, and not have had to kill him. Boggs had been looking for her, though. She couldn't hide in the city. She was the only Japanese girl she knew of in the city. He would have found her.

'Still, I could have left the city.' She had said this argument several times as well. The thought had popped into her mind several times before she had killed Boggs. She wasn't positive she knew how she could leave the city. Miho had never felt trapped in the city before, but the truth is she didn't have any money to speak of. She was a child and couldn't travel like an adult could, and she didn't really have anywhere to go. If she had run, she would have feared Boggs in every dark shadow, in every scary place for the rest of her days. Plus, there was her father, and apparently her mother as well. Boggs paid for what he did to her family.

Miho took a deep sigh and closed her eyes. She didn't want to be a murderer. She thought about the men she had killed. There was the man in the hallway before Boggs' death. She hadn't even seen his face. There was also the Bobby on the Wall who came after them when they tried to free Jen. Then there was Nate, the rabbit-faced man, and Boggs, the three who had her father thrown off the city. She didn't want to kill anymore. She didn't want to be a murderer.

"But Boggs worked for the mysterious S.C.," the cold voice in Miho's mind said. "S.C. hired Boggs to kill my parents. One more death won't change the other five."

"No," Miho said to her knees as she stretched out her legs again and felt the ache. "I will try not to kill S.C. if I can help it at all." What she wanted now was proper justice for her family, not revenge.

Then Jen's words came back to her. The words that had made

her lose her way the past few days. The words that had cut her deeper than any blade. Miho took a deep belly breath and let her face sink beneath the cooling water of the bath. She would either have to heat the bath back up again (something she had done a few times now), or get out soon.

"He's alive, for now," Jen had said to her outside of Dr. Portens' clinic. "The doctor says that the cut could turn sour and kill him. We can only try to keep the area clean, and hope."

Jen had looked horrible. She was still weak from her sickness, but now stress and worry added to her pale, haggard appearance. Huge tears filled her pale brown eyes as she spoke. "The doctor says he may never speak again. If the cut is deep enough to sever his vocal cords... we'll just have to see."

Miho had hobbled to Dr. Portens' clinic directly from killing Boggs. Dr. Portens looked startled by her appearance.

"Young Lady Ba," the doctor had said when she opened the door to find Miho. Miho was still annoyed by this name and title, but before she could say anything, the doctor had swooped down on her with concern in her expression.

"My God, you look a mess," she said, staring into Miho's eyes. "Come in, let me tend to you."

Miho hobbled inside. She felt like she could pass out from exhaustion. The doctor spoke as she wiped away the blood and attended to Miho. "The boy is currently being treated by my daughter, Patience. We've sutured the cut to his throat, and will apply poultices to try to keep the wound clean and clear of infection. He has lost a lot of blood."

Miho had nodded, only half aware of what the doctor was saying. Once she heard Arty was alive, all the energy had left her. After a couple of minutes (or it could have been a lot longer), Jen had shown up, and they had gone outside to talk.

"Is it done?" Jen had asked eventually. Her eyes drying and turning hard. Miho nodded.

"I'm glad it's finished, but I wish the cost hadn't been so high." Jen looked at her with fire in her eyes, and with anger and grief.

"Death and pain seem to follow you, Miho." The words hung in the air like a heavy weight. "If Arty dies, I don't think I'll ever forgive you. All this was for revenge, so you could kill a murderer, but what does that make you?"

Jen continued to vent her frustrations and grief. Miho hadn't argued. She stood there and let Jen unload on her. Miho felt she deserved it, and more. When Jen started to cry quietly, and stopped talking, Miho walked away into the night. Dr. Portens' clinic was in a section of the city that had open skies above it. The stars could be seen above the city tonight. Miho stumbled away without looking back. She couldn't think. She couldn't react.

"What does that make you?" Jen's voice had echoed in Miho's mind for days. Jen's anger and pain stabbed at Miho's heart. It was Miho who was responsible for Jen's sickness, and for the burns on Jen's arms and body. It was Miho who was responsible for Arty. Even if he lived, he too was now scarred for life. What had been the cost of finally killing Joseph Boggs? Miho closed her eyes, and the thoughts chased themselves around inside her mind. She wasn't aware of time passing, but when the door to the bathroom opened, she noticed the water was much cooler.

Ama walked in with a concerned look. "May I speak with you?" she asked in a soft tone. Miho shut her eyes again and nodded her head. She felt Ama sit on the edge of the tub.

"Miho, dear, something has been bothering you for days. Will you talk to me?" Ama's voice was quiet but echoed through the open bathroom.

Miho sat in silence as a thousand thoughts chased each other through her mind. Every time she thought about saying one, another jumped up in its place. Finally she heard her voice across the surface of the water. "As a soldier, you have to kill people."

"Yes."

"Does it ever bother you? To kill someone?" At this, Miho opened her eyes to see how Ama reacted.

"Every time," Ama said flatly. "I never enjoy it, but it's what I have to do." "Why do you have to?"

Ama had a small smile as she let out a single, silent exhale. It wasn't really a laugh. "Your mother and I used to talk about this subject."

Miho sat up and looked at Ama with her full attention. She knew that her mother had been an ace pilot with Ama. They were both members of the Valkyries, the city's top airship pilots. Miho wondered how her mother would feel about her child taking another's life.

Ama seemed lost in thought for a minute, then spoke again. "I'm a Valkyrie, and so was your mother. She was one of the best pilots this city had. She might have been the best in all of England. Kana-san was amazing. She was gifted. I watched her do things in an airship that I didn't think possible, but your mother never enjoyed the kill. You see, the Valkyries have a pretty high turnover rate. We have a lot of girls come in and either die or quit pretty quickly. Sometimes we get a girl who loves 'the kill.' You can always tell the ones who enjoy it. Kana didn't enjoy it, and neither do I."

A shadow had fallen behind Ama's eyes. She continued speaking even more quietly than before.

"When you first start, you tell yourself that you are protecting the people you love. You tell yourself that you are saving hundreds, or even thousands, of people in the city. You tell yourself that your actions are saving the very city itself. It makes your actions justified, maybe even noble. After a while though, that reason doesn't really have the same meaning. You know, there are dozens of pilots out there fighting to protect the city. One day, my flying days will be over. It's very possible that one day, I'll go out and not come back. Just like Kana-san didn't come back. My family is my reason for always wanting to come back. I'll fight 'til my last breath, like I know Kana did, just to make it back to them."

Ama shifted and looked at Miho. "Sometimes I still focus on protecting my family, and that sits well, but more often than not I realize that there are people out there who are going to do harm. They are going to hurt others, or kill others. If no one is there to stand against them, they will do a lot more harm than if people stand in their way. Sometimes we get to stop them altogether, but other times they get away with it. I will do what I can to stand in their way. In the end, each soldier must make their own peace."

"What did my mother do to make her peace?" Miho asked quietly.

"Kana-san was a wise woman, and my dearest friend," Ama said. "She said that one day, in this life, or another, she would have to atone for her actions. She said she tried to live her life without regret for when that day of atonement came. She said that she hadn't always been able to achieve that goal, but mostly she was alright with whatever karma was going to come back to her, because she was doing the best she could to be a good person - even if that meant she had to do bad things sometimes."

Miho thought about these words. It sounded like her mother had done things in her life that she wasn't proud of, either. She wondered if her mother had ever murdered someone for revenge. Murder versus killing – in the end, does the difference really matter at all? The outcome is the same.

"All life is precious." After all, that is what her father had said. There was so much she didn't know about her mother and father, but even when he had said those words, he had admitted that sometimes there is a need to take another's life. All of her troubles these past few days boiled down to wondering when it was acceptable to take a life, and when it was not.

"Are you missing her, dear?" Ama asked with a kind expression.

Miho realized that Ama thought Miho was missing her mother, and that was the reason she had been hurting these past few days. Miho didn't think she was ready to talk about Boggs, about everything. She didn't want to lie to this woman, though. She decided to say something that was true, even if it wasn't what Ama was trying to figure out.

"I miss my mother and father often."

CHAPTER 42

The trip across the channel had been dreadful. It had taken Jiro days to find passage. He finally found a fisherman willing to take him across, but the ugly little man wanted a king's ransom for a fee. They set off from a little village outside Brighton, and then the seas seemed to fight and punish the little boat for daring to cross. They had spent hours struggling against the currents, with the wind and chop pushing them constantly away from France. Finally they had made it.

The fisherman took his money and said he thought they landed near Yport, northwest of Paris. Jiro never wished to set foot in that pitiful excuse for a boat again.

Jiro had known it was about a two days' walk from the coastline to Paris. He had set off at once, and his leg wasn't slowing him down too much. He had looked for a road, hoping to find a cart or merchant that might be heading into Paris. If he could try to ride with someone, it might save his tired legs. He had walked for a couple of hours when the sun started to sink. They had left the English coast after dawn, but the journey across had taken far too long. He shifted his thoughts to finding a place to sleep for the night.

That's when he found the farmhouse. His apprehension grew as he saw a dark-haired man with hard eyes glare at him as he approached. The language barrier was a problem, but after he pointed to the barn and shook his money satchel, everything went smoothly. The man brightened up and his wife came out of the house. She was a pretty woman in her late 40s, Jiro guessed. She had a warm smile. Jiro gave her a few coins, and she showed him to the barn. It was very clean and smelled of fresh hay (and only a little of manure). She pointed to a full rain barrel and mimicked washing her face and armpits. He understood and started to set up for the night. His leg was getting stiff, and he felt the weariness pull at him.

The sun was down and darkness was deepening as he pulled out his blanket and candle a little while later. The couple appeared carrying a lantern, a small bundle and a plate of food for him. He could smell the food above anything else around him. The chicken was still steaming, with fresh vegetables and bread. Jiro took the plate gratefully and bowed low, thanking them. The parcel was a loaf of bread and some dried fruit. They smiled and spoke to him in French. He didn't understand, but they were kind. They left the lantern when they returned to the house. Jiro devoured the food like a ravenous animal.

As he was feeling sleep approaching, he was wandering around the space in small, slow circles. He was lost in his thoughts and memories. He would start to head for his sleeping area with his blanket, but then think about something in his bag and shuffle over to it. Jiro was overly tired, and he knew it. He remembered being this tired on the journey from Japan. The four of them had barely enough room in the little airship. They'd mostly traveled at night to avoid anyone following or reporting them. Kana was still weak from childbirth, and Machiko attended to her and the baby. Every time the child cried, Jiro was sure they would be found. If that had happened, Kana would be returned to her father. He'd been pretty sure he, Machiko and the baby would be killed.

He hadn't known what it was to be a father then. He had only held the baby a few times. It was small, smelly and loud, but it meant everything to Kana—and she meant everything to him. He had walked in circles then too, he remembered with a smile. His movements took him from the controls to the women, to their supplies, and back to the controls again. After he had done this a couple of times, Kana smiled and quietly laughed.

"You are exhausted, my husband," Kana was beautiful in the moonlight. The small bundle was in her arms asleep. "Come, sit next to me for a minute."

Jiro just obeyed. His mind was blank, but also full of the

thoughts that had been chasing themselves around and around in his head. He felt her gently put the bundle in his arms. The baby stirred and moved, but then settled. It was warm and didn't smell bad at all at the moment. He sighed deep, and the baby sighed just as he did.

Kana exhaled with a small laugh. "She's your daughter," she whispered, stroking the baby's head. "She is the best parts of you and me combined."

Jiro looked down and saw the tiny form illuminated by the moonlight. Machiko's snores quietly filled the silence, and a wave of emotion flooded over him. This little human was the cause of so much trouble. She was the reason they had to hide; she was the reason they must flee in the night like criminals. Yet, she was the product of the love they felt. That love that Jiro would die and kill for. The little nose, the tiny eyelashes, were so delicate and yet so beautiful. He tried to see any features that looked like Kana, or even himself, but it all just looked so different.

"I don't know how to be a father," he'd said as hot tears stung at the corners of his eyes. He'd felt afraid, so afraid that he was sure his heart would break out of the bars of his chest and run far away.

"It starts with love," Kana had said quietly. "The rest will come."

He'd looked up from the baby, although it was hard to take his eyes off the little form. He'd looked into the face of the woman he loved. She was the most beautiful woman on Earth. She glowed with life and resolve. More tears ran down his cheeks. He loved her, and he loved this little baby that was theirs. He was scared about what lay ahead, but so thankful he had the two of them.

She had nodded her head. "I'm scared too. We will constantly be hunted. We cannot ever let our guard down. We must survive as a family, and we must protect each other."

Jiro had nodded and felt the weight of the tiny bundle in his arms.

"We can now only trust each other. No one else," Kana had said quietly.

Jiro's thoughts returned to the barn around him. They had made that pact so long ago. He mustn't forget it. He moved himself up into the loft and pulled up the ladder. It wasn't that this couple was untrustworthy, but he must always remember that he, and what was left of his family, were always hunted. They must be on their guard. Why hadn't he explained everything to Miho long ago? He had always thought that there was time, and he didn't want to spoil what childhood she had left. That would replace the comfort and security she felt with concern and caution. He knew now that he should have told Miho the reason they had fled Japan so long ago. He had always worked to give her a fighting chance in this world, so had Kana. As long as he still had breath, he must do what he could to return to, and protect Miho.

The next morning, he greeted the couple near dawn. He bowed deeply to respect them for their kindness and said the one word that really mattered: "Paris?" They pointed in a direction with many words he didn't understand. He thanked them and set off. Less than an hour later, he was on a road. Sometime after that came the merchant in the cart. He flagged the man down and said "Paris?" while offering two English ha'pennies. The man eyed him suspiciously, but jerked his thumb behind him. The rest of that day went smoothly. He had simply ridden among the bolts of cloth and wares, while the cart and horse did all the work. His mind was always on Miho, and how each step the horse took away from England was leading him closer to her.

That night, as the sun sank, the driver pulled off the road to make camp for the night. Jiro couldn't explain the feeling of unease he felt, but he knew enough to trust it. He just didn't like the look of the driver's eyes. The way the man kept glancing at him. Jiro considered his options and decided that it was time to make his way without the other fellow. He marched off into the night in the direction of Paris. Jiro didn't need help to know where the city was. He could make out the lights and the unmistakable signs of a major city. He was a few miles away, but at last he could find Mr. Lerox.

After a week, Jiro had begun to lose hope. Mr. Jamison, that squat little troll of a man, had told Jiro to seek Mr. Lerox in Café Francaisé, which he said was located in central Paris. Jiro had no concept of just how many eateries named Café Francaisé there were in central Paris. So far, he had visited at least a dozen, and in each one asked for Mr. Lerox. He had been met with strange looks each time. He wondered if Lerox was a common name, or perhaps not a real name at all. Jiro wondered if the pock-faced Mr. Jamison was laughing at him now.

He had learned of yet another Café Francaisé in the North-East section of the city, along the Seine River which twisted its way through the sprawling city. Jiro took his time walking along the Promenade and enjoying the beauty of the morning. The city was old, and full of life. Few cities in Europe had this kind of history and character. Hundreds of years ago, when the largest cities were moving into the sky, the lower cities often fell into ruin, but not Paris.

Through a strange series of events, High Paris had fallen three times throughout history. The last time was some 20 or more years ago during a massive revolution. Many of the country's wealthiest were killed and their castles and cities in the sky were pulled down and destroyed.

Paris was beautiful and alive, and Jiro wondered what the world would look like if all the sky cities were brought down. He imagined skies without constant cloud cover. It would look like today in Paris. It would be beautiful. He wanted Miho to see this place. He wanted nothing more than to find her and take her from that terrible city they had lived in for so many years.

Kana and he had talked, when they first came to Europe, about where to settle, and where they could hide. They decided that the wealthy from around the world often flocked to the high cities of Brittiana. They would blend in better among that crowd. Ama was African, Kana and Jiro were Japanese, and there were many others from all over Asia who, for whatever reasons, had come to this area. It was the right move at that time, but now? Kana was lost to him, and her absence was still a dark hole in his heart. The other half of his heart beat for Miho. He needed to focus on what he had, and not on what he had lost.

A warm tear escaped his eye without him knowing it was there. He felt the stinging in the corners of his eyes as more tears wanted to flow. Kana, his sweet Kana. How could he do what needed to be done alone? He had no idea how, but he knew that he must.

He spotted a battered little café across the street from where he walked. Its weathered and battered sign had fading letters that showed this Café Francaisé was one of the easiest ones to forget due to its miniscule size and overall shabbiness. As he crossed the street, avoiding the horse-drawn carriages, he noticed the little café was mostly empty. He had come a long way, so he might as well ask the shopkeeper if he knew his contact. He limped towards the front door as a voice called to him over a newspaper.

"I hear you have been looking for me?" said a man's voice in clear English, but with a thick French accent.

Jiro looked at the man, who lowered his paper and looked back. He was a handsome, dark-haired man in his 40s or 50s. He was well built and thin. The only thing that made Jiro think he was that old was the greying of his hair and the lines at the corners of his eyes. His eyes were sharp, and behind the thin rimmed, round glasses was intelligence that could clearly be seen.

"Mr. Lerox?" Jiro asked, looking around him for anyone else.

Mr. Lerox smiled and nodded his head. "Please, join me for breakfast."

CHAPTER 43

The sun was unusually bright as Miho made her way through the open part of the city. The sky above only had clouds churning at the edges of what she could see. She peered up at the brilliant blue vastness and felt the heat of the sun warm her face and exposed skin. The air was clear and crisp. It was the single most beautiful day she had seen in a long time. She made her way down the street of the East district and soaked in all the bustling signs of life around her. The familiar clip-clop of horses as they pulled their various carts, the men in their suits, the ladies in their dresses, and the sounds of children playing — it all wove together into a tapestry of life.

Miho felt both a part of it all, and also separate from it. She was used to the unusual looks that always framed upon the faces of people who looked her way. She stood out, and she knew it. Today she wore layers of deep indigo blue. Ama had hired dressmakers and tailors to outfit her with a new wardrobe. The problem was that Miho refused to wear Western women's dresses. She preferred more simple clothes that allowed for freer movement and comfort. Her pants were wide enough and cut in such a way that they appeared to be a skirt. This prevented scandalous looks from both men and women on the streets. Her tops were usually composed of kimono style shirts and jackets that were layered and tied around her. She had specifically instructed how these clothes were supposed to fit her.

Many of the dress makers took the challenges on with alacrity. They almost seemed excited by the prospect of working on something new. Some tailors had wrinkled their noses and flat out refused the work, though not many. It was a testament to Ama's standing that rarely would anyone disrespect her unusual requests. Miho didn't take for granted the fact that she owed Ama an enormous debt. There was a benefit to being in the household of one of the city's Valkyries, the most elite pilots of the air defense. Miho knew from her time living in the Underbelly that no matter how she was dressed, she would always stand out, so she decided to embrace her differences and dress with full respect of her history and heritage. It didn't really matter to her that she didn't remember Japan, or had never seen any other Japanese people besides her mother, father, and Machiko.

Miho held her head high and walked with purpose. She was headed to Dr. Portens' clinic to visit Arty, and it was a beautiful day. She remembered the first time she visited Arty at the clinic. The difference between how she had felt, and the weather that day, couldn't be more extreme. It was a colder, darker day. Dark clouds had circled as she walked the streets that day. With each step, she felt the weight of her responsibility and guilt. By the time she reached the clinic door, she was ready to throw up from her nerves. It took her a long time to work up the courage to ring the bell, but she did in the end. She had to see Arty. It had been two weeks since he had arrived, and each day, each hour that passed without her seeing him, was like a blade cutting her own throat.

She must face Arty, and she must give her life to him. It was the only thing she could do to make up for what she had inadvertently done to him. When she heard he was taking a turn for the worse, she knew that if he died without her seeing him, she would never forgive herself. She remembered the looks on the faces of Jen and Dr. Portens' daughter as she opened the door. She had only glanced at them because her eyes were only for Arty. He looked as thin and fragile as a glass skeleton under the covers. His face had sunken in and his eyes were dark and unfixed as they stared straight ahead. He didn't look at her, and the sight of him stabbed her soul. His chestnut hair looked dull and stuck to his head. He looked like a soul ready to die. His thin mouth was puffy, and his white lips chapped and cracked. The bandage around his neck looked like the scarf of a noble, but she could see the pale pink of still seeping wounds.

Her heart was heavy in her chest. She only vaguely heard some of what Jen was saying. Snippets of "He was doing well until a few days ago, but then something changed" and "... we can't tell why he won't eat or drink…" floated to her ears from far away. She still couldn't take her eyes off Arty. Miho knew. She knew what this was, even if the other girls didn't. He had given up.

She knew how it felt, and she knew how it looked. His eyes said it all. He had given up and was ready to die.

"Please let me have some time alone with him," she heard herself say out loud.

She didn't look around, but felt the two girls leave the room. Miho edged closer to his bed and knelt beside it. What could she say? What could she possibly do to help her friend? Her guilt and anguish at what she had done to this boy hardened inside her and locked her throat as tears fell silently down her cheeks. She lowered her head to his hand. It lay thin and bony on the bed. She couldn't even look him in the eyes. The pain and emotion crescendoed in her ears. It was like the howling of a storm growing louder and louder until she heard a pained cry leave her.

She let out a deep guttural sound of her soul's pain as the tears flowed out of her. "Arty," she started, but her throat was too tight to continue. "Arty, I'm sorry," she finally managed, and then the storm inside burst out of her.

Miho was a river of tears and anguish. She said disjointed things that just came to her as the river of emotion flowed out of her. "My fault… I'm so sorry… You never deserved this… You deserve better… And I ruined it all… You… Jen… Everything…"

After what felt like an eternity of emotion and tears flowing from her after her dam broke, Miho felt the soft weight of his hand on the back of her head. She looked up to see him looking at her. Not with anger, or pain, but with a soft kindness in his sunken eyes and a small smile on his chapped lips.

"You can't smile at me," Miho said, upset. "I'm the reason you are like this."

Arty's thin smile widened by just a fraction as his eyes showed a spark of life and he very gently shook his head from side to side.

"Don't tell me no!" she snapped, feeling anger grow inside her and she stood up, wiping her puffy face. "You would be safe, and happy, and whole if it weren't for me!"

A shadow passed for a moment behind Arty's eyes at her words, but then the light came back stronger and his soft smile faltered just a little and he shook his head more firmly. The smile grew again, but a fraction. It had kindness and pain in its shape. Miho couldn't understand what was happening inside him, but she knew what she was feeling. She whipped out a knife and held it between them. She made sure it was pointing like a line that separated them. She didn't want him to feel like she was threatening him.

"Arty, in my country, when a warrior fails the one they are supposed to protect, the only way they can make up for this failure is to take their own life."

She was about to continue with the speech she had practiced in her mind all the way here when Arty reached out his bony hand and closed it over her hand that held the knife. His eyes burned with life as he stared into hers and he firmly shook his head from side to side.

Tears leaked out of the corners of her eyes as she put away the knife and sat on his bed, looking at him. She grabbed his hand in both of hers and asked him, "Tell me what I can do to make up for this?"

The small, bemused smile returned to his lips as his left hand came up to almost touch his throat. The expression in his eyes simply said, "I can't tell you."

Miho reached into her bag and brought out the small wrapped bundle. Inside the linen cloth was a small dark-grey piece of slate, and a bundle of white chalk. Arty looked quizzical.

"You asked me a while ago to teach you how to read and write. I thought now was the perfect time."

Arty looked up at her with an amazed expression. It was clear that he hadn't even considered this possibility. Miho looked into his eyes and said, "Arty, I will come here as often as I can, and I will teach you, but you can't give up. You need to eat, and drink, and get stronger. You are not done yet."

He stared into her eyes for a good long time and then slowly nodded his head. She felt a weight lift from her and she stood up quickly.

"Good. I'll ask for some food and water, and we can begin!"

She had come back every few days over the past three weeks. Arty was a man on fire with focus. He doggedly practiced for hours. A few days ago, the last time she visited, his face was less sunken and his skin was a much better color. There was a life in his eyes. Miho felt he was climbing back out of the pit inside his mind.

Miho's heart was smiling. Perhaps that is why the world seemed brighter, the people more inviting. She arrived at Dr. Portens' clinic and saw Arty outside in the garden. He was sitting alone. Her joy was heightened by seeing him sitting on a bench among the plants and flowers.

"Arty-san!" she exclaimed as she got closer to him. Arty looked healthy and strong. He smiled as she got closer. He quickly bent over his slate board and popped back up with a shakily written, but clearly legible "Hi." His chestnut hair was clean and blowing in the light breeze. His neck had a thinner bandage around it that looked clean. It warmed Miho's heart to see him looking so good.

"Artimus, I've returned!" they both turned to see the youngest Portens, Patience, coming around the house with a tray carrying lunch. Miho looked back at Arty, whose eyes lingered on the girl. He then turned to Miho and blushed slightly. Miho felt one of her eyebrows rise with her thought of "Oh, really?" Arty blushed a little more.

"Oh, Lady Ba," Patience stopped walking while holding the tray. "I did not know you were here. I was bringing Arty some lunch. Should I take it back..." and she turned slightly as if to return to the house.

"No!" Miho called, and she smiled at the girl. "I'm not staying. I was just in the area and decided to check in with Arty."

"Oh," Patience looked uncomfortable. "I see."

Miho turned away from Patience and faced Arty with a "You rascal" expression. "Well, Arty, I'll come back for another lesson soon."

"Oh, Lady Ba," called the meek voice of Patience as she edged closer. "I do hope it's alright, but I have been working with Arthur on his reading and writing. I wasn't trying to impose upon your lessons." Patience looked even more uncomfortable.

Miho smiled warmly. "Not at all," and she bowed deeply to the girl. "Arty-san enjoys your lessons, I am sure, and what matters most is that he learns. I thank you for your kind attention."

Patience's face reddened so much that Miho thought she might be giving off heat.

"Not at all," the girl said with an awkward bow. "I have enjoyed our time together."

Miho turn and looked at Arty while saying, "I'm sure you have. Art-timus can be very charming." Miho smiled with a 'you rapscallion' look on her face, and almost laughed out loud at Arty's smile of embarrassment.

Miho took her leave of them in the garden. As she turned one last time before they were blocked from view, she saw Patience putting out a picnic lunch for them, and Arty trying to help with a sweet smile on his face. Miho's heart warmed.

"Let him be happy," she said a soft prayer inside her heart and hoped that any kind spirit would listen.

CHAPTER 44

Ama looked inside the folds of paper at the dress the tailor had made for her daughter. It was shades of cream and light browns that would go well with Adana's complexion. The gala was in two days, and everything was falling into place. She glanced across the room at the boxes containing her husband and son's new suits. Then she looked to Miho's formal kimono. It was a dazzling array of silk and layers of colored cloth. Overall, the shades were of sunset orange and red, but with crisp white layers on top that draped the shoulders. Patterns of strange flowers began around the waist and became more prominent near the bottom of the robes. The flowers were stitched in green and purple threads.

Ama had recovered most of the possessions of her friend when she learned what had become of them. The Market Street museum's curator had been disappointed to see the items go, but had reluctantly given in to Ama's insistence. All the Michitakas' belongings had been seized and taken after Jiro was Grounded. Ama had been out of the city when it happened, and the household was picked clean by the time she had returned. She had never learned what had happened to their possessions, or Miho's fate. No one could give her any information, only rumors and bits of second-hand accounts.

But Miho had stumbled across their possessions, and Ama was able to recover them all. She had most of the belongings packed up and safely waiting for Miho to claim them when she was old enough. Some of the more precious items she put in Miho's room to be of comfort. She looked at the Kimono that had once belonged to her friend Kana and smiled at the thought of Miho wearing her mother's robes.

The tailor had nearly cried when Ama had brought the robes to be adjusted for Miho. The woman had marveled at the detail and beauty of the ensemble. She was very reluctant to cut and remove cloth to make it fit Miho, but Ama had insisted. The coming Gala was very important and now that Miho had said she was ready to enter society in full, Ama wanted her to make a big splash at her debut. She was determined to set Miho on a path that would most benefit the girl in the long run. Ama had promised herself to do as much as she could for Kana's daughter.

The smell of cannon smoke stung her nose in memory of their promise. She remembered the wet, humid smell of the cloud and the sounds of the unseen battle. Ama rubbed at her forearm that had been cut so deeply and the whole thing came back to her with a rush. It had been an intense battle with a series of Norse raiders a few years back. Every now and then, a group of them would cobble together a cluster of ships and raid the cities along the English coast. They had been doing this for hundreds of years. The raiders were quite good at it. The Norse were vicious fighters and loved everything to do with combat. Like the Vikings of old, these fools were in love with raiding, killing, stealing and raping their way across the skies.

The Valkyries had been dispatched along with the City Guard to protect the city during the raids. This batch of raiders was different in that their ships weren't just a haphazardly thrown together collection of junk and armor, set with skystone and made to fly. These were warships, and a lot of them. These raiders had more than 25 warships and were trained in using them. They were coordinated, fierce and deadly.

During the first few moments of the foray, Ama had taken a solid hit to her port wings. The Valkyrie fighters looked just like giant dragonflies. They have long metal bodies with fabric and metal wings. There are two sets of wings per side. The skystone produces steam that is captured by the engine and that moves the wing's metal support pole. The fabric is stretched taut behind the pole.

Ama's port wings were shredded, and her fighter couldn't move. All she could do was hover in place and fire her cannon. She was a stationary target, and that meant death. She had almost accepted her fate and decided she would fire as many shots as she could before she died when, out of nowhere, Kana had swooped around her in a long arch. Kana fired off a shot at the nearby enemy and come to land on top of Ama in one fluid movement. It reminded Ama of a mother hen sitting on an egg. The sound of her ship being squashed as Kana's wings pushed them both downward was like a great monster roaring in the sky. Ama closed the iris that kept her aloft and both ships sank below the fight.

The clouds swallowed them both, and she heard Kana's cry to her in the mist. "Ama, are you alive?"

"Yes, I'm still here!" Ama had shouted in reply as she looked down at her bleeding forearm. When her wings were shredded, she had been thrown around inside her cockpit like a rag-doll. Her arm had been cut on some broken glass of her canopy as it had shattered. The blood flowed deep red as she saw her life flow from her body. Now that they were hidden in cover, she needed to stem the bleeding. The first thing she had to do was to dig the glass shard out of her arm, and she couldn't actually bring herself to do it yet. She was building up courage. Every second she waited, she bled more, and the chances of them being found increased.

"That looks scary. Do you need help?" Kana's voice was calm as Ama looked up to see her friend grabbing onto the back of her ship like a monkey.

"What are you doing?" Ama had cried in surprise.

"Coming to get you," her friend had said with a smirk.

"You might fall, Kana."

"I'm tied off." And sure enough, Ama could see the rope tied around her friend's waist. Kana's aircraft was still sitting directly on top of Ama's, but the cloud cover was so thick that Ama couldn't see more than five or six feet. "Do you need me to come down there and take that out?"

Ama had stared at her friend in amazement - Kana never hesitated. She just acted on what she needed to do. Ama realized she admired Kana for that and so many other aspects of her personality.

Realizing this wasn't a time to build up courage, that she knew what must be done and she needed to just do it, Ama had grabbed the glass shard and pulled it out of her arm. It had hurt a lot, but it wasn't as deep as she had feared. The blood didn't spurt out, but rather just continued to ooze. Ama took her scarf and wrapped it around her arm and tied it off one handed.

"Don't make it too tight," Kana had said as an explosion of cannon fire went off somewhere above. "Just tight enough to stop the bleeding."

Ama didn't respond as she finished tying the knot. "Now what?" she'd asked, as she looked up at her friend. Kana was inspecting the shattered wing.

"I don't think we can repair your wings here," Kana had said with a nod, as if making up her mind. "And I don't have room for you if you abandon your ship, even if you do bring the skystone with you."

Kana had sat up on the tail of her ship and unslung a second coil of rope she had around her body. She tossed it down to Ama as she started attaching it to her aircraft's tail. "We'll have to tow you back."

"Are you insane? They will shoot us both out of the sky!" Ama had shouted.

"It's possible, but we'll have to try. Go ahead and tie your end off."

"Kana, just leave me here. Come back for me after the battle."

"That's not an option. The longer you are out here, the less likely you are to get home. We are doing this."

"Promise me you'll look after Abe and my kids if I don't make it back," Ama had said, looking from her cut arm to her broken skyship, to her friend's eyes.

"I would think that we wouldn't need to make that promise. You know I'd watch over your family as if they were my own. I know you would do the same for mine."

"I just need to hear you say it," Ama had replied urgently.

"I promise, my friend. If anything ever happens to you, I'll protect and watch over your family, always."

"I promise you, too. Thank you."

"Now then, let's get you back to that handsome husband of yours. You know he'd be lost without you."

Ama had laughed and started tying the rope around her airship. They had made it back. Kana flew like a graceful bird and Ama had blasted anything that got too close. By the time they half landed, half crashed into the hangar of the Valkyries, they were both out of cannon shot. When they embraced on the flight deck, they were both black from the smoke and looked nothing less than disreputable. They drank a toast and returned to combat later that day.

Ama heaved a deep sigh. She missed her friend. While she remembered that day, she moved close to the kimono. She rolled the soft layers of fabric through her fingertips and thought about Kana's only living relation.

Ama would do everything in her power to help keep Miho safe and to set her up for as good a life as she could have. Miho had already seen so much of life's hardships. Ama knew the girl was sparring with Abe almost daily. She knew Abe enjoyed having a partner, and he confided to her that Miho was a skilled fighter. Miho was smart, skilled and cunning, but there was so much going on behind her eyes that Ama still didn't know. She hoped the girl would open up to her. She needed to heal if she was to move forward.

CHAPTER 45

The night of the Gala came and the entire Ba household staff worked all day to prepare its family for the event. Miho hated the entire experience. She had suspected for a while that the maids and other staff of the Ba household disliked her, but after a day of constant torture, they convinced her of it. Miho had been in serious fights that had left her bruised and bleeding for weeks after, but she didn't remember any pain like having three maids brush and treat her hair, pluck her eyebrows and scrub her skin raw, or wrap her so tightly in layer after layer of cloth 'til she thought she would die from lack of breathing.

Of course, the men got off easy, those rats. They didn't have makeup and the hours of attention to detail. Miho was fuming. By the time they told her she couldn't wear her swords, she was ready to kill someone. Ama had to step in and smooth things over. Miho still didn't have her swords, but she tucked enough blades and shanks into her folds that she felt confident she could defend herself if needed.

Miho didn't care about fancy dresses and makeup in the least. It wasn't until one of the maids held up a looking glass that she totally stopped and took in her appearance. She looked like an image of her mother in her memory. It had been several years ago, but she remembered her mother with pale face makeup and beautiful robes of blue. Miho had thought she was exquisite, and so had her father.

"Like the moon over the sea, you are a light unto this world," he had said in Japanese when he looked at her.

Her mother had smiled demurely and hid her face behind a fan. She had looked at Miho and winked. Miho had giggled at how

252

Father was behaving. He was gushing over Mother and Mother was allowing him to gush.

"Getting dressed up is a rare treat, Miho-chan. It can have its uses and its benefits," her mother had said, as Father reached for her hand with a cry, "My heaven, my stars, you are a living poem."

"You look beautiful, just like your mother Miho," Ama said as she entered her room sometime later.

"I remember Mother dressing like this once, years ago."

Ama nodded. "That must have been a state dinner. Usually, the Valkyries wear our formal dress uniform as I do tonight, but for some dinners and parties we are asked to dress like women, not soldiers. Your mother always turned heads, both men's and women's, when she dressed like you are now."

Miho looked at Ama's uniform and remembered her mother's uniform too. Ama was tall and very dark skinned, even for an African woman. Her form was light and powerful, like some sort of cat. Her eyes were sharp and exotic. They were the color of amber and sparkled like cut stone.

Ama's boots were brightly polished and the puttees that wrapped around her legs, starting at the heel of her boots and stopping near the knee, were a soft brown color. Her trousers were a deep green that were almost black, and her dark brown shirt was adorned with the badges of her position and achievements.

The Valkyrie wore a sort of ceremonial backpack when in full uniform. Miho had always loved playing with her mother's. It was a slender wooden box about half a foot wide that was polished to show the grain of wood it was constructed from. Polished brass gears could be seen by anyone who stood behind the wearer. A small handle was in one side near the small of the back, so the Valkyrie could reach and pull the handle down. All the gears turned and two wings of brass would unfold from the top of the box. They didn't have feathers, but instead just ribs of brass, like a bat's wing with no skin. Each rib was connected to the ones beside it by a delicate wire that, when unfurled, arrayed the wings in a striking skeletal span of brass and wire.

At the moment, Ama's "wings" were still contained in her backpack and she wore no helmet. Normally, the Valkyrie wore a thin helmet of leather to keep their heads protected and their hair out of their eyes. They also wore flying goggles, but for the sake of tonight's party, Ama wore her hair in elaborate patterns of waves and curls. Her hair was beautiful and looked like it had been oiled into the unique patterns. Somehow, she looked both feminine and like a powerful warrior all rolled into one.

"Tonight's very special to me, Miho." Ama knelt down to look her in the eyes. "Tonight, we place you onto the stage of the powerful, the rich, and the influential. Tonight will be the first step on the next phase of your journey."

Miho nodded. She had a few plans for tonight as well. Ama lightly squeezed her shoulder and asked if she was ready to go.

"Ama," Miho spoke quietly before they left the room. The warrior woman turned with a warm, motherly expression. "Thank you for all that you have done for me."

Ama broke into a large smile and led Miho out of the room.

When they arrived in the foyer, the entire family was waiting for them. Abe wore a long tunic that was woven of deep patterned cloth of many bright colors. Henry wore a Western style suit and looked like an uncomfortable smaller version of his father. Adana was adjusting her hair in a mirror, looking very fashionable in her Western cream-colored dress. Ama led Miho next to Adana and spoke to them both.

"We will arrive at the gala in two carriages tonight. You two girls will be in the first carriage, the rest of us will be behind."

Miho wondered at this. It would be a tight fit, but the five of them could fit in a single carriage. "Why must we ride together, Mother?" Adana asked, with a slight edge in her voice.

"I want you two to be noticed."

As Adana continued to ask her mother questions, Miho noticed

Abe approaching. His slow and quiet nature always calmed Miho.

"You two girls look very beautiful tonight," Abe said with his thick accent. His voice was low and had a slight rasp to it. Miho thought it sounded like a favorite pair of boots felt - reliable, trusty and well worn.

"But you both are missing these." And with that, he withdrew two fans from his robes.

Adana took hers with a dismissive, "Thank you, papa," and set off toward the front of the house. Miho realized that she was gazing at this strange present with a questioning look. Why on earth would she want a fan?

Abe drew back the object and spoke in his slow, melodious voice, "Do not dismiss the many uses of a well-made fan." As he finished his thought, he moved his hand containing the fan out to his right. With a loud "Brrrrt," it opened wide to reveal a hand painted scene of Japanese artwork. It looked like people standing around a garden at sunset. "It can be used as a distraction."

He moved the fan to cover his face, as a lady would. "It can be used to hide your expression," he said, batting his eyes rapidly. Miho laughed at the sight of him. He lowered the open fan to his waist and said, "It can be used for cover." He dropped the fan down and revealed his other hand holding a knife at the ready. He replaced the fan to cover his hand and quickly moved it again, and the knife was gone. It was so fast and fluid, it could have been a magic trick.

Abe raised his hand with the fan, closing it as he moved in a straight line up in front of his body; then with a flick of the wrist, the fan spread out again as he twirled it over the back of the hand that had started moving back down again. "It can be used as a tool," he said, catching the fan as it looped around his hand - and in one quick movement the fan was closed again to rap his other hand on the back with a loud crack. "And if all else fails...," he said, spreading the fan out quickly with the familiar "Brrrrt" sound, "... you can use it if you get hot," and he fanned his face playfully.

Miho giggled at the performance.

"You have a smile that lights up a room," Abe said sweetly, as he handed the fan to Miho. "You should share that smile with the world more."

Miho felt embarrassed, as Ama called them over. She couldn't remember the last time she had smiled or laughed. The more she thought about it, the harder it was to remember. She thought of Arty and their time in the Underbelly. She had relaxed and felt like she had friends. People she could trust.

Miho respected Ama and her family, but she didn't feel like family here. She knew that Abe and Ama were working to make her feel that way, but in Miho's heart, she didn't see herself staying in this life. She figured she would use the position of Ama to help find the mysterious S.C., but once that was done, she assumed she would be on her way trying to figure out why S.C. had hired Boggs to tamper with her mother's airship, and get her father flung off the city to his death. Why was this man, or woman, so committed to ripping her family apart?

As thoughts of S.C.'s motivations circled around in her head, Miho climbed into the carriage with Adana. As they lurched when the horses moved, Miho turned her thoughts to the most recent step in her journey. It had started the last time she visited Arty. Patience and Arty seemed to always be together now. His lessons were coming along very well under her attentions.

Patience had given Arty and Miho a few minutes alone, and it was good to see him getting stronger and healthier. As Miho was leaving, Dr. Portens stopped her to have a chat.

"Your friend will be able to leave our ministrations soon. I know you will be happy to hear this. I can't say that I have enjoyed all that you have brought into my clinic, but I am grateful for the work and attentions that you have garnered. Assisting a pilot in the City Watch's elite is a significant feather in the cap of my clinic. It adds credibility and value to our name."

Dr. Portens gave a stiff movement that might have been an

attempt at a bow. All Miho could say was, "Thank you for all your attention and assistance."

"The other day I was treating a man who works in the Cobbler District," Dr. Portens said. "He had sustained a series of lacerations to his hands and I was mending them as best I could. It's a rather uncomfortable procedure, so he was inclined to talk a great deal to keep his mind occupied. Of interest to you perhaps was his story that the magistrate of his district is not very highly regarded. It is apparently well known that he is working for criminals." She paused for a moment, cleared her throat and pressed on, "Even going so far as to have a Chinaman thrown off the city."

Miho had tightened at these words.

"I have no idea if this information would be of use to you, but I felt I had a debt to you, and you seem to be working toward some goal." Dr. Portens looked as if she were deeply uncomfortable by this entire conversation. "I am not one to partake or pass on gossip, but, as I said, if this information can assist you... "

Miho had bowed low and thanked her for the information. It took her two days to locate where the Magistrate of the Cobbler District had lived. The visit had been very productive, to say the least.

"So you lived in the dregs of the city for months, by yourself?"

Miho had been pulled out of her thoughts by Adana's question. The other girl was watching the city pass by outside the window. Miho couldn't believe she had heard the girl right. Adana never talked to Miho unless she had to. Miho got the impression the girl didn't like her. Looking back, Adana had always seemed a little spoiled, proud even, and had always treated Miho like she was better than her. Because of these traits, Miho didn't mind that they never talked.

"Yes, I did," Miho said.

"I can't imagine it. I would die. I would just die if I had to do that."

"There were times where I thought I would die."

"How do you come back from that? Living like an animal," Adana turned to Miho with a disgusted look on her face.

Miho was suddenly very angry, but she didn't let that anger reach her face. Miho pictured her friends, and the children under Jen's care. Little Elizabeth, and Otter, and the twins. She saw the old lady who always gave her broth. She saw the men after working all day at the wheel. They would be covered in sweat and grime, but they would still laugh and help each other. Adana didn't see these as people. She saw them as animals. Miho took a deep calming breath and looked the girl in the eyes.

"All it takes is the right misfortunes, and a queen can become a beggar, or a princess a prostitute. I am very thankful that you have never known misfortunes. I hope you never do, but don't refer to those less fortunate as animals."

"Oh, I didn't mean any insult. I just can't believe that you survived that ordeal, and you are as normal as you are now," Adana quickly said as she looked out the window. "Oh, it looks like we are close. Would you mind? I'll get out first, and then if you would wait a moment before you come out." She then added in a false sense of kind tones, "I'm just worried I'll trip with my dress."

Miho looked daggers at the girl. She couldn't bring herself to actively hate Adana, but she deeply disliked the shallow, spoiled child before her.

The carriage came to a halt and Adana leapt out almost as soon as the door was opened. Miho noticed that she didn't seem to have trouble with her dress at all. Miho didn't mind: she wanted some distance between them. She didn't want to lose her temper. When she had slowed her heart rate with a few deep breaths, she stepped out of the carriage into what appeared to be another world. The lights, the sounds, the smells were all so different from anything she had ever experienced. She reached the ground off the last step and took in her surroundings.

She stood on a highly manicured gravel driveway about 20 feet from a set of intricately patterned wrought iron gates. To the sides of the gates were high walls of brown stonework. Crowds of people stood behind roped off barriers on either side of the gates. The people cried out and called to the party guests as they exited the carriages. Two long rows of carriages disappeared off to her right, awaiting their chance to drop off their passengers. The sky above was a dark and teeming mass of clouds that churned and twisted. Miho could see patches of stars now and then.

A man in white stockings and some sort of velvet uniform of plums stuck out a gloved hand to Miho. "Madam, if you will, please allow me."

Miho took his hand with her left and immediately opened her fan to hide her face, which was in total shock. She said a silent thank you to Abe as she peered over the fan into the expansive gardens beyond the gates, where hundreds of people of all kinds strutted and stood. Some were obviously guests in their dresses and suits, some were workers in plum coats with trays of food and wine, some were performers of instruments, or jugglers, and she saw some that were singing or reciting poems or plays. From the trees hung lanterns and festive paper of many colors. Her plum-colored guide stopped walking at the edge of the gates and led her to continue on. Miho walked across the gates and into the strangest scene she had ever witnessed.

CHAPTER 46

Ama almost pulled Abe along as she tried to look for the girls. Henry skulked along beside his parents. He didn't complain, but it was clear that he didn't want to be here. Ama was beyond frustrated. She hadn't counted on their carriages being separated in transit. How could she have let this happen? She had to find the girls and quickly.

"I believe you are scaring the people that you pass, my dearest. Perhaps you could be less intimidating," Abe said softly beside her.

Ama whirled on him in a suppressed rage. "I have to find the girls," she said as calmly as she could manage, but she felt her jaw clenching shut.

Abe gave a soft smile. "And we will, love, but the girls are not the only ones on display tonight. You look like a lioness about to kill anything close to her cubs, and you are crushing my hand."

Ama released his hand and started breathing deeply. Abe knew how important tonight was to her. She and Abe had been together for nearly 20 years. They had escaped their home country together and had been through so much. Abe was her rock. He almost never got emotional and rarely lost his temper. Ama, on the other hand, was a hothead by comparison. She valued his wisdom and his gentle spirit, but she knew he could be deadly when he had to be. After a few breaths, she felt like she was calming down a little. "Thank you, dear. I'm calmer now. Let's find the girls."

They made it through the gates, and Ama scanned the crowd. She spotted Adana almost at once. Her daughter was in a conversation with several women that she knew from Adana's social society. Ama took a deep breath. One down. She kept scanning the outskirts of the crowds, looking for Miho. The poor girl was most likely hiding alone and feeling totally out of her element. Abe started talking with Henry as Ama passed over faces both unknown and familiar.

The Gala was occurring on the grounds of Arundel Manor, which is the largest house and grounds in the city, and home to the Duchess of Norfolk. The Manor was immense and opulent, having been built around 1200-something. Over the resulting 600 years, High Hastings had been added to and grown, but Arundel Manor was one of the earliest estates to be built in the sky. The primary structure resembled a small castle or fortified manor. And while the castle itself was enormous, the sprawling grounds and gardens were truly breathtaking.

There stood large swaths of shrubs, plants, and flowers open to the sky. These were all connected in orderly fashion by gravel or oyster shell pathways and broken by small clusters of terraces, pergolas, small greenhouses of iron and glass for the growing of herbs and specialty plants.

There were fruit trees and living grottos made from vining plants. One could spend days walking the grounds and not see all the details. This garden was the best kept and most luxurious in all the high cities of England.

For tonight's Gala, there were hundreds of lanterns, hung from every high place. Thousands of candles and lamps were scattered around the grounds as if to mock the stars themselves. Those stars could easily be seen this high in the city, as the swirling mass of clouds that usually enveloped the city rarely reached this high. Everyone who could swing an invitation was out in full regalia tonight. Of course, there were the Lords and Ladies of the city, with their trailing echelons of servants and attendants. Also in attendance was every family that aspired to climb the social ladder and join the ranks of the city's most powerful. Folded into this mix were artisans, guests of special interest, performers, and servants laden with trays of food and drink.

Ama was used to it all, but at the moment, she was scanning the crowds with frantic determination to find one small girl. Miho should stand out. She'd look like a porcelain doll tonight, her vivid colors and small frame attracting the eyes of the curious and the hungry. For despite all their social rules and posturing, Ama considered all the city's most powerful and influential social class to be hyenas. They were hungry for new stimulation, and would launch themselves upon poor Miho like a pack of animals. Ama was planning on being by her side to help guide her and protect her. These parties were necessary, but they could also be very dangerous. Why had she insisted on the two carriages? She was kicking herself for the decision as her panic built inside her.

"I see Miho," came Abe's soft voice beside her.

"Where?"

"Near that fig tree with a group of people. She seems to be alright, but I know you want to be near her. I'll stay with the children and you go check on Miho."

Ama turned to her husband, feeling relief and her heart lightening. "Do I tell you often enough how much I love you?"

Abe's eyes sparkled as he replied, "I do not know this 'often enough' you speak of, but I am always happy to hear you say that." And with a quick squeeze of his hand, they went their separate ways for now.

As Ama started picking her path to where Miho was, she realized why she had missed the girl in her first few passes of looking. Miho was blocked from view by an extremely fat man. He was well dressed, and gave off an air of royalty, but Ama didn't know him. As she got closer, she could see that he was the center of attention in the small group, but he was giving his attentions to Miho.

"... Spent a month in the Emperor's court as a guest. Such an amazing experience. The food, the culture, so different from what we are used to here in England, you know." The man's voice was deep and melodious. He spoke with an educated tone and loud enough that people far away could easily hear him. Ama guessed he was some sort of professor or researcher. As she got even closer to the group and moved to stand behind Miho, she saw up close the man was wearing a very fine suit that was almost too small for him. The quality of the tailor could be seen readily as the buttons on his waistcoat looked like they were soldiers holding back a savage ground attack. They appeared at any minute they could lose the battle and fly off like cannon shot.

He was a short man with a massive mustache that looped down to join his sideburns. His chin was bare, which to Ama was a bad call, as his chin was rather weak. At least the first one or two chins; there were several. He wore a monocle in one eye and took his hat off occasionally to mop his sweating, balding head. He spoke with a passion and conviction that drew in the listener.

Miho looked at Ama and bowed her head in acknowledgment of her approach.

The man was looking at two girls who were hanging on his every word. When he paused just long enough to draw breath, Miho interrupted him.

"Dr. Atkinson, if I may, I'd like to introduce you to Lady Ba," Miho said in a clear, soft voice and the large man spun around with a smile on his pudgy lips and a twinkle in his watery eyes.

"Ah Lady Ba, High Valkyrie of the City Watch and Protectorate, winner of the bronze star and the medal of valor. High priestess of Dakar. It is an honor, my lady."

"You have me at a disadvantage, sir," Ama said as the man kissed her gloved hand.

"Dr. Humphry J. Atkinson III. A senior Fellow at the Royal Institute of Aerogeology. At your service mum," he said with a practiced bow. "Are you acquainted with this lovely girl?" he turned his attention to Miho.

"Ms. Michitaka is my goddaughter, and a member of my house."

"Ah-Hooo," Dr. Humphry sparkled with a smile as he turned to Miho. "Michitaka-san eh? Ha- gee-me-mas-teh," he said clumsily with a bow.

Miho returned the bow and said behind her fan, "It is a pleasure to make your acquaintance as well, Dr. Atkinson. Thank you for your kind words. Your Japanese is very good."

Ama couldn't believe Miho's grace and poise. She was perfect in every way. The large man almost giggled with delight.

"Doctor Atkinson, what brings a senior fellow of the Royal Institute of Aerogeology to our city, if I may ask?" Miho said, keeping the man's attention focused on her. The surrounding others were listening with rapt attention.

"Oh, the Institute is dedicated to the study, acquisition, and recovery of the ore commonly known as skystone. I am working with the Duchess to mount a recovery mission in this area."

"Recovery?" Miho prompted him to continue. Ama was sure that he loved to talk, and would do so at the very slightest prompt.

"Oh yes, as Lady Ba can attest I'm sure, the cities along the coast of England are those most often raided by various parties who are after the Empire's resources and wealth. The City Watch is responsible for protecting its people, but also the recovery of skystone at all costs. You see, the ore is extremely rare, and no new veins have been tapped in a good long while. The nation, or Empire, that controls the majority of the ore, controls the world, as it were."

He took a deep, lumbering breath and continued. "It is my job, you see, to travel the world and assess the quantities and qualities of known ore. I have been very blessed in this regard, and the Queen herself has rewarded me with praise for my work. But I digress, recovery. As I was saying, when the cities are attacked, as they are, sometimes the City Watch cannot recover the ore during a battle, and if an airship is damaged, the ore may break free and rise beyond our standard recovery methods."

"So the ore rises so high we can't reach it?" A girl wearing an enormous blond wig attempted to interject into the conversation.

"Quite right," Dr. Atkinson nodded. "The air becomes very thin the higher you climb. Skystone begins to rise when it is exposed to air, but when it reaches a certain altitude, it will stop climbing because the air is too thin to sustain it."

"Then why cannot we go get it if we use skystone ships? They should go to the same height, shouldn't they?" the blond girl asked with a vacant stare. This conversation was obviously taxing her mental capacity.

"Ah, but unfettered skystone can reach a higher altitude than any ship, and so, therefore, was previously untenable. Until now!" Dr. Atkinson boomed, shaking a fat finger. "The instate has devised a new method that we believe will allow us to recover the precious ore."

The group lightly applauded his boisterous announcement. Dr. Atkinson bowed with a rolling, "Thank you. Thank you," when a young man wearing a plum half-cape interjected, "Dr. Atkinson, it's nearly time."

"Yes, yes, thank you," the doctor said dismissively. "Ms. Michitaka-san, please give me a few minutes of your time. I should dearly love to introduce you to someone."

"I would be honored by your introduction," Miho said softly.

Ama was so impressed with Miho. Why had she been worried? The girl could handle herself in battle, whether it be with swords or with words. She looked to find Abe and her family in the crowd. Abe was near Henry, who was talking with John Potter, the city's farming administrator. Adana was still in a large group of her social club, chatting away.

Miho stuck out a hand to take Dr. Atkinson's arm. Her kimono was so long that her hands were hidden when her hands were down by her side. Ama saw the delicate fingers lightly rest on his large meaty forearm as he led her away. Ama felt deflated. She wasn't really needed at all. Her children, her husband, and Miho could do just fine without her. All this stress had been pointless. She glanced around at all the different people. The rich and powerful, those who had power, and those who sought power, and she wanted to just leave and fly off somewhere. She thought back to the beautiful waters of her home. The warm breezes and the cool waves on her feet as she stood in the tide. It had been years since she felt the ocean. Perhaps she could go back, she and Abe, and enjoy those waves again.

They were about 20 feet away from Ama when Miho stopped them. Dr. Atkinson was droning on about his world travels but stopped when Miho stopped walking. She turned to look for Ama. They locked eyes and Ama could see clearly when no one else could see. Miho was a mask showing no emotion, but Ama knew the girl. Her eyes were pleading for Ama to come, too. Ama took a deep breath and nodded. Perhaps she was needed, after all.

CHAPTER 47

Miho focused with everything she had on her breathing. She felt so out of her element, and the sights and sounds around her were like those of a fever dream. Forcing herself to breathe slowly and deeply, she willed her heart to beat at a slow and steady pace. The truth is, she was panicking. As soon as she walked through the gates of the Gala, she was overwhelmed by everything she saw.

There was a fat woman with so much makeup on, that her face seemed unreal. Around this woman's neck was a necklace that floated and drifted. Miho guessed it was constructed with a tiny amount of skystone. The jewelry glinted as she lumbered about. It floated here and there with gold, jewels, and intricate patterns. The woman's dress was an assault on the eyes of lace and layers. Miho turned away to see a group of men with painted faces and wearing gowns and dresses. Beyond them were a few men in the regal uniforms of some army or another. They were old men with hair growing out of their ears and noses. It was white and bushy, like their eyebrows.

Miho turned again and saw a couple in regal clothes looking strange and outlandish, but not out of place in this crowd. She was an enormous woman with multiple chins and an equally enormous wig upon her head. It must have weighed as much as Miho, for inside the wig was a scene of ships with sails, masts and rigging. The ships seemed to be engaged in a naval battle using the hair of the wig to give the illusion of waves, like the sea. On her right hand was a tiny little man who was almost Miho's size. He was short and thin and even in his luxurious suit of silk and jewels, you could almost overlook him entirely because of her bulk and his lack of stature on her right-hand side. And behind the massive woman, in her enormous and garish wig, was a servant in dark velvets carrying a large pillow with a disfigured animal perched upon it.

Miho had heard that dogs were a luxury for the city's wealthy. Through the countless years of being in the sky, with so few animals to breed with, the inbreeding had made this horrible creature almost repugnant to look upon. Miho saw limbs sticking out at odd angles and heard the ragged breathing of the beast. She couldn't bear to look at the poor animal and turned away yet again. Everywhere she looked, she saw people attempting grandeur, but it all struck Miho as grotesque. She was just about to make her way back to the gate and flee this horrible scene when Dr. Atkinson approached her and started discussing her kimono.

She had been so relieved when Ama had arrived. Now the doctor wanted to escort her deeper into the nightmarish party, and Ama was staying close. When Miho had turned to make sure Ama was coming, she almost cried, but a wave of gratitude washed over her as Ama looked her in the eyes and seemed to understand. Dr. Atkinson seemed oblivious to Miho's state. She thanked Abe yet again inside her mind for his gift of the fan. Miho was determined to keep a blank, emotionless mask on her face. She would not allow her emotions to show.

"... Just returned from the American colonies you know..." Dr. Atkinson seemed to work best when left to just drone on by himself. He required very little interaction. Miho offered the occasional interjection of interest, and the man did the rest.

"Governor Lincoln, a very striking man you know, very tall, very unusual features. He is doing the best he can to keep the 17 colonies running smoothly. What with the native nations attacking any who move near the treaty lands, both above and below. I tell you, they are quite the sight to see. Never seen a people use skystone like that. The 'Mapiya Sheboyan' as some of the tribes call it. They have enormous birds you see, all around the Americas. The indigenous people have combined the skytone and suites like giant birds to help them soar through the skies. They are a very cunning people, and very in-tune with the natural world."

Dr. Atkinson put out a hand to help Miho around a tree that had no fewer than 50 lanterns hanging from its branches. People talked in little groups. Laughter and exclamations would occasionally rise above the constant hum of conversation. Yet still they walked on. They passed another group of people, but Miho couldn't easily identify them as men or women. This group seemed to be a merging of the two. They had overall feminine clothes and makeup on, but clearly some were men. Miho had never seen such a thing. Ama caught her eye. Ama was looking serious and walking a couple of steps behind them. Miho tried asking Ama about the strange people, but either Ama didn't understand her gaze, or didn't want to talk about it.

Dr. Atkinson's voice broke the silence with his loud tones. "Lady Ba, thinking about the native nations of the Americas reminds me of some of the tribes of Northern Africa. Such an amazing people. You hail from the Western shores of that land, do you not?"

"I do," Ama said in a cool, flat tone. "That was long ago."

"I should like very much to return to Africa someday. Such an enormous place. I don't feel my last visit did it justice." The large man drifted in thought as they approached closer and closer to the large house that looked like a castle. Their destination seemed to be a small courtyard beside the building proper. Miho saw numerous men and women standing around the perimeter of the courtyard, which struck her as odd. These men and women weren't enjoying the party, but standing with their backs to the courtyard and looking out among the crowd. Miho realized they must be guards.

Inside the courtyard were several small clusters of people. These people seemed different from the others. It was like they weren't so garish or outlandish, or perhaps the make-up and fancy clothes just looked better on them. There were about 25 people who were inside the well-guarded courtyard. Dr. Atkinson didn't even slow down as they passed the guards. Miho saw several men and women in armor with swords on their hips. She wanted to see their swords up close, but she doubted she would get a chance. Dr. Atkinson slowed and looked around, muttering to himself. Then, spotting the person he was looking for, he led them on with a quicker pace.

"Ahoo, Sam, I found you at last," the large man said with glee as he approached a small group. Miho found herself once again not knowing if this was a man or a woman. There were four people standing together – a couple that looked like man and wife, a slender white-haired woman with breathtaking eyes and the mysterious Sam. Sam quickly opened a large fan hiding most of the face behind it. Miho felt this move had become one of her favorites during the night and smiled inwardly at seeing someone else do it.

"Dr. Atkinson, have you met Natalie Rothchild? She is visiting from Minsk," Sam's head tilted to the side, showing the white-haired woman on their left. Sam's voice was falsely high, like a man speaking as a woman. He (Miho's current guess) had a smaller frame, and only stood about five feet and perhaps six inches. Sam was not a very tall man at all.

"Ahhhhh, Minsk," Dr. Atkinson said with a hand on his heart and a dramatic flair. "The setting sun through the windows of the Sky Red Church will stay with me for a lifetime."

Ms. Rothchild smiled at the doctor's performance. She was an older woman, Miho guessed, but only because of the weathering of her features. Her eyes were inescapable though. They seemed to give off the energy and light of eternal youth. She wore a beautiful gown of lilac and subtle hues of gray. It was perfectly fitted to her compact frame, and by the standards of this gala she was almost ordinary, but Miho saw that the dress was actually very intricate with its stitching and overall assembly.

"I agree Minsk is exquisite, Herr Doctor. I was there recently on business, but I got to enjoy the city a little," her voice was strong but quiet. It was clear to Miho that in this crowd of people who were trying to stand out and be noticed, Natalie Rothchild had no such interest or need.

"Oh I see, visiting Minsk on business, and where do you call home, my lady Rothchild?" Dr. Atkinson asked with interest.

Ms. Rothchild smiled. "Well, for the past couple of years I've called my yacht home, as I've traveled all over Europe setting up Beit Ha'Tikvah, or Houses of Hope. These houses take in orphans or stray children hoping to provide them a better life."

"Such a noble endeavor!" Dr. Atkinson exclaimed, "Sam, you enjoy your yacht very much, don't you? You are always going on about it."

"Indeed," Sam said behind his fan. "Once you get out beyond the cities, flying through the clouds is the most amazing sensation. Although there is no ship to compare with Stargazer in the whole of south England, I don't know if I could bear the life of yacht living for years at a time. It speaks to your fortitude and determination, Lady Rothchild."

The conversation quickly turned to flying and the sky cities. They pulled Ama into the talks and she seemed quite comfortable talking about flying and city defense. Miho spotted Abe and the kids quietly join Ama and soon Adana was voicing her opinion about city life.

"Honestly, I don't know why they don't just cut the bottom of the city off and let it fall to the ground? We don't need that sort of riff-raff at all." Adana's voice seemed to rise above the smaller conversations that had broken out among the group. Miho felt her blood grow cold.

"Quite right!" said the old man who Adana had been talking with. "I daresay the crime rate would disappear overnight!"

"Harold!" his wife shot him a reproachful glare.

After an awkward moment, the conversation seemed to heat back up again. Miho noticed Ms. Rothchild had said nothing, and seemed, like Miho, to be purposefully avoiding that topic of conversation. Miho decided that she would speak to the woman. She still felt nervous in this crowd.

"Lady Rothchild," Miho asked, and the woman turned her cool blue eyes upon her. Miho almost thought she saw irritation behind her eyes, but once she looked at Miho, it seemed to disappear. She smiled at Miho and asked "Yes?" quietly.

"Can you tell me more about your Houses of Hope?"

"They are orphanages we set up to take in those who are lost or living at their lowest. I've spent the past few years traveling around Europe to fund such places," she said in a cool tone.

"Are you here in High Hastings to establish such a House?" Miho asked.

"I am," Ms. Rothchild gave a brief nod. It seemed she was keeping her answers short. Perhaps she thought Miho felt like others around them, and that those in the Underbelly weren't worth helping.

"I know someone who currently does much of what you are talking about, but with no assistance," Miho said.

Lady Rothchild's whole demeanor seemed to change. "You do?" she asked.

"Yes, she is a young woman who takes in all the children who have no one else. She cares for them and provides for them as best she can."

"How many children would you say she is caring for?" Lady Rothchild asked.

Miho thought for a moment. "When I was living with her, we had 11 children ranging between about a year old to two who were almost adults."

"You lived with her?" Lady Rothchild seemed stunned.

"I did," Miho said. "I helped with the gardens and the general care and protection of the children. I'm sure Jen, that is her name, would be a good contact for your efforts."

Lady Rothchild reached inside her shirt sleeve and produced a small piece of paper. "I would very much like to talk with her. Please have her call upon me. This is where I'm staying in the city."

Miho took the card and saw it had Lady Rothchild's name and address on it. She pocketed the card and thought about seeing Jen as soon as she could.

She was about to ask Ms. Rothchild more when she heard Dr. Atkinson's booming voice over all the conversations.

"Sam, I brought you a treat! This is Ms. Michitaka, whose family moved here from Japan. She speaks fluent Japanese." Dr. Atkinson was beaming. "Ms. Michitaka, this is Sam Caldwell, one of the city's most important citizens, a tremendous donor to several causes around the city, and a lover of all things Japanese."

It felt to Miho as if until now Sam had been purposefully ignoring her, but now after a formal introduction, they had to acknowledge each other. Sam turned his head in Miho's direction and nodded ever so slightly.

"Pleased to make your acquaintance."

Miho felt Sam's tension. Her instincts put her on high alert. She almost felt like she was in danger. She bowed her head and said, "Good Evening..." Miho suddenly realized that she didn't know how to address Sam. Mr. Caldwell? Lord Caldwell? Sam was clearly dressed like a woman, so perhaps he wanted to be addressed as such. She quickly realized that Japanese would cover for her, not knowing the social nuances and finished "... Caldwell-san. It is a pleasure to make your acquaintance."

The Japanese "-san" is a formal, non-gender-based honorific. She could use it in this instance because of Dr. Atkinson's announcement that Sam Caldwell loved all things Japanese. As Miho was thinking this and finishing her bow, a bolt of lightning struck her. "Sam Caldwell" could be "S.C." who was sending instructions to Boggs. This could be the person who ordered her parents killed, but it could just as easily not be that S.C. Miho needed to be careful. She needed to let nothing show on her face.

After what felt like a long moment, Dr. Atkinson boomed, "Come now, Sam, weren't you just saying the other day how you missed speaking in Japanese and needed to visit the area again?

I've brought you someone who speaks the language fluently, and I must say, that Ms. Machitaki is a delightful girl."

Sam hid behind his fan and batted his eyes. "It would be rude to those around us to speak in a language they didn't understand. Perhaps another time."

Before Dr. Atkinson could respond, there was a palpable change in the energy of the people around them. Hushed voices whispered, "It's the Duchess," and similar sentiments. Miho looked around and spotted a small crowd of people moving towards them. There were four armed guards with swords and pistols on their hips. Inside these guards were assistants and servants surrounding a striking woman in a regal gown of hues of purple and lilac, who must be the Duchess. Behind this woman were other people, including the largest woman Miho had ever seen that was draped in the robes of a nun.

The Duchess inclined her head and everyone in the vicinity bowed or curtsied deeply. Miho felt torn between showing respect with a bow in the Japanese way, or curtsying as a lady of the city. She did a little of both and figured no one was looking at her, anyway. As she rose from her half bow-half curtsy, she saw the Duchess looking directly at her with a smile. The Duchess looked around quickly and spoke, but returned her gaze to Miho.

"Good evening everyone, how goes the running of my city?"

CHAPTER 48

There was no denying it, this was excellent tea. Jiro had grown to accept western tea in the more than ten years he had been living in Europe, but he never stopped yearning for the tea of his home. There had been sacrifices when they fled Japan. They all knew that they would most likely never return. They had given up positions of power, wealth, all the things of beauty they had ever known in order to save the life of their child. Even Machicko, that pillar of kindness and strength, had grown dark and somber when their tea had run out somewhere over the east Mediterranean Sea. That was one of the most beautiful areas Jiro remembered in their journey, but all of them had grown quiet as they drank the last taste of home.

Jiro remembered Kana had surprised him for his birthday with a gift of green tea. Machicko and Kana had giggled like young girls as they averted their eyes from his face as he smelled the familiar scent. Jiro had grown quite emotional. For one brief, beautiful moment, Jiro was sitting at the kotatsu in his childhood home, a warm blanket covering his legs and a hot cup of tea in his hands as he watched the snow falling on the garden outside. The edges of his eyes prickled and stung as he felt the emotion of that moment clench his heart. Even now, so many years later, he could catch a brief scent of the mossy trees right before a bloom, or the smell of the ink in his calligraphy well. He smiled at the memory of his wife, who was so proud that she had procured such treasure as a gift to him.

Jiro's heart hardened at the thought that he had not been able to protect her, to keep her safe. Kana had been taken from him, and then he had failed to protect their only daughter. He had to get back to Miho. In the smallest, darkest, quietest part of his heart, a tiny voice prayed that she was alive and safe. He quickly shut the door on such thoughts. He hardened every part of his soul for the job of returning to Miho, who must be safe and waiting for him. Jiro looked up into the eyes of the man sitting opposite him.

Mr. Lerox was a kindly looking fellow. He was tall and lean with chestnut hair that somehow was short and appeared long at the same time. His eyes sparkled with amusement and humor, but were also lined with years of work and grief. He had a wisdom about him. The round spectacles he wore amplified his intelligent appearance. He was in a simple indigo sweater that looked very comfortable and obviously well worn, rough spun trousers of brown and polished brown shoes. His outfit didn't speak of money, but it was all well-made and maintained.

"I hope you will forgive me," Mr. Lerox said with his thick French accent. "I do not speak any languages of the Orient."

Jiro smiled and bowed as he said, "If you will forgive me for not speaking French."

"We will settle for the 'orrible English, eh?" Mr. Lerox asked amused. "You should learn French though. It is a language that sits well on any tongue."

"I shall attempt to pick up some French," Jiro said. "For now, 'Merci', the tea is excellent."

"Ah trés bien, you have begun a journey into a fantastic world," he said animatedly. Then he dropped his energy and looked at Jiro seriously and said, "Now, what brings you to France in the first place, and to me?"

Jiro knew that while Mr. Lerox was still speaking with a light and casual air, the mood had shifted. It was time for business. He considered whether it was a good idea to speak openly about what he wanted to discuss, but if Mr. Lerox was asking point blank in this café, then he must think it was private enough.

"I am here because I have been led to believe that you have some experience getting to the Sky Cities... and conducting business there."

The smile widened on Mr. Lerox's face. "Ah, business, this is a good way of putting this. And what if I have experience reaching the cursed cities for my business?"

Jiro took a moment to consider his next approach. He felt very much like he was playing a game of chess. His next move would dictate several moves and counter moves after. Jiro was impatient. He didn't want to fence with this man; he wanted to speak plainly with him to see if he could be of assistance, and if not, Jiro didn't know where to look next. Cautiously direct seemed like the best approach to take.

"I need to make my way back to a Sky City."

"Back, you say," Mr. Lerox looked at him without expression.

"Yes," Jiro said flatly. "Until recently, I have lived in High Hastings, along the southern shore of England."

"May I ask why you are no longer there?" Mr. Lerox said, but then cut himself off. "No, more importantly, what has brought you across the channel to me in order to return?"

"I will answer both your questions," Jiro said. "I was wrongly accused of crimes I didn't commit, and I must return because my daughter is still there."

Mr. Lerox looked at Jiro and thought about his response. "When was this?" "Almost a month now."

"And what will you do when you return? Do you think you will be welcomed back with open arms?"

Jiro half smiled. "No. I don't think this. I will take my daughter and we will go."

Mr. Lerox was quiet for a while before suddenly saying, "What do you know about the cities in the sky?"

"Quite a lot. I was an engineer there for almost 12 years."

This surprised Mr. Lerox. "Mon Dieu, this is very interesting news. However, I was interested in your knowledge of the story of the cities."

Jiro was a little taken aback by this, but answered, "Well, the oldest ones have been aloft for hundreds of years. Skystone was discovered somewhere around 1000 to 1100 A.D."

Mr. Lerox nodded, "Very true, and now 700-800 years later, look how the world has changed, eh?"

Jiro nodded. It was known that the tremendous cloud cover around the cities in the sky made it harder for vegetation to grow below the cities.

"The seas and rivers are lower than they should be. The crops, they will not grow. Cities dump their waste, and God knows what else, for the people to sift through. It is an abomination against the way the world should be."

Jiro tightened. Mr. Lerox was sounding like some sort of fanatic.

"Look around you," Mr. Lerox said calmly as he gestured outside the café. "High Paris has fallen three times in the past 600 years. Now there is no more upper and lower city. We have beautiful waters and crops, the people are healthy. Life is good. There are still the rich and poor. There is still injustice, yes, but the lands are not dying."

Jiro had to admit that there was some truth in this.

"So, Mr.... I'm sorry. How do you pronounce your last name?" Jiro smiled and sounded it out slowly "Mee-chi-ta-ka"

Mr. Lerox nodded. "Mr. Michitaka, I can help you return to your daughter. In return, I'd like you to help me take that entire city to the Ground."

CHAPTER 49

The Duchess looked around the group and nodded to each person in kind. She listened to those who spoke to her, but Miho kept feeling like the woman's attention was on her. Her eyes kept taking in Miho's kimono, or her hair. The Duchess didn't stare, but as she swept from person to person in conversation, her eyes would linger for just a moment on Miho. Miho felt very uncomfortable. This was the most powerful woman in the city. In fact, she was the most powerful woman in the entire south of England. Why was she looking at her?

She took a calming breath and told herself to relax. She knew she stood out. Her appearance had drawn attention all night. Dr. Atkinson had paraded her around so long that she felt she had met everyone in the entire city who was a member of high society. Just then Miho began to feel it all. Her feet ached. Her face felt like a porcelain mask from wearing her makeup all night. She finally listened to the pains in her back and shoulders where she had been holding herself stiffly all night.

Miho had to admit, she was tired. This carnival of strange sights and odd people had worn her down, but it wasn't over yet. She took a moment to take in the details of the Duchess and her entourage. The Duchess looked as fresh as a morning flower. She didn't appear to be tired or worn. This woman had a strength to her. She appeared to be in her element. The four armed guards weren't looking at anyone in this group, but their eyes kept scanning around them. They were on the outside of the cluster of people, obviously ready for anything. The Duchess also had two thin men that were in suits of green and yellow silks. Their waistcoats were elaborately embroidered, with butterflies on one man, and dragonflies on the other.

The two slender men looked to be in their 30s or 40s; with their makeup on, it was hard to tell. They, like Sam on her left, wore makeup to appear more feminine. They each had beauty marks drawn on opposite sides of their faces, but otherwise the two men might be twins. On the other side of the Duchess was a young girl in a plain but pretty dress. Anywhere else, and it would have looked very nice, but tonight was about being ostentatious. This girl looked almost drab by those standards. She was of average height, with light brown hair and a pretty face that somehow looked very familiar to Miho. She tried to place where she might have seen this girl before when the Duchess spoke to her over her shoulder.

"Mary," The Duchess had a very commanding voice, and the girl snapped to attention. "Make a note to have a meeting with the Banker's Guild next week, would you?"

The girl nodded and pulled some paper and a black fountain pen. Miho looked past the girl Mary to see a brooding face on the comically large nun behind her. Miho couldn't remember seeing a man or woman this large in her life. The nun wasn't fat, just bigger than a normal person. Miho couldn't tell what color her hair was, but she guessed dark brown from the nun's eyebrows.

Besides being larger than a normal person, she seemed to stretch her nun's habit over broad shoulders and obviously rippling muscles. The woman just stood out. There was no way she could ever blend into a crowd. Miho felt a pang of sympathy for her. She knew all too well how that felt.

"Dr. Atkinson, are you enjoying the city so far?" The Duchess addressed Dr. Atkinson on Miho's right. The large man jumped and bowed very low with a flourish of his sweaty, beefy hand.

"Oh I am, your grace. Thank you so very much for your hospitality," he spoke to the floor as he was still bent over. Dr. Atkinson straightened up and gestured to Miho in a practiced fashion, as he had been introducing Miho all night. "Your Grace, may I have the pleasure of introducing you to Miss Michitaka who I have only just met tonight."

He turned to Miho and said "Miss Michitaka, may I introduce you to Her Grace, Duchess of Norfolk, and Earl of Arundel, Earl Marshal and Hereditary Marshal of England, Josephine Margaret Alexander Howard."

"My goodness Dr. Atkinson, you don't need all the titles, we'll be here all night."

The Duchess seemed to have enjoyed his formal introduction despite her words. "Good evening, Miss Michitaka, it's a pleasure to make your acquaintance finally."

Miho bowed very low to hide her confusion at the word "finally," but as she was trying to find a good response, the Duchess asked, "Are you comfortable at Lady Ba's home? Do you have everything you need?"

Miho felt shocked at this. How did this woman know anything about her? "Lady Ba and her family have been very kind to me. Thank you, your grace."

"Ama was looking everywhere for you after that incident with your father. She almost tore the city apart. I've never seen the Night Rose so worked up. Hey, Ama?"

"Yes, your Grace. It's true," Ama answered with a bow and a half-embarrassed smile. "And when I had all but given up hope, Miho found me."

The Duchess turned her gaze once again to Miho. "Is it true you were living in the Underbelly?"

"Yes, your Grace," Miho nodded low. She didn't know how many times she was supposed to bow to this woman. She felt totally unprepared for this situation.

"But now you're settled," the Duchess went on. "What are your plans for your future moving forward?"

Miho didn't know what to say. The directness of this question took her completely aback.

"Any plans to follow in your mother's footsteps? Join the City Watch and perhaps become one of the Valkyrie? I know Kana spoke of you becoming a pilot one day."

Miho dropped all attempts at curtesy and looked at the Duchess. "You knew my mother?" The Duchess smiled widely. She had perfect teeth and a beautiful smile. "I knew her well."

A moment of silence followed this statement. No one spoke and everyone was watching Miho and the Duchess. Then a voice came from behind the painted fan of Sam Caldwell.

"I'm sorry to say this, your Grace, but the child of a convicted killer could never become a Valkyrie. This girl's father was Grounded for his crimes."

"Miho is of my house now," Ama said rather loudly. "She might as well be my daughter, and if she wanted to become a Valkyrie, or anything else, I will ensure that happens."

The tension was tight enough to feel around the group. Miho was wondering how everyone here seemed to know so much about her. Then she had an idea. Before anyone else could speak, she whipped her fan out with a loud "Brrrt" ensuring all eyes focused on her.

"As grateful as I am to Lady Ba and her remarkable family for their care and acceptance of me, my father's false accusations will no longer be an issue, as his name has been cleared."

When she spoke this, Miho was looking in the vicinity of Sam Caldwell to gauge his reaction. As she suspected, Caldwell's eyes went wide.

"What?" it was a confused Ama who said this.

Miho looked between Ama, the Duchess and passing over the other faces to land on Caldwell's as she said, "The Magistrate who passed the conviction of my father was pressured by a man named Joseph Boggs, who was threatening the Magistrate's family to get things he wanted. When I informed the Magistrate that Boggs left the city several weeks ago, and saw that his family were returned to him, he immediately overturned my father's conviction and confessed everything."

Sam Caldwell's face seemed to grow more sunken as his eyes went vacant. All the color drained from his face as he tried not to show any emotion.

"My God, what a story!" Dr. Atkinson seemed flummoxed. "Miss Mitchitaka, you have led quite an extraordinary life for one who is so young."

As Miho turned to look in the direction of Dr. Atkinson, she saw Ama with a look that she couldn't read. Miho felt bad that Ama had learned this in this manner. She had wanted to tell Ama, but with all the prep for the party, and everything else that was going on, she just hadn't felt the time was right. Ama looked at Miho, and Miho tried to tell her she was sorry with her eyes.

"Well, this is a lot of news all at once, isn't it? Of course, Lady Ba is right. As a child of her house, you can join the City Watch, and could even become a Valkyrie, perhaps. But with this news of your father being wrongfully convicted and Grounded, I feel this city and I owe you a debt."

Everyone was looking at the Duchess, and not a sound could be heard but for her clear voice.

"Your mother was a personal friend, and a damn fine pilot. She defended this city, and was a knight of the kingdom. She was a lady in every respect. If you wanted to follow in her footsteps, I would give you my personal endorsement to join the city elite and fly yourself. I cannot do anything to return your father to you, but if there is anything I can do for you, you have only to name it."

CHAPTER 50

The carriage rattled as it wound its way through the streets. Ama and Miho sat in silence, looking out the windows as the city passed them by. Abe and the children were in another carriage behind them. Everyone was tired. Ama wanted to say so many things, but she didn't know where to begin. She was upset that Miho had been working in the shadows, and she didn't tell her about them. It also impressed her. This wasn't some child whose head was filled with dreams of princes and castles. Miho was working toward goals, and she wasn't asking for help. She was an independent young woman.

"It's too much, too soon," Ama thought to herself. Her anger burned away with all other emotions as sadness fell into her heart. "She has had to grow up too soon. I don't know the last time I saw her laugh. I can't let her do all of this alone." She was going to say, "I can't let her do this," meaning fighting, and scheming, and God knows what else. But if she was honest, Ama knew she couldn't stop her.

"Ama, I'm afraid."

Miho's voice was quiet and small. It was full of emotion. She kept staring out the window, but her face looked like she was fighting to keep back the emotion.

Ama moved beside the girl. She was so small. She put her hand on Miho's. "Oh, Miho, please tell me what you are thinking."

"Everyone in my family was taken from me." The small girl seemed to have a shadow that crossed her face as she spoke slowly. "I couldn't do anything to stop it from happening."

Her hand went to her chest near her heart, and Ama knew that she still carried her mother's last gift to her, a gift that she herself had delivered. Ama's heart cracked. It was a promise she and Kana had made to each other. Ama never had wanted it to become true. She still remembered the tiny girl when she had handed her the tin. How could that child be the same young woman in front of her now?

Being a mother was one of Ama's favorite aspects of her life, but it came with a terrible fracture to one's perception of time. She saw double in her heart almost every day. When she looked at her children, when she talked with them about their desires and their plans, she always saw them in her arms as infants, wrapped in their small blankets and totally dependent upon her for life. At this moment, she saw Miho the infant, tottering after Kana, trying to hold on to her mother's robes, and at the same moment she was a young woman in a beautiful kimono of silk, with her face like a porcelain doll.

It was a cruel web that wraps itself around a woman's heart and squeezes at the most unusual of times. She wanted to scoop this girl into her arms and protect her, but she knew that wasn't what the girl wanted–or needed–right now.

"Oh, sweet one," Ama said. "You have had to deal with more than most people do in a lifetime, and I'm sorry you have known so much pain."

"You have been so very kind to me," Miho said, "I don't want you to feel that I am ungrateful. I know I should tell you more about what I've been doing, and why, but I'm afraid."

Miho fell silent, lost in her thoughts. The carriage wheels bumped and shifted as they continued to roll them down the street.

"What are you afraid of, darling?" Ama thought the girl was afraid of being chastised. She was afraid of getting into trouble. It was a difficult situation. They had a tenuous relationship. Miho wasn't her daughter. She didn't have to listen to Ama, she didn't have to obey her. But Miho was trying to live by her rules. She was trying to fit into the house without clear guidelines as to what her role actually was.

"I'm afraid that if I think of you as family, you'll be taken from me, too," Miho turned to face Ama and her expression made Ama's heart crack down the middle. "I don't know if I can lose anyone else."

Ama didn't think, she just folded her arms around Miho and felt the girl give in to the tempest of emotions she had been holding at bay. For a long while, they just held each other while Miho wailed. It was a floodgate that was opened. Once opened, she had to empty what was behind it. Ama let her cry, and wail, and scream. It was messy. It was raw. Ama didn't speak, she just rubbed the small girl's back. She could feel the knobby bones of her tiny spine through the silk. The carriage lumbered on. Eventually, the cries became sobs, and the flow ebbed.

Ama pulled a piece of cloth from one of her stashes and pressed it to Miho's wet face. The girl took the pale-yellow cloth and mopped her face. When she was done, the cloth looked like a war zone. Makeup and tears and snot covered it so that no hint of its yellow color could be seen. Miho laughed. Ama laughed too. It was the escape of laughter at the end of an emotional flow that could so easily become hysterics.

"Miho, I can't promise you I won't be taken from you, or Abe, or the children. I think you of all people know what a dangerous place this world is. I don't want to make you a promise I can't keep, but I do know that the people we lose are not truly lost to us. Your mother and father live on inside you, just as the people I've lost live on inside me. That doesn't really help when you want to have a conversation with them, or when you want a hug from them. In truth, nothing can really help those times. You do have the blessing of those feelings though, in your memory. I don't know how much comfort that is, to have had these wonderful things and lose them, versus never having them in the first place. But for me it is a comfort to know that I knew love, and I can always take that feeling with me, even if I can't experience it in the same way as before."

Ama thought she wasn't doing this as well as she wanted to, but she kept trying.

"Miho, I can't promise you that nothing will ever happen to us, but I can promise you that for as long as I breathe, I will love you. I will try to be there for you, if you allow me to be. You cannot be so afraid of loss that you never trust anyone again. Our lives are precious because of our connections to each other."

The girl nodded slowly. She looked so small and fragile. Ama hugged her again and when Miho had calmed down more, she asked the question that had been burning within her for weeks.

"Miho, what's going on? What are you up to?"

The girl wiped her face again and looking at the soiled piece of cloth, she took a deep breath.

"Joseph Boggs was the head of an Engineering team like my father," the girl said, looking into the cloth like she was looking into the past. "He was also a criminal involved with smuggling and murder. He pressured Magistrates and avoided the law. I know he was taking orders from someone with the initials S.C. and that someone owns at least one warehouse used for shipping alcohol and other goods. I assume it's someone in upper society."

Ama didn't say anything. She just listened. She still had one hand on the girl's back, but she had stopped rubbing.

"The two other men who testified about my father worked for Boggs. Boggs said he was hired to kill my father and me. He also admitted to tampering with my mother's airship."

Miho reached inside her kimono to the tin that held the last of her mother. Inside the tin she pulled out a small piece of cloth and when she unfolded the cloth, a light hissing noise came from the small piece of skystone that lay within. The skystone almost glowed a faint electric blue in the carriage's dimness. When she uncovered it, it at once floated away from the cloth and rose slowly upward. A small amount of vapor seemed to emit from the stone.

Ama's heart, already cracked and emotional, hardened. She was a pilot of an airship. She was a Warden of the City Watch, and commanded a battle wing of Valkyries. To know some pathetic worm of a man had tampered with one of her sisters' aircraft, with Kana's airship, put murder in her heart.

"He stole this from my mother's airship. He helped her die and then tried to kill my father and me," Miho said in a flat tone.

The two women stared at the unnatural-looking stone that slowly rose into the carriage.

The moment was over, Miho wrapped up the skystone and put it back in her tin. Ama was awash in emotion. Finally, something settled in her mind.

"Miho, are you in danger now?" This came from years of being a soldier. The ability to sift through a flood of information and choose the most important thread. Ama was sure this was the correct thread to follow. Establish what danger exists and then deal with it.

"Not from Boggs, or his crew," Miho said with her eyes down. "But whoever hired Boggs must still want me killed."

"Miho, where is Boggs now?" Ama asked. "How can you be sure he's not a threat?"

Ama needed to hear the answer. She hoped Miho wouldn't say what she knew she would say. Ama wanted the job herself. She wanted Boggs to be alive somewhere so she could kill him herself. But Miho looked up and straight into her eyes and breathed.

"Because I sent him to my father."

CHAPTER 51

The carriage jostled and bounced on the stone streets as the gaslit pools of light strobed by the window in a hazy wash of color and motion. Miho sat in the silence after her statement, waiting. She waited for Ama to say something, but Ama just seemed to be lost in thought. The moments stretched on. The clip-clop of the horses' hooves and the ringing of their tack were the only sounds.

"I'm glad that you're not in any immediate danger," Ama said slowly in low tones. "I'm sorry that you had to take care of this matter alone."

"Thank you, Ama," Miho whispered.

"You're sure," Ama asked quietly. "You're absolutely sure that he is gone?"

"Yes," Miho said just as quietly. "I'm absolutely sure that he, and the two other men who Grounded my father, are gone forever."

A long silence stretched on as both of them seemed lost in thought. "What are you planning to do next?" Ama asked.

Miho considered this question. She had asked it of herself for what seemed like a while now. Miho felt like she was somewhat lost, now that Boggs, Nate and the rabbit-faced man were gone. She knew of a mysterious "S.C.," and suspected Sam Caldwell from the party tonight, but suspicion isn't knowing. There was no knowing without proof.

"I'd like to find out who this S.C. is and why they wanted my family dead," Miho said, but she didn't know how to make that desire become reality. Where should she start? How would she prove S.C. was Sam Caldwell, or find out who it was if it wasn't him? "Until I learn more about them, I have to assume I'm still in danger."

"Well, if you're convinced they are in upper society, I can see why you'd think that," Ama spoke matter-of-factly. "They are able to give orders to a City Engineer, have influence over the City, magistrates... to keep it all quiet...

"Plus, they own at least one warehouse, and I believe based on this note that they have more."

Miho pulled the note from S.C. out of a hiding place. She still lived by the rules of the Underbelly, and kept the most important items she had on her person at all times. While she couldn't carry the pistol, or her swords to the gala, she had her mother and father's portrait, several blades, and this letter on her.

Miho had brought it along because she hoped it might somehow help her discover who S.C. was tonight. She handed the note to Ama, who leaned closer to the glass window for better light to read the handwriting.

"Where did you get this?" Ama asked with a perplexed expression.

"It was hidden along with a pistol under Joseph Boggs' bed, in his apartment," Miho explained. She decided that now that she had opened up to Ama, she wouldn't keep things from her any more. She felt a weight lift from her chest at the thought of having Ama as a confidant.

Ama stared at Miho for a minute before saying, "You broke into his apartment? Miho, that was very dangerous."

Miho stared back at the woman. Many thoughts and feelings went through her in a rush. She felt like Ama was reprimanding her, but then she also felt that Ama was impressed. Miho remembered that this woman was also a mother, and worried like a parent. That thought made her think of her own mother. Her mother could never reprimand her again. She felt very sad at that thought, but also very thankful that she had someone who worried for her safety right in front of her.

"Yes ma'am," Miho whispered.

Ama shook her head slowly and said, "You've had to do so much on your own. I'm so sorry. You've been in danger, and you've done these things, and I wasn't there for you."

"I wasn't alone," Miho said, trying to reassure. "I had help."

I'm so glad you had people you could rely on. Miho, I want to help you too, if you'll let me. I can't promise that I'll support everything you are doing, but I hope you will trust me enough to let me give you my insight and perspective."

"I do. I am," Miho said. "I do trust you."

Ama reached across and hugged Miho tightly. They stayed in the embrace for a long time before Ama leaned back with wet eyes and said, "Thank you."

Miho felt her own eyes sting with emotion, but she didn't cry. She didn't think she had any tears left after the outbreak she had had a few minutes ago.

"You'll need to join the upper society to investigate this person," Ama said, handing the note back. "And just being in my house, or in your own house, may not be enough. You will need to get invited to functions and socials. Have you considered the Duchess's proposal to join the City Watch elite, to try to become a Valkyrie?"

Miho thought about that for a moment. Would she want to become a pilot? Her mother had loved flying. Miho knew it could be dangerous, but she wasn't really afraid for her safety. Ama was right though, as a Valkyrie, Miho would be in the topmost sphere of high society. The Valkyries were celebrities. They were soldiers, to be sure, but the upper class admired them. Their kill ratios, number of combat missions, and so many other details of their service to the Empire were followed like the stats of athletes. There were fan clubs and celebrations of their service.

Miho hated attention. She hated the idea of a spotlight on her and of people following what she was doing, but being a Valkyrie would get her invited to every social event in the city. There was no better way to seek out S.C.

"I think it may be useful," she said. She wasn't convinced it was what was best, but it offered many paths forward.

"I'll help you any way I can," Ama said strongly. "It won't be easy. For every 20 girls that apply, only one will become an actual Valkyrie. We have a high failure rate, a high turnover rate, and most girls won't be able to make it. But you've already shown that you are made of sterner stuff than the average girl."

Miho bowed her head, embarrassed.

"The Duchess's offer for an endorsement is an enormous help," Ama said. "It would normally cost a small fortune to purchase your own airship, skystone, supportive workers, pay the fees and various taxes, plus the training... Oh, the training begins in just a few weeks! Miho, we have so much to do."

Miho felt nervous at the idea. A whole new world was about to open up to her. No matter what happened to her, though, she knew she wasn't alone. She had friends, some as close as family, here in this enormous city among the clouds.

End Book One

ABOUT THE AUTHOR

Daniel Harrell was born into a family of actors and storytellers. A third-generation television Producer-Director on his father's side, and a family of yarn spinners around the fire on his mother's.

His father left the stage to pursue television as an actor-writer- and producer. Some of Daniel's earliest memories were trying to keep quiet in television studios while watching magic be made.

He began writing in high-school, and has enjoyed it ever since. He has published short stories, written countless television scripts, and now tries his hand at novels. He lives in coastal Virginia with his wife, enjoys the outdoors and the company of their cat (Pasha) and dog (Bella), who do not enjoy each other.

www.ingramcontent.com/pod-product-compliance
Lightning Source LLC
Chambersburg PA
CBHW030426180626
46812CB00005B/2192